D1058429

THE
DARKLING

THE
DARKLING

R. B. CHESTERTON

PEGASUS CRIME
NEW YORK LONDON

For Debby Porter Pruett, DeWitt Lobrano, David Haines,
Boris Karloff, and my crazy, ghost-hunting family.

✽✽✽

THE DARKLING

Pegasus Books LLC
80 Broad Street, 5th Floor
New York, NY 10004

Copyright © 2013 by R. B. Chesterton

First Pegasus Books cloth edition 2013

Interior design by Maria Fernandez

ISBN: 978-1-60598-458-2

10 9 8 7 6 5 4 3 2 1

Printed in the United States of America
Distributed by W. W. Norton & Company, Inc.

Prologue

In the 1940s, Coden, Alabama was a hideaway for movie stars—an isolated playground tucked among live oaks and the placid bay waters where pleasure and vice could be indulged. When Veronica Lake or Errol Flynn came to play, bedazzled lawmen turned a blind eye to the excesses that ride the coattails of fame. Coden was a backwater with incredible natural beauty, the old Paradise Inn, fitted out for royalty, and silence that could be bought.

No one asked questions.

In the summer of 1974, the hotel was abandoned and the stars had found other, more exotic backwaters. The poor were poorer and the rich were gone.

Like most of the rest of the kids around Coden, I'd grown up on tales of glamour lost. While the past intrigued me, I had a more practical bent. "Mature beyond her years" was the description most often attached to me. Not exactly the attributes of a popular young woman. I didn't care. I was the live-in tutor for the Henderson family, a job I'd held for three months. Only twenty-one and fresh out of college, I found myself in residence in the grandest house in south Mobile County with a family that looked like it stepped out of *House Beautiful*. Berta, the mother, kept the kitchen filled with the scent of home cooking. The children were bright and willing to learn. And Bob, oh, he was a handsome man accomplished as an architect, but also a man who loved his wife and children and never failed to show it. The Hendersons were everything I'd been denied—a perfect family. They brought hope that new prosperity had come to Coden.

My grandmother, Cora Eubanks, and most of the residents, pinned their dreams on Bob and Berta Henderson and the belief that they could bring back what had once been lost.

Coden was a dying community, a left-behind fishing village on the small and placid Portersfield Bay of the Mississippi Sound. Like all towns built around water and a fishing industry, it was remote. Much different from Mobile or even the coastal towns of Mississippi. The families of Coden had been there for generations, a mixture of old French and Spanish with a smattering of Irish and Scot thrown in.

In the summer of 1974, Vietnamese families had begun to move in, a point of controversy amongst the "natives." The Vietnam War was too fresh, the losses of young men from the area too bitter. Still, whether old line stock or newly arrived Asians, these were fishing families that shared a way of life, a relationship with the water and a sunup-to-sunset work ethic.

Not so with the Hendersons, a family of golden blond Californians, as exotic as any of the strange blooms in the garden of Belle Fleur, the showcase home they bought and renovated at the water's edge. They were outlanders. Outsiders. They had wealth, looks, education, and, most telling, different expectations. While they were viewed with suspicion by many, it couldn't be denied that the family brought the promise of better times to come. Bob Henderson's renovation of Belle Fleur was the first step in his master plan. Seeing the old house restored on the rise of land that led down to the Sound made everyone in Coden feel that better times were coming. Bob's dream of bringing the Paradise Inn back to life was the hottest topic of talk in town that summer.

Even I, working in the bosom of the family, believed that the Hendersons would change the luck of Coden. The old stories, the tales of big bands, rollicking parties, movie stars water-skiing—somehow by bringing the Paradise back to life, Bob would bring back the flush times. Instead, the Hendersons opened a door to the past that should never have been unsealed. Their arrival initiated a tragic chain of events and unbearable suffering.

I'd thought never to tell this story. I vowed never to think of it again. I changed my name and left, for who would hire a tutor who'd been on the scene of five grisly murders and continued to claim she saw . . . what? An evil child? A murdering child? An imposter who moved into the heart of a family with only the goal of murder?

So I refused to talk. Not to reporters or therapists. Not to anyone. At last they left me alone. I found another post with a family in Ocean Springs, Mississippi, and I saw their children through to college and then found another family in Biloxi, and another in Gulfport. My duties moved me farther along the Gulf Coast rim until I hit a little town south of Corpus Christi, Texas, where I baked in the full glare of the Gulf Coast sun.

At night, I drank. Vodka couldn't keep the memories at bay, but it did dull them to the point that I could sleep. Aside from the brutal murders that haunted my dreams, I worried a point of guilt. What role had I played in the destruction of the Henderson family? What role had my grandmother, Cora Eubanks, enacted?

Such dark thoughts are less terrifying in the heat of the late summer sun. So it is now, in the August of a new decade, the second of a new century, that I've taken on the burden of putting my story on paper. The written word has tremendous power. I hope that by writing this I can . . . I'm not certain what I hope to accomplish. Put my demons to rest? Warn others? Leave a written legacy that might carry more weight than my spoken words? Or perhaps I'm following in the footsteps of Cora, who once left me a document that was the key to the past.

I only know that the long summer days offer me some comfort from the terrors of the dark. I must write fast. Time is running against me. When I'm tempted to back away from this story, as I often am, I remember that I have seen her. Only last week. As young and innocent as the first day she stepped off the bus at Beauchamp's Grocery in Coden in 1974.

As long as the August sunlight heats the woods and fields of southern Mobile County, I force myself to the task of recounting the events of nearly forty years ago. In the darkness of the night, I drink. When the sun is gone, I dare not call forth the images of my past for fear she will sniff me out. She has the acute senses and cunning of a wild animal. And she has no mercy, not for a child or me.

How did she manage to get back to Coden? That's a question I pursue even as I chronicle her story. Annie. Such a simple and beautiful name. There is no word in the English language that can strike such fear in me.

To properly tell her story, I must go back in time. The memories of youth in the 1970s would be wonderful, were it not for the events I must remember. My grandmother was the fulcrum that set it all in motion.

1

JULY 7, 1974

A whipping summer gust blasted off the water, sending a paper bag skittering across the parking lot of Beauchamp's Grocery. I couldn't see the water from the parked car where I waited with my grandmother, but I could smell it. That tang of salt and fish and a wildness from the marsh grass that made me long to get out and stretch my legs in a brisk walk.

"It won't be long," Cora said, patting my leg. "Don't fidget."

My grandmother was a social worker for the Department of Pensions and Security, later renamed Human Resources. Annie had come to her attention when she was picked up on the streets of downtown Mobile. At first it was thought she was a teen prostitute, but Cora claimed she was an amnesiac, a girl with a big imagination, a talent for storytelling, and no one to love her, no memory of where she'd come from or what she was meant to be doing. Cora had a soft touch for mistreated children, but she wasn't in the habit of dragging them home. Annie was different, though. Something about her had tugged at Cora's heartstrings.

I was already working as a tutor for the three Henderson children—a job I'd held since the previous May. In the short weeks of my employment, I had found my place in the family. I taught lessons, but more than that; I was valued and respected as part of the family.

I went to work the day after my college graduation, eager yet also unsure. Now I'd gained my footing, but the addition of another teen gave me concern. Cora would hear none of my worries.

"She's a teenager with no place to turn. Give her a chance, Mimi," Cora said. "You may discover you have things in common."

The things I'd have in common with her would be that I would have another charge to educate. My life with the Hendersons was nearly perfect—I didn't see the need to include another child.

Shifting on the car seat to better see my grandmother, I asked, "Why did the Hendersons agree to take her in?" Most families I knew would never consider harboring a strange child, especially a sixteen-year-old girl who had no memory of who she was or where she'd come from. Annie was the only name she'd give.

Grandma, who I'd grown up calling Cora, believed in the power of love. All of my life, she'd told me how love could heal any wound, patch any hole in a person's soul. Love was her miracle drug.

"The Hendersons have room and plenty of love. Once Annie feels secure, her memory will return. I suspect she's been through a terrible trauma. The doctors believe her amnesia comes from some shocking event or accident. The Hendersons are the perfect family to help her heal. Belle Fleur is the place for her. You'll be a part of her healing, Mimi. Perhaps you, too, will find the experience curative."

I wasn't certain that was true. Even after thirty years as a social worker, Cora wanted to believe the best of people. I was only twenty-one, just out of college, and I knew better. But I said nothing. Cora was a figure beloved in the Coden community. She'd asked the Hendersons to foster Annie, and so they would.

Cora had gotten me the tutoring job, a full-time position that required me to use my education degree from the University of South Alabama to its maximum potential. I was the compromise between

Bob and Berta Henderson. Bob loved old Belle Fleur, the house of his dreams and the perfect project to show his architectural and renovation abilities. He'd bought the property against Berta's wishes. He'd completed the renovation before she'd consider moving here. Bob wanted the slower pace—and perceived safety—of a small, rural Alabama town to raise his children.

Berta, a California girl through and through, refused to send her children to the Alabama public schools. She was more than a bit horrified by the curriculum, not to mention the prevalence of "portable" classrooms, essentially trailers. Before she'd move from the heaven-on-earth of Cambria, California, to Alabama, she negotiated a live-in tutor, four week-long trips to "cities with culture," an in-home movie theater, and piano and violin lessons for all the children. I was young, unattached, and credentialed in teaching. Though I'd been living with Cora, I also longed for a family, something I found nestled in the brood of blond Hendersons. I felt as if the job had been created especially for me.

The three children, Donald, nine, Erin, twelve, and Margo, sixteen, were not spoiled, but they were willful. Donald quickly became my favorite. Erin charmed me with her energy, and Margo challenged me. How would this new child, this orphan, fit into the mix? I wasn't sure this was a good idea.

"The bus is late." Cora frowned. "When I was a young woman like yourself, the bus was the only way to get into Mobile. Folks didn't have cars like today. We relied on the bus, and it was on time. I know I sound like a fuddy-duddy, but this whole country is going to hell in a handbasket."

We were only six years past the terrible murder of Dr. Martin Luther King, a man my grandmother revered. His death shook her faith in her fellow countrymen and the basic goodness of America, but she didn't stop trying or believing. Girls like Annie—the abandoned, the thrown away, the damaged goods—this was where she made her mark. America might have lost its way, but Cora knew the steep and rocky path she was meant to trod.

The bus pulled in front of the grocery store on a belch of black smoke. It looked as old and worn as the setting. I was about to step out of the car when a gust of wind caught the heavy Pontiac door and slammed it with vicious force, almost catching my hand.

When I looked up, Annie was standing beside the car. Dark curls batted about her small, pinched face. She was beautiful, elfin almost, and she looked so lost. The word that came to mind was "stray." Like a dog or cat hungry for love and attention. I opened the car door, pushing against the wind that tried to keep me safe inside. She simply stood there, as if she didn't know how to help. At last I got the door open and got out.

I extended my hand. "I'm Marie Bosarge. You can call me Mimi," I told her. "I'm Cora's granddaughter. I'm the tutor at the Hendersons."

She shivered in a gust of hot air, and I realized she was nervous. Her too-short dress exposed long legs, lean but shapely. She was sixteen, and she looked starved. She came with only one suitcase, a battered brown thing that had once tried to pass itself off as leather before the surface had been scraped and the cardboard beneath revealed. I picked it up and put it in the spacious trunk.

"Climb in," Grandma ordered. "The Hendersons are waiting."

Annie clambered into the back seat, teeth chattering. Cora turned off the air conditioner and away we went, racing down Shore Road ahead of the storm that brewed to the south. The squall had blown in quickly, as marine gales are wont to do. In the summer, we worried about hurricanes, but the Gulf was empty of the whirling tempests that could wreck a coastal town and kill hundreds with high winds and water.

With the air conditioner off, the car was like an oven, and I rolled down my window for a moment of fresh air. Seagulls cried and cawed, circling the marshy shore. The wind seemed to have confused them because they swooped at the car as if they meant to attack. They were curious birds, but not stupid. The erratic behavior puzzled me.

"What's wrong with the gulls?" Cora asked.

"It's almost as if they're disoriented. Maybe something to do with the storm." I'd spent a bit of time bird-watching, and I'd never seen gulls pursue a car. "Or maybe . . . blind." They acted as if they'd lost their ability to see.

"Maybe it's the car," Annie said from the backseat. "They're following us."

It was true. The birds moved down the road with us. To my complete horror, a gull came straight at the car like a missile. I reached over and honked the horn as Cora applied the brakes.

"Good lord!" she jerked the wheel, sending my head banging into the passenger window. In the backseat, Annie slammed against the door. The bird hit the windshield with a bloody smack as Cora brought the car under control and stopped.

I got out quickly and checked the bird, but it was hopeless. The impact had killed it instantly. The other birds wheeled and cried, circling above me and the car, but they made no attempt to get closer. I moved the carcass to the side of the road. When I got back inside, Cora's hands shook on the steering wheel.

"I can't believe that happened," Cora said. "I've driven this road my entire life. I've never hit a gull."

"Something was wrong with it," I said. In my family, the death of any creature was cause for grief. I was partial to birds and I'd trained as an amateur ornithologist. I wasn't an expert, but I knew gulls didn't deliberately dive into the windshields of cars traveling fifty miles an hour.

Cora was shaken but tried not to show it. "It had to have been sick. I'm sorry, Annie. I don't want that to spoil your arrival here in Coden."

"I don't believe in omens. At least it was a quick death," Annie said. "It didn't suffer."

I hated it when people mouthed platitudes. A quick death. What did that mean? Annie had no clue what she was talking about, but I wisely kept quiet. Cora was struggling to regain her composure, and I didn't want to do anything that would make it harder for her.

She put the car in DRIVE and we started along Shore Road at a more sedate pace. When I glanced back in the side mirror, I saw a dozen other gulls pecking the corpse. They tore at it with a savage frenzy. Gulls were scavengers, but I'd never seen them feast on a freshly dead comrade. My gaze connected with Annie's in the rearview mirror. She watched me with cool calculation.

"What's wrong?" she asked. She was so calm, I could only imagine what hardships she'd endured to gain such composure.

"Nothing." I had no desire to spoil her arrival at Belle Fleur. The Henderson family was waiting, a happy occasion. Cora had planned this for days. The bird's death was unfortunate, but there was no reason to mar the remainder of the day.

"Wild creatures are unpredictable, don't you think?" she asked.

"Seagulls are hardly wild creatures."

Annie broke her gaze from mine. "Will the Hendersons like me?" she asked Cora.

"I'm certain they will. This is a big day for them, too. I've told them all about you."

Out of the corner of my eye I watched Cora put aside her shock and assume her professional demeanor. "All we know," I added. "There wasn't a lot to tell since you can't remember anything about your past."

"They'll be charmed by you," Cora said. "And you will adore them."

"Will they adopt me?" Annie asked.

Cora hesitated. "We've talked about this, Annie. You're sixteen. That's a bit old for adoption. They may foster you until it's time for college. That would be a wonderful outcome for you."

"Yes," she said.

I couldn't see her expression, for her face was hidden behind a blowing strand of dark curls, but her voice sounded less than sure. She merely wanted to be loved, I thought. Who could not love a child so beautiful and damaged?

2

WELCOME, ANNIE

The banner hung in the live oaks that lent the front lawn of Belle
Fleur an air of grace and elegance. The house, surrounded by oaks,
camellias, azaleas, and other hardy shrubs, faced the road and the
water. To me, it looked like a photograph, something captured on film
from a bygone time when houses were built with care and attention
to detail. As we drew closer, I could see the love Berta had showered
on the house in the hanging ferns along the front porch, the freshly
painted wicker furniture, the pots of geraniums that bloomed blood-
red. Bob had loved the house first, but Berta had grown to love it
over the summer.

Cora stopped the car a dozen yards from the five Hendersons who
stood beneath the banner. Bob and Berta wore welcoming smiles.
Donald had his typical open friendliness that always made me think
of Huck Finn or Tom Sawyer. He was all boy, all adventure, all happy
to include a poor waif with no memory. Erin was unsure. Margo was
trouble. The instant Annie stepped out of the car, Margo took her

measure and a sneer crossed her face. I couldn't say I blamed her. Annie and Margo were the same age. No matter how hard Berta worked at it, both girls would compete for her love. It was the way of the teenager.

"Annie!" Berta came forward, extending the joyful welcome of a California goddess. Berta was sun and oranges and blue-eyed beauty. She was a perfect match for Bob, who could have played Robert Redford playing Gatsby.

The two of them had produced three children as golden and blond as the loins from which they sprang. Against them, Annie appeared foreign and dark, a dainty child compared to the tall Nordic Hendersons.

Berta engulfed her in an embrace. "Welcome."

Annie clung to her. Her thin arms circled Berta's neck and she didn't let go until Bob offered her an embrace. She almost disappeared in his hug. Donald and Erin seemed amused. Margo rolled her eyes and mouthed the word "baby" at me.

Introductions were made and we went into the house for cake and ice cream, a treat Berta reserved for birthdays and special occasions—sugar wasn't normally allowed. Berta had brought a head full of crazy California ideas with her. She believed in "healthful" treats like apples and pears, but Annie's first day with the family was a momentous occasion and would be celebrated as such.

We gathered round the dining table for the welcome fete, and at first, chatter animated the room. Cora sat beside Annie, and she glanced at her often, the guardian of a lost child's safety. Cora was worried, though she did a good job of hiding it, and I wondered why. Annie seemed okay. She attacked the cake and ice cream as if she were starving, and I had to wonder how long it had been since she'd had enough to eat. While I refilled coffee cups and laughed with the others, I watched Annie. She seemed eager to fit in. Maybe Cora was right—this wouldn't be a problem, but a joy.

As we relished the delicious pound cake Berta had baked from yard eggs she'd raised, the chatter died and an uneasy quiet settled over the dining room. When Berta offered Annie a second piece of cake, she nodded eagerly.

"Mama made pound cake because she said everyone liked it," Donald said. "What's your favorite, Annie?"

For a brief moment she looked like an animal caught in the headlights of a fast-approaching car. "I don't know. This is delicious."

"But what's your favorite?" Donald pressed. "Erin loves chocolate. Margo likes coconut pie. What do you like?"

Annie looked around the room as if she might read the answer from someone's face. "I don't remember. Probably pound cake. I could eat the whole thing."

"And then you can waddle around the house," Margo said.

Berta shot her a warning look, but Margo ignored it. In the last few weeks, she'd begun to defy Berta. And to a lesser extent, me. She was falling behind on her studies and was often on the phone. The move had been hardest on her, tearing her from her teenage companions. At sixteen, she was legal to drive and wanted to have more of a social life than Coden could provide. Of all the children, she missed California the most. When she was banned from the phone, she wrote endless letters to her old classmates and lately had taken to sneaking out of the house. To what end, I didn't know. There was nowhere to go and nothing to do in Coden. The town shut down at five o'clock.

Though I'd never been a problem teen, I empathized with Margo and felt she was simply testing her wings for that leap of flight from the nest. Still, she behaved like a brat, and Berta was fed up with her conduct.

"Do you remember anything about your past?" Margo pressed Annie. "I mean, surely someone must be missing a wonderful child like you. Cora has been singing your praises for weeks." The edge in her tone made Berta push back from the table.

"I know some things," Annie said. "I get dressed and I know how to read and do math. I think I know how to drive . . ." she shrugged. "It's strange because I don't know what I know until I try it."

"Do you know how to ride horses?" Erin asked, oblivious to the darker undercurrent between the two older girls.

"Maybe." Annie's smile was wan. "I'd know if I tried."

"But not today," Berta said with meaning. She stood and began to gather the dishes. "Margo, why don't you show Annie her room? Mimi, you can give her the books you picked out for her studies."

Margo's chair raked the hardwood floor as she pushed back with unnecessary vehemence. She hadn't touched her cake. Without a word she stalked to the staircase. Ten steps up, she turned. "It was supposed to be my room, you know. Are you coming?" she asked Annie.

Berta carefully put the dishes down on the table. Her blue eyes shot fire at her daughter. "Perhaps if you asked nicely," she said in a tone that brooked no sass.

"Annie, may I show you to your room?" Margo's tone was barely civil.

"I can find it myself. I feel as if I know this house already," Annie said. "Don't worry, Margo, but thank you. I think I'll chat with Berta and Bob a little more."

"And I have to go." Cora rose from her chair. "Annie, Berta, Bob—call me if you need anything." She began the ritual search for her purse, and then the search in her purse for her keys. Cora's mind was razor-sharp, except for keeping up with her glasses or keys or purse.

"Can I take Annie to the water and show her how to fish?" Donald asked.

"Maybe another time," I said. My protectiveness for Donald was instant. Annie, while Cora might vouch for her, was still a stranger. I didn't want her taking Donald off.

Donald looked at me and then his mother.

"Mimi wants to introduce Annie to her studies, Donald. Besides, I'm sure Annie wants to see her room and settle in." Berta put her hand on my shoulder. We were a team.

"It's okay, Mrs. Henderson. I'm not tired. I'd love to see the property. Then I'll focus on my new books. I promise." As naturally as if they were siblings, Annie took Donald's hand. "I'll tell you a story," she said as they went to the front door.

"Twenty minutes," Bob called out. "And don't leave the front lawn."

"Sure thing." Donald pushed open the door and held it for Annie. "You're gonna love it here," he said as they left the house.

I glanced at Cora, and I wondered if I had ever seen her happier. She was deeply invested in Annie's tenure with the Hendersons. Despite the truth that all the years had handed Cora, she still believed in a happy ending.

"Mother, may I go and ride?" Erin stacked her empty saucer on top of the other. She was a fanatical equestrian. She rode every day and thought of little else. It was all I could do to keep her mind on her lessons, but I'd learned to associate countries, cultures, historical facts, and even math with horses. Anything horse-related held her attention.

"You may."

"Thanks!" Erin bolted from her chair, gave Cora a squeeze, and sprinted from the room. She was slender but solid, and as she pounded up the stairs to her room to change into her riding clothes, I realized she likely weighed more than Annie. One thing for sure, Berta's cooking would put some meat on Annie's bones. When the children were gone, Berta sighed. "I don't know what to do, Cora. Margo is determined to dislike her."

"Annie is invading her territory." I understood it clearly. Bob and Berta were dream parents. Margo had no desire to share. "Margo is threatened by Annie. They're the same age, and now Margo has competition. It's a hard place for her."

"That's unacceptable, Mimi. My children have everything and Annie has nothing. I don't want them to grow up to be selfish." Berta picked up the stack of dishes. When Cora moved to help, Berta shooed her away. "You were headed out the door. I can manage this."

"Your children are exceptional, Berta. That's why I wanted Annie to come here," Cora said. "Give them time to adjust. Annie is almost grown, and so is Margo. This will be hardest on them. The younger ones will view Annie as a big sister. Mimi's right. Margo sees her as competition."

"I won't tolerate selfishness." Berta almost dropped a bowl of melting ice cream, but Bob caught it.

He took the dishes from her hands and put them on the table. "They're still kids. Children *learn* to be givers, they don't pop out that way." He grabbed Berta's wrist and pulled her into his lap. He kissed her neck until she laughed. "They'll get used to Annie and before you know it, she'll be part of the family. Just like Mimi."

"Bob's right," I said, warmed by his words. I *had* become part of the family. I picked up the dishes before Berta could. "Annie's going to stick out like a sore thumb in this family, but everyone will adjust." I, too, had a darker coloring and was aware of the stares that came my way whenever I was in town with the Henderson brood.

Berta kissed Bob on the forehead and pushed to her feet. "She's a beautiful girl, Cora. We'll help her as long as she wants to stay."

Cora patted Berta's hand. "I knew I could count on you." She found her keys in her purse and shook them with a sigh. "I think she'll be a rare blessing."

3

After Cora left, I wandered to the front porch. The view never failed to move me, either to joy or melancholy. The front lawn of Belle Fleur slanted gently for a quarter mile down to the bay. Clusters of live oaks contrasted dark green against the bright green August grass. Bob had given me free rein to plant Oxonians and resurrection lilies around one of the oaks as part of a history lesson, and come next spring, my special garden would show life. My gaze wandered down to the edge of the beautifully maintained lawn, where marsh grass danced on the breeze all the way to the water.

The sky, a lighter shade of steel, pressed down on the bay. The storm still hovered out near the barrier islands, a wall of gray so dark it looked almost like night. It was only three o'clock. Far too early for darkness to fall.

At the edge of the water, Donald showed Annie how to cast a lure past the marsh grass. Their antics made me smile. While Berta and the girls still missed California, Donald had adapted to his new home. He loved the freedom to fish and roam. The Hendersons owned a section of land, six hundred and forty acres of pine timber, pastures, sloughs, marshes, natural springs, a creek, and the old dilapidated hotel, a place of legend in Coden. I stepped off the porch and walked down to join Annie and Donald. While Berta was the mother, I shared in the responsibility for the younger children.

Casting a glance over my shoulder, I noticed Margo in the second floor window of her room. She, too, studied Donald and Annie, but if her expression was any indication, her thoughts were far from pleasant.

She saw me staring up at her and pulled her curtains closed. Her window was like a dead eye. The rest of the house, a warm butter yellow with green shutters, was open and inviting. Shaking my head, I changed course and started down the path that led to where the old Desmarais family had planted the original gardens. Local legends said the family arrived from France in the first half of the nineteenth century with the dream of creating flower gardens to make perfume. The subtropical climate of South Alabama allowed a growing season unheard of in the French region where the family originated.

Though nearly two hundred years had passed since the Desmaraises settled in Coden, many of the plants had survived. Despite my bulb patch, birds, not plants, were my thing. While I couldn't name the exotic flora that bloomed unexpectedly on the Belle Fleur grounds, I could appreciate the beauty, especially those varieties hardy enough to survive the sweltering south Alabama summer. Shades of yellow and orange peeked out from the tangle of vines as I sauntered toward the old hotel.

Berta had taken an interest in the gardens, and I could see where she'd fought hard to clear some of the beds. If anyone could tame the vegetation, it would be her. She was iron-willed, a trait I appreciated. She demanded respect and obedience from her children, but she tempered her expectations with love. Berta made my job a pleasure, and I had come to believe I was a big help to her. I enjoyed our time in the kitchen, cooking and talking. She missed California, but she wasn't the kind of person to whine. She had begun to build a new life. I admired that.

The path wound through the dark green forest of trees, under-growth, vines, and some valuable plants. Twenty minutes later, I came upon the ruins of the old hotel, a plantation-style building with granite columns of a five-foot circumference down the entire front. Above the wide porch were balconies along the second and third floor, though the stairs to the upper levels were gone. A natural hot spring had fed water to private baths and from what I gleaned from local tales, there had been croquet courses, tennis, water-skiing from a natural bayou that was deep enough for large sailboats to dock at the front lawn of the hotel, and then the darker activities of gambling, hard drinking, and sex—the romantic kind and the acts money could buy.

It took little effort to imagine the place in perfect condition and filled with Hollywood royalty. Cora said Lana Turner had been a regular when she was very young. The Andrews Sisters had sung there during the war. Paradise Inn had been a place to splash and play, and also for assignations. There was—and still is—only one road down to this part of the coastline, and no one today or in the past would choose to walk through the marshes in an attempt to gain unauthorized access. Alligators own that marshy land.

Bob had killed one in June when it came up onto the front lawn. The sheriff, Benny Delchamps, had issued the order to execute the reptile because it displayed aggression toward Margo. Or so the girl had said. In my experience, the gators did everything in their power to stay away from humans. Margo had insisted the six-footer had lunged at her as she walked along Shore Road. Bob had shot it with a degree of expertise that surprised me.

Thinking of the gator made me anxious about Donald, so close to the edge of the marsh. Annie wouldn't know to be alert for the reptiles. I threw a last look at the hotel and turned back. My sense of anxiety grew, though I knew it was unfounded. Still, I pushed from a brisk walk to a jog.

When I came out of the woods and onto the edge of the lawn, I thought my heart might choke me. Donald ran toward the house. His blue eyes were wide with terror, and he ran almost as if he were in a trance. He didn't see me at all.

"Donald!" I called out to him and ran to intercept him. "What's wrong?"

He seemed not to hear me.

"Donald!" I reached from him and caught hold of his shirt. "Donald!"

His eyes, blinded by some inner fear, turned toward me.

"Donald!" I shook him lightly.

He drew in a deep breath and for a split second I thought he might cry out, but he stopped himself. It took real effort, I could tell, but he swallowed the scream. Instead, he clung to me, holding me so tight I almost couldn't breathe.

"You're okay. Donald, what's wrong? Where's Annie?"

He turned to look back at the water. Annie stepped out from behind a tree, concern on her face.

"Donald!" she called out to him. "Are you okay?"

"What happened?" I tried to focus him on me, but he kept twisting to look at Annie. When she was abreast of us, he finally relaxed.

"I'm not afraid," he said. He eased back from my arms, but he still clung to my hand.

"Afraid of what?" I'd never seen him in such a state.

"Of anything." He looked at Annie but then dropped his gaze in what seemed embarrassment. "I'm not a baby."

"Of course you aren't," she said, kneeling so that she was eye-level with him. "There's nothing to be afraid of. You aren't a pantywaist, are you, Donald?"

Her tone was off. It seemed to hold a warning, but of what I couldn't determine. "Did you see an alligator?" I asked.

"Maybe," Annie said. "We saw something. Or maybe we just imagined it." For the first time I noticed the dimple in her cheek. She was stunning when she smiled. "I think Donald and I got carried away with a story. It was just something I made up. I didn't mean to upset him so much."

Donald took a deep breath and nodded. "I'm not upset. Annie is a great storyteller." His smile was genuine.

"Let's go into the house," Annie said. She stood and extended her hand. Donald took it without hesitation. As they ran toward the house, they giggled like happy schoolchildren.

I stood for a long moment, tempted to go down to the water and look for myself. Instead, I followed them into the house. Berta would be preparing dinner, and I liked to help her. It gave me a chance to discuss the children's school progress. It was also our time together, something I had come to value, for Annie was not the only one on the property who was an orphan and wanted to be part of a loving home.

4

The storm broke as we all sat at the table for dinner. The lights flickered, but the power remained on, much to the disappointment of
the children. I'd taken care to use the fine china and linen napkins.
I was curious about Annie's table manners. She couldn't remember
a moment of her past, but she seemed at ease in the midst of a new
family. She displayed none of the awkwardness of a normal teenager.

We joined hands around the table. Bob and Berta were not religious, but they gave thanks as a family for the blessings of good food
and good health. Bob had installed central air and heat in the house,
one of the first homes in Coden to have the luxury, but often, like
tonight, Berta opened the windows to allow a crossdraft to swirl
around us. Belle Fleur was blessed with excellent airflow, and even
on the hottest days we opened the windows.

Because it was a celebratory dinner, the official welcome to Annie,
I lit candles. Berta prepared a fresh salad, crisp and delicious, from
her garden, along with slices of smoked turkey. The weather was too
hot for heavy meals.

I watched with interest as Annie shook out her napkin and spread it on her lap. She helped herself to the salad and passed it on, acting without thought, a true indication of manners. Wherever she'd come from, she'd been taught table graces. Bob poured wine for Berta and me, a merlot that Berta loved. He said I had a "natural palate" for wine, and he enjoyed introducing me to new vineyards. He held up his glass and we joined him. "We welcome Annie. I hope your stay here is filled with love and joy. And I hope you remember something about your people, Annie. I know they're missing you."

Margo put her iced tea on the table. "Has anyone checked to see if the cops are looking for her? Teenagers don't just drop out of the sky."

Bob slowly pushed back his chair. "Please excuse Margo and me for a moment." He went into the kitchen. When Margo followed, stomping every step of the way, he closed the door. Margo's voice rose in anger, but she stopped in mid-sentence. Bob's low voice, unclear but forceful, could be heard.

"Annie told me a story today. It was the best scary story." Donald spoke too loud. He was a kind-hearted child and was attempting to smooth over Margo's rudeness.

"What kind of story?" Berta picked up the thread of conversation. In the kitchen, Bob continued to lay down the law to Margo. She'd just gotten her driver's license, and I had no doubt he would take her keys away.

"About the old hotel and a ghost. A lot of things happened at The Paradise Inn. Annie knows all about the old hotel. Lots of movie stars hung out there. Some of them even *died* there."

"Do you know about the Paradise?" I asked Annie. How was it possible she knew my history but not her own?

Her smile was apologetic. "I could see it from the water, the big old columns and all of the vines. It must have been beautiful once." She signaled me with a wink to let me know she was fibbing. "I told Donald a tale about the ghosts of people who once visited there."

"A ghost story!" Erin was thrilled. "Tell us! Tell us!"

Donald paled slightly, but he joined in with the demand.

Berta was amused. "I'd like to hear the story, too."

Annie shrugged. She motioned us all to lean in closer, and I noted that though she was shy, she could manage the limelight. "There was once a beautiful movie star named Madeline who came to the Paradise Inn. She was the most beautiful star in all of Hollywood, but very young. She'd filmed two movies, and she'd come to Coden to meet with a director, a man from Germany who was highly respected."

Annie might not know her past or her family, but she had a good handle on telling a story. I sipped my wine and leaned back, prepared to enjoy a gothic tale.

"Madeline was a strong swimmer, and each morning she got up and would swim down the bayou and out into the sound to a small buoy with a bell. She would ring the bell and swim back to shore. It became a routine for the first week she was there because the director was delayed in Berlin, something about the war. Finally, on Saturday night, Madeline was told he'd arrive on Sunday."

I wanted to ask Annie where she'd gone to school. She had a sense of the world unusual for a teenage girl found wandering the streets. I didn't interrupt. Donald and Erin were enraptured. Even Berta was caught up in the story.

"The morning the director was supposed to arrive, Madeline went for her swim. It was a foggy July morning, and the people in the hotel heard the bell on the buoy ring. At noon, when the director arrived, he went hunting for Madeline. No one could find her."

A peal of thunder exploded, and everyone around the table jumped. I looked up to see Bob standing in the door. There was no sign of Margo, and I assumed she'd gone up to her room.

Once the giggles subsided, Annie resumed her story. "By the afternoon, people had begun to search for the young star. When night began to fall, search parties with lights went out to check the shoreline."

"Did they find her?" Erin was on the edge of her seat.

"She was never found," Annie said. "But to this day, fisherman see a young girl with dark hair floating in the deep pools of the bayou.

They say Madeline's spirit remains near the old hotel, waiting for her chance at a movie."

"I saw her." Donald's eyes were nearly black, only ringed by a thin edge of blue. "She was in the marsh grass." His chest rose and fell rapidly, and I pushed back from the table and went to him. He was almost rigid with fear.

I turned to Annie. "You've frightened him half to death. You shouldn't do that to a child."

Annie blushed. "We saw something. In the water. Just a shadow or dark cloud. It wasn't anything. Donald's imagination jumped to conclusions."

Donald leaned forward. "That's not what I saw. She wasn't in the water, Annie. She was down the shore, hiding in the marsh grass. She was watching us. A girl with dark hair. Didn't you see her?"

Annie seemed afraid to breathe. Seconds ticked by in the silence that weighted the room. "It was just a story, Donald," she said at last.

Berta hesitated. "I don't like for the children to be frightened." It wasn't exactly a warning, but it was a clear direction.

"Yes, ma'am." Annie looked as if she'd been kicked. "It won't happen again."

Oblivious to the mood around the table, Bob refilled his wine glass and Berta's. I shook my head when he tipped the bottle in my direction. I'd learned something interesting. Annie was facile with a tall tale, and she was a quick study with local landmarks. It troubled me. I'd heard plenty of tales about the Paradise, but none about a drowned actress. "I should take Donald up to his room. The multiplication tables are calling his name," I said. "Annie, I left your books on the desk in your room."

"Annie's story has piqued my imagination." Berta twined her fingers through Bob's. "I think the Paradise Inn might make an interesting topic for research, especially since my husband is determined to bring it back to life. If the ghost of Madeline is there, we should know."

"I've lived here my entire life and never heard of Madeline."

"Maybe we can research the story of Madeline." Erin was suddenly eager.

Berta stood and put a hand on Erin's head. "Enough ghost stories. Let's clear the table. How about a game of Crazy Eights? Erin? Mimi beat the socks off all of us the last time we played. I think we deserve a rematch."

"I want to watch *Sanford and Son*," Erin said. "Margo loves that show."

"No television for Margo," Bob said. "She needs to reflect on her behavior, and some time alone in her room will do her good."

Dinner was over. As we carried the dishes into the kitchen, I noticed Annie staring out the windows at the front of the house. She stood, a small, solitary figure, enthralled by something in the night.

5

My suite of rooms occupied a portion of the second floor. Night had fallen, and for a moment I went to the door that gave onto a set of exterior stairs that also went to the third-floor room Annie now used. The staircase allowed me to come and go as I pleased. Bob and Berta wanted me to have my independence—not to seek permission for social activities. So far, though, I'd had no late dates or occasions to come home and slip inside unseen. I loved my rooms and had everything I desired at Belle Fleur.

Bob's renovations included a lovely old clawfoot tub, marble inlays in the bathroom, a spacious bed, and antique mahogany furniture. Cora had turned Berta on to a stash of antiques Bob bought for a pittance because "they might have really been in Belle Fleur."

He'd also added a huge walk-in closet. Since I had no living expenses, I could indulge my fashion wants—hip-hugger jeans, knit tops, sandals, shorts, and lots of prints with hippie influence. But I wasn't a girl who advocated drugs, sex, and rock and roll. My longing for family and acceptance undercut any rebellious need to express my independence in negative ways. I yearned for Bob and Berta's approval, therefore my wardrobe was simple, and I was careful not to go beyond a certain boundary because I feared I would influence Margo toward too-revealing clothing. She already had a penchant for short shorts and halter tops.

Some of the local teenagers had discovered marijuana and rock and roll back when I was in high school. A couple of boys I knew ran a business selling homegrown weed. The woods around Coden offered good soil, seclusion, and not much interference from the law. Drugs never interested me. I'd gone to college. I'd had other ambitions, and sometimes I'd been mocked for that. Mimi the Mouse was one nickname, because I was quiet.

The last laugh was mine; I now had probably the best job in town—room, board, a very generous salary, and the pleasure of being with the Hendersons. I also had the advantage of knowing which kids to guide Margo away from, though I wasn't always successful. She was sixteen and determined to prove she was grown.

The house settled into a soft quiet. I thought to stop by Margo's room and speak with her. I knew she was sore about the dressing-down Bob must have given her. While I didn't approve of her conduct, I did understand that sharing is something that doesn't come easily when love is at stake. To Margo, Annie was an unnecessary interloper who sucked up the air and the love and the attention. In a way, I agreed with that thought. But no matter, Annie was here and Berta meant for us to be kind to her.

I crept down the hallway, listening to the sighs and whispers of the house as the timber contracted in the cooling night. At times, I would have sworn the house had a consciousness. It sheltered the Hendersons, holding them close.

Margo and Erin shared a room large enough to include two desks and chairs, beds, their own private bath, and a game table as well as dressers and vanities. There wasn't a sound from the sisters. I cracked the door and peeked in. Both girls had agreed upon the blue-checked bedspreads and décor, but Margo had outgrown the childish frills.

Each daughter was bundled under her checked spread, sound asleep. I eased the door closed.

Part of Margo's anger at Annie's arrival involved the third floor. It had been promised to Margo once Bob finished the renovation. Now Annie was installed there and Margo was stuck with her kid sister.

Farther down near the stairs and across the hall from me was Donald's bedroom, a true boy's paradise of model planes, erector set creations, toy soldiers, and a train that ran around the entire room. Often, in the middle of the night, if I heard him stirring, I went to his room and told him stories until he fell asleep. It wasn't part of my job, but I enjoyed those times when it was just the two of us. Donald was an intuitive child. I thought he was Berta's favorite, and he was certainly mine.

Moving downstairs, I paused outside Bob and Berta's master suite. Berta had wisely chosen the bedroom that controlled the stairs and the front door. Even the best children are prone to mischief. It also gave the adults a bit of privacy, since the master suite was accessed only from a hallway that ended in the bedroom.

Sometimes, late at night, if I went to the kitchen for a glass of milk or an apple, I would pause outside their door and listen to them giggling like children. I wasn't really spying, but I couldn't help my fascination with their marriage. I'd seen Bob work his magic on Berta when she was in a bad mood. A whisper, a kiss, a tickle—he had a way with her. If I ever married, I wanted a man just like Bob. Tonight, though, they'd fallen asleep, judging from the lack of sound. It seemed I was the only person up and about.

Feeling like a sneak, I cut a big chunk of pound cake and headed back to my room. I was almost at my door when I heard footsteps behind me. I glanced back, but there was no one there. Still, the steps had sounded distinctive. I walked to the stairs and looked down and then up to the third floor. Nothing. I took a bite of the cake and listened. The house was quiet.

Back in my room, the cake consumed, I picked up my guitar and went out on the balcony. Perhaps I'd heard Annie on the exterior stairs, but it didn't matter. I might teach her, but I hadn't been charged with babysitting her.

The earlier storm had dropped the temperature, if not the humidity, and while my windows faced the old gardens and the place where Bob had built Erin a stables and riding facilities, I still caught some of the salt tang from the Sound.

My guitar skills were minimal, but I enjoyed picking and strumming the tunes of Bob Dylan, Jesse Winchester, John Prine, Simon and Garfunkel, and Arlo Guthrie, the poets of my generation. Coden was a place with few opportunities for young men, so a number of older boys I'd known in school had died in the humid jungles of Vietnam. While I kept my political opinions out of my job, I had strong feelings. Paul Dubois, a boy I met in college, left medical school to go into the Marines, one of the last to join the fight. He felt a civic duty to serve his country. And he had died in that faraway place. I could still see him so clearly, his dark hair and eyes. Funny that his image was etched in such detail when other things had slipped away.

"Mimi?" Donald stood at the threshold of my room.

I put aside the guitar and went to him. He wore pajamas covered in Casper the Ghost. "What is it?"

"I can't sleep. I heard someone in the house."

"I'm not surprised you're having bad dreams." I tousled his hair. "Stories about dead starlets aren't good for sleeping." I couldn't stop myself. "Donald, what did you really see? Annie said there was a shadow in the water, but you said you saw someone in the marsh grass."

He took my hand and we walked back to his room. "I saw a girl. Dark and pretty, like Annie. She stared at me like she wanted something. Are ghosts real?"

It was a question without an easy answer. I wasn't certain what I believed. There had been times when I was positive I'd seen my parents in the shade of an old tree or standing in a dark corner of Cora's house. But were they ghosts, or were they manifestations of my desperation? I couldn't say for certain, because to be honest, I couldn't remember what they looked like. They'd died a long time ago. Cora said it was better for me not to remember, that the fire had been a terrible tragedy and only the quick actions of a neighbor had saved me.

"Are they real?" he pressed, dragging me from my memories.

"I think Annie is a marvelous storyteller, Donald, but she made that story up. She doesn't know anything about the Paradise Inn or Coden or anywhere else. She'd never even heard of those places until she got here today. She's a lonely girl with a big imagination."

He climbed beneath the sheets I held up for him. As I tucked them around him I could see he was still disturbed.

"I didn't imagine the girl I saw. She was there, watching me."

"Even if ghosts are real, they can't hurt you." I kissed his forehead.

He looked toward the window. He was so pale, so agitated that I put a hand on his cheek. He was cool to the touch.

"Annie told me about Madeline while we were fishing. Only she told me different things." He hesitated. "Madeline was a slut."

I couldn't have been more shocked had he slapped me. "Do you know what that word means?"

His blue eyes were wide. He knew he'd upset me. "It's a bad girl. A girl who does bad things."

"Yes, it is. Who told you that?"

He closed his eyes, long dark lashes fanning out on his cheeks. "I don't remember."

"Did Annie tell you Madeline was a slut?" I had no idea where Annie had been or what hard things she'd endured in her brief life, but it was inappropriate to use such language with a child. I would have a talk with her first thing tomorrow.

"No. I don't remember. Don't be angry."

I hadn't the heart to be too hard. "I'm not angry, but words can hurt. And that's a word you shouldn't know and certainly shouldn't use."

"Okay." He turned to look toward the window. His room gave onto the Sound side of the house. With the windows open, the rush and kiss of the water could easily be heard.

"This girl you saw, what did she look like? Maybe it was Margo messing around."

He shook his head, his china gaze riveted into mine. "No. It wasn't Margo. She wore a white dress. She was really sad, and I think she was lost. I think she belongs here, at Belle Fleur."

Fear prickled along my arms and neck. "Annie's story has upset us both. Our imaginations are excited. Tomorrow, we'll look for evidence of this mysterious girl. I suspect it's a trick of the light or a very active imagination. We'll get Annie to help us look." I also intended to tell her that she was to share no more ghost stories. Donald was too impressionable.

"She already knows someone was there," Donald said. "She saw her too but she won't admit it."

6

Despite the upsets of the night, Donald woke with a voracious appetite and a sunny smile. He was at the breakfast table with Berta when I went downstairs, lesson plans in hand. One joy of private tutoring was the freedom to take our classroom outside. I didn't doubt Annie's verbal or language skills, but I wanted to test her knowledge of biology. The woods and swamp around Belle Fleur were the perfect place to do so—and I could also warn her of the natural dangers. Alligators and poisonous snakes of the deadly moccasin family were abundant during the summer. Huge timber rattlers slithered among the pines further inland. There were also wonderful king, black, garter, and many other "helpful" reptiles. Knowing the difference could mean life or death.

I took my place at the kitchen table where breakfast was always served. This was one meal Berta insisted that she serve "all of her children."

"Mama made blueberry pancakes. I picked the last of the berries this morning." Donald crammed a huge forkful into his mouth. He

loved the natural life—picking berries, fishing, boy things. Sometimes, when he rode Cogar with Erin, his natural grace and ease with
creatures large and small made me wonder where in life he would
find his true path. He was a child out of time, drawn to activities and
thoughts from the first half of the century, not the latter.

I poured maple syrup over the short stack Berta put in front of me.
Bob had eaten and gone to his office in Mobile. He had a new client
interested in renovating the old Bienville Hotel in downtown Mobile.
The port city, as Mobile was known, was one of the oldest settlements
along the Gulf Coast. Influences of early French and Spanish settlers
made the downtown area a delight for architectural renovators like
Bob. His passion was preservation, and the Bienville offered a chance
for him to show his stuff in a city with a growing tourist industry.

Once the social center of the port city on Mobile Bay, the Bienville
had withstood the ravages of the War Between the States and Yankee
occupation, but time and neglect had almost finished the old girl off.
Bob saw great potential and hoped it would be the project that would
garner national attention and bring in backers to fund the renovation
of the Paradise Inn.

"Erin is riding." Berta rolled her eyes. "She'd rather ride than eat."

"It's good for her. She has talent." I knew Berta was afraid of
Cogar, a large Connemara-cross with a strong will and a talent for
jumping anything in front of him. She also viewed the horse as a bribe
to get Erin to love Alabama.

"I'd prefer a violinist or maybe an opera singer to an equestrian."

Berta was teasing, but I understood. Violins didn't weigh fourteen
hundred pounds and buck. "She isn't afraid. Fear is the most dangerous
thing about riding. Don't ever let her know how much it scares you,
Berta." I glanced around the kitchen. "Where are Margo and Annie?"

"Margo is asleep. Annie must have gotten up at the crack of dawn.
She left a note saying she was going to explore and would be back by
seven-thirty."

Just as the clock in the hallway struck the half-hour, Annie
appeared in the doorway. I hadn't heard her footsteps in the hall.

"Sorry I startled you, Mimi. I went out to check around the marsh grass by the old hotel." She looked at Donald. "Not a trace of a ghost anywhere." Her hand rumpled his hair. "Am I too late for breakfast?"

She wore jeans, sneakers, and a cotton shirt in stripes of primary colors. It was an exceptionally bright outfit, something that surprised me. I'd expected a more demure palette.

"Not a bit." Berta lifted pancakes hot from the skillet and put them on a plate in front of her. She tore into them as if she hadn't eaten in at least a week.

Berta and I smiled over the top of her head. Nothing is more gratifying to a cook than someone who enjoys food.

Margo entered the room dragging a dark cloud behind her. She took a seat at the table and waved away the pancakes. She wasn't a cruel girl, but she was sixteen, a time when independence had to be won no matter the cost. She hadn't yet realized she didn't have to kick free of Berta and Bob. They were willing to let her go, because they understood it was their job. They required only that she engage her brain and keep herself safe so they could drop the reins with some degree of confidence that she wouldn't harm herself.

"Juice?" Berta asked, ignoring Margo's frown.

"Just coffee."

I began to clear the table. "Today we're going over to Paradise Inn. We'll identify some plants and discuss the local ecosystem."

"I'm not going. It's too hot. I hate sweating and the mosquitoes are as big as wrens."

Margo dared me to contradict her, but I didn't have to open my mouth. Berta loved her children, but she brooked no impertinence.

"Yes, Margo. You *will* go and you *will* be polite, courteous, and obedient. If I hear otherwise, you won't drive for two months." Berta stacked the plates on the table. "Annie, would you please take the garbage outside?"

When the door closed on Annie, Berta rounded on Margo. Before she could say anything, Margo lashed out.

"Why are you so mean to me?" Margo pushed back so hard, her chair flipped over when she stood. "Everyone else is perfect, especially

Annie. I'm the one who's always at fault. Why is that, Mother?" She didn't wait for an answer. "We've been to the hotel a hundred times. This is for Annie's benefit, isn't it, Mimi?"

Corporal punishment wasn't a part of the Henderson family, but I itched to slap her face. Margo had no idea how lucky she was, how much I'd give to be loved and coddled as she was. "I want to make sure Annie understands the dangers of the snakes and alligators. This is a dangerous place for someone who isn't aware."

"It wouldn't hurt my feelings if an alligator ate her," Margo said. "The entire house has turned upside down to make Annie feel good. What about me?" She turned to Berta. "What about your real children? We don't count for much anymore since you have Perfect Annie and Mimi the Do-Gooder."

Berta wiped her hands on a dish towel. "Margo, put on your boots and go to the front porch, where you'll wait for Mimi and the other children. Not another word. I'll discuss with your father an appropriate punishment for your behavior. You will learn to control your emotions or you will become a social recluse."

Berta had struck a deathblow. Margo had hard-to-get tickets to the Black Oak Arkansas concert in Biloxi. If Berta grounded her, she would miss out on an event she'd planned for weeks. She paled and left the room. The front door shut softly.

"She must learn to think before she speaks," Berta said. "Yes, she's an emotional teen, but in two years she'll be away in college, far from my ability to help her. She has to start using her head."

I couldn't argue with that logic and didn't want to. "I'll pick up Erin when we pass the stables. I'm ready to start the lessons."

"I'm going into town for supplies. I thought I'd let Margo and Annie prepare dinner tonight."

I swallowed. It wasn't the game plan I'd have chosen, but Berta was the boss.

"I've been thinking, Mimi. The children and I really dragged our feet when Bob moved us here. Listening to Annie's stories about the old hotel made me realize that we don't really know the history of our home or the hotel. I'm going to stop by the library and see if there are any books on Coden. It might be a good project for the children. Annie can learn the truth about Belle Fleur and the Paradise Inn along with the children. Put that ghost story stuff to bed. I know Annie doesn't mean any harm, but I don't like to see Donald so scared."

"That's an excellent idea." I was instantly caught up in the potential of the project. While Cora had told me many tales about Coden and the landmarks here, I'd never actually thought to explore the facts through research. In high school, we'd studied Alabama history, but Coden had hardly gotten a mention. "We'll battle the ghost stories with facts. It's a wonderful lesson in combating superstitions with knowledge."

Berta's fingers combed through my dark hair. "You're an unexpected blessing, Mimi. We were so lucky when we ran into Cora and she told us you were graduating as a teacher. I don't think I could have found anyone better."

Her praise made me dizzy. "Learning can be exciting. If I teach the children that, they'll never lack for an education."

"You make lessons fun. That's a gift. No matter where you end up teaching after these children are grown, you'll be a star."

"Thank you, Berta." It was a big compliment, but it also rattled me. I'd never thought that the Henderson children would grow up and my services wouldn't be necessary—that I would become their past. Of course it was the natural course of life, but it still made me sad.

"Hey, did I upset you?" Berta asked.

"Of course not. I just stepped into the future for a moment. It was a little disconcerting."

"Well, soon enough you'll be immersed in the past. I'll get all the books I can find at the library."

7

"Tell us about the gardens, Mimi." Erin grabbed my hand and held it as we walked beneath the live oaks that formed a canopy over the path. I'd decided to head for the natural springs, an area filled with plant and aquatic life. The swamp lilies, an amazing plant with white blossoms that smelled of heaven, were in bloom. The marshy land was also a primo location to find the native Alabama birds, and to that end I'd brought along my binoculars. It was also the habitat for moccasins, the most deadly of Alabama's snakes. There were rattlers aplenty, but they at least gave a distinctive rattle. The cottonmouths and copperheads were sneaky. They hid and then struck without warning.

"One reason Henri was drawn to Coden was the climate and the vast assortment of plants that grow here. We get more rain than any other place in the United States. While it makes humidity a problem, it's great for plants."

"I hate it here." Margo lifted her hair off her neck. "My hair is already starting to frizz and we haven't gotten out of the yard."

I ignored Margo's whining. "The swamp lilies, or Cahaba lilies as they're also known, were going to be one of the premier perfume plants of the Desmarais family's plan to create exotic and original scents." I lectured as we walked.

I threw a glance at Annie. This was a continuation of a history lesson started in the early summer, and I wondered if she might be lost. She gave me a smile that said she was willing to catch up as I told it.

"Henri Desmarais was the man who built our house and the Paradise Inn," Donald told Annie.

"Suck up." Margo reached out to pinch her brother but thought better of it when she saw I was looking.

"You're a bitch, Margo." Erin was angry. "Why do you have to act so awful to Annie?"

"Why do you have to act so awful?" Margo mocked her.

I grabbed Margo's arm in a none-too-gentle grip. "Stop it. Now."

She wanted to defy me, but she didn't. I was only five years her senior, but I was her teacher and I had the authority of her parents behind me. She broke free of me but kept her mouth shut.

I caught Erin's shoulder. "And your language is unacceptable."

"Did the Desmarais family ever make money on the perfume?" Annie stepped smoothly into the breach.

"The family suffered much tragedy, which is part of the local legend of Belle Fleur and the Paradise Inn, but they did create two original scents. I never thought to ask if they actually made a profit." That was a point we could look up in the library books.

"Tell Annie about the perfumes," Erin said. "I wish I could smell them."

"One perfume, named Belle Fleur for the house, resembled a blend of wild white jasmine and magnolias and was said to be the favorite of the confederate officers." I loved this part of Belle Fleur's legend.

"Chloe Desmarais, the young daughter of Henri and Sigourney, was the first to wear it, and Cora said that it could cast a spell on a man. Chloe had many suitors, from what I understand." It was Annie who spoke, and I turned to her in amazement.

"How did you know that?"

"When Cora said she was bringing me to Coden and the family lived at Belle Fleur, I went to the main library on Government Street and looked up the Desmarais family. In 1860, the newly created scent, Belle Fleur, was produced and had begun shipping to Northern markets as well as the South. The war, though, ruined the family perfume business."

"That's remarkable, Annie." She was so matter-of-fact with her eager knowledge.

"What? That I would look up the history of the place I was going to live?" She made it sound so logical, but it struck me as strange.

"It's very . . . mature."

"Belle Fleur is *my* home, and I don't give a damn what kind of perfumes they made here two hundred years ago. Knowing about Belle Fleur won't make it your real home, Annie. Can we get this field trip over with?" Margo wiped sweat from her forehead. "I have a date tonight and I don't want to have to reset my hair. If we fart around here all morning, I'll have to wash and roll it."

"Your wish is my command." I gave her a low bow. "Lead on."

"Stop a moment," Annie said. "I can smell the flowers. Incredible."

She was right. The intoxicating scent of the swamp lilies was suddenly all around us. When we rounded a bend in the path, I saw the lilies. They bloomed everywhere in the natural springs that bubbled around the roots of the trees. The smell was intoxicating. Had the war not destroyed the entire economic structure of the South, the Desmarais family would have been millionaires.

The rat-a-tat-tat of a woodpecker stopped us in our tracks. With the help of the field glasses, I was able to find the rare pileated woodpecker halfway up a dying wild cherry tree. The bird hammered the bark with its beak. I handed the glasses to Erin, who looked and then passed them to Donald while we stood hushed and observing.

"Note the bird's size—it is the largest of the woodpecker family. And the red hood. Both the male and female are colorful, and both hatch the eggs and feed the young."

"Very modern," Margo sniped. "Mommy and Daddy both parent. The baby peckers will be so well adjusted."

"I'm telling Mother on you." Erin glared at her older sister. "There's no reason to be ugly to Mimi. She's only trying to teach us."

"I don't want to learn this shit. I want to be a lawyer. Who cares about woodpeckers?"

"It's okay." I didn't want the other children reporting that I couldn't control Margo. I faced her. "I don't appreciate your conduct, Margo."

"Oh, I'm not perfect like Annie. Too bad."

"I'm going to tell Daddy now," Erin threatened.

"Tattle-tale." Margo curled a lip.

Erin was about to step forward when Donald pushed her aside, sending her stumbling backward and sprawling into me. I caught her. "Hey!"

He stopped us all and pointed. A huge brown snake coiled on a limb right at head level. Had Erin gone a step farther, the snake could have bitten her right between the eyes. From the musky odor, I knew it was a moccasin.

"I've had enough of this *Mutual of Omaha* wilderness shit." Margo turned back down the trail. "These woods creep me out. I'm going home."

"I'd be careful, Margo. Someone is waiting down the trail. He's been watching us for a while." Annie pointed down the path.

"Someone *is* watching us," Erin grabbed my arm and pointed where Annie pointed.

I tore my gaze from the snake to look to the west. The woods were close, the lighting poor. But I saw something. A shadow moving among the darker shadows of the woods.

"It's a deer or a stray dog." I couldn't allow the children to feel the surge of irrational panic that gripped me. Donald pressed against my side.

"It's the girl. She's watching us all." He clutched at my shirttail. "She's hiding in those bushes."

For one moment we all stood rooted to the spot. "What a bunch of horseshit. I'm outta here." Margo pushed Annie out of her path.

"We will stay together, Margo. We're all leaving, but we'll go as a group." My voice had a quiver and I couldn't help it. Maybe the earlier talk of ghosts had unnerved me, but I felt a keen sense of danger. Tucked deep in the shadows, I saw something shifting.

"I'm not afraid." Margo started down the trail. "You're on your own. I hope the bogeyman doesn't get you."

"There is someone there." Annie was calm. "Don't be foolish, Margo. We can all go home together. It's safer."

"I'll take care of myself and you take care of you," Margo said, plowing ahead. She disappeared around a bend in the path.

"What are we going to do?" Erin was truly frightened, and so was Donald.

"We're going home. We just spooked ourselves, that's all. It was just the wind moving the tree limbs." While I spoke boldly, I couldn't resist looking back at the place I'd seen the shadow moving. There was nothing there except an old hackberry bush and a dogwood, the blooms long since fallen. "Just a shadow. Let's go home."

"Let me gather a few flowers," Annie said. She ducked beneath the snake without hesitation. Donald started to go after her, but I grabbed him and pulled him back. My authority might not sway Annie to common sense, but I could protect Donald.

In a moment she was back with a cluster of exotic blooms in her hand.

"I'm not waiting!" Margo called from far ahead. She was out of sight.

"Why aren't there perfume factories here?" Annie asked. "Were they built and destroyed?"

"I don't know." And to be honest, I'd never given it a lot of thought. Coden was a fishing community. The waters teemed with shrimp, crabs, oysters, and dozens of fish species considered delicacies around the world. The Gulf was a demanding and dangerous mistress, but it was the heart of the area. Perfume seemed so . . . alien, so fancy compared to the life I'd grown up witnessing.

"Maybe Bob will rebuild the perfume factories," Annie said. "Wouldn't that be the best? Belle Fleur could be what she was once supposed to be."

I couldn't focus on the fantasy Annie wove. I was on high alert, looking for someone in the shadows. I wanted to call out to Margo, but I wouldn't give her the satisfaction of letting her know she'd worried me. Above us the trees made a shelter from the hot sun, but nothing could help the humidity, or the mosquitoes. Margo's complaints were justified, and as sweat trickled down my back and into my jeans, I wished I'd listened to her. By the time we got back to Belle Fleur, I'd be a soggy mass dotted in insect bites.

"Let's stop by the cemetery." Donald was happiest outside, and the old wrought-iron-enclosed burial ground for the Desmarais family held no horrors for him. We'd done tombstone etchings, and I found the marble statuary melancholy but also an interesting art form. Since our biology field trip had been a bust, the cemetery might yield a history lesson.

"Annie might be interested," I said.

"Margo went on to the house." Erin was slightly miffed that her older sister defied the rules and seemed to get away with it. "It's hot and the mosquitoes are feasting on my legs."

"Berta won't be pleased with Margo. Let's give some time for the dust to settle," I said. Margo had to learn, and the lesson would be as painful as she made it. "Part of growing up is learning that there are consequences to our actions. Margo is about to learn that in spades."

"You're right. Let's stay outside for a little longer." Erin didn't like confrontation.

We veered down a narrower path. Hoof prints told the story of Erin's latest ride. His fear forgotten, Donald ran ahead and pushed open the wrought-iron gate to the cemetery, an enclosure that covered a couple of acres. The perimeter had been planted in cedar trees, and as we entered I touched the gnarled trunk of a tree over two hundred years old.

"Mimi!" Donald's cry brought me to full alert.

"Donald!" He'd ducked behind one of the larger, more ornate monuments, and I couldn't see him. I found him a moment later standing beside the broken image of an angel. The marker had graced the grave of Sigourney Desmarais, Henri's wife. As I stepped closer, I felt a chill of distaste. The figure once had all of the accoutrements of a heavenly host, but she had fallen into ruin. The marble eyes were blackened by mold. She lay on the ground, her wings snapped from her body.

"What a shame," I said. I doubted the markers were monetarily valuable, but they were of historical interest. They'd been created at a time when statuary was a mark of wealth. The more ornate, the more revered the dead person.

Donald knelt beside the fallen angel. His hand traced the words at her base. "Death has not marred your physical beauty, and God have mercy on your soul."

"Do you think Sigourney was beautiful?" Donald asked. "She must have been. She had the biggest tombstone of all. She had an angel, but now it's broken."

"Maybe Bob can repair it," I said.

"I want to be cremated." Erin glanced around. "I don't like this place. I don't want to be buried anywhere."

"Dead people can't hurt you," Annie said. "It's the living you have to keep an eye on." She stood back from us, almost as if she were reluctant to get too close to the graves.

"Do you really think Dad can fix the angel?" Donald was deeply worried.

"We can ask."

"Henri and Sigourney were the . . . founders of the family here." Donald talked to Annie. "They had a daughter, Chloe. She's buried over there." He pointed toward a tombstone with a lamb lying beside a lion.

"That's an ornate marker, too," Annie said. She walked over, slowly. "Born 1858, died 1874. A hundred years ago." She looked at me. "She was only sixteen. What did she die of?"

I shook my head. "We've looked for records of her death, but we can't find any. According to my grandmother, Sigourney fell down the stairs in the house. Henri died of a fever. But we couldn't find the records for the daughter, Chloe. She was said to be ravishing, but shy. There are lots of local stories about her beauty and how Henri meant to create the most original scent in the world and name it for her. It is strange that no one knows what happened to her."

"Maybe she didn't really die," Annie said. "Maybe she ran away or something."

It was a peculiar thing to say. "But the tombstone has a death date."

Annie shrugged. "Rich people can make things look exactly as they want them to."

"Do you think the police would come and see who pushed over the angel?"

Donald was all but obsessed.

"We'll tell Bob. He'll know what to do."

Erin looked concerned. "We aren't far from the barn. What if they messed with Cogar?"

"Bob will take care of it, but we'll stop by and check on your horse just to put your mind at rest."

"You don't know how lucky you are to have a father like that," Annie said to Erin. "And a tutor like Mimi."

I was about to comment when in the distance I heard a scream so shrill, I winced. My gut reaction came a split second later. "Margo!" She was the only one of my brood who'd wandered away. While her pique might have sent her down the path alone, I'd allowed it.

"Come!" I grasped Donald's hand and ran toward the path Margo had taken.

The scream came again, high-pitched and frightened.

"What the hell?" I muttered under my breath.

Annie, so thin and dainty looking, shot past me. She ran like a gazelle. I'd never seen a human cover ground so quickly and effortlessly.

"Annie! Wait! It could be dangerous."

She didn't pause or look back. She disappeared behind a cluster of oak trees, and I was left trying to keep up with Erin and tugging Donald behind me.

8

We broke through a thicket of wild azaleas and stumbled to a stop. Margo stood in the center of the path, her arms wrapped around the neck of a dark-haired boy who kissed her with a passion that bent her backwards. He hugged her to him tightly, lifting her and spinning as they held the kiss. Margo's blue canvas shoes flew from her feet into the bushes. Annie was not a yard away and they totally ignored her.

"Margo!" I spoke sharply.

She broke from the embrace, flushed but bold. "I suppose you're going to tell Mother about this, too. I don't care. I'm sick of doing everything she says. I'm old enough to know what I want."

Arguing with Margo would be spitting into the wind. "Andrew, you should leave. Now." I recognized the boy. He'd graduated from high school this past year. Andrew Cargill, captain of the Coden High School football team and the owner of a muscle car that ripped down the county roads at breakneck speeds. He was a bad boy through and through with no ambitions. The military draft had ended—no hope he'd be called up for duty. He'd been sniffing around Margo all summer and would continue until someone put a stop to it. Or he got arrested for dealing dope. It wasn't a well-kept secret in town that he made a little extra cash, on top of his mechanic job, with the weed he grew in the woods.

"Good to see you, Mimi." He grinned. The boy had the very devil of charm in his smile.

I nodded. It was clear he had no fear of, or respect for, me. He kissed Margo's lips briefly. "See ya later, babe." He sauntered down the path.

I caught Margo's wrist. "Did he follow us down to the swamp?" I asked. "He was in the woods watching us, wasn't he? That was Andrew sneaking around." That he'd made me afraid roused my anger.

Margo shrugged as she felt around in the bushes for her shoes. "He jumped out of those azaleas and almost made me pee my pants." She laughed. She was hooked on the boy and saw no reason to hide it. "Are you going to tell Mother?"

"Why would you kiss him knowing we were coming along behind you? You wanted to be caught. You should tell your mother yourself."

She shrugged. "I'm tired of sneaking around. I've been seeing Andrew since May. He's cute and sexy and he treats me like I'm a person and not a child. Mother has Annie to be her little baby girl now. She can let me be free."

"Berta won't approve of Andrew, especially not if you're sneaking around." That was an understatement.

"She'll never approve of me. You're so perfect, Mimi, and Annie is so wonderful. She doesn't see me, not me, separate from her. She thinks I'm going to UCLA, her alma mater. I'm not. Not unless Andrew goes. We're going to get married."

"Not likely. Annie, please take the children to the house." I motioned the children to go ahead of us. I wanted a serious word with Margo. When we were alone, I grabbed her arm, and not gently. "Listen to me. You are about to screw up your life. Andrew doesn't have the ambition, the finances, or the drive to go to a top school. You do."

R. B. CHESTERTON

"No, I don't. Mother does. That's what she wants. That's her fantasy of my life. That's what she did and she thinks I should follow every step she took. Lot of good it did her. Look at her now, tending her vegetable garden in Coden, Alabama. The freaking back woods without even a movie theater. I'm not living her life over for her so she can get it right. I'll join the Reverend Sun Myung Moon and sell roses at the crossroads before I turn into her. At least with the Moonies Andrew and I can be together!" She dashed her sweaty bangs off her forehead.

Her reference to the North Korean businessman who'd recently moved to Bayou La Batre and started the Unification Church, an organization that most locals viewed as nothing more than a cult, showed me how desperate she'd become. Members of Moon's church, Moonies, worked for no wages, living within the framework of the church. Margo's threat, and threat was all it was because she couldn't go a day without her cosmetics, fine clothes, and luxuries, would torment Berta, though.

"That's something you should take up with your parents," I said calmly. The temptation to argue was strong, but I didn't. This was Bob and Berta's battle, not mine. I was responsible for her safety when she was in my charge, but I couldn't govern her personal life. I brushed past her and continued to the house. At least the mystery of the person watching us at the lilies was explained. Andrew Cargill. Berta would not be pleased that the young man was lurking around on Henderson property with the clear intention of seducing Margo.

Berta returned from town before lunch, and we threw together sandwiches and lemonade. The children were reading the stories I'd assigned them, and Berta turned the radio on in the kitchen so we could listen to the local Mobile disc jockey's humorous ramblings. Doctor Love was a show Berta and I both enjoyed at lunch time. The local spin jockey, who took calls from listeners, handed out ridiculous advice for teenagers in love. The silly radio show had become part of the daily routine at Belle Fleur. We listened as we prepared lunch, and Berta often offered counter-advice, which was sensible.

"Can I help?" Annie stood in the kitchen doorway.

"We've got it, Annie. Are you through with your book?" I'd assigned her *To Kill a Mockingbird*.

"Yes. I love that story. I read it before."

"Oh, really. When?"

She frowned. "I don't know. I only know I remember the story. Atticus Finch, a lawyer." She went to the counter and began to shake out the lettuce Berta had washed. "He was a good man. He reminds me of Bob."

"Except Bob is an architect and isn't Southern."

"But Bob would stand up for what's right. He would. Even if it cost him."

Berta stopped behind Annie and pulled her wild hair back and began to loosely braid it. "That's a nice thing to say, Annie. Bob will be flattered."

"Did Mimi tell you what happened in the woods today?" Annie asked.

The bottom dropped out of my stomach. Andrew Cargill's influence on Margo weighed heavily on me, but I wanted to give Margo a chance to tell Berta herself.

Berta dropped Annie's hair and tilted her head at me. "What happened?"

"Erin nearly walked into a moccasin in a tree. Donald saved her."

"I hate the snakes here. Everything is just so . . . lush. The grass, the trees. There's too much of everything, and it's soft and wet." She shook. "Maybe you should stay out of the woods until winter."

Berta was overreacting, but it would be nothing compared to what she'd do when she heard about Andrew Cargill. I gave Annie a warning look, but her expression was all innocence. I wondered if she was so naïve, or if she meant to get Margo in trouble. "Did you get any of the library books?" I changed the subject.

"I did." Berta washed her hands and went to her book bag and withdrew several volumes. "I found this local history on south Mobile County that showed the area as it had been from the boom period of the 1880s up to 1906, when the 'second September storm' struck with tides ten feet and above." She shuddered. "I hope we don't have a hurricane while we're living here. Anyway, Coden was devastated. Some thirty people drowned."

I'd heard about the numerous hurricanes that hit around Coden, but it was the 1906 storm that extracted a high cost in my little community. "The storms are horrible. Some summers, they hit all around us. But Belle Fleur has withstood all the storms since it was built." I looked up to see Donald and Erin standing in the doorway. "Come and look at the history book on Coden your mother found."

With Donald and Erin on either side of me and Annie at my shoulder, we leafed through the local history volume. I noted the author was Chad Petri, a Coden native. I knew his grandson, Trevor.

"And one of the grandest homes on the Coden shore was that of Henri and Sigourney Desmarais. . . ." I flipped the page, only to find that the story had jumped to shrimp production.

"The pages have been removed." Erin pointed to the thin stubs of what would have been two or three pages. Checking the page numbers, I saw she was correct.

"Who would deface a history book?" I closed it.

"They cut out the story of our house." Donald was disappointed.

Berta came over to look. "That's awful. Who would do such a thing?"

"I'll see if the library can order another copy." I put the book aside. Another idea came to me. "If we can't get the information from a book, maybe the author will remember. I know the Petri family. Mr. Chad is still alive. Cora will know if he's in a good mental state. If he is, maybe he can tell us the story of Belle Fleur."

"That's even better than reading a book." Donald was all about field trips.

"I'll call Cora and see if she can set up an interview with Chad. It would be an excellent report for each of you to write." I glanced around the room, aware that Margo was missing. Lately she'd been pulling a disappearing act whenever my attention shifted. She was setting herself up for serious trouble with her parents.

A knock at the front door sent Donald flying down the hall. His sneakers gripped the hard wood floor, squeaking, as he raced. He swung the door open without looking first. "Cora!"

"Erin, see if you can find Margo, please." I spoke softly. In a way I felt sorry for Margo. The phase that had settled on her was unpleasant for her as well as everyone else. She wasn't a bad kid, she was just headstrong and used to getting her way. I'd had a few problems with her at the first of the summer, but ever since Annie had come into the house, Margo had been impossible. The hard truth was that she only made matters worse for herself by sneaking away and back-talking. She was going to end up confined to her room.

Donald and Cora came down the hall singing a song about Daniel Boone. I gave them a round of applause before I put on a pot of coffee. I was glad to see Cora. She might have some insight into Margo and how best to handle her. She'd certainly know more about Andrew Cargill than I did.

"We're doing a report on Belle Fleur," Donald told Cora. "Can you make us an appointment with Chad Petri? We want to tape-record him when we ask questions about Coden and the house and all the things that happened here. Maybe he'll know about the movie star girl who drowned."

"What's the sudden interest in local history?" Cora gave me a curious look.

"Actually, it's because of Annie and her stories that Berta got the idea to study the area. It's a wonderful chance for the children to speak with a living source." I grinned at Berta as I talked. "Annie did some research and she's whetted our appetites to know the whole truth about Belle Fleur."

"Mimi, you know all about the house," Cora said. "There really isn't any history. It's mostly folklore and legend now. I doubt you'll find much written down. So many records have been lost, thanks to hurricanes and such."

"Researching Belle Fleur will be good for the children," Berta said. "It's like a mystery. I was thinking about this, and maybe Margo can do something with film. It would be wonderful for her to really create an oral history, capture some of the people who lived this history. So many of the older generation are passing on."

"Berta, I can see you're enthused by the project. I just wish there was something more interesting about Coden." Cora patted Berta's hand. "And, Annie, how are you? How are you fitting in?" Cora was more interested in her charge than any interviews.

"I love it here." Annie blushed, a dark rose of color climbing her cheeks. "I've never lived anywhere so . . . wonderful!"

"That you can remember," Cora pointed out. "Still not even a glimmer of a memory?"

"I'd know it if I had a family like this." Annie spoke with palpable sadness. "I never want to leave Belle Fleur. Never."

Berta laughed out loud. "For right now, Annie is a part of the Henderson family. When she gets old enough to go to college, she'll find a career she loves. Until then, she's one of us." Berta closed the door on the topic and got a bowl of fresh strawberries from the refrigerator. "I bought some pork chops, and garden-fresh squash and tomatoes. Annie, I think you and Margo should collaborate on dinner tonight."

"I love to cook." Annie seemed surprised by the revelation. "I don't know how I know, but I can cook." She nodded with a wide smile. "We can grill the pork chops and I can make a squash casserole with sliced tomatoes."

"That sounds delicious." Berta looked at me. "Where's Margo?"

I hesitated a second too long. "I don't know. She was with us when we came back from the field trip. I was hoping she'd gone to talk with you."

Donald had no compunction about keeping his mouth shut. "She met that Andrew boy in the woods. They were kissing like in the movies. He picked her up and swung her around until her shoes flew off."

"Is this true?" Berta's gaze bored into me.

I hated to rat Margo out, even though it was for her own good. I looked to Erin and then Annie for some help, but they both kept their gaze on the floor. "Yes. I told her you'd be upset. I don't think she arranged to meet him."

"No, he just happened to be wandering around our property and stumbled upon you."

When she put it like that, I saw that Margo must have called Andrew before we set out. She'd planned the meeting, playing me for a fool. "I broke it up and told her she had to tell you."

"Sometimes it's best to let something like this go to the finish," Cora said gently. "Margo is headstrong like most teens. If you forbid her from seeing this boy, she'll only be more determined."

While Berta might value Cora's wisdom, she was angry at Margo. "I'm afraid my eldest daughter is going to have to learn the hard way that I mean for her to obey me."

Cora sighed. "Girls are easier up until this age, then all hell breaks loose. I don't envy you, Berta." She put an arm around Annie. "Don't you dare start any behavior like this."

"Annie isn't as reckless as Margo, and you can't tell me Mimi gave you any trouble," Berta said, trying to lighten the pall that had fallen over the room. "She's the most sensible young woman I've ever met."

"Yeah, that's me. Sensible." I hated it when I was made to sound like vanilla pudding. Old Mimi, reliable, responsible, always wanting to please. There was more to me than bland sludge. For one wild moment, I hoped Margo made a break for a life with Andrew.

"Oh, she had her moments." Cora reached across the table and brushed a strand of hair from my face. "Every child has a hard time finding her path. Every one. The smart ones, like Mimi, don't fall in the ditches but once or twice."

"We shouldn't talk about my past." I stood up suddenly. Everyone in town knew about the fire that had killed my parents, but I didn't want the Hendersons to think of that every time they saw me. I'd learned the hard way that tragedy could stick to a person like stink on a turd. I'd gone through school ignoring the whispers, the sympathy, the cruelty. Cora knew how sensitive I was.

"Everything worked out for the best." Cora drained her coffee cup. "Margo will work it out the same way Mimi did."

"Margo is a different kettle of fish," Berta said. "But I thank you for your encouraging words. If she turns out half as lovely as Mimi, I'll be a proud mother."

"Don't forget Mr. Petri," Donald said to Cora. "We want to tape-record him. That would be fun. To do like a radio reporter asking questions. We can pretend we're on WABB."

"I'll speak with him this week," Cora promised. "I might come along, too. As long as I've lived in Coden, I've heard stories about the old days when Belle Fleur was a showcase and people came from miles around to see the gardens. I was always told that Belle Fleur was the original pattern for Bellingrath Gardens."

She referred to a local home that had been turned into a tourist attraction offering a vibrant show of flowers year-round. The sixty-five-acre gardens and "Southern Renaissance" home had opened for public tours in 1934, long after Belle Fleur had fallen into disrepair. Bellingrath drew tourists from all over the world. But once, Belle Fleur and the Paradise Inn had been the queen attraction on the upper Gulf rim.

"We went to Bellingrath last spring," Berta said. "Beautiful. I loved the butterfly garden."

"You could do a similar garden here," Cora reminded her. "The plants are in the ground—far more than sixty-five acres. There must be at least three hundred acres of formal gardens here at Belle Fleur. They're just overgrown."

"It would take hundreds of workers to reclaim. . . ." Berta looked out the window. "Is that Margo?"

I almost dreaded looking. I walked to the kitchen sink where I had a good view of the backyard swing. Margo leaned back and Andrew Cargill stood behind her and held her in his arms. He kissed her with a raw, wild passion that made me dry-swallow.

"I'll go get her." I started toward the back door, but Berta grabbed my arm.

"I'll take care of this."

I almost reminded her of Cora's words of wisdom. Pushing Margo right now might not be smart. On the other hand, Margo was pushing Berta, which I knew for a fact was not intelligent.

"Margo! Get in the house!" Berta slammed the back door as she strode across the lawn. Annie, Erin, and Donald joined me at the window. "Andrew! Leave this property now and you are not invited back. If you come here again, I'll have you arrested."

"I told you to find her," I said to Erin.

She shrugged. "I did. I told her to come inside. She told me to kiss off. Mama is gonna make her sorry for being so ugly."

No doubt about that. But in the end, Margo's rebellion was the least of our worries.

9

The excitement of Andrew Cargill and Margo's defiance led to a supper fraught with tension between Margo and Berta. After I'd cleared the table and put the dishes away, I found the defaced book and put it on the hall table to take back to the library the next day. The other members of the family had gone to their respective rooms, and I had no interest in television. The conflict in the family was distressing.

That night as I played guitar on the balcony, it was Annie who came to my room. She slipped down the exterior stairs like a wraith. Surprised, I started to put the guitar down, but she stopped me.

"We like the same music," she said. "I want to write songs."

I strummed a few minor key chords. She'd just stepped on my secret ambition, one that I'd never voiced. In my most private fantasies, I was a famous songwriter. "Do you play the guitar?"

"No. It wasn't allowed."

"Allowed?" I put the guitar on the bed. "So you remember something."

Annie turned to look out the window. "I remember there were rules. Lots of rules. No music, no dancing, no laughing." She faced me and shrugged. "Is that a real memory or just the lack of memory? I can't distinguish."

"Why is your past such a secret, Annie? Did you do something wrong?"

If the question irritated her, she hid it well. "I don't remember. I don't think so. If I was punished, it's gone from my brain. I just know the place I lived wasn't like this house." She looked around my room, taking in the books and a few stuffed animals I'd brought from Cora's. "This is the best place in the world."

I knew then she wasn't leaving. Not ever. She'd come to stay, seeking the love that I also needed. We were both desperate for the bounty of Belle Fleur. "You'll grow up and want your own life."

"You're grown, Mimi. And beautiful. But you don't date. Margo can't stand being away from boys for a minute, but you don't seem to care at all."

Cora had sometimes prodded me to date. I'd gone to movies or dinner, but never more than twice with the same young man. The spark of romantic love had failed to settle on me. The boys in Coden bored me. "If I knew someone worth dating, I'd date."

"What if I flirted with Andrew Cargill?" Annie asked. "I could break them up. Men like me."

"Margo would snatch your hair out." I couldn't help but smile at the thought. Annie had a point, though. When we were all in town together, men would do a double-take when Annie walked by. She was thin and gangly, but she had something men responded to.

"Berta would be happy if I broke them up."

"And you would be dead because Margo would kill you. You can't interfere like that."

"It was just a thought." She went to my record collection and started to look through the albums. "I wish I could play and write like John Prine." She held up his album, *Diamond in the Rough*. "He's a genius."

"You can borrow my guitar if you want." I regretted it the moment I said it.

"I'd like that." She touched my guitar, a fine old Gibson that I'd bought second-hand. The guitar deserved a more talented owner, but I enjoyed trying to play.

"Try it." I showed her a few chords and helped her sing a verse of "Blowing in the Wind." "Your voice is true." She blushed at the praise.

Her fingers touched the strings. "I don't ever want to leave here," she said. "I don't care who I used to be. Like you, I'm not part of the family, but we belong here. I don't know how I know it, but my parents are dead. It had to be something awful or I'd remember. Cora said your parents are dead, too."

I hated that Cora had shared my past with her. It felt like a violation. "I've forgotten the details."

She perched on the edge of my bed. "You don't remember anything?"

I didn't, but I'd been told. It was better to deal with this head-on than have Annie asking Berta about my past. "There was a gas leak and when my dad started the car in the garage, the house blew up."

"And you got away?"

Something in her tone made me look into her dark eyes. "I don't know how. I don't remember." The only image of that night that I retained rose up behind my eyes. Flames danced from the windows of the small frame house. Inside someone was screaming. I dropped a curtain over the memory.

"I knew something bad happened in your life." She touched the deep furrow between my brows. "When you worry, which is a lot, your have a mark here."

"I try not to frown, but thanks for the beauty tip." I stood up and put the guitar back in its case. This was too close to the bone, too personal. She had no right to stomp around in my private pain.

"Sometimes you can't help what the past does to you." Annie handed me the pick. "See you in the morning, Mimi."

When she was gone I played a Beatles tune, "Yesterday." I was only twenty-one, but I'd had sea shifts in my life. Cora was the only constant. Until the Hendersons. Like Annie, I never wanted to leave.

❦

The gulls screamed across the water and marsh grass. They circled and spun, white wings outstretched and black markings nearly invisible as they blurred by. In the distance a shrimp boat trawled the rich Sound waters. Another covey of gulls circled the boat, swooping down for any debris. In the distance, their calls sounded like laughter.

"What type of gull is it, Donald?" I asked as I drove the station wagon along Shore Road. It was a beautiful August day. Too hot, really, but the wagon had air-conditioning and so the heat devils that shimmied on the asphalt were merely a distant bother.

"Those are laughing gulls. Black heads show maturity." Donald loved birding as much as I did.

"Erin, are the birds herbivores?"

"Carnivores. They survive on small fish and crabs, the debris from the fishing vessels and what they can steal from other creatures or humans. Some gulls have been known to use tools."

I nodded. "For example."

"The larger white gulls have been filmed using bread to lure small fish to the surface so they can be caught." She flopped around on the backseat. "It's horrible. Something is always eating something else."

Erin retained information better than any of the other children. She was also the most tenderhearted. A vegetarian, she ate seafood but no other life forms. Berta had resisted at first, but now Erin's prefer-ences were part of the family.

"Nature is cruel," Annie said. "In this world, it's eat or be eaten. It isn't just animals, either. People are like that, too."

"Spoken like the little parasite you are," Margo, who was in the front seat, turned back to speak to Annie.

"You're a stupid cow, Margo. Life doesn't have to be awful." Erin was only twelve, but she had strong feelings. "Mother says that love and compassion can change anyone."

"You are such a goody two-shoes," Margo reached back and pinched Erin's leg.

Berta wouldn't apply that to Andrew Cargill, but I kept my mouth shut and my comments to myself. Innocence was a privileged state, and I would allow Erin to stay there as long as she could. "Why don't you guys grab an ice cream while I take these library books back and show them the damage? Margo, if you continue to torment your sister, I'll have to tell Berta."

"Oh, another black mark. What now? She'll make me scrub floors? Like that's ever going to happen."

We parked at the library and Margo, Annie, and the children tumbled out of the car and headed down to Swenson's Ice Cream shop. Coden had little to offer in the way of shopping. For clothes and such, we drove into Mobile. Beauchamps stocked the basic groceries, and Bobinger Hardware carried the essentials of home maintenance. Other than that, there was a bait shop, two restaurants, one beauty salon, and the ice cream shop, which was open only in the summer months.

It was with a sigh of relief that I stepped into the air-conditioned library. Quiet surrounded me. I put the books I was returning on the counter and then searched the stacks for other history books. Away from the bickering children, I lost myself in thoughts of the past, when the Paradise was up and running. Then there had been clubs and sailboats and a sense that life was opening up for Americans. Before the Paradise, there had been another hotel, the Rolston, which had been destroyed in a hurricane.

"May I help you, miss?"

The librarian was Cora's age, a trim woman with steel-gray hair and a twin set the color of her hair. I walked back to the counter and got Chad Petri's book and showed her the damage, which drew an exclamation of dismay. "This book is irreplaceable."

"Surely Mr. Petri might have additional copies?" Or know how to get some. "He lives right around here."

"I'm afraid not." She ran a finger down the spine of the book as if she could heal it. "There was a fire last night and his garage burned to the ground. All of his extra books went with it. Everyone is so upset."

"That's terrible." I was surprised. Fire was an event everyone in Coden learned about, yet I'd heard not a word. "Was anyone injured?"

The librarian shook her head. "It's the strangest thing. He fell in his garage late last night and struck his head. When he came to, he was on the floor of the garage and flames were all around him."

"I'm so sorry to hear that. Is he okay?"

She shook her head. "I'm afraid he isn't." She leaned closer. "He keeps insisting that someone pushed him down."

"He's my grandmother's age, just a nice old man. We were going to interview him about his history book. Who would want to harm him?"

The librarian shrugged one shoulder slowly. "There wasn't a sign anyone else was in the garage. They think the trauma has unsettled his thinking." She leaned closer. "Don't talk this because of the insurance and all, but Mitch Lowell, the fire chief, thinks Mr. Chad was in the garage smoking. Somehow he knocked over the gas can for the lawnmower. Mitch thinks Chad is just confused about the sequence of events."

"When was the fire?"

"After midnight. It was on the news this morning. WKRG sent a camera crew, and the *Mobile Register* sent a photographer. Mr. Chad gave an interview to the TV reporter, which I think his son should have stopped. Poor old thing looked senile. He was so upset about the books burning. Said he'd paid to print them out of his own pocket and now it was all gone."

"Thanks." I left the library though I'd intended to check out additional history books. I wanted to talk to my grandmother, but she would be in Mobile, at the office, or possibly en route to a client's home. It would have to wait until tonight, after dinner. For now, I wanted to round up the children and head back to Belle Fleur.

10

It was my turn to cook, and my grilled chicken salad was uninspired and limp, but we struggled through the meal. Berta cast glances at me but said nothing. Chad Petri and the fire occupied my brain. I'd driven by the Petri property on the way home from town. The fire marshal from Mobile was there, as well as some federal officers. Coden seldom attracted attention from Mobile's authority figures. We were a backwater, a poor fishing community, and as such we were left to our own devices when it came to the rare criminal act. A sheriff's sub-station, with office space for three deputies, had been added in Grand Bay to keep an eye on the Unification Church. Mark Walton, a Coden native, and a couple of other young officers rolled through south Mobile County to "maintain a presence" and keep Rev. Moon aware his "religious" endeavors were being watched.

Other than fistfights and public drunks, there was little crime in Coden. The minor burglars and drunk drivers were arrested and sent to Mobile for trial or punishment.

"Mimi, it's a shame about Mr. Petri and his books," Berta said. "Have you talked to Cora about it?"

"Not yet. After supper I'll drive over and find out what she knows."

"Good plan. Bob is going to take Annie for a night drive. Leave the station wagon and take the convertible, okay?"

I loved driving her car. "Sure."

Margo slammed her napkin into her salad bowl. "I'm not allowed to drive, but you're giving Annie a lesson?"

Berta pushed her bowl away. "You're not allowed to drive, Margo, because you've shown you don't have good judgment. When you start to act mature, you'll regain your driving privileges. And they are privileges, they are not a birthright."

"You think you can punish me into obedience, but it isn't going to work. You've jammed Mimi down my throat and now Annie. There's just no room for me here anymore." She stood up. "I hate all of you." She picked up her salad bowl and hurled it against the barn-red wall of the kitchen, then fled the room. A large smear of Thousand Island dressing slid down the wall.

"She is really pissed," Erin said.

"Not nearly as pissed as I am," Berta said. Her tone was calm, but she gripped the table, a bad sign. "No one cleans up that mess." She pointed to the wall. "Margo will come down and do it."

"Can I still have my night lesson?" Annie asked.

Bob hesitated, but Berta spoke up. "Of course. Margo's bad conduct shouldn't interfere. You and Bob go ahead."

"I think we should wait." Bob was troubled. "Another time, Annie. Soon. But I want to talk with Berta. We've got to find a way to deal with this problem, and so far, our tactics aren't working."

"Margo is spoiled," Annie said quietly. "She has to learn she can't be so ugly to the people who love her. Why is she acting so awful?"

"She's jealous of you," Berta said. "For no reason. But enough is enough."

Dinner was over. I gathered the dishes and took them to the sink. The person who cooked also cleaned up. House rules. I hurried, eager to get down to Cora's before she prepared for bed. She was over seventy, though she didn't show it, and she often turned in early to read.

"I'll do the dishes." Annie stood at my elbow, and I realized that we were close to the same height—I was only a couple of inches taller—strange since I viewed her as short and frail.

"It's okay. It's my night." My resistance was also peculiar. I was eager to get to Cora's and washing dishes wasn't one of my favorite pastimes.

She took the stack of salad bowls and started running water in the sink. "I'll take care of it. Go ahead." She smiled. "Do you have a date?"

The thought of dating was so far from my mind that I smiled too. "Of course not. I'm really going to see Cora. I wouldn't fib about a date."

"Sometimes we protect others by lying. A date would be more fun."

"I don't have to lie, because there's no one I'm interested in. Besides, lying isn't a good habit." And it was an easy one to fall into.

Annie's smile hid a secret. "When we were in town, I saw that deputy checking you out. I thought he was going to wreck his cruiser, he was so busy watching you."

"What deputy?" I had no idea what she meant.

"The tall one with the dark hair. You know, beautiful eyes, nice jaw, looked like he would be tall if he stood up. He was across from the library in his patrol car and he watched every move you made. It's funny, because he was playing 'Little Red Riding Hood' on the radio, and he was so wolf-like when he watched you."

I loved the Sam the Sham record, and I knew who she meant now. I was secretly pleased at her description of Mark Walton. He'd been several years ahead of me in high school, and I'd lost touch completely when I went to college. Mark was from a farming family, a hard worker with the most incredible hazel eyes with thick lashes. In the days when I'd crushed on him, I fantasized I saw my future in his gaze. Much water under the bridge since then, but he was still handsome. I'd seen him in his patrol car cruising the town, but he'd never seemed to notice me.

"How do you know he was looking at me?" Asking revealed my interest, but I couldn't help myself.

"There was no one else coming out of the library. He was almost panting. Why don't you ask him out?"

"That's not the way things are done here in Coden." Her idea shocked me. "Girls don't ask boys out." The pill had given women a lot of sexual freedom without the dire consequences of an unwanted pregnancy, but women were not the aggressors in a dating relationship. That would never happen in Coden. *Playgirl* and *Cosmopolitan* could advocate for sexual liberation all they wanted to, but Coden men had only one use for forward girls.

"You aren't a girl, you're a woman, and why shouldn't you? If you want him, you should let him know." Annie's eyes held a dare, and I wondered if she was baiting me, and to what end.

"You have a lot of romantic chutzpa for a sixteen-year-old." I meant to tease her gently in return.

"I'm not stupid. There's no guarantee you'll be around a week from now. Or a month. If you want him, you should grab him." Her words carried a lot of heat. "Hey, I was only kidding you." I put a hand on her thin arm and she bit her lip.

"Sorry. I'm a little sensitive. People don't take me seriously because I look like a kid, but I see things. That deputy likes you. You should take the first step if he won't."

I nodded. "I'll think about it."

"Go see Cora. I'll finish the dishes for you."

"Okay." Why argue against what I really wanted to do? "I'll be back in an hour or so."

Cora's favorite spot on earth was her front-porch rocking chair. She'd been born on the cusp of a new century, and during her life, she'd seen the invention of cars, telephones, air conditioning, tractors—a total revolution in lifestyles. Her youth had been spent sitting on the front porch of the home she now occupied shelling peas, rocking, and talking with older female relatives and passing visitors. In those days, neighbors stopped by for a glass of lemonade or water on the way to town and back. Cora wasn't one to dwell in the past, but she missed that connection to community. Things moved too fast for her now, though she didn't complain.

I found her rocking and watching Shore Road, which seldom saw a car these days. After the Paradise Inn died, there was no reason to drive on Shore Road, which ultimately dead-ended into a bayou. Now that the Hendersons had arrived, Bob drove his sedan and Berta her convertible. I used their station wagon to haul the kids to the library, field trips, and sometimes to the Capri Theater in Mobile for a film. They were generous with the vehicles and had given me access to keys for all three.

"What brings you home?" Cora asked, rising to give me a hug. "Life is more exciting with those young Hendersons than here with an old woman. Or maybe you're on your way to town to socialize with some friends your own age?"

"I love you." I kissed her cheek and held her tightly. Cora was my rock. I owed her my college education and so much more. "I'm here to spend some time with you. I miss you."

"What's wrong?" She pointed to another rocker.

"Why do you think something's wrong?" I asked.

"Your face tells everything, Mimi. Spill it."

I told her about the defaced book and about the Petri garage fire. The news didn't surprise her. "You knew, didn't you?"

"Yes. Gossip travels fast in Coden. I heard it this morning before I left for work." She rocked a little faster.

"What's wrong?" Cora was upset.

"I just found out the fire marshal has decided it was arson. Someone deliberately burned Chad's garage. Lucky the house didn't catch."

"Someone burned Mr. Petri's garage? That's terrible."

"Chad said he heard something in the garage. He went out to check. He was struck on the head and pushed down. He's lucky he got out alive. As it was, the trauma nearly did him in. He's in the hospital in Mobile. I'll stop by to see him tomorrow if he's up to visitors."

"Who would do such a thing? And why?"

Cora rocked a spell. The frogs and crickets sawed loudly in the marsh grass. Cora's house was only a hundred yards from the water, only a mile from the Henderson place. It was possible that she bordered their land. I'd never thought to examine the boundary lines.

"It could be a prank. Young people don't think things through. This might have gotten bigger than they expected."

She had a point, but she was missing mine. I wondered if she was deliberately ignoring the parallels. "That Mr. Petri's history book would be defaced *and* his garage—full of those books—would be selected at random for arson is sort of . . . convenient."

"What are you getting at?" Cora asked.

I shook my head. I didn't know what I was intimating. Why would anyone care about history books? "I feel like a conspiracy nut."

Cora laughed. "Maybe we'll learn more once the authorities finish processing the scene. Until then, best not to jump to rash conclusions."

"There's trouble in the Henderson house, too. I just thought you should know."

"Is Margo still head-over-hills for young Cargill?"

"She seems determined. Berta and Margo are fighting, and Margo is acting like a real bitch. She says she and Andrew are going to join the Moonies."

Cora chuckled. "That girl wouldn't last four hours. Those Moonie kids work."

"Margo's obstinate."

"She'll outgrow Andrew in three weeks if Berta doesn't push her into his bed. Back when I was a girl, I could be shamed into proper conduct. Today, children are rebelling. Push them too hard and you get the opposite of what you want. Birth control pills. Bah! If girls give it away free, the whole fabric of society will unravel. Consequences are what keep folks on the straight and narrow."

Cora might be old, but she wasn't naïve or a prude. It had occurred to me that she'd never had the traditional birds-and-bees talk with me. She'd assumed I would behave and value myself. Had I met someone who kissed me the way Andrew did Margo, I wonder how well-placed her trust would be. "Margo is determined to defy her parents. You're right about that. Maybe you can make Berta see that. If she would just ease up. . . . Honestly, if they don't quit bickering, I have a terrible feeling something awful is going to happen."

"Don't say that!" Cora got out of her chair so fast I was afraid she'd fall over.

I jumped up to steady her. "What in the world? What's wrong?"

"Nothing." She started into the house.

"What is it, Cora?" I grasped her elbow and held it. "What's going on? This is more than Chad Petri being hurt or Margo and Berta bickering." I examined her face. "What was in Chad's book about Belle Fleur?"

"Belle Fleur has a troubled past, Mimi. Folks around here don't talk about it. I read Chad's book when he first had it printed, and I disagreed with some of the things he hinted at."

"Like what?"

"The Desmarais family had a number of . . . issues."

"What kind of *issues*?" I'd grown up in this community and heard only the stories of parties and perfume. Town history painted the Desmarais as a rather eccentric French family that came to Coden with a dream—to grow the flowers that would produce the world's most exquisite perfume. They were town heroes of a sort. The gardens employed dozens of workers. Belle Fleur was a showcase, an attraction that rivaled some of the antebellum houses of Mobile. This was the first time I'd heard anything negative about the mansion.

Cora took off her glasses and rubbed them on her blouse. Her pale blue eyes seemed weak without the lenses. "I don't know why you've suddenly decided to poke into the past of Belle Fleur, but I'd rather you hear this from me. There was talk of abuse. The daughter died very young. At sixteen."

I could read Cora's face as easily as she could mine. "She died, or she was murdered?" The word gave me a chill.

"That's a harsh accusation, Mimi. All of this happened long ago. Before I was born. There's no truth, only speculation, and Chad was wrong to speculate. I'm sorry he was injured, but I'm glad that book is gone. No one ever checked it out, but it was always there, waiting to stir up trouble."

"Was Chloe's death in Chad's book?"

"No, well not the outright accusation. But there were hints at it. And as I remember, a number of photographs. The family was physically striking and very particular about the things said of them." Cora fidgeted in her rocker. "I can only imagine how angry she'd be with me now for talking about this. She was a terror."

"Who?" I was confused. Every member of the family was dead.

"Sigourney."

"But no members of that family are alive today, right? Who else would care about rumors from ancient history? Every family has horse thieves, scoundrels, and champions. You act like a family member might sue or something."

"Old habits, I suppose. Sigourney's primary emotion was pride. Chloe was an only child. She died young, and Henri not far behind her. Sigourney lived to be an old, old woman." Cora looked out toward the woods. "I was a teenager, and I was terrified of her. She was very mean. She'd walk in the grocery store with her cane and if a child got too close, she'd strike us."

"And she was never arrested?" I was outraged.

"She was old and alone. People realized she was mentally unstable. Back in those days parents expected their children to be seen and not heard. We knew about her and we knew to keep out of her way. If she whacked us with her cane, it was our fault, not hers."

I looked toward the woods. Dusk had fallen as we talked, and above the tree line the first star winked in the night. "When he gets out of the hospital, I'm going to take the kids to do an oral interview of Chad Petri. I hope he can remember about Belle Fleur."

"Chad's not rational about Belle Fleur. He might upset the children. I think this is a bad idea."

"But it's the history. It's—"

"It's an old man's interpretation of history, and he was one of the children Sigourney was so mean to. Why spoil the joy of the house for the Hendersons? Once you open that door, Mimi, there's no taking it back. And the house has nothing to do with the people who lived there, but the taint will linger."

She was right. "I can come up with another oral history project, I suppose."

"Why not talk with Si Bailey about the Paradise Inn? He has some wonderful photographs." Her face softened. "You can see the old girl in all her splendor. She was a showplace, Mimi. I spent many an evening dancing until I wore holes in my hose."

I could imagine it—the big band music, so romantic. Cora was a looker back in the day. She'd been in her thirties—close to Berta's age. It somehow didn't seem possible. I nodded. "That's what we'll do then."

Cora sat back down in her chair, her face suddenly alert. "I think someone is in the bushes over there." She pointed to the dense woods. "Do you see them?"

Night hid the fine details of the landscape. The woods were a black blur against a sky rapidly going dark. I couldn't see anything, but Cora was not one to arouse fears without cause. "Shall I call the sheriff's department?"

"Get the flashlight."

She kept a powerful light near her bed. Storms often kicked the power off, and everyone along the shore kept emergency lights and good batteries. I fetched it and swung the beam into the woods. For a moment I picked up a pair of eyes, bright yellow. The creature stared at me, unafraid, almost as if it dared me to come and investigate. And then it was gone.

"Probably a coyote or stray dog," Cora said, unruffled. "Go on back to the Hendersons."

I didn't want to leave her. She seemed suddenly old, vulnerable. "I can stay tonight with you. We can make popcorn and watch old movies." I was homesick for the days before I went to college. I loved the Hendersons, but I was one of many in the household. With Cora, I was the only one. "Cora, did you tell Berta and Bob about the fire?"

"Chad Petri's fire?" She was confused.

"No, the one . . . my parents." It was hard to say it, even to her. She'd taken me in like a daughter and raised me after my own parents burned to death.

"Why does it matter, Mimi?" she asked.

"I don't want them to pity me."

"You don't have to worry about that. No one who looks at you would ever pity you. You're a beautiful girl, Mimi. Bright, responsible, talented. Your whole life is ahead of you. The Hendersons know the basics. No more or no less. But they see you as my granddaughter and a lovely, smart young woman. And that's how we'll leave it."

"I love you."

"Be off with you." She swatted my arm. "I'm going to bed to finish my Taylor Caldwell novel. Wonderful writer."

"Are you sure?"

"Go."

"I'll stop by tomorrow with some fresh vegetables from Munch's garden."

"Bring me a watermelon. A Shouting Methodist." She laughed. "Those are the sweetest. And some tomatoes. And some okra and Vidalia onions."

I laughed with pleasure. Cora loved her fresh vegetables, and it was a small thing to get for her. "I'll do it."

11

Annie was in the kitchen when I returned to the Hendersons. Donald and Erin sat at the table, schoolbooks open while Annie wiped down the counters. As she worked, she recited a poem:

"To all the little children, the happy ones and sad ones; the sober and the silent ones; the boisterous and glad ones. The good ones—yes, the good ones, too. And all the lovely *bad* ones."

She hit the last words hard.

"Where did you learn that poem, Annie?" Erin asked.

"Oh, I can't remember." She winked at me. The children hadn't seen me in the doorway yet.

Donald snorted. "That's funny. You can't remember where you came from, but you can remember a poem."

"Do you want me to tell it?" Annie asked.

"Yes!" both children chorused.

There was a pause, and then she began in an intimate voice that boded a spook at the end.

"Little orphant Annie came to our house to stay, to wash
the cups and saucers and sweep the crumbs away."

She put a lot of emphasis in her recitation, which I approved heartily of. Memorization and recitation had fallen out of favor in the public school system, but I used it with the Henderson children because I felt it exercised the brain and also taught confident public speaking. I waited outside the door, not wanting to interfere.

"An' shoo the chickens off the porch,
an' dust the hearth, an' sweep.
An' make the fire, an' bake the bread,
an' earn her board-an'-keep."

"You don't have to do that stuff, Annie." Donald spoke with confidence. "Mama would never make you work like that."
"Shut up and listen to the poem," Erin said. "Don't interrupt."
Annie's intimate tone continued,

"An' all us other children, when the supper-things is done,
we set around the kitchen fire an' has the mostest fun.
A-listnin' to the witch-tales that Annie tells about,
and the Goblins will git you—If you don't watch out!"

Donald and Erin squealed with pleasure. Like most children, they enjoyed a good ghost story, and this was one I recognized. While James Whitcomb Riley's poem was scary, it wouldn't leave Donald with nightmares.

"Wunst there wuz a little boy wouldn't say his prayers,
an' when he went to bed at night, away up-stairs,

his Mammy heerd him holler, an' his Daddy heerd him
bawl . . ."

Dramatic pause.

"An' when they turn't the kivvers down, he wuzn't there
at all!"

I almost laughed as I imagined Donald's face. Now that the focus
was on a little boy disappearing, he wouldn't be all that bold.

"An' they seeked him up the chimbly-flue,
an' ever'-wheres, I guess.
But all they ever found wuz just his pants an' roundabout."

Another pause.

"An' the Goblins'll git you, if you don't watch out!"

Chill bumps marched along my arms. I stepped through the
swinging door that led to the kitchen and both Donald and Erin
squealed with fright. "Something wrong?" I asked with a grin.

"You scared us!" Erin was delighted.

"I'm really going to scare you if you don't get your homework
done," I said, tapping her book. "You have a lot of reading to do."

"Why are they in school during the summer?" Annie asked.
"Aren't most children out?"

"Because we're homeschooled, we can learn all year," Donald
answered for me. "We don't want Mimi to leave, and if she wasn't
teaching us, she wouldn't be here."

"That's right." Erin leaned her head into my hip. I brushed my
hand down her sleek blond hair. How was it possible that the entire
family looked like some commercial for Sun-In?

"I love learning," Annie said. "Especially literature."

"Sounds to me like you have a pretty good memory. You were reciting, not reading."

She shrugged. "I love narrative poetry. That short poem tells a complete story." She hesitated. "I love to tell stories. Sometimes I imagine what I tell comes true." Something flickered across her face that stung me like a bee.

"Then you must only tell good things," I said. "We don't want any goblins running around Belle Fleur."

"I'm afraid they're already here," she said, swinging her gaze out the window. "I'd be careful outside in the dark. All of you. There's no telling what lurks on the grounds of Belle Fleur."

Erin squealed and Donald crowded up against my side. "You shouldn't frighten the children, Annie." She'd creeped me out, too, but I wasn't going to show it.

"I disagree, Mimi. Sometimes fear is the only thing that keeps you alive. There are goblins. You know that as well as I do."

"What goblins?" Donald asked.

"Look what you've done." I didn't bother to hide my anger. "Belle Fleur is isolated enough. If you make the children believe in some foolishness about goblins, they'll be prisoners in the house." I held Donald close. "There aren't any goblins. Annie is pulling your leg."

"Maybe not goblins." Annie put the dishcloth in the sink. "Maybe something worse than goblins."

I was mad enough to punch her. "That's enough, Annie. I'm sure Berta will want to have a word with you—after I speak with her."

"It was a joke." She wiped her hands on a dishtowel and pushed open the back door. "I'll be back in an hour or so. I'm going for a walk. See, I'm not afraid."

"But you already went for a walk." Donald's puzzled face revealed his incomprehension that anyone would walk in the dark for no good reason, especially after talking about goblins.

"Maybe she's smoking a cigarette," Erin said, which told me that Margo was experimenting with tobacco—or worse. That Andrew Cargill, no telling what he'd gotten Margo into.

"Nothing as wicked as a cigarette," Annie said. "I won't be long."

And then she was gone. I settled at the table and helped Donald outline a book report for *The Case of the Missing Chums*, a Hardy Boys mystery. Erin worked on percentages. The old clock above the stove ticked away the minutes. The house was too quiet.

"Where's Margo?" I asked. She sometimes did her studies in her room.

"Upstairs. She's mad." Erin tapped her pencil against the page. "She went into Annie's room and threw some of her clothes out the window. Mother caught her, and she's grounded for the rest of the year, I think. Daddy had a talk with her about Andrew Cargill. She started crying. She said she was going to do what she wanted to do and no one was going to stop her. She told me to get out of the room. She said she'd make everyone sorry for the way we'd treated her."

I closed Donald's book. "Let's call it a day and get some sleep. We'll finish the book report tomorrow."

"When will Annie return?"

"I don't know and right now, I don't care," I answered as I prodded him up the stairs in front of me. Erin followed behind.

"Maybe a goblin will get her," Erin said, and there was a hint of dark spite in her voice. I didn't blame her. Annie had deliberately frightened them and then left.

"Maybe," I told her. "One thing for sure, we won't be awake waiting to find out. If there are goblins out there, Annie can handle them."

We'd made it to the second floor landing, where the beautiful stained-glass window was muted by the darkness outside. Donald stopped and grabbed my arm. "What was that?"

"What?" I'd barely gotten the word out when I heard something on the third floor. It sounded like a dog's nails clicking on the hardwood.

"Did you hear it?" Donald was truly frightened.

"I did." Erin took my other hand. "Let's get Daddy."

The sound came again, and I imagined something running the length of the hallway beside the rug. Click, click, click—it moved down the hall. "I'll check it out."

"No!" Donald held firm. "What if it's a goblin?"

That was enough to force my hand. Now I had to investigate or the children would be terrified. When Annie returned, I would have a discussion with her, for sure. "It's not a goblin. More likely it's Annie trying to scare us. She probably sneaked up the servants' staircase to get ahead of us."

Together, the three of us crept up the stairs to the third floor. The minute we got to the top step, the noise stopped. I found the light switch and light flooded the hallway. The empty hallway.

"What was it?" Erin asked.

"I don't know." What I didn't tell the children was that I saw strange claw marks—as if little sharpened dog paws had made them—beside the hall runner. The marks stopped at Annie's door.

"Will you tuck me in bed?" Donald asked.

"Absolutely." We headed back to the second floor, but I deliberately left the lights on. I didn't know what tricks Annie had gotten up to on the third floor, but I intended to ask her about them.

12

Around me the house was unnaturally silent. The children were upstairs in bed. Donald had finally fallen asleep after I read to him for half an hour. Erin was in the room she shared with Margo. I remained downstairs in the kitchen, unable to relax enough to sleep.

Annie had washed up the dishes, but I picked up a cloth to dry them and put them away. Bob had offered Berta a dishwasher, but she felt it was good for the children to have chores. The dishes were part of a master plan of instruction and responsibility.

Once the drainboard was empty, I took a seat at the table. The kitchen settled into a ticking silence, the clock my only companion. There was a TV in the family room, but it was seldom turned on, a fact I greatly admired. Margo was the only child who complained about the restricted TV hours. She had girlfriends who were deeply invested in *Happy Days* and *The Six Million Dollar Man*. Not watching made her feel excluded from her peers. It didn't bother the other two children. Erin rode and Donald tramped the woods near the house.

Unable to sit still, I went to the cupboard and began pulling out the dishes. I intended to organize them. Berta's everyday dishes contained a border of colorful roosters on a white background and a cornucopia in the center of the plate. I loved the pattern and weight of each dish. When I had my own house and my family, I would have dishes like these. So many things at Belle Fleur perfectly reflected my taste.

As I worked, I hummed "Take Me Home Country Roads," thinking about the history of Belle Fleur. Cora's hints at a darker past were more annoying than troublesome. The house felt like home to me. Berta didn't ask me to do many of the chores I did; I enjoyed putting things to right. I could pretend it was my house—I was as beautiful as Berta with a family that loved *me*.

I held a plate in one hand and a wet cloth in the other. When I went to the sink to rinse the cloth in hot water, I glanced out the window. Movement in the yard caught my attention. My first thought was deer. It was unusual to see one—the rednecks had hunted them to near extinction. But something large moved just on the edge of the woods, where the open lawn began but behind the first fringe of undergrowth.

My reflection gazed back at me, a pale shadow of an image cast in the clean glass of the kitchen window. Beyond me, movement. Whatever it was crouched and ran. Furtive. I froze, knowing I was highlighted in the kitchen window and whatever was out there could see me far better than I could see it.

For a split second it stepped out of the underbrush, almost as if it meant to be seen. I couldn't breathe. All I could do was look. Dark hair blowing in the breeze from the bay, she faced me. She lifted a hand and pointed. Right at me. And it seemed she smiled, but I couldn't be certain. Hair obscured her face.

Behind me the front door slammed with such force that I screamed. The plate went flying from my hand and crashed on the split-brick floor of the kitchen. I yelped with fear and surprise. Footsteps ran toward me and Bob appeared in the kitchen.

"What's wrong, Mimi?"

"There's someone in the yard."

"Who?" Bob went to the window and looked out. I knew the yard would be empty. "Who did you see?" Bob pressed. "Was it that Cargill boy?"

"A girl." I tried to organize my thoughts and words.

"A girl?" Bob retrieved a flashlight. "Who was she?"

I shook my head. "I've never seen her before."

"Probably one of Margo's freaky friends," Erin said. She'd come down the stairs and stood in the kitchen doorway. Berta and Donald joined her. Annie, too, had come back in the house and was gathered with us.

Bob opened the window and played the high beam of the flashlight across the lawn. Nothing. Not a trace. The woods that surrounded the yard seemed to absorb the light.

"I don't see anyone."

My heart ached, literally, from the jolt of pure adrenalin. I'd seen what I'd seen, but convincing the Hendersons would require evidence. I bent to clean up the broken plate. "I'm sorry, Berta."

"They're everyday dishes," she said easily. "Let me help." She got the broom and a dustpan. "I heard the front door slam. Was someone outside?"

"That was me," Annie said. "The wind blew it out of my hand. I'm sorry."

"Where's Margo?" Berta asked, suddenly realizing her eldest wasn't caught up in the excitement.

Without a word she handed the broom to Erin and started up the stairs. In a moment I heard an explosive, "Damn!"

I knew then Margo was gone. She'd slipped the leash that Berta had been trying to train her to accept. Which might have explained the girl in the yard, had she been a tall blonde.

"Was it Margo?" Bob asked. "Is she out there in the woods?"

I shook my head. I couldn't tell him who had been in the woods, but it wasn't Margo. Likely one of her friends she'd made arrangements with to pick her up. Margo was headed for a world of trouble.

13

By morning Berta was frantic with worry. The eldest Henderson child had not come home. As I anticipated, Margo's behavior made Berta more determined to bring her daughter into line. Worry bred anger. Bob, too, was exasperated. While I suspected he'd taken up for Margo with her desire to see Andrew Cargill—in a very restricted way—now he could do nothing but back Berta's play. Margo was well and truly screwed, and when she came home, she would spend the rest of her summer on restriction.

I cooked breakfast for Erin and Donald, and we set out for town. I'd set up an interview with Si Bailey, as Cora had suggested, and Bob and Berta needed some privacy to determine how to handle Margo's disappearing act. Berta was nearly sick with anxiety that something had happened to her child. Bob was merely angry. They had discussed calling the sheriff to report her gone, but Bob was reluctant to involve the law when he felt Margo would return on her own, and there was no indication she'd left unwillingly.

Erin, Donald, and I piled in the station wagon. In the past, Margo would have driven. Berta and Bob had planned on giving her a car for her seventeenth birthday, but that was out the window now. Margo would be a passenger, or walking—Berta would never trust her with her own vehicle.

Annie had opted to stay at Belle Fleur and wait with Berta. It was a job I didn't envy her. The slow sweep of the minute hand around the clock face was not for me. I was relieved to be out of the house and headed to dig around the history of Coden.

Si Bailey had agreed to let the children tape-record him as they asked questions about the Paradise Inn. I drove along Shore Road, hoping to see Margo headed home. She'd left on foot, which meant nothing. She was sixteen and some of her girlfriends had access to a vehicle. The most likely sequence of events involved her making arrangements for a friend to pick her up after she'd sneaked out of the house. If not a girlfriend, then Andrew Cargill. She would ride high on the feeling that she'd put one over on Bob and Berta—until she started to realize she had to go home. Then her actions would take on new shadings and fear would replace arrogance. Every child has moments of rebellion, and every child pays the price. Margo would be lucky to get out of her bedroom by the time she was nineteen.

As familiar landmarks passed by the car window, my concern multiplied. Defying one's parents and showing independence was one thing. Worrying them to the point they were frantic was nothing more than stupidity.

We passed no one on the road. The shore was beautiful and isolated, except for the gulls and a nutria that ran in front of the tires, making me swerve dangerously. The damn thing stopped and tried to stare me down, the orange buckteeth glowing against the gray road. Nasty creature. It was nothing more than a giant rat. Still, I didn't want to smash it. I didn't like to harm any living thing.

I even drove through town, hoping to see Andrew Cargill's vehicle at the Esso station where he pumped gas and worked as a mechanic. The black mustang was nowhere to be seen. Had Margo and Andrew run across the state line to Lucedale, Mississippi, to get married? Surely they weren't that foolish. Then again, Margo had an iron will. And she was spoiled. It never occurred to her that she could do something her daddy couldn't fix for her.

Marriage might be her first reality check.

After driving around Beauchamps—with no sign of Margo—we went to Si's house, an old Creole shotgun shaded by three majestic live oaks. The marsh grass whispered as we got out of the car into the oven of August heat. The door and windows of the house were opened wide for any trace of a breeze. Si seated us at the kitchen table and I listened with interest to the questions Erin and Donald asked.

"Did movie stars really come to the Paradise?" Erin was smitten by the idea of famous people in her back yard.

"They did, girl. And plenty of them. Gangsters, too. Back before the hurricane took out the Rolston, it was a hotbed of political intrigue and such. Then the Paradise came along and things cranked up again. Liquor and gunrunners, celebrities and public officials. They had a live band every Saturday night and the local folks turned out. I worked as a valet parking those fancy cars. Sometimes I slipped inside and had me a dance or two with a few of the pretty gals."

"With Cora?" I asked. I took his measure as he talked. He was in his seventies, still straight and tall. Trim. His face was freshly shaved, and his clothes pressed, though he'd been a widower for twenty years. After his wife Greta died, he'd never remarried. His words piqued my interest.

"Your granny was one beauty," Si said. "Like you, with her dark hair and fair skin. Those eyes with golden flecks. You could be a movie star yourself, Miss Mimi."

Erin giggled at my compliment. "Mimi is pretty. She could have any man around. That's what Mama says." She pushed the tape recorder closer to Si. "Tell us about the movie stars and big bands."

Si led us into a glamorous past where elegance ruled and Coden played host to the rich and famous. The minutes ticked by as he recounted the world of his youth.

"That's enough stories about the way things used to be." Si shifted in his chair.

"Do you know any stories about a young actress named Madeline?" Donald asked.

"Not off hand." Si checked his watch. "We should call it a day, I think."

"Are there any stories about Belle Fleur?" Erin asked.

Si hesitated for the first time since we'd arrived. "Oh, there are some old tales. I wouldn't put any stock in them. Cora told me you were interested in the old hotel, not Belle Fleur."

"The children are naturally curious about their home. We've had a little difficulty finding any written facts, so we'd like to hear your stories."

He shrugged, discomfort settling into his features. "Nothing to talk about."

"Tell us." Erin tapped the tape recorder. "We want our parents and Annie to hear. She tells us ghost stories, and we want to find some good ones to pay her back."

"Donald and Erin are connoisseurs of ghost stories," I said. "Me, too."

Si grinned. "That's right. Young folks like a little spookiness, don't they?"

"Please," Donald begged.

"I guess I can accommodate if your teacher says it's okay? Miss Cora told me not to get you all goosed up over bogeymen."

I stuffed down my sudden unease. "There's nothing bad to tell, except Sigourney was mean, right? I don't see the harm."

"Sigourney was mean. No denying that. But there's more to Belle Fleur. More to the history of that house and the family that lived there."

Donald and Erin were leaning forward, eyes wide. I nodded for him to continue. I was as curious as the children.

"Well, they say that sometimes, just as the sun is setting, if you look up at the third floor windows, you can see a young girl standing there. The wind blows in off the Sound and the curtains flutter around her."

I felt again the tightening in my chest, the sense that something restricted my breathing. Si's words were harmless enough, the simple stuff of classic ghost stories. "But the third floor was an attic. No one used it until Bob renovated it," I said.

"Back in the day, it was Chloe's room."

"The daughter?" Erin asked.

"That's right, Chloe Desmarais." Si shifted in his chair. "'Course it's most likely just a trick of the sun."

"Why would Chloe haunt the house?" Erin asked. "We found her grave. She was really young. Only as old as Margo. She must have had an accident to die so young."

"Folks say Chloe had a hard life." Si frowned and I knew he'd stepped into territory that gave him discomfort. I wanted to stop this, but I didn't know how.

"Why?" Donald had to ask it.

"She, uh, made some mistakes. Sometimes it's not as easy to fix things as you might think."

Funny how his thoughts paralleled mine—about Margo.

"What did she do?" Erin's question was direct. "We have to find out, for our project. History isn't something that can be changed to make people happy. There was slavery in this country. It's a fact. The Irish were treated like vermin. It's a fact. We destroyed an entire culture when we wiped out the Native Americans. So what happened to Chloe?"

I was proud of Erin. I'd taught her that history couldn't be compromised to spare the feelings of a few people. Still, Si might not subscribe to my doctrine, and I didn't want to make Erin afraid of her own home. "I think we've bothered Mr. Bailey enough for one morning." I stood and put a hand on Erin's shoulder.

"But we haven't gotten the whole story." Erin's jaw set. "You taught us not to halfway do a project, and we need to know what happened. What mistakes did Chloe make that no one wants to talk about?"

"She got herself pregnant and then it seems she fell down a flight of stairs." Si blurted it out. "She was only sixteen, and it killed her and the baby. Grief killed her father. He died only a few months after she was buried. The loss of both Henri and Chloe sent Sigourney over the edge. She became mean and took pleasure in frightening children in the town." His words were rushed, and he stopped abruptly.

Donald and Erin sat so quietly, I could hear the tape recorder spinning. They hadn't expected the vehemence of Si's answer. Neither had I. But this was part of the lesson. History, for all intents and purposes, might be dead, but people's reactions to it weren't.

"What an awful tragedy. Thank you," I said. "Children, we should go."

"Does Chloe's ghost haunt our house?" Donald asked.

Si, knowing we were headed out the door, had regained some of his humor. "Now why would you ask something like that?"

"Annie says she does."

His words stopped me in my tracks. "Annie? She doesn't know anything about Belle Fleur or Coden. She's only lived there two minutes! And she was told not to tell stories that scared you two."

My tone was too sharp, and Donald stepped back.

"I'm sorry." I tried to ease him out the door, but he refused to budge.

"Are there any pictures of Chloe?" he asked. "Annie said she was really beautiful."

"That I don't know, young man." Si's gaze met mine over Donald's head. "But I can tell you it was said she was a rare beauty. Dark hair and beautiful eyes, old French blood. Delicate bone structure. There was a photo of her in Chad Petri's book. Damn shame about that fire. Makes me wonder what this community is coming to."

"It's terrible about the fire. I'm so glad Mr. Petri wasn't more seriously injured." I nudged the children toward the porch.

"Damn strange if you ask me." Si was agitated now. "I told him it would do no good plundering around in the past. But the book was printed ten years ago. Doesn't make sense someone would hurt him because of it now."

"Come on, children," I said. They'd gathered the tape recorder and their notebooks, but they were dallying. Si Bailey was a source of much information for them.

Si stopped inside his screen door as we went onto the porch. "Folks say it isn't Chloe who haunts the house, but that bitch Sigourney." He realized he'd cursed in front of the children, but he waved it away. "Bitch she was. Hit me so hard I lost an entire summer in a cast. For no reason. All I did was speak to her."

I pushed the children along the porch and down the steps. This wasn't the way I intended for the interview to go. The children shouldn't be exposed to cursing and anger and foolish stories of ghosts. "Thank you," I called as I ushered them into the car.

When we backed out of his driveway, I saw him behind the screen, watching. He seemed to have shrunk in size, a man defeated by the bitter taste of the past.

14

We crossed the small bridge over the bayou and I parked beneath the shade of a big cypress. Ever since I was a child, I'd loved this spot. It was right in the middle of Coden, yet isolated. I could identify the type of vehicle passing by the sound it made on the old bridge. On the summer days when Cora had been at work and I was left to my own devices, I'd walked to town and brought a lunch to eat beside the bayou. No one noticed me, hiding among the weeping willows and cattails. In a small town, secret places are hard to keep.

The smell of burgers and fries wafted from a fast-food joint up the street, and a breeze kicked off the water, bringing the odor of fish and brine. Somehow, it was comforting. I decided to keep the children in town for several hours. Maybe by the time we got home, Margo would have come to her senses and returned. With all my heart I wanted my Belle Fleur family reunited in the house, laughing and happy. A sixth sense warned me that that was not to be.

The day was sunny and stifling hot. Erin's shirt stuck to her back as she squatted beside the bayou. She and Donald examined the shallows for aquatic life while I rested on a bench in the leafy shade of a sweet gum. When I saw the patrol car pull up and park beside the station wagon, my gut clenched. Was it word about Margo? It couldn't be good if a uniformed officer had to deliver it. Then I realized who was driving the car.

A flush ran up my cheeks as I remembered Annie's observation about Deputy Mark Walton. She'd seen what I missed. Or perhaps she'd made it up.

Mark sat behind the steering wheel and watched Erin and Donald. He knew who they were. They were so obviously not of Coden that everyone knew them by sight. I climbed the steep bank and walked over. Mark rolled down his window and tilted his head. "Mimi Bosarge," he said. "Back from college."

I couldn't tell if he was complimenting or baiting me. For some in the Coden community, the idea of college, especially for a girl, was a sign of a family getting above itself. Cora had earned her bachelor's degree in social work, but she'd done it after Grandpa Willis passed away. Education was fine for a widow woman who had to fend for herself. A young girl, though, was expected to marry and go under the care of her man. I'd defied those expectations, and there was talk about me in town. The whispers and speculations were ugly, and only respect for Cora kept them tamped down. The thought depressed— and aggravated—me. I'd wanted to fit in, but I couldn't help that I reached for more of life than others did.

"I am home," I said. "At least for a while."

"I heard you got hired by the Henderson family. Going to bring some Alabama learning and culture to those Californians."

His smile told me he had no ulterior motives. His comments weren't intended to cut. "They're a great family. I'm lucky to have the job."

"I'm headed out there. Got a call from Mr. Henderson about his eldest daughter. Seems she snuck out of the house and took a runner. What's your opinion? Is this serious, or is she just acting up?"

I swallowed a lump of dread. Bob and Berta were obviously frantic to involve the law. "Margo is wild, but she isn't stupid."

"I sure hope not. There's just so damn much meanness in the world today. Here in Coden, it's pretty safe. Worst things going on here are those Moonies holding group weddings and a couple of fistfights at the Bahama Breeze. If she took it in her head to get up to the highway and hitchhike. . . ." He didn't finish the thought.

"She has a boyfriend. Andrew Cargill."

"So I've been told. No sign of him either. He didn't show up for work today."

I couldn't decide if I felt better or worse with that information. "Do you think they ran off together?"

"It looks that way, but I'm not jumping to conclusions."

"Has anyone seen them?"

He shook his head. "Mrs. Henderson is pretty worried. She doesn't know this community and I think she sees more danger than there is here."

"She's protective. It's the way mothers should be." My tone was harsher than I intended. "Sorry, it's just that she loves her children. She has a right to be worried."

He winked at me. "I'll cut her some slack. You, too."

Mark had learned how to flirt. Back in high school he'd been shy. "Would you tell Berta the children and I are fine?" I leaned closer and caught a whiff of English Leather. Some of the college boys had worn that cologne. "I'm keeping them out of the house. The tension and all."

He nodded. "Will do. And that's a smart idea." He began to roll up the window to save the air conditioning that was blasting in the car but stopped halfway. "Hey, Mimi, would it be okay if I called you sometime?"

I hesitated, suddenly unsure. My dating know-how amounted to zip. Mark was a grown man, a sheriff's deputy. What use did he have for a girl like me with no experience? "Now isn't a good time. Everything is up in the air with Margo missing. Maybe when she comes home." I was surprised at the sweep of disappointment. I wanted a date with him.

"Now that's incentive to find the wayward teen." His smile was quick and filled with good humor. "I'll have her home before dark."

He finished with the window and backed away from me. In a moment he'd disappeared over the bridge.

"Mimi's got a boyfriend!" Erin looked like a wicked little sprite. Her eyes danced with mischief. "Mimi's got a boyfriend!" she sang.

Donald took it up, too. I ignored them. My knowledge of men was limited. No father. No brothers. I hadn't dated in high school or college. I'd avoided the situation, uncertain how to behave with the opposite sex and the feelings men brought out in me. Cora hadn't pushed me, at least not hard. She'd arranged a few introductions that went nowhere. She'd always said I would find the right path in my own good time. It occurred to me that maybe Mark was the path. But how was I supposed to know? He did make my stomach jitter and my palms sweat, but was that good or bad?

Donald took my hand and tugged me back toward the water. "Why didn't you tell the deputy about the girl in the woods? The one you saw last night." He looked up at me. "I saw her, too."

I'd convinced myself she was a product of my overactive imagination. "What did you really see?" I asked him. We moved into the shade. Sweat trickled down my back and into the waistband of my jean shorts, but I pulled Donald onto my lap. "Tell me everything." I had a sense this was important.

"Just a girl. She was watching the house. Like the girl I saw with Annie. The one in the marsh grass that frightened me. She pointed toward the house."

So Donald had seen what I saw. It wasn't the wind or my imagination. "Did she look like anyone you know?" I'd seen her, but I didn't have a clear memory of anything except her hair. Maybe she was one of Margo's girlfriends waiting for her to sneak out.

Donald stared at me. "Her hair was wild. All around her face. It was dark and curly, like Annie's." He took a strand of my hair. "Like yours."

"Annie was walking down Shore Road and I was in the kitchen. Do you think our mystery girl was someone Margo knew? Think about friends Margo may have talked about."

He shrugged. "Couldn't tell. It was so dark. Margo has a lot of secrets, you know. She doesn't want me to know her friends."

"All teenage girls have secrets." I could tell Margo had hurt his feelings. She'd done a damn good job of hurting everyone at Belle Fleur. She'd learn one day that pain always came back in spades. "Don't take it to heart, Donald."

"Will you tell the deputy about the girl?"

"If it looks important I will." I eased him to the bench beside me. "I think it was someone waiting for Margo to give her a ride."

Donald nodded. "I think she was waiting for someone to come outside." He stared at me. "Or maybe she was waiting to come in."

15

Because of the poverty and lack of opportunity, Coden saw its fair share of "missing" teens. Most of them packed up and moved west or north, looking for a new life, one with broader dimensions. Margo was a child of privilege, so law enforcement took her strange disappearance seriously, hence the attention of a Mobile County sheriff's deputy.

When I pulled the station wagon into the front yard, I found Mark talking to Annie on the front porch. They'd pulled two rockers so that they faced each other. She leaned toward him, her face filled with intensity. When I started up the steps, she stopped. Mark stood and walked toward me.

"Could I have a moment?" he asked. "Annie tells me you saw someone in the yard last night. You should have mentioned it." His earlier playfulness had evaporated.

"Go inside," I told Erin and Donald. "Tell Berta about your interview with Mr. Bailey, but don't mention that he cursed, okay?"

For once they didn't argue. They banged into the house calling for their mother.

"I wasn't certain what I saw." I had to tread carefully. Annie was up to something. Painting me as a fool or liar. "It was dark. Bob looked outside, but no one was there." Behind Mark, Annie rocked slowly. She smiled at me.

"I have to be honest, Mimi. This isn't looking good. Sheriff Delchamps has put out a missing persons bulletin on Margo."

This was more serious than I'd anticipated. "And Andrew?"

"He's a person of interest in her disappearance."

I must have looked stunned because he took my elbow and walked me away from Annie. "You can't believe Andrew took her unwillingly," I said. "If she's with him, she went because that's what she wanted. It's not like he kidnapped her. If anyone instigated this, I can assure you it was Margo." Andrew Cargill was a bad boy, but he didn't deserve a kidnapping charge.

"He's twenty and she's sixteen."

"Mark, that's not right." The unfairness made heat jump to my face.

"If we find them, chances are the charges won't stick, but the Hendersons are upset and angry. Mrs. Henderson is. . . ."

He didn't have to finish. Berta would be hysterical, and angry, and determined to make someone pay, especially the boy who'd gone off with her eldest child. "Did Annie tell you anything?"

"Only that she was outside for a walk and didn't see anyone or any vehicle on Shore Road but that you'd seen someone in the yard. We'd just gotten started when you drove up. Let me finish talking with her." He motioned me toward the front door and then held it open for me. "I'll have to talk with the other children, too."

"Is that really necessary?"

"I'm afraid it is," he said. "I could sure use a cup of coffee if there's any in the kitchen."

I took the hint and went into the house, but I didn't go far. I shamelessly eavesdropped as he continued his interview with Annie.

"You were along the road. Did you hear a vehicle? Anything out of the ordinary?"

"Not really. I was looking at the stars and smelling the water. This is the most beautiful place I've ever lived." She hesitated. "There was something strange, though. Banks of clouds passed over the moon, but sometimes it was bright enough to see clearly. The water shushed against the shore, like a gentle kiss. I love that sound. The last of the summer insects droned and sang. I remember the cry of an owl. But. . . ."

"But what? Tell me, Annie." Mark's voice was gentle. He sounded truly concerned.

"There was another sound. Like something running in the tall grass just out of sight. It followed me all the way home. I never saw anything. Do you suppose it was a fox or something wild? Or maybe someone bad."

I glanced through the screen and saw the mingling of sadness and fear on Annie's face.

"Why would someone bad follow you, Annie?" Mark asked softly.

"Maybe I'm bad."

It was broad daylight, but her words frightened me. I fought the impulse to slam and lock the door. To shut her out of the house. But I didn't want to leave her alone with Mark. Men were drawn to her. She hadn't lied about that.

"I doubt that. You're just a kid. Who's following you?" Mark kept it steady, easy, no reaction. He was better at the police work than I'd anticipated.

"I know it sounds . . . crazy." Her voice grew thick with emotion. "Before I came here to Coden, I . . ." she reached across and touched Mark's arm. "I can't remember, but Cora says something bad happened to me. She says that's why I can't remember." Her hand lingered on him, and he looked down at it but didn't remove it. "I feel safe when you're here."

I couldn't believe she was making a play for Mark. I stepped onto the porch. "Annie, is something wrong?"

Mark looked up at me, frowned, then stood. "Annie was telling me something." He was annoyed at my intrusion, but he covered it.

"I'm sure it's just my imagination. You know how it is at night, with the wind and the tide slushing up to the shore." Annie stood.

"I'll get that coffee for you, Deputy. But Mimi did see someone in the yard last night, like I told you. I'm surprised she didn't tell you. You should ask her."

Mark's eyebrows rose. "Mimi, I think we should talk."

I waited until Annie went in the house. Her behavior disturbed me. I couldn't tell if she was truly going after Mark and trying to get me in trouble, but it had certainly looked that way. "I saw what looked like a girl with long dark hair." I shuddered. "Donald saw her, too. But Bob checked and there was no sign of anyone in the yard. I figured it was Margo's friend, someone who'd come to pick her up."

Mark cleared his throat. "I'll take a look behind the house. With the wind blowing at night, it can get tricky. If someone was back there, I'll find evidence."

His reassurances calmed me. "I'll walk with you." I glanced at the front door and saw that Annie had taken my place. She stood beside the sidelight and eavesdropped on me and Mark.

"I'll show you," I said. Together we walked off toward the back yard. I led him to the place I'd seen the stranger. The house had been landscaped with azaleas and camellias, hardy evergreen plants with thick leaves that had endured storms, droughts, and scorching summers. They stood over twenty feet tall and surrounded the house, which had been built a good six feet off the ground. To my knowledge, the area had never flooded, but Henri and Sigourney Desmarais had taken no chances with the beautiful Victorian.

In the back yard, the swing on long chains hung from a two-hundred-year-old live oak. I'd often watched Bob and Berta playing here. He would swing her and then steal kisses. If I ever married, I wanted what they had. At times they were more like young lovers than the parents of teenagers, eager for a touch or kiss or shared look.

"You're sure it was a girl you saw?" Mark asked.

But now, I wasn't. I remembered the animal at Cora's. I'd thought for a moment it was a person. "I saw her hair."

"Could it have been someone in a windbreaker with a hood?"

I hadn't considered that possibility. "Maybe. Someone like Andrew Cargill?"

"Margo probably left with someone. It's a logical leap." Mark left me beside a wisteria vine as he carefully searched the ground in the area I indicated. He worked slowly, methodically. He found several snapped twigs in the undergrowth, and at last he stopped and called me over. "Look at this."

The ground where he indicated was raked by claws. Something with powerful nails had dug up the ground. "What did that?" I asked.

He knelt and studied the mark. "Dog, coyote, armadillo, gopher, turtle. Anything like that. But human, no." He patted my shoulder. "It's hard to see at night and you said you didn't have a flashlight. You probably saw the bushes moving, that Spanish moss blowing, a dark shadow."

Maybe he was right. I nodded. "It could have been. Donald must have seen the same thing. But where is Margo?"

"Most likely with Andrew. The two of them are in plenty of trouble."

I didn't say anything as we walked back to the house. Berta watched us from the kitchen window, and from high above on the third floor, Annie watched us, too.

Mark looked up to the window. "I'm going to check into Annie, too," he said softly. "Someone is surely looking for her. She's smart, educated, well-raised. If she has amnesia, like Cora says, there must be a reason behind it." He lightened the heaviness of his words with a touch on my elbow. "We'll find her. In the meantime, I'm glad to spend a little time with you."

16

Night dropped over the house like a damp, heavy cloth. The normally starry sky was obscured by clouds, which suited the mood of the family. There had been no sign of Margo. None of her clothes were gone, but her purse was missing, the only indication that she'd left under her own power. Otherwise, it was as if someone had snatched her up—a goblin, perhaps.

Berta had taken to her bedroom, so frantic with worry that she didn't want to upset Erin and Donald. Annie and I prepared a simple meal of sandwiches and iced tea. We worked in silence. The children were safe in their rooms, and I took a tray of food to each, checking to be sure the windows were locked. Perhaps it was a foolish precaution, but the sense that something dangerous lurked outside had me unnerved.

As I was about to leave her room, Erin caught my hand. "Do you think Margo is okay?"

"I do. But she won't be when Berta gets hold of her." I had to keep it positive. Berta's emotional reaction had terrified Donald and Erin.

Bob had his hands full with his wife, and Erin and Donald had only me to comfort them.

"What if something bad got her?"

"What do you mean, some*thing* bad?"

"Like in the poem. A goblin. Annie told us the rest of the poem. It was about a girl getting snatched up and taken." She started to weep silently. "It's almost like the poem told what would happen to Margo. Do you think something bad snatched her?

Cora had often recited the poem to me, and I knew the verse Erin meant.

"One time a little girl would always laugh and grin,
and make fun of everyone, an' all her blood-and-kin.
And once when there was company and old folks wuz there,
she mocked 'em and shocked 'em and said she didn't care.
And just as she kicked her heels and turned to run and hide,
there wuz two great big Black Things a-standing by her side.
And they snatched her through the ceiling 'fore she knowed
what she's about.
And the goblins will get you if you don't watch out."

"It's a poem meant to scare children. It's not real." I sounded short of breath. Margo *had* disappeared just as if she'd been snatched away. Though I knew that wasn't possible, I couldn't bear the imagery the poem evoked. "Eat your sandwich. I'll come back up later." I had to get away, to find a quiet moment to compose myself.

I returned to the empty kitchen and sank into a chair at the table. I focused on trying to take a deep breath. Annie had probably gone to her room, and I was glad to be alone. I had to conquer the fear that had taken me over. The clock tocked away in the hall. That was the only sound except for the creak of the house settling into night. I hoped for Bob's footfall on the stairs, but no one else in the house stirred.

"What do you think happened to Margo?" Annie asked.

Her sudden appearance made me gasp. I hadn't heard her footsteps. "You scared the shit out of me. Don't do that!"

She repeated her question as she walked to the kitchen sink and looked out over the dark yard.

"I think she's with Andrew." I would not allow myself to think anything else.

"Do you think she'll ever come back?" Annie stared out the window.

The question stunned me. "Of course. She may be angry with Berta, but she isn't stupid. She has college ahead of her. She wants to be an architect like her father. Andrew is a passing fancy. Once she realizes he's a dime a dozen and has no future, she'll tuck tail and come home."

Annie dumped a bag of chips into a bowl and put it on the table. "I don't think so. I think she's gone for good."

"That's a terrible thing to say." I rounded on her.

"I'm not saying that's what I want to happen, but think about it. She must have had some money stashed away. Bob and Berta are generous, you know. Once she's gone a few days, she'll realize that if she comes home, Andrew will go to prison. Margo is prideful. She won't back down."

Annie had observed plenty in the short time she was in the house. She'd pegged Margo's selfishness. "Pride isn't very filling. When she runs out of money, she'll be home." I spoke with far more assurance than I felt.

The phone rang, startling me so that I jumped. Annie laughed as I hurried to the hall phone table. Mark was on the other end.

"Just wanted to update you. We've got a report of a black Mustang with a couple of kids in it over near Slidell, Louisiana. The deputies there are checking it out. Maybe we'll have her home before midnight."

The relief made my knees weak and I sank into a chair at the table. "Thank goodness."

"We should have the facts in half or hour or so. I'll give a call back."

"Thank you, Mark. Thank you!" I gripped the phone so hard my fingers ached. I hung up and faced Annie.

"Good news?" Annie asked. There was something in her tone that made me wonder what she really knew about Margo's vanishing act.

"I think so, but I'm not going to tell Bob and Berta until it's certain." False hope was the worst of all. "Mark said he'd call back in a little while."

"Looks like we'll be keeping a vigil." She brought an open bottle of wine from the refrigerator. "Want a glass?"

"You're too young to drink."

"So was Margo, but she did." Annie got a wine glass from the shelf.

"You'd better not." I had no real authority over Annie, but I was also the tutor, the person supposed to watch over the children and set a good example. Technically Annie wasn't one of my charges, but I felt responsible.

She poured the glass of Chardonnay. Lifting it to her lips, she smiled. Instead of drinking it, she put it on the table. "For you, silly. I'm too young to drink."

"And I don't care for wine." I pushed the glass away just as the phone rang again. There were extensions in the kitchen, Bob and Berta's bedroom, Margo's room, and the hall. I picked it up.

"Mimi, it's Mark."

In the ten minutes between calls, his tone had changed completely. "What's wrong?"

"Let me speak to Mr. Henderson."

"What is it?" I wanted to drop the phone and run, but I couldn't.

"I'm on my way out there."

"Have you found her?" I couldn't stand it.

"I really have to speak to Margo's parents. I'll be there in twenty minutes."

"Mark, what did you find? Don't do this to me!"

"Jesus, Mimi." He sounded in pain. "The car in Slidell belonged to a young married couple. It wasn't Andrew and Margo."

Something else hung between us. "What? Tell me."

"A fisherman brought up a human hand in his shrimp net. He just got back to the dock and called it in. It's male. We think it might be Cargill's, but we can't prove it."

"Where's the rest of him?" It was a stupid question.

"Don't jump to conclusions. There's a ring on the hand. We're hoping someone can identify it."

17

The grandfather clock in the hallway, an heirloom of Berta's family, chimed midnight. Mark and I sat on the front porch. Dr. Albert Adams was still with Berta. He'd given her a sedative. Bob was with the children upstairs, trying to console and calm them. Annie had gone to her room.

"How does a sixteen-year-old girl vanish? There's not a trace of where she went." Margo was now officially gone more than twenty-four hours. What had seemed like an act of teenage rebellion had taken on a darker coloring.

At the sheriff's order, Mark had brought the pinky ring the coroner had taken from the severed hand to see if Bob or Berta recognized it. It was a ring made from a silver spoon handle, a popular type of jewelry with teenagers, with the initial M engraved. Though none of us had ever seen the ring, the initial was enough to send Berta into a panic.

"There's no proof anything bad has happened," Mark said, but his voice lacked confidence.

"How was the hand found?"

"Robert Dray caught it in his shrimp nets. He wasn't far off the shore, near the old hotel." Mark's wrists rested on his knees. He looked tired and worried. "The sheriff is bringing in the Alabama Bureau of Investigation," he said. "Maybe the FBI. We've got a body part and nothing to go on. Maybe it isn't related to Margo, but we're concerned about those Korean followers of that Moon fellow in Bayou La Batre."

"They're weird, but they aren't killers. Besides, Margo's not with the Moonies. Not in your wildest dreams. Margo's a princess."

Mark nodded as if he agreed. "The other possibility is a kidnapping. Folks here see the Hendersons as wealthy. Someone might have taken her for money."

"And chopped off Andrew's hand? Why?"

"We don't know it's Cargill's hand."

"If it was a kidnapping, wouldn't they have called for ransom?" I asked.

"Yeah." He let it drop.

"Do you think the hand belongs to Andrew?" I simply couldn't understand why someone would sever a limb.

"I don't think talking about this is a good idea. It's only upsetting you more."

I shifted to confront him. "How? Not knowing is even worse, and someone has to ask these questions."

"His mother couldn't identify the hand. Fingerprints are worthless, because Andrew doesn't have any on record. There was grease that would be normal for a car mechanic beneath the fingernails. The thing is, the hand was sliced off clean. Took someone with great strength to do that."

My stomach surged, but since I'd eaten nothing, I only gagged.

Mark put his arm around me and I turned into his chest. He smelled like starch and sweat and the lingering odor of aftershave. He seemed a cocoon of safety. "I'm sorry, Mimi." His hand stroked my hair, and I felt a longing so intense it was almost irresistible. Turning my face up to him, I invited a kiss.

"Hold on there." He stood up. "I want to go out with you, Mimi. But I'm on duty, and you're really upset. That would be taking advantage."

Shame washed over me. Margo was missing and I was trying to seduce the man who should be out looking for her. I wasn't the kind of girl who threw herself at a man. I couldn't explain what had come over me. "Sorry."

"Hey, don't be sorry. You're upset. You're looking for comfort. It's a natural thing." He sat back down. "I'd really like to get to know you, Mimi. Even back in high school I thought you were beautiful. I just didn't know how to tell you."

"I know. This isn't the time." The comfort of his thigh against mine was solid, real. In a world gone haywire, he made sense. He was right, though. Rushing wasn't smart. His attention needed to be on finding Margo. "Tell me everything you can about the search."

"We've got a couple of leads on Andrew's car. Tomorrow we'll explore a tip about Dawson Slough. Some kids looking for mudbugs say they saw a car matching the description of Andrew's."

"That's near the old hotel. It's on the Henderson property." I glanced toward the east. The night was cloudy and there was no moonlight. Even in the bright sun, the hotel was too far away to be seen. "Could Margo be that close?"

"We're starting grid searches tomorrow. We'll have volunteers going through all the marshes and we're putting up fliers around Mobile. The TV stations are going to carry the story of their disappearance with photos, and Bob is offering a reward. A big one. Even the Moonies would turn her in for it."

He was trying to make me feel better but it wasn't working. "If someone kidnapped her for money, they would have called by now."

"If a ransom call comes in, the FBI will take over." He rose smoothly to his feet, lifting me with him. "I have to get busy." He handed me the empty tea glass.

"Want a sandwich?" I didn't want Mark to leave.

He put his hat on. "Thanks anyway." He hesitated. "I'm glad we're getting to know each other, Mimi. I kept up with you through Cora. She's really proud of you."

"I know, but thanks for telling me."

He tipped his hat and walked across the beautiful lawn to his patrol car parked beneath an old oak.

I stood, preparing to go inside. My hand was on the door when I heard a giggle. It was soft, sweet, and childish. Donald was too old for that type of merriment. I slowly turned around and faced the water. There was no moon or stars, and the water was a lighter shade of black that extended to meet the sky. There were boats on the water, but I couldn't see any of them. I could hear the water, though, a susurration almost like a living, breathing thing.

The giggle came again.

"Who's there?" I called into the night, my fear overcoming my desire not to bother Bob and Berta.

The only answer was another giggle.

There was someone out there, someone watching the house. Was it possible it was Margo and that she was having a fine laugh at how upset we all were by her disappearance?

"Margo!" I was ready to kill her. "Margo!" I screamed her name.

Above me a window slammed shut with great force. Footsteps shook the porch floor as someone heavy pounded toward me. The front door flew open and Bob raced to grasp my shoulder.

"Is Margo out here? Is she okay?"

My vocal cords seemed frozen. The depth of Bob's despair and worry paralyzed me. "I heard something."

He released me and stepped in front, shielding me. "What did you hear?"

"I thought it was someone . . . calling out." I couldn't say giggling. I couldn't. He would think me mad.

"I'll get a flashlight."

Before I could stop him, he went inside and returned with a high-beam light. Side by side we walked toward the water. I took his hand for courage, and he held mine tightly.

"Where?" he demanded.

I pointed to the dense azaleas that lined the driveway. "Over there. It was just a noise. I maybe jumped to the wrong conclusion."

He led and I followed as he checked beneath each huge shrub. He didn't call Margo's name. He couldn't bear to do so, because he knew she wouldn't answer. Halfway down the drive he stopped. I walked over to look and found the strange claw marks similar to the ones Mark and I discovered in the backyard.

"What kind of animal is that?" he asked.

"Coyote." I didn't know, but a definite answer was required. Bob expected me to know such things since I was a native of the area.

"They wouldn't . . . attack a human, would they?"

Again, I was no authority on coyotes, but he needed reassurance. "No, Bob. They're mostly scavengers and they prey on small animals like rabbits. Not humans."

He searched for another ten minutes before he gave it up. We'd turned to go back to the house when I heard the giggle again, so soft it could have been the whisper of the wind. I stopped.

"What is it?" He halted too, waiting for me.

"Listen," I said.

We stood for a long moment as the gentle surf sucked at the marsh grass to the south and the wind sawed through the live oaks around us. Crickets churned and the frogs made a variety of noises. Some sounded like cries, others like the grind of a motor.

"Mimi." The voice was almost a purr. "Mi-mi."

I tensed and Bob caught hold of my arm. "What is that noise?" he asked.

"You heard it? Like someone calling my name?"

He shook his head. "Not like that. Like something suffering. Like a small creature in pain."

I clutched his hand like a terrified child. "Let's go inside." I hustled us forward, afraid to look back and see what might be watching us.

18

It's hard to comprehend how time passes when every second is spent waiting. Belle Fleur became a house filled with listening and watching, hoping for the glass-pack muffler of a black Mustang or the ring of the phone. But those things didn't happen. Margo was gone, vanished as if the words of James Whitcomb Riley's poem had come to life and she'd been snatched by two great big black things. And Andrew Cargill, too.

Mark kept me apprised of the investigation. There were leads, but none panned out. To his credit, Sheriff Delchamps kept up a nightly appeal on the local news stations. He did love seeing himself on television, but he was working to find Margo.

Berta suffered. She stayed in her room more than was healthy, and some days she didn't bathe or dress. Guilt ate at her, because she blamed herself for Margo's disappearance. Not even Bob could anchor her in the swirling vortex of emotions. She refused to believe anything except her eldest was alive and living with Andrew somewhere in California. Margo hated Alabama, and it was logical she'd flee back to a place she loved. That one fantasy kept Berta from going insane.

But I wasn't certain. While I hoped for the best, logic told me Margo wasn't able to come home. When Erin was riding and Donald was busy, I examined Margo's belongings, hoping for some evidence of her whereabouts by what she'd left behind. The problem was that she left everything behind. She'd been wearing shorts, a red top, and blue canvas shoes when she left. She hadn't even taken her cosmetics. She had no money to speak of. It didn't make sense.

Mark's visits became more personal than professional. He had little news. New leads didn't turn up, and the severed hand was a dead end. But Mark's presence seemed to comfort Berta, a sign that the law officers hadn't given up hope. But I knew Mark came to see me. And for the first time in my life, I found myself dating steadily, if somewhat restrictively. We kept our feelings under wraps. The hours I stole with Mark made me feel more fully alive than I'd ever known.

Bob worked later and later—the renovation of the downtown Mobile hotel was in full swing. Bob could either meet his obligations or trash his career. He didn't speak about it, but I understood his dilemma, as I also understood that Belle Fleur was not a welcoming place any longer. Watching Berta deteriorate was too brutal—he loved her so much and he was powerless to help her.

The care for Erin and Donald fell to me and Annie. Bob was too wrapped up in Berta to notice that Annie had begun to change. I'd caught hints of it, but with Bob and Berta both distracted, a much darker Annie peeked out. I no longer trusted her with the younger children for extended periods. No matter how many times I told her not to scare the children, she persisted in telling her ghost stories. On more than one occasion, I woke up to find Donald and Erin both creeping into my bed, terrified by some tale Annie had spun. It seemed to me that Annie took pleasure in tormenting them.

Two weeks after Margo disappeared, I officially accepted a public date with Mark. We had plans to go to a high school scrimmage game to mark the beginning of the school year. In Alabama, football is god, especially high school. I had no real interest in the game, but it was an excuse to escape the tension of Belle Fleur.

The night was unbearably hot. August in Coden was like walking through damp gauze. Watching the players run across the field and the cheerleaders jump and yell, I wondered how they did so when I felt as if someone was pressing lightly on my lungs.

Mark and I sat at the fifty-yard line, and he explained the intricate plays, trying to keep me interested in what seemed to be aimless running back and forth. "The red team quarterback has a great arm," Mark noted.

"He did make some good passes." I was pleased to be able to comment.

Mark put his arm around me. He'd been very patient with my shyness. He liked it that I wasn't experienced, that I held back. "Would you like to drive into Mobile, maybe have a drink? There's a new pub at the mall that folks say has great sandwiches."

The invitation was tempting, but I'd been gone for three hours already. Annie had promised not to tell any stories, but I'd discovered that Annie didn't always keep her word.

"I should go home. The children—"

"May need you." He tightened his arm around me. "Do you think you'll be that worried about your own children?"

"I can't imagine being any other way."

We drove back to Belle Fleur with me pressed against him. Even in the heat, I enjoyed the feel of him. When we pulled into the yard, I knew something was wrong. Donald stood in the second-floor window of Margo's room. He was crying, and he waved to me to hurry inside.

"What the hell?" Mark said. When I tried to run into the house, he grabbed me and held me back, stepping in front of me.

As soon as we were inside, I called out for Donald. Still crying, he appeared at the top of the steps. When he saw me, he ran into my arms and slammed against me so hard I almost fell backwards.

"What's wrong, buddy?" Mark asked. He scanned the room, moving slowly to check out the den and the kitchen.

"Annie said Margo was dead." He clutched at my smock top. "Erin got so mad she locked herself in your room, Mimi. She wouldn't let

me in. And then I heard something in the hall, scratching at my door."
He was almost hysterical.

"Where is Mr. Henderson?" Mark asked over Donald's head.

I shook my head. Surely Bob and Berta had heard the commotion.
Why hadn't they come out to attend their children? I was a tutor, not
their mother. "Let me get Erin." I disentangled Donald, and Mark
scooped him into his strong arms.

"Get Annie, too," Mark said.

Erin was indeed locked in my room, but she flew out when she
heard me calling her name. Tears streaked her cheeks and her eyes
were wild. "Where's Annie?" I asked her before I sent her down to
Mark.

"In her room." Erin was getting a grip on herself. "She said she saw
Margo's ghost out on the front lawn. That meant Margo was dead."

"She doesn't know any more than anyone else."

"She shouldn't say such things." Erin followed me as I went to
the staircase.

"No, she shouldn't. Go on down to Mark. I want to have a word
with her alone."

Erin scampered down the stairs, and I climbed to the third floor.
I could feel the pulse of fury in my jaw. Annie had gone too far this
time. I tried her door without knocking and found it locked. She
answered immediately, though.

"You look like you're about to explode." She stepped into the hall
and closed the door. She'd become very secretive about her room.

"The children are frightened and upset. What did you tell them
about Margo?"

She took her time assessing me. "The truth. Berta wants to pretend that Margo is living in California, some little hippie flower child
running around with her mechanic boyfriend. That's Andrew's hand.
Everyone knows it. What happens when someone's hand is cut off,
Mimi? They bleed to death. If Andrew is dead, chances are good that
Margo is too. It's time for everyone in this house to face reality and
stop pretending."

I drew back to slap her. It was an automatic impulse, but her hand was lightning-fast. She caught my wrist in a punishing grip. "I wouldn't try that."

"I will see to it that you're put out of this house." I snatched my wrist away from her. "Cora can find you another place to stay."

"I wouldn't count on that, Mimi." She tilted her head. "Berta adores me. While you've been minding the children, I've been tending Berta. We're very close." She opened her room and stepped back. "If you make it a contest between us, you'll be the one leaving." The door closed softly.

When I returned downstairs, Mark had Donald and Erin engaged in a game of Uno at the kitchen table. I joined them, and in a few moments, Annie appeared in the doorway wearing baby doll pajamas that showed her long, slender legs to advantage. She wasn't the least disturbed by Mark's presence. I hadn't recounted our conversation to Mark. I didn't want to upset the children again.

"Donald, Erin, I didn't mean to scare you," Annie said. She held her hands behind her back and brought them forward with an Almond Joy in each one. "I am sorry." She handed one to each child.

Donald tore into the candy. Erin put hers on the table.

"Berta doesn't like for them to have a lot of sugar," I said.

"It can be our secret." Annie grinned. "A candy bar every now and then won't hurt anyone." She turned in the doorway. "Now I'm going to bed." She took her time walking away.

"She's really grown up," Mark said.

"Maybe a little too much." I had no doubt that Annie was sending me a private message. I'd seen her flirt with Mark before, but now she was letting me know how far she'd take it.

With Annie's conduct so questionable, I wasn't comfortable leaving the house often, and Mark spent many an hour munching Jiffy Pop and watching the network movies on television in the Henderson living room with me and the children. When Mark was in the house, Annie kept to her room or else she went walking along Shore Road or exploring the overgrown grounds of the Paradise Inn. She was looking for something.

When Bob was at work, Annie spent most of the day with Berta. Erin and Donald took all of my attention, and the shut door of Berta's bedroom was like a hand in my face. Even when I knocked to deliver coffee, Annie took the tray. The glimpses I caught of Berta told me she was mired in her worry and grief. Had I wanted to talk with Berta about Annie, I was thwarted at every turn.

In the evenings, when Bob was home, Annie was at his side. If he went to the Paradise to take measurements, she was his helper. She was versed in architectural styles—from books she'd gotten from the library—and she delighted Bob with her interest in his work. Trouble was brewing there, but I saw no way to stop it.

In late August, Sheriff Delchamps staged a raid on the Unification Church. Margo was just an excuse to do so, and he found no trace of her or anything else crime worthy. Still, some days I'd see the Moonies selling their roses at the corner of 188 and Hwy. 90 and wonder if Margo and Andrew had been spirited away, assisted to a new life as flower vendors on some sunny California street. Then the vision of the severed hand would return. No one had proven it was Andrew's—the ring wasn't familiar to the Cargill family. But Andrew was the only missing male in the community. While no one said it, I knew everyone thought it was Andrew's hand and that the young couple was dead.

August gave way to September, and Erin enrolled in the public school. A thin shadow of herself, Berta resisted, but Bob persuaded her that it was temporary, until the household regained balance. She gave in with surprisingly little resistance, and each of my days developed another hole, another void. I missed Erin's enthusiasm, but I redoubled my efforts to give Donald the best education possible. I kept him out of the house as much as I could.

A spree of bank robberies and the murder of a Mobile city councilman at Shady Banks, a reputed whorehouse, turned the sheriff's attention at last. Margo slipped from the news. The posters that Bob printed and put all over south Mobile County grew tattered and disappeared from the trees and posts on which we'd nailed them.

The same was true for the Cargills. Andrew was replaced as a mechanic at the Esso station. The fabric of life was re-knit with little to show that Andrew had ever been a part of the community. While Bob had the funds and influence to keep the pressure on for Margo, no one seemed to worry about Andrew.

One morning I borrowed the car without revealing my destination. There was no evidence that Margo and Andrew had left together, but it was hard not to draw that conclusion. Mark had talked with Andrew's family regularly, and they had heard no word from their son. I put a basket of fresh muffins I'd baked into the station wagon and drove to the clapboard house on the south side of town.

Mrs. Cargill met me at the door. She was only a few years older than Berta, but she'd spent days in the sun working on the dock when her husband returned with the day's catch. Her skin was leathery and her brown eyes haunted. She took the basket of muffins I offered but didn't invite me in. Like Berta, she seemed on the edge of life, no longer a real participant but a wraith sentenced to watch from a distance.

"Mrs. Cargill, do you have any idea where Andrew might be?" I asked. It had occurred to me that perhaps Andrew—if he was alive—was communicating with his family. It was a foolish hope that Mrs. Cargill might tell me what she wouldn't tell Mark or the sheriff. Looking at her, though, I knew her son was as gone as Margo. Still, I had to ask. If there was any chance, I had to try.

"I told the sheriff and the deputy, we've had no word from Andrew since the night he disappeared. Not a word."

"We still believe Margo is alive," I told her.

"Andrew wouldn't hurt that girl," she said.

"I don't believe he did. None of the Hendersons do. Berta wants to believe they're together, happy somewhere."

She shook her head. "Andrew's not the kind of boy to run off and not call home. Since my husband died, Andrew helped take care of the family. Folks never knew what kind of boy he was. They looked at him and thought the worst, but he was a good boy. He's dead. I know it." She put a hand on her heart. "That girl was the worst thing coulda happened to him. Spoiled, used to the best. She put him in a spot he didn't fit. He didn't hurt her, but she got him killed, and herself too."

She dropped the basket of muffins and closed the door.

I didn't tell Bob about the encounter, but I told Mark when he stopped by the house on Wednesday night. He'd come to collect me for a movie date. *Young Frankenstein* was playing at the Loop, and he thought I could use some light entertainment. I was reluctant to leave the children, but I was also exhausted with the emotional turmoil of Belle Fleur.

Mark's car, a restored 1964 Dodge Dart, rode low and fast, and we cut through the dense pinewoods and across creeks where frogs screeched at a high-pitched whine as we blasted by. Mark drove fast, but he had a get-out-of-jail-free pass with his badge.

The movie, shot in black and white, made me laugh. For a couple of hours, I forgot everything about my life and sank into the antics of Gene Wilder, Marty Feldman, and Teri Garr.

The moment the lights came up, though, my anxiety returned. The drive from Mobile took forty minutes, so we headed back to Belle Fleur. Though I tried to hide my worry, Mark knew.

"The house isn't going to disintegrate without you there for an evening." He reached across the seat and took my hand. His thumb worked slow circles across my knuckles. "You can't let their problems overwhelm you, Mimi."

He was right. Unfortunately, he offered no solid suggestions as to how to accomplish what he said. For a while I let the whisper of the tires on the asphalt lull me. The night was soft with stars and a misty humidity. We drove with the windows down, and I let the breeze catch my hair and toss it in all directions. "Did you ever learn anything about Annie?" He'd offered to look into her past.

"She's a riddle. We can't find a thing about her. That could give you some comfort, Mimi. If she had a record, we'd be able to track it. I can only say she was damn lucky to run into Cora on the street. How many unwanted kids end up living in a place like Belle Fleur with a family like the Hendersons?"

"She has to have a past." My tone earned me a hard look from Mark.

He drove in silence a moment. "I'm sure she does, but without a direction or clue from her, we don't even know where to begin looking. She's a sixteen-year-old girl who's a little . . . strange. What is it about her that troubles you so much?"

"The timing." A chill ran down my arms and I rolled up my window. "Annie shows up looking for a home and Margo leaves. Like there's not room for both of them." The minute I said it, I realized the accuracy. "It was as if Annie's arrival had precipitated Margo's departure."

Mark reached across the seat and pulled me closer to him. "Forget about Annie and the Hendersons. Just for a little while. It's like you're obsessed, Mimi. You work there, but they aren't your family."

"I know." I sighed and snuggled against him as he drove. I closed my eyes and tried to forget Belle Fleur.

We were still several miles from Coden. On both sides of the road, dense pines stretched into blackness. Mark pulled off the road onto a narrow path that led into the woods. He killed the motor and turned to me.

Our make-out sessions had grown increasingly intense. Still, I resisted going all the way. There was no opportunity at the Hendersons, but here, alone in the woods, Mark pressed me. I pushed away.

"I should get home." I liked kissing Mark, but that was as far as I wanted to take it.

Mark blew out a breath, but he straightened up. His arm was still draped over my shoulders. "I don't understand, Mimi. You seem to like me."

"I do." How could I explain what I didn't understand? "I don't know what I feel about this. It scares me, Mark. I'm not ready. Please take me home."

"It's only ten o'clock." He pulled a stick of gum from his shirt pocket and offered it to me. I unwrapped it while he did the same with another. "You're a college graduate, Mimi. Surely the Hendersons don't have a curfew on you."

"No. They don't. It's that Bob has no one to help him with the children. I have to go home. Now."

He removed his arm and started the car. "Belle Fleur isn't your home, Mimi, but I'll take you back to the Hendersons."

It angered me that I felt pressed to explain my actions. "You shouldn't punish me because I'm responsible. Bob and the children have no one to turn to but me. This will pass, Mark. Berta will get over this. Right now, though, *I* have to shoulder this burden."

"No, you don't. You're the hired tutor, not a family member. Take this on if you must, but at least recognize it's a choice."

"I try hard to be a good person, to do the right thing, and no one sees that. Annie is a little beast, and everyone thinks she's perfect." No matter how hard I tried, I always fell short of what was expected of me.

"Sorry. I'm behaving like an ass." He caught my hand and raised it to his lips. "I've been looking forward to this evening."

The tension eased. "Me, too. I'm sorry I'm acting all weird, but I miss Margo, too. It's just a rough patch until she comes home."

"Maybe we can play some putt-putt. The course over in Biloxi is fun."

I just wanted him to take me home. Something niggled at me, a darkness that blotted out the pleasure of Mark's company. "That would be fun," I said automatically.

As he pulled out onto the road, I caught a glimpse of a deer in the headlights. The doe bolted, zagging left, then right as if something deadly trailed her. It didn't seem like a good omen to me.

⚶

Erin moved her belongings to a small bedroom at the far end of the second floor. She'd never wanted that room, because it was removed from the rest of the second floor down a narrow hallway. The room had a lovely view of the Sound, though, and a huge oak tree grew right beside it, offering shade in the heat of the summer. She seemed to thrive at Coden Middle School, and she was making friends. Donald had adjusted, but Berta seemed to grow more distant. I tried everything I knew. Cora stopped by regularly, but none of us could shake Berta from her lethargy. When Bob began to talk about possible medical intervention, I knew something had to be done, and quickly. Berta's absence, emotional and physical, was pushing Bob to the brink of a tragic decision. Unless things changed, the family would collapse. Bob would take them all back to California if Berta didn't pull herself together.

I paced my bedroom at night trying to think of remedies, and bad dreams disrupted my sleep. I heard creaks and noises, and I found myself patrolling the second floor of the house, checking on Donald and then Erin, watching them sleep, then quietly slipping downstairs to stand outside Bob and Berta's bedroom. Dr. Adams had given Berta something to sleep, and it knocked her out as effectively as a tire tool to the head.

As for me, I dreaded sleep. The unidentified hand crept into my dreams, an artifact like a saint's shriveled appendage kept in a box. Nightmare imaginings of the blow that severed the hand, the screams and blood—none of it real—tormented me. Annie, too, was restless. On more than one occasion I caught her slipping around the house. She said she heard things, strange noises. My distrust of her grew.

It was a cool morning in late September when I went to the local hardware store to pick up a faucet for the watering trough. It was a simple matter for Bob to replace it, but I thought I'd surprise him by having all the parts ready.

I was exploring the different faucets when I overheard Mrs. Waylon and her husband whispering at the register.

"I don't know what's going on at Belle Fleur, but it's like the mother disappeared from the face of the earth. We never see Bob Henderson without that girl. She's like his shadow, and I can tell you if some teenage girl started following you around like that, Vernon Waylon, I'd put a stop to it."

The picture they painted took my breath away. Annie had become Bob's little helper, in a way that was drawing attention from the community, not just me They were always together. People had noticed.

"Now, Bell, don't be jumping to conclusions," Vernon said, but without conviction. "The girl's an orphan. Maybe she's just attached to someone who showed her a little kindness."

"She comes in here, never speaks. She's not natural," Bell insisted. "And she may be a teenager, but she looks like a young woman. Berta Henderson had best get over her grief and tend to her family—before she loses it."

The community gossip forced me to acknowledge what I knew but had been unwilling to really confront. The weeks of good food had rounded Annie's curves. She was no longer the knobby-kneed teen, but a young woman whose body now could be called lush. I dropped the faucet I'd selected and left the store before they saw me.

For a long time I sat beside the small bayou under the bridge. I thought at first to confront Bob with the gossip, but I realized that wouldn't work, and it might plant a dangerous seed. No, I was going to have to do something.

One Wednesday evening, I left the Hendersons and went to spend some time with Cora. The disappearance of Margo had hurt her, too. I brought her some carrot cake Annie had baked, a delicious treat. Annie turned out to be quite the cook. She could remember exactly how to prepare a complicated recipe, but she had no inkling of her past. Or so she claimed. Now, I doubted everything about her.

I'd done a little research on amnesia at the library and had come to consider Annie's lapse as more convenient memory than true memory loss. I intended to talk to Cora about it.

The days and nights were still hot as hell, and instead of the porch, where mosquitoes as big as crows buzzed around our heads, we went inside to her cozy living room. She sampled the cake with a wide smile. "Delicious. I'm glad to see Annie has found a niche in the Henderson house. I hope she's a help to you."

"Have you given up?" I asked. "On finding Annie's family?"

Cora looked surprised. "It hasn't been a high priority. Why? Is she making trouble for Bob or Berta?"

I shook my head. I'd decided not to broach the issue of Annie's conduct with Bob, her constant bird-dogging of his every move. It was better to take a different tack. "It's just that we're so sad there. I know Annie's suffered and now she lives in a house where everyone tiptoes or whispers. She may not remember the details of her past life, but she's surely got some kind of family. She's been well schooled. And she can cook and clean. Someone spent time with her. I thought it might be happier for her if we could find her home." I could be manipulative, too.

Cora smoothed the crocheted doily on the arm of the sofa. "What's wrong, Mimi? What is Annie doing that upsets you?"

"My concern is for Annie. The house is sad. Berta is distraught and stays in her room. Erin is going to public school, and there's only me and Donald." I'd underestimated Cora's astuteness, but I had no choice but to press on.

Cora was nobody's fool. "And Bob. How is he holding up?"

"Fine." I said the word too sharply. "He's exhausted. Sometimes he drinks at night, after Berta is asleep. His judgment is impaired." What I didn't say was that Annie was often with him when he drank. If I listened at the door of his study, I often heard them whispering.

"I see." Cora assessed me. "I'll renew my efforts to find out about Annie's past."

"It would be for the best, Cora. For her and the family."

"When I saw Bob recently, he mentioned what a help Annie was. He said he couldn't get along without her. She's just sixteen, Mimi. She's still a child. I had really hoped the two of you would become close, that you would help each other."

I met her gaze directly. "She's no help to me. I don't want her at Belle Fleur. She doesn't belong."

"If there's something more you want to tell me. . . ."

I shook my head. I'd said enough.

19

Driving back to Belle Fleur, I thought about what I'd done. When she'd first arrived at the Hendersons, I'd been willing to welcome her. Now, though, I viewed her as a danger. She scared the children, and worse than that, she had set her sights on Bob. She was capable of managing on her own—a fact she'd demonstrated. She was sixteen and mature for her age. Too mature. She had to find a home or a husband of her own. Not Belle Fleur and not Bob Henderson.

The night was crystal-clear. A tropical storm had surged through the day before and left the air clear and the water calm and gentle. For the first time I thought I could smell fall in the air, though I knew we had at least five more weeks of hot temperatures. Summer in South Alabama extended from the first of May until the end of October.

I slowed the car, Berta's sporty Thunderbird convertible, as I drove along Shore Road. For the most part I drove the station wagon, but Bob had asked me to take Berta's car since it hadn't been driven for weeks. I loved the sounds of the water at night all around me in the open car. The gulls were silent, but there were other birds out. Night birds. Owls and hawks. Predators.

On my right, marsh grass ran down to the edge of the water, a rippling field of silver-tasseled green in the moonlight. To the left, the long blades of the cruel saw-grass led to the dark embrace of the woods. Above was the spangled sky, and I stopped the car to examine the constellations. Now that fall was approaching, astronomy would be fun for Donald and Erin. I wasn't nearly the storyteller Annie was, but I loved the legends of the Seven Sisters and Orion, who pursued the sisters across the night sky.

A bit of poetry from Hesiod came to mind. "And if longing seizes you for sailing the stormy seas, when the Pleiades flee mighty Orion and plunge into the misty deep and all the gusty winds are raging, then do not keep your ship on the wine-dark sea but, as I bid you, remember to work the land."

It was time to reconnect Erin and Donald with a structured fabric of life. While the house had not returned to normal—would never until Margo's disappearance was resolved—it was incumbent upon me to try to put things to right as much as possible. To that end, lessons would bind us. We could invite Bob to join us in a star search. And a bird-watching adventure. We could explore the architectural details of the Paradise Inn, and maybe do a book of pressed leaves and flowers for botany. Maybe Berta would like that.

Excited by the prospect, I put the car in gear and pressed a bit too hard on the gas. The powerful sports car lurched forward. To my horror, a young girl stood directly in front of the car. She'd come out of nowhere. I hadn't seen or heard her approach. I slammed on the brakes, sending the car into a sideways slide in the loose gravel of the road.

For several seconds I fought to hold the car from slipping into the marsh on one side or the ditch on the other. When at last I brought it to a halt, I'd spun in a complete circle. Had I hit her? I hadn't felt anything bump beneath the wheels.

Shaking, I got out of the car and leaned against the door. In the moonlight, the road was empty in both directions. Feeling queasy, I looked beneath the car, expecting to find a crumpled body.

Nothing.

I stood up and calmed my thudding heart. I'd seen her. Where had she gone? I looked around the car and finally got a flashlight from the glove box. The tire marks were clear in the road where I'd slid. It was easy to find the place I'd slammed on brakes. From there I tracked east twenty feet.

In the glow of the light, I saw disturbed earth. Not footprints. Not a sign of a dark-haired girl. Instead, there were claw marks where something wild had dug up the road in an attempt to avoid being struck by the car.

Some six feet distant, just at the edge of the ditch, I found more claw marks that led to the waist-high saw-grass. Shining the light, I picked up two yellow eyes nearly fifty yards away. They stared at me, and then came a horrible high-pitched giggle. The eyes disappeared.

20

That night I slept in fits, and when I woke up I had an agenda. It was a school day, so Erin ate the breakfast Annie cooked and went to catch the bus that trundled down Shore Road just for her. Bob offered—each morning—to drive her on his way to Mobile, but she liked the bus. It gave her an opportunity to laugh and gossip before classes began. The one bright spot in the household was to hear her on the telephone, conspiring with her new buddies.

Bob left for work, and I set Donald to a page of percentages. He was particularly bright at math and enjoyed working the problems. I went to the kitchen and dried the dishes Annie had washed.

"Would you take the car into town and get some fresh squash and turnips?" I asked Annie. "There's a pork roast in the refrigerator and I want some vegetables for supper."

"Why don't you go?" Annie assessed me, as if she could read something ulterior behind my request. Or perhaps my guilt only made it seem so. "I don't have a driver's license," she reminded me.

"I could, but I thought you might enjoy being in town without the rest of us. Nobody in Coden is going to bother you unless you do something stupid like speed. Bob went to a lot of trouble to make sure you could drive. He'd be disappointed to know you wouldn't help me." I let that sink in.

"Okay." She dropped the dishcloth and palmed the keys from a peg by the door.

I gave her five dollars from the stash in the canister Berta kept for incidentals. "For Bob's sake, you should get a license." It was odd that Annie never cared about driving. Margo had been wild to get behind the wheel and gain her freedom.

"Bob has a lot more on his mind than a silly driver's license. He'll get to it when the time is right." She jammed the money in her pocket and headed outside.

From behind the front door, I watched as she eased out the driveway toward town. When she was gone I went to Berta's room and knocked on the door.

"Come in."

I felt like I was entering a sick chamber. Berta sat in a chair by the window where she could see the water. She still wore her nightgown, likely the same one she'd had on for several days. It had been four weeks since Margo's disappearance. Each day, Berta called the sheriff's office and was told the same thing—no leads, no news.

I didn't ask permission. I went in the bathroom and drew water in the tub. "Get up, Berta."

"I'm tired. I don't feel like dressing."

"I know." I grasped her wrist not so gently and pulled her to her feet. My strength surprised us both. "You have two other children and a husband. Go clean up. When Bob comes home tonight, he's going to find his family waiting for him."

A cry broke from her. "Not his family! Not! His! Family!" She tried to pull free of me, but I restrained her. "Not Margo!"

When she crumpled, I held her on her feet. I gave her several moments, but then I shook her lightly. "Stand up!" I shook harder.

"Stand up! You're going to lose everything if you don't pull yourself together."

Her pale gaze searched my face, and I knew she thought I'd turned into a monster. "You're very cruel, Mimi. I had no idea you could be so hard."

My hand itched to slap some sense into her, but I merely dragged her to the bathroom. "Margo is gone, and we don't stand a chance of finding her unless we start looking." I pulled the gown over her head and nudged her toward the bathtub. "Get in."

She did as I told her because I'd frightened her.

"You're going to get cleaned up. We'll take matters into our own hands." I'd hatched a plot during my sleepless night. "The cops aren't looking any longer." Mark had told me as much. Mark hadn't given up. On Margo or me. He called almost every day to talk about his efforts to find the missing girl. Unwilling to risk another argument about my duties at Belle Fleur, I kept him at a distance. I missed him. At night I longed for his kisses, his touch, the safety of his arms. But I couldn't choose him over my family. My adopted family.

Mark continued to chase leads and follow up on reported sightings of the teenagers, but to the sheriff Margo was a spoiled kid who'd run away with the town's bad boy. The severed hand had never been connected to Andrew's disappearance, and all efforts to find the body missing a hand had failed.

"What can we do?" Berta sounded like a lost child.

"We'll hire a private investigator and start our own search. Someone devoted only to finding Margo."

"A private detective?" Hope sounded in Berta's voice.

"Yes. A good one." He could search for Margo, but I also had something for him to do. Annie. Where had she come from, what was her past? I had to know. The incident on Shore Road the night before had left me almost paralyzed with fear and dread. Somehow, all the strange things that had happened—continued to happen—at Belle Fleur were connected to Annie. Life at Belle Fleur had been paradise before Annie showed up on the doorstep. Patterns were emerging, and Annie was at the center of them.

"Did Bob agree to this?" Berta asked as she washed herself.

"He doesn't have to know." I went to her closet and pulled out Capri pants, flats, and a red jersey top. I put them on the counter in the bathroom. "Hurry. We have a lot to do."

She nodded.

I left her there and went to check on Donald. I had no idea what forces we were battling. What was Annie's connection to the dark-haired girl both Donald and I had seen haunting the perimeter of Belle Fleur? The girl had appeared when Annie arrived, like her woodland doppelganger. Annie's evil twin. Whoever she might prove to be, I had no doubt we'd entered into a war. Someone, or something, had taken Margo.

21

Jimmy Finch carried too much weight around his middle, and his polyester pants had seen better days, but he struck me as someone who could handle himself in a physical confrontation. I nodded to Berta. I'd made a list of three local P.I.s, and Finch had the best reputation.

"What's your fee, Mr. Finch?" she asked.

"Fifty a day, retainer of three hundred. You cover any out-of-pocket expenses."

We sat in his office, which was a small house surrounded by oleander bushes and ligustrums, in Pascagoula, Mississippi, near the Jackson County Courthouse. In my research, I'd discovered that Finch had cracked two missing girl cases and had recovered another from the Moonies, though that case had ended unhappily in the girl's suicide once she was returned home.

I didn't believe Margo was mixed up with the Korean cult leader, whose top aide had been the former deputy director of the Korean CIA. But I'd applied myself to digging up facts about the Moonies, and what I'd found was disturbing. Sometimes it was best to go through channels outside the law.

"Will you take the case?" Berta asked Finch. She looked so pale and troubled that I wondered if Finch considered her mentally deficient.

"I will. I'll start out talking to the deputies. It's strange to me they dismissed the severed hand. I mean it's not every day a hand turns up in these parts at the same time a girl and a boy go missing. You're sure your husband isn't going to get upset about hiring me?"

Finch was concerned for his fee. "Bob will be glad we thought of it," I assured him, though I wasn't sure enough to have asked Bob first. I'd opted for begging forgiveness later—if at all. Some things were better left untold.

"I'll report at the end of the week," Finch said, tucking the check Berta handed him into his coat pocket.

"Thank you." We stood and I took Berta's elbow. She was still unsteady, but taking action had done a world of good for her. Perhaps the P.I. was a waste of money, but it had given Berta new life.

I took her to the car, then hesitated. "I forgot my purse," I said. "I'll be right back."

I hurried to the office and entered. "Check into this girl," I said and gave him a photograph I'd taken of Annie. "She's living with the Hendersons. Claims to have amnesia."

He studied the photograph and then me. "'Claims'? You don't believe her?"

I shrugged. "Her name is Annie. She was found wandering the streets of Mobile with no memory of who she is or where she came from. My grandmother works for Pensions and fostered her with the Hendersons. Not too long before Margo went missing."

"The cops looked into this yet?"

"I don't know." Mark had made some effort, but I wasn't sure how rigorous. Annie's past was difficult to track. "This information on Annie. No one should see it but me."

"Strange that a family with three children would take in a total stranger. A sixteen-year-old stranger."

I didn't like what he implied. "The Hendersons have a lot of love to give. My grandmother pushed Annie on them."

"And she's still there. You think this might be what prompted the daughter to hit the road?"

Finch was quick to catch on. "Margo didn't like Annie. I don't think the dislike was strong enough for Margo to leave her family and the cushy life she had. Not leave *voluntarily*." He understood me. "When you report, I want a copy."

"I thought you were the tutor." He sat on the edge of his desk, his flat green gaze assessing my true role.

"I'm a bit more than a tutor. This family is important to me." I hesitated, resisting the urge to tell him about my nighttime fears. "Margo's disappearance is the most obvious evidence something's wrong, but . . . things aren't right at Belle Fleur."

"Care to expand on that topic?"

"That's your job—to find out what happened. There's a stranger hanging around the house. A girl. I've seen her and so has Donald, but no one else has. It's just a glimpse, but she's connected to Annie."

"Can you get a photo of her?"

"I can try."

"That would be helpful. What do you think happened to the daughter?" He watched me carefully.

"I hope she ran off with Andrew Cargill. If she didn't, I expect she's dead. Like I said, things aren't right at Belle Fleur."

"No, I can see they aren't." He kept his gaze on me until I picked up my purse and left.

❦

For the first time in weeks, Berta assumed her role in the kitchen. While I washed the turnips and put them on to cook, Berta sliced the squash and onions and put the pork roast in the oven. Annie chopped pecans for the German chocolate cake icing, a treat of chocolate, pecans, and coconut. Berta had once limited the sweets in the house, but Annie was an exceptional baker. Now we had dessert almost every night.

Erin was riding Cogar, and Donald was outside, refitting his tackle box. He'd saved his allowance and bought three exotic looking lures. He called them Yellow Sallies, and he was positive he could catch the trout that lurked in the spring-fed lake behind Belle Fleur. We'd all seen the trout swirl in the water, his scales catching and reflecting the light. Donald had named him Old Pike and was determined to hook him.

For one shimmering afternoon, the house regained a semblance of the old rhythm, the old feeling of love. Berta was back, and the last of summer had graced us with golden sunshine and crisp air.

As Berta pushed the roast into the oven, she put a hand on Annie's thin shoulder. "How are your studies coming? I've kept you so busy with my worries that I'm afraid you're falling behind."

I kept my back turned. Annie had resisted my attempts to pull her into class work. She said she knew enough, and I didn't have the authority to force her. She'd somehow convinced Bob that she could take a high school equivalency exam and move on to college when the time came.

"I'm scheduled to take the GED in a few weeks," she said. "I can pass easily."

"Are you sure that's smart?" Berta wiped her hands on an apron. A flush touched her cheeks, and she looked better than she had in weeks.

"I won't attend that stupid high school, and I won't burden Mimi with trying to teach me. I'll do fine on the GED. I read a lot." That was true. She had her nose stuck in a book all the time. She was endlessly checking out library books, especially biographies about Antonio Gaudi and Le Corbusier, and studies of art nouveau.

"If you're in my care, I want to provide you with an education so you can go to college or get a job. It's part of my responsibility."

Annie nodded. "If I don't do well on the test, I'll . . . revise my plan."

Berta didn't agree, but she dropped the subject. Instead we talked about the fall and the relief that another hurricane season was passing without a bad storm in our region. Hurricanes had struck to the east and west but we'd been spared any major winds—those over a hundred miles an hour.

"I'll get Donald and Erin," I said. The food was nearly done and Bob would be driving up. I wanted dinner on the table and smiling faces to greet the man of the house. He should remember his family with smiles, not tears. It was wrong that we had to campaign to win him back from Annie's clutches, but win him we would.

I left out the back door and walked toward the woods. The spring-fed lake we called Crystal Mirror was about a half mile from the house. The stables were between the two, and when I drew close, I stopped and rested one foot on the rail of the jumping ring and watched Erin and the big gray horse fly over the five-foot hurdles as if they were nothing.

Erin rode with total concentration. I wasn't certain she saw me until she finished the course and trotted up to the fence. "Good job," I said.

She patted her horse's neck. "He's a star. I'm going to the big show in Gulfport. Daddy said I could. Annie helped me convince him that I deserved a chance to try. He's hiring a trainer for me so I'll be ready."

I nodded, wondering if Berta knew. She was afraid for Erin to compete on the high jumps, and the Gulfport show was semi-professional. Erin was talented enough—and Cogar was bred for it. Still, it was a dangerous sport.

"Dinner's almost ready. Hose Cogar off and head to the house." I smiled. "Your mother's back in the kitchen. It's wonderful."

"She is!" Erin whooped with joy.

"I'm after Donald. I'll join you in a bit." I pushed off the fence and ambled on toward the lake.

I was almost there when I heard Donald cry out. I couldn't tell if it was fear or pain, but something had upset him.

"Donald! Donald!" I ran toward him.

"Mimi!" He called to me. "Help!"

Branches slapped my face and tore the exposed flesh of my arms and legs. I ran without regard for anything. "I'm coming!"

When I burst into the clearing around the lake, I saw him. He was sitting on the grass, hunched over, rocking back and forth.

"Donald!" I couldn't see his face. "Donald!" I grasped his shoulders and pulled him upright. His hands were over his face and blood streamed from between his fingers. "Donald!" I pulled his hands away.

A fishing lure hung from his cheek. The barb had gone through, and the hooked end was inside his mouth. He gagged and spit blood all over the ground.

"Help me." He cried, only making the situation worse.

"We have to get home." Wire cutters would snip the barb and I could remove the lure.

"It hurts," he said, crying harder. He was only a small boy. Most of the time he was tough, and it was easy to forget he was just a kid.

"Hey, it's okay. We can fix this. It isn't terrible. I promise." I told him how we'd cut the barb and then pull it out without hurting him. As I talked, I pulled him to his feet and started walking.

"Remember the time Margo slammed the car door on her hand? It turned out okay. She didn't even scar. You're going to be just fine." I shielded his injured cheek so that underbrush didn't slap at his face.

Donald sniffled and walked beside me. We were close to the stables when I saw someone standing ahead of us on the path. For a moment I could have sworn it was Margo. She was tall and slender and blond. Her hair glistened like spun honey in the sunlight that filtered through the canopy of trees. There was a glow about her, a sort of haze. Donald, walking with his head down, didn't see her.

I didn't want to alert him, but joy touched me. Margo! She'd come home! I wanted to hug her and then spank her within an inch of her life. She'd worried us all to the point of illness, but at last she was home. I was about to yell her name and point her out to Donald, when something felt wrong. Her features were obscured by the strange aura. I couldn't trust my own eyes.

She stood still, waiting, as we moved ever closer and I got a better view. I glimpsed the angle of her jaw when she turned her profile, the straight nose. I thought of an angel, until I realized the face was amorphous. Androgynous. Not Margo. Not any living person. More like a fetus. Slowly the features sharpened into Margo's beautiful face.

Donald stopped stark still. "What . . . ?"

I froze, too.

"Hey!" He started forward, but I held him back.

"Stay close to me." I had no idea what was in the path staring at us, but I knew it was dangerous. It wasn't Margo, though it had taken on her face. The creature giggled.

Donald's fingers dug into my arm. "Mimi, what—"

To shield him, I used my body to block his view. "Don't look!" When I turned back to the path, it was empty.

"It was Margo," Donald tried to get away from me and run to the spot where the creature had stood, but I held him back. The Yellow Sally jutted from his blood-streaked cheek.

"No, Donald. No!" I folded my arms around him and held him tightly. "It wasn't Margo. It wasn't."

"We have to get Dad and Mom. They'll find her. She's here, in the woods." He fought like a wild thing against my restraining arms.

"Donald!" I knelt so that we were face to face and shook him lightly until he stopped struggling. He was panting, but I lifted his chin so that he looked me eye to eye. "That wasn't Margo, and you can't tell anyone."

"We have to tell Dad! He'll get help to find her."

I shook him harder. "No! That wasn't Margo. I swear it."

"Who was it?"

I was frightening him, but I had to do it. For his own safety, I had to do it. The creature in the path was evil. It was somehow connected to Annie and her evil twin. Whatever it was, it had taken on Margo's appearance to upset the family, to undo the progress Berta had made. One whisper of a creature roaming the woods with Margo's face, and Berta would be in a mental ward. I would likely be right behind her. Such inhuman evil was enough to unravel the strongest mind.

"It isn't *who*, it's *what*. There's something out here in the woods. Something wrong. It's trying to trick us, and we *cannot* tell anyone. If you want your mother to get better, you have to keep this to yourself."

"But it was—"

Before he finished the sentence, I dragged him to the path. "Do you think Margo would make a footprint like this?" I pointed at the narrow lane. "You know about the animals in the woods. Is this human or animal?"

The ground had been savagely rent by claws.

Donald's hands fell to his side. "We should tell Daddy."

I stroked his hair. "We can't, Donald. Not now. Not yet. Your mother has been really sick, and she's getting better now. We have to be very careful not to upset her. Promise me you won't say a word about this."

"It looked like Margo. What was it?"

I searched the surrounding woods, wondering if the creature was watching us. It certainly enjoyed toying with me. Frightening me. "I don't know what it was, but I promise you, I'll find out."

22

The dinner Berta had worked so hard to prepare was left on the table, untouched, as she rushed Donald to the doctor's office. She didn't trust me to snip the barb, and she was smart to insist on a tetanus shot and medical expertise.

Erin rode with her.

Annie and I were left alone, waiting for Bob to come home. He'd called, saying he was delayed.

"Come up to my room," Annie suggested. "You don't look well, Mimi. Did something happen?"

I was still reeling from Donald's injury and the creature we'd seen in the woods. I was nauseous with a blazing headache, but I followed Annie up the carpeted stairs to her room. I hadn't been invited to the third floor since Margo had disappeared. I'd heard Annie above me, moving furniture, hammering. She'd been the only person in the house with energy to do anything, and I was curious to see what she'd been up to. I also hoped to glean details of her past. The link between Margo's disappearance and Annie's appearance held firm in my head, even if no one else could see it.

We took coffee upstairs. Berta made at least three pots a day, and I'd fallen into the habit of a cup after dinner. Though we hadn't eaten, I needed the jolt of caffeine.

When she pushed open the door to her room, I stopped. Yards of different fabrics hung from the ceiling, creating a dreamy swirl of colors and textures around the room.

"Do you like it?" She entered and twirled, dancing through the floating material. "I've been reading about Isadora Duncan and the freedom of modern dance. The arts were alive then. Dance, painting, architecture, it was all so alive." She wove in and out, her body fluid and graceful. "I'm not sure I did it right, but I found the fabric really cheap. It makes me feel like I'm safe in layers and layers. My cocoon. I'm like a chrysalis. One day I'll emerge, complete and beautiful like a butterfly." Her gaze cut toward me. "Like you."

"It's nice." I sat on the edge of her bed. The room disconcerted me. The hanging cloth could conceal almost anything. "Was this what your room was like at home?"

She gave me a blank stare. "I don't know. Maybe."

"Annie, are you sure you don't have any memories of your past?" It was too blunt a question. Rushing into this discussion would serve no purpose, but I couldn't help myself. Her amnesia wasn't real and I was weary of the pretense of it. "Why don't you just tell the truth? You can't remember some of the things you say you remember and then none of the pertinent details. Berta isn't going to send you away no matter what your past was."

She walked to the windows on the front of the house. They opened onto a small balcony. Margo had lusted for that balcony. Now she was gone and Annie lived in the room. "I do have some memories, but they scare me."

I put my coffee cup on the bedside table. This was either progress or a tease. Annie was never straightforward, but if she gave me anything, even the smallest detail, Jimmy Finch could follow it up. "Scary how?"

"I think someone hurt me. When I try to think about the past, my brain just shuts down. It's like being underwater in a storm, great surges of fear and panic."

"You don't see anything you remember? No images. Like a street. Trees, houses. Flowers." I tried to come up with pleasant things.

She shook her head. "I keep having this dream about fire, though. It's terrifying. Orange blazes are all around me. I hear screaming, but I think it's me. I don't know which way to find the door."

I didn't believe her for a minute. She'd heard about my past and was trying to steal even that from me. "Were you in the fire? Were you burned?"

"Not burned, but trapped. I don't know how I escaped, and I don't have any scars." She glanced down at her arms and legs. "Not a single mark on me."

She was simply using *my* past to her advantage. That would be something Annie would do. "That's a terrible memory. How old are you in the dream? Maybe something like this happened when you were a little girl?" Enough rope to hang herself was my thought.

Annie's smile was amused. "Why are you so interested in my past, Mimi? I'm happy here. Maybe I don't remember the past because it was awful."

"Maybe you have parents who love you and miss you."

Her smile slid off her face. "I don't think that's the case. I feel certain no one is looking for me."

"But they could be." I pressed too hard, I saw it in the spark in her eyes. I'd made her angry, an emotion I'd seen little of since she came to Coden.

"I'll tell you what, Mimi. You don't meddle in my past, and I promise to stay out of your future." She paused a beat. "I saw Mark in town today. He asked about you. He seemed puzzled that you haven't had time to see him lately. I gave him a little attention and comfort. He liked that."

The audacity of her statement was like a slap. I'd seen her turn on the charm, and I knew how effective she could be. Bob's devotion to her was living proof of her feminine powers. "How dare you."

"You don't want him? He's cute."

"You're sixteen, Annie. Mark is too old for you, and surely he has sense enough to know that."

"I'm not interested in Mark. He's lonely, Mimi. Why don't you be nice to him?" She went to the window and looked out to the Sound. "He really likes you. I was only trying to help. Men just want you to 'be nice.' How hard is that? Berta hasn't been very nice to Bob lately, either."

Annie was a lot more mature than anyone thought. She might pretend to be an innocent sixteen-year-old, but she was far from that.

"What did you tell Mark?" I asked.

"I told him you had things on your mind, but I didn't say what things." She sat beside me on the bed and pushed back so she was resting against the headboard. A breeze off the water ruffled the gauzy material around her bed, causing it to undulate with a sinister energy. "What are you thinking when you wander around the house in the dark?"

"What are you talking about?" I did wander the house, checking up on her, but I wasn't about to admit it.

"You don't sleep, Mimi. You're worried all the time. Mark is concerned for you and so am I."

I stood up. She was a kid, a stray with no real claim on the Hendersons or anyone else in Coden. I was a grown, college-educated woman. "Don't worry about me, Annie. I'm taking care of Donald and Erin. Berta is coming back to herself. Things will get back to normal. You focus on your own life and what you're going to do with it."

She stretched out on the bed. "I know what I want, Mimi, and I know how to get it. Whoever I was before, I've learned a lot. Now I'm going to apply it."

✥

Berta returned with Donald, his cheek bandaged and his blue eyes full of mischief. "I have a story to tell now," he said. "Annie tells us lots of stories, but I have my own. Mom helped me with it coming home. It's about a giant fish that throws hooks back at fishermen."

We heard Bob's footsteps on the porch, and we all ran out to greet him. His eyes clouded at Donald's bandaged face, but when he saw Berta, it was as if a long storm had cleared. "Berta!" He swung her in his arms until she laughed.

Erin and Donald danced around them. "Let's picnic in the yard," Donald said. "It's cool enough now. It's almost dark. We could eat on the table in the back."

"Okay," Berta agreed. We all rushed to carry the food outside. It was September and the worst of the heat had passed for the day. As we filled our plates and sat down to talk, I felt a sense of peace that had been missing for weeks. Margo's absence was a living thing around the table, but we had put some distance there. Enough so that we could at least share a meal with a bit of laughter. Even Annie was smiling, but I detected a curl of cunning at the corner of her lips. What did she have in store for later?

Erin spoke of her day at school. She'd made friends with Peggy Cargill, Andrew's younger sister. It wasn't a friendship I would have fostered, but Erin had her mother's independence. "Peggy wants me to spend Friday night," Erin said.

"I don't think so." Berta's face showed tension. "Why don't you invite her here instead?"

Erin frowned. I thought she'd defy Berta. Something changed her mind, though. "Okay. She wants to meet y'all, anyway. And see Cogar. She says that Andrew talked about the house here a lot. She's curious."

And so was I. Peggy Cargill might know something that she didn't even realize she knew. A visit would give me a chance to ask questions.

We finished the meal without further controversy. Donald told his story about the Yellow Sally. For a moment he seemed to lose himself in some dark thought.

"What is it?" Bob asked.

I held my breath. Under the table, I nudged Donald's foot with my own. I mouthed the words "you promised."

"I thought I saw someone in the woods." He spoke almost in a monotone.

"Who was it?" Bob asked, his tone indicating he thought this was part of Donald's story.

Donald shook his head. "I don't know. She was too far away for me to see."

"You saw a girl?" Berta came up out of her seat. "Was it Margo? Did you see Margo?"

The eager desire in her voice and face scared Donald. I'd warned him what would happen, and now he saw I wasn't lying.

He pushed his plate away as if he'd lost his appetite. "Maybe it wasn't anyone. It must have been the wind blowing the undergrowth."

"Tell us what she looked like." Berta was almost demanding.

"It was just a shadow. That's how I got the fishhook in my face. I was casting when I saw . . . something and it messed me up so the lure went into a tree. I pulled it free and it came right into my face."

"Let's stay out of the woods for a while," Bob said slowly. "And a lesson to you about jerking on a line. Be careful, Donald."

"Bob, can we go inside? I want to talk with you." Berta stood up and took his hand. She had regained her composure, but I could see the struggle in her face. "Erin, Donald, help Annie and Mimi clean up." She gave me a look to let me know she'd decided to take the bull by the horns about the private detective.

"I'll go wherever you say, beautiful." Bob kissed Berta's hand as he rose. Out of the corner of my eye, I watched Annie. At the kiss, she turned her back on Bob and Berta.

"I have to tell you something," Berta said.

She was going to tell him about hiring Jimmy Finch, though I would have waited. I didn't want Annie to know about Finch. "I'll clean up, Annie. Why don't you all enjoy the swing before it gets dark."

"As you wish," Annie said, but I felt her gaze drill a hole in my back as I carried the food and plates into the kitchen.

23

On Friday I arranged for Annie to take Donald to a new Disney movie. In their absence, Jimmy Finch brought a typed report to Berta. If Bob was displeased with the hiring of Jimmy Finch, I never heard. No matter—I knew I'd done the right thing. Berta was healing and taking positive steps toward figuring out what had happened to her daughter.

The P.I. sat on the sofa and sipped the coffee I made while Berta paced the room as if all the days of inactivity were pent up inside her, fighting to get out.

Finch said, "I got the report from the sheriff, and I'm satisfied that Margo isn't involved with the Moonies. I have a few contacts inside, and no one has seen a girl matching her description, so we can cross that off the list."

"She could have dyed her hair, used an assumed name." I knew Berta wanted Margo to be somewhere, anywhere, alive and safe. Even the Moonies were preferable to an unknown fate, or worse.

"Anything's possible," Finch said diplomatically, "but I don't believe she's there. I have to operate off my best assumption based on the evidence."

"I'm sorry." Berta perched on the edge of a chair.

"A buddy of mine in the FBI ran a few checks for me. There's a problem with the way individual states report runaways or missing children, I won't pretend otherwise. But with the information we have, there are no reports of Margo or the Cargill boy found dead in other places. No unidentified bodies matching their description have been found."

Berta was on her feet. "I—I didn't—" she stammered.

I got up and gently led her back to her seat.

"I'm sorry, ma'am, but these are the places I have to check first. I've discovered Cargill supplemented his income by selling marijuana. If he crossed someone's boundary, he could've gotten himself hurt, and the girl with him. These drug dealers are dead serious about their turf. Cutting off a hand is the mark of some of the more vicious cartels. . . ." When he saw Berta's face, he stopped.

"Berta, he isn't saying that's what happened." I put a hand on her shoulder. "Andrew Cargill was a small fish. I doubt any vicious cartels were interested in him."

"You're probably right," Finch said hurriedly. "Like I said, I have to check. So now I'm turning my attention to checking service stations doubling as mechanic shops in a four-hundred-mile radius. Cargill has to make a living. If they've holed up somewhere, maybe I can find him that way."

Berta relaxed slightly.

"Does your daughter have any means of making a living?" he said.

Berta looked at me as if he'd spoken Latin, so I answered. "She could be a sales clerk in a clothing store or cosmetics counter. She could tutor children." I racked my brain thinking of things Margo could do to earn a living.

"That's a help." He stood. "I don't mean to upset you, Mrs. Henderson. I'm doing my job."

"I know." She managed to nod without crying. She handed him a check she'd prepared before he came.

"I'll walk you out," I said.

He got to the Rambler Hornet Sportabout, a distinctive green with tri-colored leather interior. The back seat of the station wagon was filled with file boxes and clothes. "Did you learn anything about Annie?" I asked.

"I spent most of the time working on the missing girl, but I have a few feelers out. She was on the Mobile streets less than a week before Mrs. Eubanks found her, but one of my sources tells me she had money for a hotel room."

"An amnesiac with money?" It struck him as odd too. I could read it in his face.

"My source, a young man, met her in Bienville Square. She was eating lunch on a bench. Paul spent a half hour or so with her, he works with one of the soup kitchens to round up the strays, but she had no interest in help. She had money for food and a place to stay. He only saw her that one time."

"Did she reveal anything about where she came from?"

He lit a cigarette before he answered. "Nothing. She didn't say she couldn't remember, but she just didn't answer any questions." He inhaled the smoke and gazed down to the Sound. "She's got a sweet deal here." He cast a sideways look at me. "So you're not part of the family and you're living here, too. It's like a halfway house."

I bit back an angry reply. "I'm a paid employee here. Annie is a ward. There's a big difference."

"Sorry. I didn't mean to lump you together. It's just that—" His eyes narrowed.

"It's just that what?" I demanded.

"Forget it." He tossed the butt and ground it into the grass. "I'll let you know if I get anything else."

I wanted him gone before Annie returned, and I could see Berta at the window watching us. She'd think he had bad news about Margo and go off the deep end if I didn't get back inside. "I'll set up another meeting," I told him.

After he drove away, I went inside to help Berta ice cupcakes for the arrival of Peggy Cargill, who was coming to spend the night with

Erin. The ban on sugar had fallen by the wayside—Berta's rigorous attitude toward healthy eating had flat-lined under the wheels of Margo's
crushing defection. Berta added the green and blue food coloring to the
icing with a hand mixer. The colors swirled. "I want Erin to be happy
and have friends," she said, almost as if she could read my thoughts.

"Even if they get high on sugar?" I teased.

"I shouldn't have been so hard on Margo. She was my first, and
I wanted everything perfect. No sugar, no sodas." She turned away
abruptly, but it wasn't too quick for me to see the blame she leveled
squarely at herself. She believed—or wanted to believe—that Margo
had left voluntarily.

I put the last dollop of butter-cream icing on a cupcake and
sprinkled it with colorful M&Ms. "Before the girls get here, I'd like
to go to the library," I told Berta.

"Take the convertible. It's a beautiful day." She tossed me her keys.
"Do you think Annie would want to go? She and Donald should be
back any minute."

"She said she was working on a project for tonight." The lie slid
out with no effort. I didn't want Annie with me.

"Be back before supper. I'm going to make chicken kabobs. It feels
like fall and Bob will enjoy grilling."

"I'll be back in plenty of time."

October danced in the occasional breeze from the water, and I felt
that I could sniff out the last days of summer. I cranked the top down
on the car and took off at a leisurely pace. When I was out of sight, I
put the pedal to the floor and let the little car fly. The wind ruffling
my hair and the dank salty smell of the air was sheer joy. I loved this
place, this wildness and even the dark past.

Coden had risen and been knocked back more than once. Hurricanes, bad economy, boom-and-bust employment. We were a resilient
people. We did not give in to adversity.

And I would not give in to Annie. I would find her secrets, and I
would send her—and whatever dark things she'd dragged into Belle
Fleur—back to the hell from which they'd come.

I parked under an oak and walked to the library. The staff knew me well, and when I asked how to search for newspaper stories about house fires, they told me that to look back any farther than two years, I'd have to go to the main library in Mobile. Disappointment must have shown on my face.

"Are you still interested in Chad Petri's book?" the librarian asked.

"I am."

"He came by today. He's out of the hospital. The fire scarred his lungs, but he's a tough old bird."

"Do you think he'd see me?"

She nodded. "Just don't tire him, Mimi. He's fragile. I worry for him. But he can tell you what was in the book." She got the copy that had been defaced and handed it to me.

According to the pin on her blazer, the librarian's name was Jeannie Holmes. She'd been at the library ever since I could remember. "Do you know if there are any legends or stories about Belle Fleur?" At her questioning look, I added, "Like ghost stories. Actresses downing at the old Paradise or young girls seen around the grounds." Since Donald's fishhook mishap at the lake, I hadn't seen the blond creature, but there was the sense that something lurked at the edge of the lawn. I believed whatever evil had come to Belle Fleur had come with Annie. But there was a chance it had been there all along, waiting for some family to bring it out.

"There's a book of ghost stories set in Mobile written by a local woman. Coden isn't mentioned, though. Most folks forget we're part of Mobile County." She walked around the desk and led me to a shelf. Running a finger over the spines, she brought out a book, *Old Mobile Hauntings*. Turning to the index, she shook her head. "Nothing about Coden or the Paradise."

"Other than Mr. Petri, is there someone else I could ask?"

"Your granny. Cora knows more local history and stories than anyone else. Mr. Petri might know something, too."

"Thanks. I'll ask both of them." I left the library and went straight to his address. He was on his front porch in a cowhide rocker, a man of Cora's generation. He was tall and too thin. His plaid shirt hung from his shoulders, and he greeted me with a worried frown.

"Who are you and what do you want?"

"Mimi Bosarge. I'm Cora Eubanks's granddaughter." My grandmother had been reluctant for the Henderson children to speak with Chad. She was afraid he'd upset them with some details of the past. Since I was alone, I couldn't see the harm.

His face relaxed. "Cora's granddaughter. Come on up and sit a spell."

Grasping the chair he pointed to, I dragged it around so I could face him. I took a seat. "Mr. Petri, I'm curious about Belle Fleur." There wasn't time to beat around the bush. Berta expected me home in an hour.

"That Bob Henderson's done a bang-up job putting that place back to rights. The man's got magic in his hands."

I couldn't help but smile. That was a compliment I'd be happy to pass to Bob. But it wasn't the current owners of Belle Fleur that interested me. "Tell me about the Desmarais family. Cora told me to ask you."

Surprise gave way to hesitation. For a moment, I thought he was going to refuse. When he spoke, it was clear his mind was back in time. "That Sigourney was a mean woman. She was beautiful, but she was mean as a snake."

I wasn't certain how to frame my questions. It was one thing to hear about Sigourney's meanness in an anecdotal way, but there were plenty of houses in Coden where mean people had lived. "Was there something special about the Desmarais family and Belle Fleur? Or was it only because the house was big and prominent and Henri and Sigourney wealthy that they drew the gossip of the town?"

"What is it you really want to know?" Chad asked. His look was direct. He might be old, but he was far from senile.

"Tell me about the house. I know you included it in your book—" I held it out to show him. "The pages about Belle Fleur were cut out."

"Damn hooligans! They burned up my shed. All my books—" He rocked furiously.

"Mr. Petri, please." I put out a hand and slowed his rocker. "I promised I wouldn't upset you. I'll have to leave if you get agitated."

He took a deep breath. A morning dove cooed from a hedgerow, and he leaned back into the chair. "I want to tell you. I need to tell someone. Folks should remember the past, so it don't slip up on them again when they aren't looking."

"You talk as if the past was alive and could . . . return."

"You think it can't?" He laughed, but it was a grating sound. "Evil doesn't die, Mimi. It just waits for the next opportunity to strike. Folks around here don't like to remember Belle Fleur and Sigourney. Most of the ones who saw it are dead or getting old. They don't want to think about the past, but if they don't, they'll see it again."

"You think Belle Fleur is evil?"

"The house is heart pine timber cut from virgin forests. Never rots. Nothing wrong with the materials put into the house, but there was plenty wrong with the people who lived in it."

Cora had taught me not to believe in evil—that humans were flawed and often cruel, but evil was a Sunday-school concept that didn't hold in real life. "Sigourney and Henri had only the one child, Chloe, right?"

"According to the birth and death records of the county."

"You don't believe that?"

"My grandmother cooked for the Desmarais family. She was friends with Cora's granny. They saw things. Heard things." He withdrew into himself. "Terrible things. Grandma Bates tried to stop them, but everyone feared the power of Henri and Sigourney. They had money, and they employed many people in the gardens. My mother said that Henri controlled the law, and Sigourney controlled Henri."

"What did they do? Did they kill people?"

"Only two."

"Who?"

"Their daughter, Chloe. And her infant daughter."

This didn't make any sense. "Why would they kill their own child and grandchild?"

"They didn't just kill her. They tortured her. They kept her a prisoner until she gave birth to the baby. Sigourney starved her, trying to force a miscarriage. When that didn't work and the baby was born alive, Sigourney threw it into an old dry well that had once been used to supply water for the flowers." Chad rubbed a finger between his eyebrows. "My mother said the baby screamed for a day before it stopped. No one was allowed to help it. Chloe was confined in the house, but she looked out the third floor window and begged the garden workers to save her child."

"That's a terrible story." For fourteen years I'd lived in this community and no one had mentioned a hint of such events—especially not my grandmother, who had been on a mission to paint Belle Fleur and the Desmarais family as some kind of folk heroes. "How could people ignore a dying baby and a girl being held prisoner?"

"Sigourney and Henri made everyone on the property complicit in murder. Nothing was ever done. No one ever tried to do anything. Chloe disappeared. I think she was starved to death in her room. Henri died. I believe the guilt killed him. He didn't live two months after. But Sigourney, she lived. She ruled the town until she died. My mother danced on her grave in that old cemetery behind Belle Fleur. You have no idea how much she was hated."

"Chloe is buried there, but there's not an infant's grave."

"A bastard child? Sigourney viewed that baby as nothing more than inconvenient rubbish. Far as I know the bones are still in the well at Belle Fleur. A child not of pure French extraction was no more than an unwanted cat to her. Chloe was to marry French aristocracy and bring financial support and a sophisticated heritage to Belle Fleur perfumes. When she got pregnant by one of the garden workers, she lost her value to Sigourney."

"What happened to the man who got her pregnant?"

"The boy? Nothing. Chloe never told his name. He never came forward. My mother often wondered if he heard his own baby crying in that well and was too much of a coward to save his child."

"This is what was in your book about Belle Fleur?" I couldn't believe that such controversial material hadn't been the topic of much discussion in the community.

"No. I didn't write that in the book. I should have, but I didn't. I wrote about the land and how Henri bought it for a pittance from the Terry family and how he built the house from trees milled off the land and how he hired the famous architect John Prefect, to draw up the plans for the house with a library and clever rooms and decorations. The blueprints for the house were included in the book. Now it's all gone."

"Why didn't you tell about Chloe and the baby?"

He gave a half-smile. "I have no proof. My grandmother is dead. Everyone who knew the truth is dead. Cora knows it, but she won't talk about it. To print that story would be to invite a lawsuit."

"They're all dead." A breeze chilled the sweat that had trickled down my spine. "Who's left to sue?"

"I always had the sense that someone connected to the Desmarais survived. Sigourney lived a long life, some of it away from Coden. She'd slip into town, and reappear, living at Belle Fleur like a queen come home. She died in that house, alone as far as anyone knew. I saw her body, sitting in that third floor room where she'd tried to starve her daughter into a miscarriage. Her face was frozen in this . . . she was terrified by something, likely the realization of her own deeds. She died of fright, and she deserved much worse."

"If there was only Chloe and the child, then they're all dead. What happened to the house after Sigourney died?"

"It was abandoned. No one wanted it. No one would think to live in it. For forty years it stood empty, going into ruin. The wood doesn't rot, as I told you, but nails rust and timber warps. Eventually she would have come down, and that would have been for the best."

"Bob had to buy the house from someone. Maybe there is family left alive."

"That's not something to wish for—or pry into." He spoke sharply. "If there's anything of Sigourney left alive in this world, stay away from it."

"You said she was evil. Do you truly believe she was?"

"I meant it. No woman could treat her own child the way she did. She murdered her grandchild. That's the work of Satan himself. She gave herself over to evil, and her blood is cursed."

A wind gusted, and the screened door behind me opened and slammed shut. My heart hammered, but I forced my mind to think logically. "Or else Sigourney was mentally disturbed and no one had the courage to confront her. This is something I'll have to ask Cora. She's kept such stories and talk from me. She doesn't traffic in gossip, especially stories so vicious, but if there was something wrong at Belle Fleur, I deserve to know." And so did Bob and Berta.

"Be careful what hornet's nest you poke with a stick, young lady." He rocked slowly now. "This land, beside the water filled with sea-food, is as close to paradise as humans are going to get. Until things get stirred up."

"Thank you, Mr. Petri." I stood. "I have to get back to the Hendersons."

"What he did for that house, it's remarkable. She looks more beautiful than she did when she was built. But don't ever turn your back on her."

"It's just a house, like you said."

"Perhaps," he said. "But no one knows for certain what the surrounding woods absorb. And be careful. Keep alert and watch out for. . . ." He stopped.

"For what?"

"For—" He stood up and almost tottered over. "Watch your step, Mimi. I heard one of the Henderson girls is missing. I can't prove it, but I don't think she's run away. I don't think she ever had a chance to get away."

He walked into the house and closed the door.

24

Peggy Cargill was a polar opposite of her brother. Where he had been dark and brooding, she was pale and smiling. She came up the lawn from the bus stop with Erin, holding hands and laughing. In the golden October sunlight shafting down through the trees, I realized Erin was still a child. She wouldn't be for long—puberty loomed. But for this moment, she was carefree and unspoiled.

"Welcome to Belle Fleur, Peggy." Berta stood on the steps with Donald at her side. I was reminded of the day Annie had come to stay. We'd welcomed her, too, and it had been a serious mistake. I couldn't know how Berta struggled to open her home to this girl whose brother may have taken Margo, but I could see the strain in her face.

We tramped into the kitchen, and Berta served cupcakes and milk. Donald, though he'd consumed at least four, was eager for more. As we ate the festive cupcakes, talk turned to birthdays.

"Erin didn't get her party this year," Berta said as she ran her fingers through her daughter's silky blond hair. "We were so upset about Margo. . . ." She turned to Peggy. "And your brother, Andrew. I suppose you've heard nothing from him."

I'd been at the sink, but I turned back to watch Berta.

"Nothing, ma'am," Peggy said. Sadness settled into the corners of her mouth. "I miss him a lot. He looked out for me. Made sure I had lunch money for school." She struggled against emotion. "He would never hurt Margo."

Berta hugged the child to her. "No, he wouldn't," she said. "We're both missing the people we love."

The sound of glass shattering made us all jump. "I'm so sorry." Annie stood among the shards of Berta's favorite pitcher. Glass and milk covered the kitchen floor.

"Are you okay?" Berta asked Annie.

"It slipped. I'm very sorry."

But she wasn't. She'd dropped the pitcher because she was jealous of the attention Berta was giving Peggy. "We could still have a party for Erin," I said as I got a broom and mop to clean up the spill before anyone was cut. "Better late than never. We could have a scavenger hunt. Those are a lot of fun."

Excited, Erin slapped the table. "Halloween night! We could all wear costumes."

"My birthday is November first." Annie knelt in the disaster of her own making.

For a moment no one spoke. Berta recovered first. "You remembered something, Annie! That's wonderful. And we can celebrate your birthday, too. Two birthday girls, what fun."

"What about me?" Donald had green icing smeared from ear to ear.

"And you, too," Berta said, rumpling his hair, "though your birthday isn't until December. Why not have a party for everyone? Mimi, you should invite Cora and some of your friends, we'll celebrate yours, too." Tears sparkled in her eyes and I knew she was thinking of Margo. Where would she celebrate her birthday?

"Thanks. A group party. Great idea." But there weren't any friends I wanted to ask. When I went to college, I became something of an outcast. My high school friends thought I'd gotten above myself. It seemed only Mark felt otherwise, and at the moment he was miffed with me. Maybe a party would be the perfect way to breach our awkward issues.

We gave Peggy a tour of the house, and I listened to Berta tell of the Desmarais family, the good version. This was the story I'd heard all my life—the French family who left a perfumery to come to the New World to harvest new, exotic blooms. Like so many things about my life, I now knew it to be a lie.

When we went to Annie's room, I saw past the swirl of fabric Annie created to the prison it had been for Chloe. But I said nothing. To invite the past into a house is never a good thing. I wouldn't be the one who opened that door. I had to believe that wood and nails were only that—materials. If evil abided in Belle Fleur, it came from a human host.

Annie and Berta retired to the kitchen to prepare dinner while I went outside with the girls and Donald. From the swing, I could see them in the kitchen, dark and light, their heads together at the sink. Annie spoke and Berta laughed. They had become closer in the last few days. The last time I'd broached the subject of finding Annie's real home, Berta had shook her head. "Don't even try. She's a joy to me."

Erin came up beside me, watching the scene in the window that I was watching. Peggy Cargill hung several steps back. "Mimi, do you think the stories Annie tells are true?" Erin took my hand, pulling me out of my thoughts and into the present. It wasn't often she played the little girl, and I enjoyed it.

"Depends on the story." Annie told of Jean Lafitte the pirate who sailed the waters of Mobile Bay. Those were true. She told of Civil War battles, also partially true. But she also had a romantic bent that I was cautious of. And there were stories that went to the dark side, scaring Erin and Donald to the point they were afraid. I had asked her not to tell those, but Annie was not inclined to obey me.

"Sometimes at night, Annie invites me and Donald to her room. She tells us about another girl who lived here. A sad girl who wants someone to love her. She said you told her about Chloe."

I couldn't define the fear that jolted through me, and I noticed that Peggy had crept up beside Erin. I fought to control my expression as I wondered how Annie had come to know things that had been hidden from me for a lifetime. "What does she say?"

"That we have so much love, and that the girl wants to be part of our family."

"I think Bob and Berta have enough children to worry with." I tried to make light of what she said though my chest felt bound with bands of iron. "You're frightening your friend, Erin. You shouldn't listen to Annie." Peggy's eyes were wide and upset.

"Is there a girl all alone and hungry out in the woods?" Erin's worry was clear.

"Of course not. Annie's just pulling your leg." And I was going to break hers when I got a chance. "Did Annie describe this girl?"

"Donald told me he saw something coming back from Crystal Mirror Lake." She swallowed. "He said you saw it, too. A girl who looked like Margo."

I'd been foolish to think a nine-year-old boy wouldn't tell. "We saw something, Erin. It was so quick, but it wasn't a girl. I don't know what it was. It could have been the light. The path there is really shady and the trees probably moved in a breeze."

She looked at me hard. "Sometimes I think I see something, just on the edge of the woods. A girl with dark hair. Like what you saw the night Margo disappeared. Before I can be certain, she's gone."

Erin was afraid, and Peggy was terrified. Any moment she'd be asking for someone to take her home. "Your father and Mark both checked for evidence of someone hanging around. They didn't find any trace of a person. Annie is scaring you. If your father knew what she was doing, he'd be really upset." I wasn't about to add fuel to Annie's fire.

"Daddy never gets upset with Annie. He thinks she's perfect. She studies all the time about houses and buildings so she can talk to him."

Annie's inappropriate attachment to Bob wasn't a topic to discuss with Erin. I turned to Peggy. "Did you spend much time with

Margo?" It wasn't a graceful segue, but I felt pressured to change the subject.

"A little. Sometimes on the way to town she'd stop by the house for a minute." She looked around as if she expected to be reprimanded. "Not a lot. Just once in a while, after she got her driver's license. I know she wasn't supposed to be there and all. Mama said she was a really nice girl."

"I only met Andrew once, here, in the woods of Belle Fleur." I forced a laugh. "He startled us. He'd hidden and jumped out. When we got over the scare it was funny." Erin homed in on my lie, but I ignored her.

"Andrew liked to play around like that. He jumped out of bushes and scared me, too." Peggy made a face. "I didn't like it when he did it, but now I miss him." She bit her bottom lip. "He wasn't as tough as he acted. He just didn't get along with Dad. Andrew wasn't going to knuckle under. He was like that. Even if Dad hurt him, he wasn't going to give in." She swallowed. "I hope he's okay. I keep thinking he'll call me or send me a letter. He told me he'd always take care of me, but he hasn't sent any word."

So Peggy assumed Margo and Andrew were together. And alive. That was something. "Have the police found any clues as to what happened to him?"

She shook her head, and I knew it was time to change the subject. I had one more question however, and though I knew it was cruel, I had to ask. "What do you think happened?"

Erin glared at me. "We don't want to talk about this anymore. If Peggy knew where Margo was, she would have told us weeks ago."

"I didn't mean to imply she knew anything." I put a hand on Erin's shoulder. "I'm only asking for an opinion. The police can't find anything. To them, Margo is just another rich, spoiled kid who didn't get her way and took off. Maybe that's what happened, and I just wondered if Andrew ever said anything. Like any plans they might have made or things they talked about. I'm only trying to help find your sister."

Peggy shook her head. "They met in the woods around here all the time. Margo would slip out at night and meet him. He said he loved her. They wanted to get married, but I can't say that. Dad would kill me."

I hadn't realized the relationship was that serious. No one had. Margo had been very sly indeed. "If she ran away, where do you think she might have gone?"

Peggy hesitated. "They talked about going to New Orleans. They wanted to get married, and Andrew said he had a friend who could get him a job on a riverboat. He'd make really good money, and he could take care of Margo."

At least it was a lead. "Thanks, Peggy. And I am sorry about your brother."

"Andrew pissed people off." A tear slipped down her cheek. "Dad thinks he fell in with the wrong crowd of people. Some of his friends were bikers and they sold dope."

I didn't say anything. Finch was already on the drug angle. I wished I could comfort Peggy and Erin with a convenient lie, but I couldn't. "I'm sure we'll find them both," I said, "but for now let's plan the birthday party."

My smile was the biggest lie of all, because Chad Petri had soured my relationship with Belle Fleur. I now looked on the house with suspicion, and I began to watch the house and Annie with a closer scrutiny.

25

Saturday afternoon, Bob went to watch Erin ride. I thought I might have a moment alone with him to discuss what I'd learned from Mr. Petri. Belle Fleur was not the home he'd been led to believe it was, and he deserved to know the true history of the house. There was something very much amiss on the property. If he chose to tell Berta, that was up to him. The true story of Chloe would likely drive Berta out of the house, but to withhold what I'd learned was a form of deception.

As I walked down the shady trail to the stables, I realized it was mid-October. Margo had been gone for two months. It truly was as if she'd vanished into thin air. Not a single trace of her had been found anywhere.

Except for that strange blond creature I'd seen near Crystal Mirror Lake.

In the split second I'd had to really look, it had looked exactly like Margo. I knew it had to be a trick of light shifting through the leafy branches of the trees combined with my desire for Margo to come home. But it had looked so much like her. Until it began to change.

My logical brain denied what could only be described as a transmogrification. The amorphous fetal features—neither human nor sheep nor fish—shifting as if the process of full development happened in a moment, a creature already birthed yet still developing into the identity of a missing girl.

The inability to explain what I'd seen and the possibility that I was losing it made me hold my tongue. The stress level in Belle Fleur was through the roof. Even though I wasn't blood kin, I suffered the loss of Margo and the impact on the Hendersons. My "vision" on the path home could be the result of fatigue, poor sleep, anxiety, or some combination of the above—and I would have written it off to that had Donald not seen it too.

As I drew closer to the riding ring, I heard Bob's voice, a business tone, and one filled with excitement. "Of course. I've already drawn up the plans for the hotel renovation. The structure that's left is solid. It's just a shell, but we can build from that. It's a grand building. A real showplace."

Another voice, masculine, asked, "You really think Coden could become a resort destination again?"

I rounded the curve in the path and saw Bob with another man. The railing of the riding ring supported a set of architectural plans Bob had unrolled. They were discussing the old hotel on the grounds of Belle Fleur, the project Bob had moved here to take on. The man was a financial backer, an investor. Now wasn't the time to talk about haunted Belle Fleur.

"Mimi," Bob motioned me closer, "this is L. J. Martin. We share the same vision for the Paradise. He's considering becoming an investor."

I nodded and smiled and listened to the men talk about the prospects and what the renovation would mean to the local economy. All of it was true. But somewhere along the way, my feelings about Belle Fleur and the property had changed. Bringing the property back to life had taken on a far more sinister tone.

Erin loped Cogar around the ring, warming up. When she began a series of jumps, we all stopped talking and watched the elegance of her riding. She completed the double oxer, a sharp turn that led to a triple jump and a final in and out and trotted over to us as we applauded.

"Mimi, would you open the gate? I'm going to take a ride around the lake. Stretch Cogar's legs."

"Sure thing."

A frown touched Bob's face. "Maybe you should stay—"

Erin's laugh stopped him. "I'll be back in twenty minutes. You'll still be standing here gabbing."

He yielded, but I could tell he worried for his daughter. I worried, too. Erin was strong and agile, but she didn't weigh more than a hundred pounds soaking wet. Riding alone in the woods wasn't a good idea.

Bob's voice jolted me out of my worry. "Mimi, would you show Mr. Martin the house?"

"Of course." It wasn't what I'd planned, but Bob was proud of the work he'd done on the place. For him, Belle Fleur was still the dream of a wonderful French family, not a prison where a sixteen-year-old girl was starved to death.

"I'll join you shortly," Bob said. "I want to snap some photos of the old hotel so we can get them developed right away. L.J. is about to sweat to death. Give him a cold drink."

The investor did look uncomfortably hot, though the weather was milder than it had been in months. "I'll fix him up."

Indicating the path I'd come down, I walked with him toward the house.

"I'm sorry to learn of the daughter's strange disappearance," he said when we were out of earshot of Bob.

"It's been very hard on all of us."

"Are there any leads? Did she run away?"

My first inclination was to snap, but I battled it down. "We don't know. I can't understand why Margo would run away, but we certainly hope that's what happened. She was eager to leave the nest, to find her own life, even if she wasn't old enough."

He glanced at me. "I've been concerned about Bob, but he seems to be pulling out of it. I can't imagine how difficult it must be."

"Please don't mention Margo in front of Berta. They're both trying to hold their lives together and move forward. It's raw."

"Absolutely."

"Belle Fleur was almost a total ruin when the Hendersons bought it." I pointed to the house, which was magnificently framed by the widespread limbs of live oaks and surrounded by the dense green foliage of azaleas, camellias, and bottle brush plants.

"It's incredible," Mr. Martin said, stopping for a moment.

In the third-floor window, Annie watched us. She spent a lot of time alone. If Bob wasn't home, Annie was in her room. When Bob walked in the door, Annie came downstairs to be with the rest of us. She took every opportunity to touch Bob, to pat his shoulder or stroke his hand or slip her arm around his waist. Berta failed to notice because she'd never consider betrayal from someone she loved. To her, Annie was just a child starved for affection.

I knew better, and I had to figure a way to get Annie out of the house. Maturity had come with her fuller figure. Sometimes, when she looked at Bob, there was a predatory glint to her gaze.

Berta's resurgence as mistress of the house and loving wife had stymied her for the moment, but it wouldn't be long before Annie struck. I'd come to see her as a viper waiting for the prey to draw close enough to swallow him whole.

"Who's that in the window?" Mr. Martin asked.

"A young girl staying here for a while. She's not part of the family." I touched his arm lightly. "Let's go inside."

We walked in and I made a gin and tonic for Mr. Martin and retired to my room while Berta gave him the tour of the house. From the conversation I overheard, Bob had landed enough investors to start work on the Paradise.

The Hendersons would not be leaving Belle Fleur in the immediate future. If I told them what I'd learned about their home, would it make a difference now?

After Mr. Martin left, I sat Donald at the kitchen table and worked with him on Alabama history. His fascination with the Native

American tribes, the Choctaws and Creeks that populated Alabama, made him an eager pupil.

"Annie says that there are lots of Indian burial mounds around here."

"Oh, really. And how would Annie know that?" I sounded shrewish, but I couldn't help it. Annie lied about everything and I was tired of her stories that twisted things to suit her purposes. I'd heard her earlier in the morning telling Erin some foolishness about Chloe Desmarais—something she couldn't possibly know but told as the absolute truth. Annie played fast and loose with facts, and sometimes attributed her information to me.

Donald frowned at me. "Are you mad, Mimi?"

I sighed. "No. I'm sorry. I just get annoyed when she blends history and fiction."

"But if the Indians lived here, they had to die and be buried somewhere."

His logic made me roll my eyes. "Very true."

"So she wasn't really fibbing, right?"

"Whatever you say."

"Why are you mad at Annie?"

If Donald could read me so easily, I had to do a better job hiding my suspicions—until I had solid proof.

"I'm not mad. You know, I just don't want you confusing facts with her story-telling. Making things up is fun and interesting, but to understand history, you have to know the real facts."

"Gottcha." He grinned. The place in his cheek he'd pierced with the fishing lure had left only a tiny white scar.

"Enough history. Let's call it quits." I had a slight headache and wanted to go to my room.

"Yay!" He jumped up, slammed his book shut, and took off out the back door. He was all boy, and he made me smile.

I climbed the stairs to my room and closed the door softly behind me. It wasn't yet time to prepare supper; I had half an hour to myself. I went to the window and looked out over the back yard. Donald was in the swing, pushing himself high into the lacy leaves of the oak.

His joy was palpable. The simplest things made him happy. I was about to turn away when I saw something moving through the thick undergrowth only a short distance from the swing.

Since it was daylight, I stared with more curiosity than concern. A dog or deer or even a large raccoon would rustle the branches. Whatever it was angled closer to Donald and the swing. I watched to see who would startle whom. Donald remained oblivious to the scuttling intruder.

I can't say why the first jolt of fear arced through me. I leaned forward and placed my hands on the cool glass panes. Donald swung to and fro, his short legs pumping higher and higher. He leaned back, holding tight to the chains, so he could look up into the tree branches that swirled above him, a small boy happy with the sun and the freedom of a swing.

At first I tried to calm my fears. Even as I argued with myself that it was some wildlife or stray dog, sunlight touched the gilded blond of her hair. She stood slowly, unsteady, as if she were waking from a long and dream-filled sleep. She was just on the edge of the dense shrubs, and she watched Donald with such intensity that I struck the glass with my fist to stop her.

While I could see Donald clearly, a diffused light illuminated her face, obscuring her features.

"Margo?" I whispered the name even as my eyes told me it couldn't be her. But the creature was the right size and shape, the right posture. I raised the window and leaned out, my gaze riveted upon the girl. Except it wasn't a girl. Not at all. It was . . . some fetal creature growing and changing as if the shrubs were an incubating womb.

Before my very eyes the creature shifted from something that looked like Margo into the spitting image of the child in the swing.

It wasn't possible. It was absolutely impossible. Yet I saw his wide-set blue eyes, the blond hair that fell over one eye, the chin that came to an elfin point. It was Donald.

While the little boy I loved and adored swung high into the air, his eyes blissfully closed, this other boy, this creature who had assumed his appearance, looked up at me.

The creature grinned, revealing teeth sharpened into points.

"Donald!" I screamed his name. "Donald! Run!" I knew instinctively that the other child meant danger. I flailed my arms out the window. "Donald! Run!"

His blue eyes opened and he stared at me, failing to comprehend the danger lurking not twenty yards from him.

"Run!" I frantically waved him toward the house.

He slowed the swing to a stop. "What?" he called up to me.

The boy in the shrubs was perfectly still, unmoving. He lifted one hand in a solemn wave, a perfect replica of a gesture I'd seen Donald make a hundred times.

"Come inside the house!" I called urgently.

My fear communicated itself to Donald and he hopped from the swing and came inside at a dead run.

When I looked back at the shrubs, there was no one there.

26

The wind whipped over the water, a fair warning of the storm that brewed just offshore. It was the third week in October, and I loved the flat gray of the Sound that met the heavy gunmetal sky. The unrelenting heat was over, at least for a few months. Fall and winter were spectacular at Coden. None of the flashy color of New England or the pristine snow of the Rockies, but the soft browns and grays of fall and winter gave me a sense of serenity. The pagans believed the seasons marked the cycle of the soul. Youth, maturity and bounty, the decline, and ultimately death in preparation for the spring and rebirth. I wasn't so sure about all the soul stuff, but I knew that energy transformed. Maybe that was soul or spirit or essence. Whatever people called it, it remained behind.

I drove along Shore Road at a leisurely pace, a little melancholy in mood. I was worried about myself, my imagination, which had taken a dark turn. After scaring the bejesus out of Donald, I searched the area around the swing and found—nothing. There was no evidence of a Donald-creature or a dog or deer or anything else. I'd upset Donald to the point of tears. Luckily, I'd persuaded him to keep the incident from the adults. I had to tell Bob, but not yet. Not until I had some way to prove that I wasn't losing my mind.

With the arrival of cooler weather, maybe our lives would regain some balance and rhythm. Belle Fleur had huge, wonderful fireplaces, and Bob had promised that as soon as it was cold, we'd build a fire. This image of Bob and Berta, Donald, Erin, and me, all gathered around the fire, was a promise I intended to make real. Hot chocolate and popcorn, laughter, maybe a game of Clue. I loved solving the mystery.

I rounded the last bend in the road and saw the outskirts of Coden. I had errands in town, and a meeting. The drive and the daydreaming had relaxed me. My shoulders were knotted from tension and recurring headaches plagued me. The sun, not too hot, and the smell of the water was what I needed.

Not far from shore, a trio of shrimp boats trawled for the bounty of the sea. The fishermen had their own cycle, based on tides and winds, storms and seasons. Except for my parents, who I was too young to remember, I hadn't experienced death. Cora was old, but she was in great shape. Without undue circumstance, she would live to see me into my fifties or sixties. Soon, though, she would begin to lose her lifelong friends, the older generation of Coden. Their cycle was coming to a close. While it was a natural progression, it was still painful. But not as painful as the death of a young person. That kind of death was out of order, abnormal.

I pulled into a parking spot by the old bridge and bayou and got out of the car. Leaves from a saw-tooth oak blasted across the road and skittered onto the brackish surface of the bayou. I sat on the cement bench to wait. Exactly at three on the dot, Jimmy Finch pulled his shiny Rambler Sportabout beside the Hendersons' station wagon. He took a seat beside me on the bench.

Before he started, he pulled a pack of Camels out of his pocket, shook one out, and offered it to me. I didn't smoke often, but I accepted it and the light.

Blue smoke curled between us before a gust of wind cleared it away.

"I gather there's nothing new on Margo or you'd be talking to Berta. So what about Annie?"

"I can't find a damn thing on the girl." He said it with frustration. "It's like she came from nowhere."

"You checked the fire business?"

"I looked into house fires in every community in South Alabama and Mississippi. There were twenty-two last year and not a single one of them reported missing a teenage girl. I checked back five years. Nothing fits with a girl her age surviving. To go back farther, I'll have to spend some time driving to the small communities. Volunteer fire departments don't keep the best records, so it'll have to be personal recall."

"Maybe the fire was just a dream. Maybe she made everything up." I inhaled deeply and let the smoke relax me. My shoulders ached, and the headache was returning.

"I checked every missing person notice for the whole Southeast. I checked with the FBI for missing children. I took a photo of her down to the sheriff's office in Mobile to see if they'd uncovered anything, which resulted in nothing. The sheriff told me quick enough he was more interested in finding the girl missing from the Hendersons instead of trying to identify a child who was well-fed and safe living *at* the Hendersons."

Finch lit a cigarette off the butt of the one in his hand and offered me the pack, but I declined.

He looked into the distance. "It's as if she dropped out of the sky. If she's pretending amnesia, there's a good reason, and she's done a damn good job of covering her tracks."

I listened with my jaw clenched. She was smart. "What about birth records?"

"She says she's sixteen. I checked with the local hospitals to find her birth record. She wasn't born around here. Or let me rephrase that—she wasn't born in a hospital or with an attending physician. There are children born at home with a midwife. Some of them don't get registered."

"I don't think you're going to find anything about Annie." I'd come to believe she was something other than an amnesiac teenage girl. I hadn't put it all together, though. She had a strange knowledge of the local area, a mainline into some of the legends and tales. Who was she talking to? When was she gathering this information? Annie had wormed her way deeply into Berta's affections, and she was Bob's shadow. The few times I'd attempted to broach my concerns, they'd brushed me off, just as Cora did. If I insisted on talking about such things, it would be me who was sent away—to a mental institution. I was the one who saw frightening creatures in the woods, the one who glimpsed the dark-haired invader. Such sightings would paint me as unreliable and unstable.

"I've pretty much exhausted my sources for Annie. I have feelers out. If anyone contacts me, I'll let you know."

"Thanks, Mr. Finch." I stood. "I think we should drop this. Focus on Margo." I relayed to him what Peggy Cargill had told me about New Orleans. He made a note and said he'd check with the tugs and riverboats on the river.

He frowned. "It's a peculiar case. Those kids were here one minute, gone the next. If they meant to run away and start a life together, why in the world wouldn't they let their families know? Margo was old enough to marry, there's nothing the law can do. No reason they shouldn't call home."

"Do you think she's alive?" I thought of the blond girl I'd seen coming back from Crystal Mirror Lake. She'd been a perfect replica of Margo. Had it been her spirit, come back to Belle Fleur for . . . what? To haunt her family? To warn us? To let us know that she was gone? But why show herself to me? To Donald? Maybe because I was the only one willing to see her. Or maybe I was going crazy. None of this explained the other creature, the Donald-thing. But I had come up with another theory. What if this creature were some descendant of the Desmarais family? Chloe was the only legitimate heir. That didn't mean there weren't other children. The knots in my shoulders jumped back to life with a painful throb.

"Hey, you okay?" Finch was staring at me. "You look like you saw a ghost."

"I'm worried."

"You'll get ulcers and you won't find that girl any quicker."

"There's something not right at the Hendersons." I watched him closely. He waited for me to continue, his sharp green eyes hiding his thoughts. "I see things. Someone."

His interest was acute. "Like who?"

"Someone outside the house."

"Someone in the shadows?" He grinned.

"Never mind." I rose, but his hand caught the sleeve of my sweater.

"What do you see, Mimi? Tell me."

My burden was so heavy. I wanted to share it with him. I really did, but he would think I was insane if I told him the real truth. "I thought I saw Margo the other day. In the woods. But it wasn't her. It just upset me."

His eyes softened. "It isn't uncommon to think you see someone you want to see badly. Cops do it all the time when they're working missing children's cases. If Margo were alive, she wouldn't be camping out in the woods. She'd be inside, begging forgiveness and trying to get back on the gravy train."

"You think she's dead, don't you?"

"It's a lot easier to dispose of a body than keep a live girl hidden." Finch rose also. "I'm telling you this because I don't want to get your hopes up. Mrs. Henderson, she's not ready to hear it, but I want to be straight with you. I think the girl's dead. The boy, too. That business with the severed hand—that clinches it. I'll check with some of my contacts in New Orleans just to explore all angles, but I don't see much hope. The last time the girl was seen was in the Henderson house by her family. The boy left his house saying he was going to Mobile to meet a friend. They'd obviously planned to meet. What went wrong? Maybe I can find that out and at least bring a little closure to the family."

"Thank you, Mr. Finch, for your honesty."

"I'm a good investigator. I'm not happy with the way this is going. I'll keep my ears open. If something turns up, I'll jump on it."

"I'll tell Berta you're investigating possibilities in New Orleans." She'd pinned her dreams on Jimmy Finch finding evidence that would lead to Margo's recovery and until a body was found, there was no reason to destroy her dream. "Before you go, could you check one more thing?"

He lifted his bushy eyebrows and waited.

"I wonder who sold Belle Fleur to the Hendersons."

"Ask your grandmother. She should know that. From what I've learned of this community, your grandmother knows everything about everything."

"I will, but I don't believe she knows. It's some corporation or holding company or something like that. Could you find out?"

"How will this help find Margo?"

"I'm not certain it will, but there's something about Belle Fleur. Maybe there's a clue hidden somewhere."

He nodded and turned abruptly, his shoulders hunched slightly as he walked in the golden light to his car.

"Mr. Finch, don't give up. Not yet."

He kept walking and never looked back.

I drove the station wagon to the sheriff's precinct in Grand Bay. I intended to find Mark. It would be awkward. I'd avoided him for the past several weeks, and it was time to rectify that. Mark was a good guy. His desire to push our dating to the next level was normal—I was the one with hang-ups. Most girls my age had a couple of kids, but I was still a virgin. *I* didn't even understand what I was saving it for. Mark was a great catch—handsome, fun, good sense of humor, and responsible. Any Coden girl would be lucky to snag him. I wanted him to know that. I also needed his help.

Instead of the precinct, I found Mark at a burger joint. South Mobile County didn't offer a lot of gourmet options. Billie's Burgers was popular with the high school crowd. Not so long ago I'd been one of the teens sitting in a small booth with my friends. Mark sat alone. My hands holding the steering wheel were slick with perspiration. I'd missed him. More than I thought. The temptation to rush in the door and kiss him and tell him I was ready for a serious commitment fought with my duties to the Hendersons. Duty trumped desire.

When I slipped into the booth opposite him, he didn't bother to hide his surprise.

"What's going on, Mimi?" he asked. "I'm surprised to see you away from Belle Fleur and the Hendersons."

I dropped my gaze to his burger and fries. "I'm sorry, Mark. I've been a little . . . obsessive. I think I've accepted that I can't change the fact Margo is gone. I have to let that go and move on with my life."

I thought for a moment he was going to be hard about it, but he smiled and pushed the plate of fries toward me. "We haven't given up hope. We're still looking."

"Really?" It came out skeptical, and I waited for him to get angry, but he didn't.

"Not like we were at first." He sighed. "That hand. It just bothers me. The sheriff decided to let it drop. You know, it's so macabre. It got all the news reporters stirred up and writing crap. We got calls from Atlanta and New Orleans. Reporters were interested in the ghoulishness, not the missing kids. But I check every week with—with the area hospitals and mortuaries."

"Tell me the truth. Do you think it was Andrew's hand?" When he hesitated, I added. "I'm not going to break down or rush back and tell Berta anything."

He took a swallow of his sweet tea. "Andrew was selling weed for a supplier out of Gulfport. He had a couple of pounds and was supposed to make a delivery to Mobile. He never made it. We think he intended to sell the dope to make money for him and Margo to run away, but we don't have any proof the girl was with him. Last people to see him was his family, and he was alone. Last person to see Margo was her family when she allegedly went up to her room. There's nothing new in that, just a few details."

"Some drug dealer could have Margo. They probably cut off Andrew's hand."

His smile was tired. "Not likely. Not over a couple of pounds of pot. There's a chance Andrew got into trouble and he and Margo took off on the run. That's what we're hoping."

I took a deep breath. No matter how crazy I sounded, I had to tell him. "I've seen someone around the Henderson house. I've been thinking . . . is it possible some descendant of the Desmarais family could still be around Coden? Someone who might not want the Hendersons in the house?"

He leaned forward, a teasing grin playing across his lips. "Who? The strange dark-haired girl? Folks always said Chloe Desmarais was a raven-haired beauty."

"Mark, you have to believe me and not think I'm losing my mind."

"Okay." He wiped his hands on a napkin and pushed his unfinished food away. "You're really afraid, aren't you?"

Even sitting in Billie's in full daylight with people all around me, I couldn't stop the cold claw of fear that traveled my spine. "I saw this girl. Not a brunette, a blonde. At first I thought it was Margo, but then she . . . changed. It was like she morphed into Donald. Only Donald with sharpened teeth. An evil Donald—" I stopped. His face had gone blank.

"Why are you doing this?" he asked. He wasn't angry, he was puzzled.

"I'm not *doing* anything. I know it sounds crazy. I know that, Mark. But I'm afraid. There's something watching the Henderson house, and it wants in."

Mark leaned forward. "How long has it been since you've had a good night's sleep? I'm going to talk to Cora and see if she can't get you out of that house, at least on the weekends. This isn't good for you, Mimi. You're a young woman and you have the entire burden of that family on your back. No wonder you're seeing things."

"I'm not crazy."

"I don't think you are. I think you're exhausted. Physically and emotionally, and if you won't take care of yourself, then someone should step in and do it."

I pushed myself out of the booth. "I thought you might listen, but I was wrong."

"Mimi—"

But I didn't give him a chance to finish. I rushed out of Billie's and ran to the car. In a matter of seconds I was on the road back to Belle Fleur. I'd tried. I'd honestly tried to get help. Now it was up to me.

27

The day of the scavenger hunt dawned clear and cold. Halloween, the night when dark spirits came out to play. It was a perfect opportunity to study the old religious beliefs that provided the genesis for our modern-day costume holiday. To my surprise, Annie joined Donald and me in the kitchen. Erin was there too. Berta allowed her to skip school since the party scheduled for that night was a late birthday celebration and we had food to prepare and scavenger clues to plant.

In the five days that had passed since my attempt to enlist Mark to help me, I hadn't seen anything strange, and I'd begun to believe that maybe he was right. Exhaustion often made a person's mind play tricks. Maybe I'd seen sunlight on a shrub or some bizarre floater in my eye had tricked my tired mind into seeing something that wasn't there. I was willing to believe that—wanted to believe it.

We were gathered around the kitchen table, the white curtains, starched and ironed, fluttering in the open window. I stuffed treats and goodies into small bags that would be party favors. The mouth-watering smell of baking tollhouse cookies filled the air. More sheets of cookies, Annie's special recipe, waited for the oven. Berta had driven into Mobile to pick up a huge birthday cake, a surprise for Erin, and left us to finish up the party details.

Erin's face glowed with excitement as she wrote out the many clues to the scavenger hunt that we'd come up with. All of her classmates had indicated they would attend the costume party, and she was basking in the warm glow of finding herself popular. "We're going to start at the old hotel and finish there, under the moon. It's going to be full tonight. And no rain. Daddy's going to make a bonfire."

Anticipation had infected me as well as the children. "I can't wait to see all the costumes."

"Halloween night, the time when the veil between this world and the spirit world is at the thinnest *and* a full moon." Annie leaned toward Donald. "Beware, little boy, that the wicked ones don't come to take you away."

"What wicked ones?" Donald cast a sidelong glance at me. Annie had spooked him again.

"The ones that hide and watch." Annie sounded scary enough that chill bumps danced along my arms. "They're out there now, watching and waiting. You'd make a tasty snack for them."

"Stop it!" I'd had enough of her stories and foolishness. "If there's someone outside watching us, you should tell Bob."

She slowly faced me. "Why don't you tell him what you see, Annie?"

I'd spoken of the strange blond apparition to no one except Mark. How had Annie—"Have you been talking to Mark?"

"He calls here every day. Someone has to talk to him. He's worried about you."

Mark's betrayal stung more sharply than a slap.

"See who?" Erin asked. "Mimi? Is there someone out there?" Real concern washed over her face. "What are you talking about?"

"It's just more of Annie's foolishness." I glared at Annie. "And it is going to stop."

"Oh, really?" She laughed. "I didn't realize you had psychic abilities, Mimi."

Her smugness was infuriating. "You will stop frightening the children—"

"They aren't afraid. You are." She stepped toward me. "What are you so afraid of? You're the college-educated one, the one with logic and reasoning, the one who sneaks off to meet with deputies and private investigators." She put her hand over her mouth as if she'd accidentally spilled a secret.

I was stunned. How did she know these things?

"I intend to find Margo." My words came out stilted. "I care about this family, Annie. I'll do whatever it takes."

She put down the tray of cookies. "I wonder who it is you care so much about. Is it really Margo?"

"What are you accusing me of?" I rose slowly to my feet, my hands itching to strike her.

"Why so defensive, Mimi?"

The children looked from Annie to me and back. Erin stepped between us and grabbed my arm. "Let's go hide the clues for the scavenger hunt. Come on, Mimi. You're too upset."

I had to escape Annie's presence or I might do something rash. Annie had driven me to the breaking point, where violence seemed a plausible solution. I picked up the basket with the clues. Erin, Donald, and I went out the back door and into the golden October sunshine.

As we walked down the trail, I forced the anger from my body. Annie never showed her true colors in front of Berta or Bob. It surprised me that she'd gone on the offensive in front of the children. I consoled myself with the thought that she was growing careless; soon, Berta and Cora would see how she undermined the family.

"Why are you so mad at Annie?" Erin's question stopped me.

For a moment I didn't know how to respond. "I think Annie is up to no good."

Erin and Donald looked uncomfortable. I wondered if she'd been talking to them. Sometimes, late at night, I knew they gathered up on the third floor. Sometimes I heard them laughing and talking. Often the children ended up in my room, frightened from her stories. Yet they wouldn't stop listening to her. It was as if she'd charmed them, too.

"You two don't understand what's going on." I wasn't about to tell them that Annie had her eye on Bob. "Just trust me. She bears watching."

"She only wants to be part of the family," Erin said softly. "She doesn't have anyone else, and she just wants us to love her."

"That sounds so simple, but it isn't that way. She's . . . dishonest."

Erin started to say something but stopped. She took the basket from me. "Donald and I are going to hide the clues." They dashed ahead of me at a dead run.

The pain of exclusion left me standing perfectly still. The children had left me behind. The canopy of trees created a tunnel of green light, and I walked on toward the old hotel. Even with my feelings hurt, I wanted to check out the bonfire Bob was building and the site for the tables Berta would set up with food.

Pushing past the hurt, I focused on the beauty of the day. October in South Alabama has the most exquisite light. Not the butter yellow of summer, but something aged with a hint of sadness. Winter hovered just in the distance.

The land around Belle Fleur contained mostly hardwoods. Pine, a money crop, was not native to the area, and where Belle Fleur had grown up in natural plants, there were oaks, wild cherry, dogwoods, maples, and sycamores. I loved the white, ghostly bark of the sycamores. Their summer green leaves changed overnight to gold and then fell, littering the path. Stepping on them caused a delicious crunch.

I took my time walking. When I cleared a huge wall of scuppernong vines, I caught sight of the pillars that remained of the Paradise Inn. Even I, who had little imagination, could visualize the façade of the old hotel. In my mind I heard the strains of a big band and saw the elegant men and women dancing in the cool fall air. The Paradise Inn, back to life.

Bob's plans for the renovation were coming along. Mr. Martin had brought in the last of the investors. The money was in place, the drawings were at the last stages of approval. Bob's excitement was contagious. He expected to start work within a week.

The giggle caught me unaware. It came so unexpectedly I spun in a complete circle. "Who's there?"

Of course there was no answer.

"I am sick to death of you." My fury erupted. "When I find you, you're going to die."

The giggle came again from a dense cluster of wild sugarberries. I stepped close to the bush, which was loaded with the juicy purple fruit.

"Come out, you little bastard." I hardly ever cursed, but I'd had it with the hide-and-seek. "Show yourself."

The bushes rattled, and my heart almost stopped. Whoever was hiding in the wild growth was only twenty yards from me. I'd never been so close.

"Annie?" Had she somehow gotten ahead of us and hidden to torment me?

The giggle again. It was so childlike, yet with a hint of knowledge of things that no child should ever know.

I picked up a stone from the path. I would kill it. Whether it was the dark girl who watched my every move or the blond thing that shifted its shape, I would kill it. Cora had taught me to respect all living creatures, but she'd also made me understand that in the natural world, we sometimes had to fight to survive.

"Show yourself." I hefted the rock.

The bushes shook like an ague had touched them, and then it stepped into the path.

I saw it clearly. It looked exactly like Donald—the same crystal blue eyes that seemed to hold a chip of the sky. The same dimpled cheeks with the scar of the fish hook. The same thatch of blond hair that fell across his forehead and into his right eye. It wore Donald's favorite red T-shirt and it lifted a hand to wave in a gesture that perfectly imitated the child I loved.

With two exceptions.

When it smiled, it revealed tiny teeth sharpened into dangerous points.

Instead of feet, it stood upon the paws of a dog.

It gave a soft giggle before it spun and bounded away. The claws dug into the dirt, raking hard and sending a spray of loam that struck me in the face.

And then it was gone.

28

It took only a few seconds for me to react. I bolted forward and gave chase. Ahead of me, the creature giggled and darted through the woods. It required no trail. With the feet of a beast, it dashed always ahead of me. I had no intention of giving up. I would catch this creature and force it to tell me what master it served, for I had no doubt it did the bidding of someone.

I didn't bother calling out. It wouldn't heed me, and I didn't have the breath to waste. The creature was fast. It could have easily outdistanced me, but it didn't. I caught glimpses of it waiting, almost letting me draw abreast before it jumped into action again.

My pure hatred of it gave me the energy to keep running. I had no idea where I was or how I would get home. Nothing mattered except that I capture this thing and force it to tell me its intention. Why was it at Belle Fleur? Why did it look like Donald, a child so sweet and innocent that it was a sick mockery? I would make it tell me.

Up ahead the creature paused, waiting. Smiling at me. The little giggle came again, as if we were playing a game. My legs throbbed with pain and my breath was ragged. Not so for the creature. It looked as fresh as when we'd started.

It stopped beneath a live oak. The dense leaves of the tree prevented the natural undergrowth. Leaning against the trunk, the creature waited for me.

When I stepped into the clearing, I sensed danger. It lounged, that's the only word. I stepped forward, and it held its ground. I took several more steps. It looked so much like Donald.

With a wild giggle, it bolted and disappeared.

I couldn't chase anymore. My body refused to obey my command to run. I stumbled toward the tree and sank against it, slumping to the ground. It had beaten me. There was no chance I could catch it. Whatever it was, it had supernatural energy and strength.

As I pressed my back into the rough bark, I saw something. At first, I didn't want to believe it. I wouldn't. It wasn't possible. Out here in the middle of the Belle Fleur wilderness, there was no way that Margo could have lost her shoe. But there it was, the slender navy flat, one half of her favorite pair of shoes.

I picked it up. The canvas shoe was covered in mud. Margo had been wearing these shoes the day she disappeared.

The creature had led me. It had lured and terrified me, slyly baiting me here, and for one purpose: it wanted me to find Margo's shoe.

29

The excited shrieks of teenagers echoed around the architectural bones of the Paradise Inn. It was the perfect night for a party, and forty or so kids in a variety of costumes, most of them from Erin's class, ran around the premises searching for the scavenger-hunt clues the children had so carefully hidden. The guests had been divided into groups and given Polaroid cameras to document each successful element they'd found or acquired in the quest for the grand prize. The hunt, as far as I could tell, was a huge success.

Donald had no friends his own age, and Annie had no friends at all. I had invited Mark, but he was working. My guest was Cora, who manned the table where Bob had put out grilled burgers and hot dogs. Berta had returned to Belle Fleur with the cake, which was hidden in the back seat of her car.

I'd told no one about Margo's shoe. I couldn't. Not in the middle of Erin's party preparations. I didn't know how to tell them. Their first reaction would be horror and pain. They'd view the shoe as a sign that Margo was hiding in or lost in the woods, so close but unwilling to come home. Then they'd imagine her barefoot for months and realize that circumstances were dire. Then they would ask why I was in that place in the woods and there was no logical answer to that. I couldn't say I was chasing Donald's evil twin. So I held my peace, knowing that tomorrow I would shatter Berta and Bob's world, and I tried to determine what role Annie had played in Margo's disappearance. She was always slipping around the woods and overgrown gardens, mooning over the Paradise and Bob's plans to resuscitate the place. I had no doubt she knew more than she'd told.

A moon, full and strong, cast shadows and edged the gentle waves of the Sound with silver. Sitting on the marble steps that now led to the hull of what was once a thriving resort—and would be again if Bob had his way—I tried to relax my shoulders. My body ached from the strain of the secret I kept.

Come daylight tomorrow I'd have to take the sheriff into the woods. I'd marked the path to the shoe with broken branches.

It had taken me a good half hour to find my way out of the woods where the wight had led me. What was this creature and what did it want? It looked like Donald, almost a perfect replica, except the imitator was pure evil. I knew it. And it was somehow connected to the strange dark girl who lurked on the grounds of Belle Fleur. A girl who looked like Annie. I could not piece it together, and I dared not tell my wild thoughts to anyone. If I spoke, the bitter irony was that *I* would be viewed as a madwoman, someone dangerous who had to be locked away. If this was my imagination at work, then I needed confinement, but then how did I explain the shoe?

A squeal of pleasure came from the old swimming pool, empty except for rain water and leaves, and I knew one of the teams had found the Barbie doll I'd so carefully hung from the diving board with the next clue taped to her perfect body. It was a riddle. I'd worked really hard on the game, and though Donald and Erin seemed withdrawn when I'd joined them to plant the clues, we'd worked through the awkwardness. Now Erin was reaping the reward of our efforts.

Down at the food table, Cora laughed, and I shifted so I could see her. As I suspected, she was thick as thieves with Annie. Somehow,

Annie had worked both Cora and Berta. All afternoon she'd been in the kitchen with Berta, mixing up the hamburger meat, preparing trays of condiments, laughing and giggling, sharing secrets. And now, she was pulling the same act with Cora. They worked at the food table side by side, putting patties on buns for the kids who would be ravenous once the scavenger hunt was complete.

Annie said something and Cora put an arm around her shoulders. My grandmother, normally astute with human nature, had been completely taken in by the orphan girl with no memory. Everyone loved Annie. To them, she was the perfect child, always on hand to help with a chore or offer a funny story. Little did they know.

Berta returned with the cake and Annie helped her set up. Even I had to admit that Berta looked better than she had in weeks. She'd convinced herself that Margo had chosen to leave Coden and her family. She'd woven a fantasy where Margo and Andrew had driven to the sunny California coast and were living in a cottage, playing house, until such time as Margo got homesick enough to come back.

The shoe I'd tucked into the fork of a tree told a different story. One not nearly so pleasant.

Annie left the women and wandered toward the grill where Bob worked. She'd chosen a ballerina costume. The pale pink leotard with the flowing tulle skirt showed off her curves. Living with the Hendersons, she'd put on at least fifteen pounds, all in the right places. She wasn't a child any longer, at least not physically. She was a woman.

She meant for Bob to see that.

Berta and Cora worked with the food, while not thirty yards away, Annie moved in on Bob. I was helpless to stop it. All I could do was clench my fists and watch from my vantage point high on the marble steps as Annie touched Bob's arm and laughed up into his face. Her body was supple, and she moved sensuously, pretending to dance. He said something she obviously enjoyed.

Rage, fed by the fear that she would ultimately destroy this good family, made me stand up. Movement at the edge of the water caught my attention.

Donald, dressed in his pirate costume, stood on a narrow band of sandy dirt that marked low tide. He stared out into the water. Not so long ago, I'd told Donald about Moonraker, the old fisherman who came out on nights of the full moon and skimmed the silver from the tops of the waves. While Annie held the title of premier storyteller, I had a few good ones. Donald loved the story.

I wondered why he wasn't participating in the scavenger hunt. He'd been assigned to the group of kids with Erin. Likely he felt like a fifth wheel. The age difference between Erin and Donald made it difficult for him. Erin had become a teen and he was still a child. I dreaded the time when he, too, would grow up and move to independence.

Dusting my hands on my jeans—I'd dressed as a hobo for the party—I started down the steps. Donald's stance told me he was pensive. It was hard being odd man out. I'd collect him and get him to help me with something.

Out of the corner of my eye, I saw something move far down the shore. A small figure sprinted along the sandy margin of land between marsh grass and water. The young boy moved very quickly. Too quickly . . . to be human.

The creature had joined the outskirts of the party. It moved amongst us.

And it was dressed in a pirate costume that duplicated what Donald wore. It stopped on the beach and looked directly at me, separated from Donald only by a jut of marsh grass that hid it from Donald's view. It lifted its hand and waved, exactly as Donald would do. Then it opened its mouth wide and moonlight struck the pointed white teeth. It snapped its jaw shut with a force I felt rather than heard.

The wildest, most excited giggle burst from it. Donald turned toward it, took a step or two and then stopped. He couldn't see the creature, but intuition told him danger hovered. Instead of going toward the giggle, he backed away.

The creature giggled again. Donald's face shifted from curiosity to panic. He was too far away for me to yell at him.

I looked for Bob, but he and Annie had disappeared. The grill was unattended and they had vanished.

Donald's future was in my hands.

I flew down the steps, moving with speed I never knew I possessed. My hobo hat flopped behind me. I dropped the stick with a bandanna full of socks tied to the end. I ran out of the big floppy shoes I'd borrowed from Bob. Ignoring the rocks and sticks that jabbed my bare feet, I ran toward Donald.

"Donald!" I cried his name. Behind me, the teens squealed and laughed, blocking out my frantic cries. Surely someone would see me rushing to the water and realize something was wrong.

"Donald! Run!" The creature intended harm. "Donald!"

The susurration of the water against the shore blocked out my cries. Donald sensed danger, but he stood without moving, scanning the shoreline in either direction and behind him, unable to determine from which direction the menace came.

My position was slightly elevated, and I could see over the top of the marsh grass that the creature was moving steadily closer to Donald. It didn't hurry or rush. Confident in its superior speed and stamina, it seemed to glide. Donald was no match for it, but it hadn't reckoned on me.

I angled so that I would intersect the strip of beach between the two. A part of me was aware that my feet bled from numerous cuts, but I didn't feel them. I couldn't allow myself to. I ran.

"Donald!" I screamed his name, and at last he heard me. He looked up and terror filled his face. "Run!" I pointed east, down the shore. "Run!"

He hesitated only a moment then stumbled toward the east. He ran awkwardly, looking back over his shoulder, his face a mixture of fear and confusion.

When I made it to the slip of beach, I ran west, toward the creature. I would confront it once and for all. Little bastard. It would pay.

I rounded the outcropping of marsh grass and stopped. The beach was empty. The water slushed against the shore and the tall grass rippled in the breeze. The creature was gone. Vanished.

Except for the marks in the sand made by sharp and deadly claws.

30

Donald shivered and I bundled him in the blanket as we sat in front of the bonfire Bob had lit. The flames jumped merrily into the starry sky, and the teenagers, plates heaped with food, sat cross-legged on the ground, basking in the warmth of the blaze as rock music blared from a radio Bob set up.

"You scared me, Mimi. That wasn't very nice." Donald refused to look at me. I'd caught up with him, panicked and fleeing along the beach, and I'd brought him back to the party. He didn't understand what I'd seen or why I'd sent him running along the tidal line.

"I saw something and I was afraid. . . ." How to explain to a young boy? "I thought it would hurt you."

"What was it?" Curiosity won out over aggravation.

"I'm not sure." I couldn't tell him it was a creature that looked like him.

"Probably a big ol' nutria."

I closed my eyes for a moment, remembering the creature. "Not a nutria, but something like that, with strange, sharp teeth."

Donald poked me in the ribs. "You're trying to scare me. Like Annie does."

"Annie tells you about a creature with sharp teeth?"

Like a summer storm, Donald's anger at me had blown away. "Sometimes. She says there are dangerous things in the woods around the house."

"What does she call them?"

He thought a moment. "She's never given them a name. May I have something to drink?"

"Stay here. I'll get you a cola." I pushed off the ground, all too aware that my feet needed medical attention. I hobbled to the drink table and poured cola over ice.

"Mimi, what happened to your feet?" Cora was at my side. "They're bleeding."

"I lost my shoes and had to . . . get back here. It's okay."

She pointed to several chairs Bob had brought over for her and Berta and Annie. "Sit down and let me look." She waved at Bob. "Do you have a flashlight? Mimi's hurt her feet."

"Stop it." I tried to push her away, but Cora could be hardheaded. "Let it go, Cora. I'll tend my feet later."

"Lord, child, those cuts will take stitches." She gently held my foot. "Annie! Bring me some water."

"Keep her away from me." I spoke without thinking.

Cora rocked back on her heels. "What's wrong with you?"

Again, the fault came squarely back to me. The unfairness almost choked me. "I just want to be left alone." The whole mess boiled inside me. Margo's shoe and the implications of that, the creature that no one else troubled to see, Annie's obvious desire for Bob—it was too much. Cora and Berta clung to their blindness. It was easier to pretend that I was somehow at fault than to address the source of the real problem. Annie.

"You need medical attention." Cora sounded so cold.

Annie brought a pitcher of water and Cora poured it over my hot and throbbing feet. She washed them with care, tut, tutting as she worked.

Berta came over to check out what was going on. "My goodness, Mimi. What have you done to your feet?"

When I looked, I saw that the wounds were far more serious than I'd thought. "It was an accident. I lost Bob's shoes in the marsh."

"Don't worry about his old shoes. It's your poor feet."

"I think we should take her home," Cora said. "Can you drive her?"

Berta nodded. "Absolutely. Will you cut the cake? I think the partiers are ready for that and then we can start pushing them back to Belle Fleur. I don't know about you, but I'm tired."

"Can Bob take me?" I asked. "I don't want you to miss cutting the cake, Berta." Mostly I wanted to get Bob away from Annie.

Berta hesitated only a moment. "If that's what you'd like."

"I think it would be best."

Annie stepped forward. "I'll go, too."

It was, of course, the one thing I didn't want.

31

Bob tried to insist that I go to the hospital, and I would have if we could have left Annie at home. She shadowed every move Bob made, reminding me of the dark-haired girl who lurked on the fringes of the yard. As it was, I put on my brakes and refused. Bob brought me antibiotic salve and bandages and left me in the second-floor bathroom to doctor my wounds. He was slightly aggravated because I wouldn't go to the emergency room.

Annie had offered to wash up the dishes in the kitchen, and for a while I heard the rattle of pans and plates. When the kitchen fell silent, I was acutely aware that the house seemed to hold its breath. I pulled the last strip of tape tight and hobbled to my feet. Pain bloomed around and ran down my calves and ankles to my toes. Perhaps the doctor might not have been a bad option.

My room was down the hallway, and I doubted my ability to get there. I had no choice. Bob and Annie had disappeared. Grasping the wall and various pieces of antique furniture, I made my way slowly toward my room.

The second-floor hallway was covered in a long, plush Persian rug. Dark burgundy, navy, and gold, the jewel tones of the pattern seemed warm in the sunlight, but at night the carpet was dark. The color of old blood. The thick pad muted my steps, but beneath the carpet a floorboard here and there creaked. Those were the only sounds in the house.

When I reached the door to my room, I was panting from pain. With my hand on the knob, I hesitated. A sound from the third floor stopped me cold. Giggling. The evil little bastard child that looked like Donald was in the house. The creature had entered Belle Fleur while we were at the Paradise Inn. It had come into the heart of this family with god knew what intent.

My first thought centered on a weapon. Bob kept a gun in the closet of his bedroom, a semi-automatic and a box of bullets. Living this far from a city, Bob had told us all, except for Donald, where the gun could be found in case of an emergency. With my feet burning with pain, I didn't know if I could get downstairs and back up to the third floor.

In my bedroom was a flashlight. Not a real weapon.

Annie had a set of croquet mallets in her bedroom, a far more effective weapon than a lightweight flashlight. I started up the stairs to the third floor.

The giggle came again, a sound so supremely confident that it ignited impotent rage inside me. Damn that creature. Damn it to hell.

Pulling myself on the banister, I made it to the third floor. The door to Annie's room was closed.

Again, the intimate sound of laughter.

Taking care not to make any noise, I limped to the door. I slowly turned the knob and pushed. The door eased open on silent hinges.

The giggle came from deep within the blowing folds of fabric. Annie—or someone—had opened the windows and the door to the balcony, and a breeze off the water set the fabric dancing. The entire room moved in swirls of red and blue and yellow muted in the moonlight, hiding the bastard creature that giggled like a titillated schoolgirl.

One painful step after the other took me into the room. The wind caught the door and blew it shut, but the click was almost inaudible.

The only light came from the full moon, but I could see the shapes and contours of Annie's room. The bed was draped in gauzy material, and it rose like a queen's chamber out of the swirling fabrics.

The giggle came from there.

The material was thick enough to hide the occupant of the bed. I saw the blurry outline of movement. A body swayed like the wind-whipped material. This was not the body of a little boy, though. From the outline cast against the gauzy material I recognized a slender waist, curved hips, and breasts that tipped toward fullness. This was a woman.

Annie.

Was she in bed with the creature?

The thought was so repugnant, I choked back bile that threatened to rise up my throat. Surely not even Annie could be so evil.

My feet burned, but I forced myself forward, a step closer to the bed. The silhouette of the woman moved in a motion as old as time. She sat atop someone.

The truth pierced me. My knees almost buckled, but I refused to yield. I held my ground, counting my breath in and out.

Beneath Annie the man stirred and sat up, pushing Annie onto her back. She laughed and said something soft and suggestive.

Bob covered her, his lean body clearly defined against the gauzy material of the bed as he lowered himself on top of her.

32

Shock kept me upright. I eased out of the bedroom, closing the door and lumbering down the stairs to my door. I wept as I entered, harsh racking sobs that echoed in the empty house. Berta's betrayal was as bitter as if it were my own.

When I went to my window and looked out, I could see the glimmer of the bonfire at Paradise Inn. The party was still in full swing. Annie and Bob were safe from discovery, except by me.

Would I tell Berta? I didn't know. The messenger who brought bad news was often shot, and it was clear Annie could manipulate Bob, Berta, and Cora to see things however it suited her. Slipping into a rocking chair that looked out toward the old hotel, I tried to calm my thoughts. I had to accept that I was a coward. I should have said something to them—destroyed their carnal pleasure by letting them know they'd been found out. But I hadn't. I hadn't.

Instead I'd tucked tail and cowered back to my room as if I were the one in the wrong. Would I have the grit to tell Berta what she so deserved to know? I rocked harder.

My view showed me the side lawn, a place of midnight magic. The old clock in the downstairs hall chimed the hour. Halloween had ended and All Saints' Eve begun. From ancient times, man had feared this season when reality lost its grip and the supernatural gained the strength to manifest.

The Henderson lawn was incredible in the moonlight. The old oaks, some of them spanning two centuries or more, waved their moss-covered branches, creating a dappled effect on the grass. The scuppernong arbor, now bare of the wild grapes and leaves, rattled its viney fingers, tapping against itself like dried bones.

An old oak limb pushed against the screen of my window, a creepy sound that made me think to ask Bob to trim it back. Or else I would do it myself. I would ask Bob for nothing. I leaned forward to check the limb. She stood by the arbor, looking up at me. The moonlight struck her full on the face, and I saw how much she resembled Annie. They could be sisters, if not twins.

Annie, with no memory and no family, had a doppelganger or, more likely, an accomplice. The girl looked up at me with a knowing smile. She made a vulgar sign with her hands and then laughed. It wasn't the giggle of the Donald creature nor was it the sexually charged sound of pleasure that Annie had made while Bob screwed her. This was something different. Something far more sinister.

⚜

I drank my third cup of coffee while the house slumbered around me. Dawn had broken, and the pale gold light of autumn tipped the slate waves of the Sound with a glimmer of liquid gold. It was just after six o'clock and I went inside and called the Mobile County Sheriff's office. I had to report Margo's shoe. I was tempted to report Bob. Surely there was some crime involved in his sexual relationship with a teenage girl who was his ward. I didn't pursue that, though. First things first.

"Deputy Mark Walton, please." I spoke softly. I didn't want to wake the house. I wanted to talk with Mark first, to show him what I'd found so we could determine what it meant.

The call was patched through, and in a moment Mark's groggy voice answered.

"Come to Belle Fleur," I told him.

Something in my tone warned him of the direness. "Did Margo call?"

"Not exactly. Just get here as quickly as you can. I'll meet you on Shore Road." I hung up and left the house. Walking was difficult. I'd re-bandaged my feet, and put on thick socks and soft shoes. I could feel the blood oozing. Walking on my wounds was my penance for the cowardice I'd shown by not stopping Bob and Annie. I was as much a part of the betrayal of Berta as they were.

I made slow progress toward the road. Somehow I would have to walk through the woods with Mark to show him Margo's shoe. I should have left a note on the kitchen table for Berta, telling her that I'd run an errand, but my brain hadn't been functioning.

I stood in the sunshine and listened to the water kiss the shore. The marsh grass whispered, and for the first time that I could remember, there was a sinister undertone. It was almost as if the Sound spoke. Gulls called as they swooped and dove, angry sounds that mingled with the murmur of the water and grass.

Moving off the road, I eased into the marsh, careful to put my feet upon solid ground. The whole area became aquatic when the tide came in. Now, though, it was low tide and the area was semi-solid.

The whisper came again. "Don-nald." It sounded almost as if the water called out. I backed away quickly. It was just my imagination, because I'd been so stressed.

"Fuck you," I said to the water as I turned my back. In the distance I saw the brown patrol car coming my way. Mark was breaking land-speed records. He pulled up and stopped while I climbed into the passenger seat.

"You look like hell," he said, a furrow between his dark eyebrows.

"I hurt my feet last night. Walking is painful."

"So why are you walking down here? I could have driven to the house to pick you up."

I shook my head. "No. I want you to see this before we tell anyone."

"What?"

"I found Margo's shoe. In the woods."

"Shit," he said softly. "Are you sure?"

"I am. Yesterday I was hiding the clues for the party and I stumbled across it. I didn't say anything. I—" Tears choked me. "I knew it was a bad sign. I—"

He pulled me against his side, and I melted against him. "Hey, let's take a look. Maybe it isn't anything."

But I could tell from his voice he knew that wasn't true. The comfort of his body against mine couldn't protect me from the truth. A teenage girl didn't disappear and leave a shoe deep in the woods unless there was a reason for it.

33

By the time the sheriff's deputies and the search and rescue members gathered on the front lawn of Belle Fleur, the sun was occluded by thick gray clouds. The storm had rolled in off the water, blown in from the barrier islands by a strong southeasterly wind that brought the tang of salt.

Donald, Erin, and I sat on the front steps. Bob and Berta were on the lawn talking with the searchers. Bloodhounds, on the sheriff's order, were brought over from the Louisiana state prison. The dogs were the best trackers in the Southeast, and Mark would use the shoe to hopefully put them on the scent.

No matter how hard I tried, my mind kept going back to Berta's face when Mark told her about the shoe, how I'd found it, how he wanted to bring in tracking dogs. Cadaver dogs, specially trained to find buried bodies. Mark didn't say it, but he didn't have to.

Margo had been gone for two months. Berta wasn't stupid. She knew the searchers and the dogs were looking for a body. When Mark held out the shoe to her, she'd slumped almost to the floor. Only Bob's quick reaction saved her from hitting the ground. If she knew the truth about her husband and Annie, she wouldn't allow him to touch her.

Now she was hugging herself, rubbing her arms, moving around. There was a frenetic element in her actions. If she stopped, she might explode.

"Is Margo dead?" Donald asked the question.

"I don't know." It wasn't exactly a lie. I had no proof. But I knew.

"Should I call Peggy Cargill?" Erin asked. "She'd want to know if Andrew is with Margo."

"I don't think so. We should wait to see if the searchers find anything." It would be worse for Berta if Andrew's family was here, terrified and waiting.

"Why didn't you tell about the shoe last night?" Erin asked.

"It wouldn't have made any difference. They couldn't start searching until today. Until daylight. So much time has passed . . . I didn't want to spoil your party."

Erin brushed tears from her face. "Why would she and Andrew go off into the woods?"

"I don't have any answers." I wanted to go inside. Watching Berta was like waiting for a dog to run out into traffic.

"Look, they're heading into the woods." Erin stood up. "Should we help search?"

"No, and neither should your mother."

"Annie's going." Erin pointed to the slender figure in a car-coat and boots running from the backyard to the path to the old hotel. She caught up with Bob and fell into step beside him. I felt the urge to chase after her. And kill her.

"Berta!" I called out to the lone figure left standing in the front yard. Berta stomped her feet and stared after the disappearing men. I understood why she hadn't gone to search. If they found what they all expected, she would never recover from the sight. "Berta!" I waved to her. "Come back to the house."

Reluctantly she came toward us. She made no effort to stop the tears. "Do you think they'll find her?" she asked.

"I don't know." I hated those words.

"Mark said the dogs could pick up a scent even if it's months old."

I nodded. Cadaver dogs weren't necessarily following a scent. They sniffed for decomposition.

"Margo never went into the woods. She was afraid of snakes and she hated the mosquitoes and she didn't like to sweat." Berta patted her face, as if she were waking herself from a nightmare.

I took her hand and urged her up the steps. When she was seated at the kitchen table, I made coffee and toast. She'd lost at least fifteen pounds since Margo disappeared, but in the last few weeks, she'd been eating better. Now it was as if that small gain had disappeared. She was gaunt and nervous. I knew there were sleeping pills in the medicine cabinet in their bathroom. It occurred to me that it might be smart to crush one up in her coffee.

"I don't feel well." Berta pushed back from the table, the toast untouched. "I'm going to lie down."

"I'll call you when we hear news."

She slipped out of the kitchen and I heard her sob before she closed her bedroom door.

"If Margo is dead, I don't think Mother will recover," Erin said. She was crying, too.

"Berta is strong. She has you and Donald to fight for and love. She may think she wants to die, but she won't." It was cold comfort.

Erin wiped her runny nose with her sleeve. "I'm going to my room."

"Me, too." Donald looked as lost as his sister.

"I'm going to walk a little ways toward the search." My feet would prevent me from walking any great distance, but the compulsion to check up on Bob and Annie couldn't be denied. Bob should be here with Berta. Instead, he was in the woods with Annie.

"Shouldn't you stay with us?" Donald asked. He tugged at my shirttail. "I don't want to be alone."

"Erin is here. And Berta." I had to get out of the house.

"Mimi, do you believe in evil?" Donald asked.

"What an odd question." Donald's timing was peculiar. "Why do you ask?"

"Annie says that some people are evil. She says they *intend* to do bad things. She says we have to be careful about them."

"Did she say who was evil?"

Donald shook his head. "But she scared me. Do you think an evil person hurt Margo?"

"Let's just wait and see if Margo is hurt before we try to decide who caused her injury." I rumpled his blond hair and kissed his forehead. "Why don't you read your Hardy Boys book? You like that, and it'll take your mind off things."

"Will you come read to me for a little bit?"

I tamped down my impatience. My job was to mind the children, and I couldn't forget that just because I was trying to birddog Bob and Annie. Just as I was about to agree, I saw the small blond creature tucked behind a bush in the backyard. He wore Donald's snap-buttoned cowboy shirt and blue jeans. I walked to the window and gripped the kitchen sink. "You little bastard," I whispered.

"What?" Donald's voice registered shock. "Mimi, I—"

"I wasn't talking to you." I recovered as quickly as I could. "I don't have time to read. I'll be back as soon as I can." Ignoring the pain of my feet, I hurried out the back door and across the yard to the place where the branches of the shrub still quivered.

34

Thunder rumbled, a sound like cannons in the distance. The creature led me into the woods. We angled toward Crystal Mirror Lake, away from the search party. Ahead of me the Donald-creature moved slower than I'd ever seen it. Almost as if it were trying to accommodate my feet. Why did it want me to follow?

When I was out of earshot of the house, I called out to it. "Hey! Hey, you! Stop!"

It ignored me, moving steadily away from the house. I had some concern for the children upstairs, left without protection, but Berta was home. She was upset, but she ought to be able to mind her children for a little while.

The creature paused up ahead. "Hey!" I yelled as loudly as I could.

It turned to face me, Donald's innocent features corrupted by a mouth filled with needle-like teeth. Saliva ran from a corner of the creature's mouth.

"Can you talk?" I stopped walking. My feet were on fire, and I could feel my left shoe filled with blood.

The creature watched me, tilting its head as if he was viewing an anomaly, some animal it had never seen and couldn't comprehend.

"Do you speak English?" I asked.

"Mimi, save me." It spoke in Donald's voice.

"Stop, damn you!"

"Mimi. . . ." It giggled. "Save me. Save little Donald. Save little Donald from being my supper." The last three words were spoken in a thunderous voice. The smell of something long dead and rancid drifted to me.

"What are you?" I gagged out the question.

Instead of answering, the creature bounded down the path. Gritting my teeth, I followed as quickly as I could. It led me north, deep into the acreage that was part of Belle Fleur. The remnants of an old trail, slightly recessed as if heavy wagons had once moved along it, could be detected, but the trees had grown so close to the road and the underbrush was so thick, I knew not even Erin had explored the area on Cogar.

The creature showed no hesitation, though, as it took a fork that was angled into the dim grayness of the day. The brooding storm moved in, and to the south lightning bloomed inside the heavy clouds. The sky could open any minute.

I lost sight of the creature in the dense foliage and gloom. It was as if the grayness had swallowed it. I slowed, wondering if I'd been lured into the middle of nowhere on a fool's errand while the creature doubled back to Belle Fleur to harm the humans I loved.

Spinning a hundred and eighty degrees, I heard a soft giggle. The little bastard enjoyed playing with me.

"I'm done with your game of follow the leader." I aimed south toward home.

"Poor Margo. Poor, poor Margo. Find her bones."

It was Margo's voice that came to me. Not Donald's. Dread settled over me, as oppressive as the storm clouds. Slowly I turned. The creature, now a good foot taller, stood in the path not thirty yards away. All traces of Donald were gone. Long blond hair brushed the shoulders of the figure, and a swirl of shifting light blocked the face. The blur began to clear and Margo's features emerged.

"Don't abandon me, Mimi. Don't leave me to rot, all alone, in the woods. Take me home to Mama."

"Margo!" I stumbled toward her. "Margo?"

Vile, vile creature. It opened its mouth to reveal rows of deadly sharp teeth. Laughter bubbled out of it before it sprang down the path, its dog-like claws digging into the rich loam and sending clumps of it flying into my face.

"Margo's gone, Mimi, but you can have her rotting flesh." The creature bolted so fast that it disappeared before I could react. This time I knew it was gone. It had led me to the point where it no longer needed me, and it had fled.

Just ahead I saw open space, and in the distance I heard the baying of hounds. I had no idea where I was on the Belle Fleur property. I'd lost all sense of direction, and the clouds obscured the sun. The clearing might give me a chance to get my bearings.

At the edge of the tree line, I was surprised to find strands of barbed wire. Bob had never mentioned pastureland. And certainly not cows. But unless my eyes deceived me, a herd of Brahmas grazed on the last of the summer grass. For a long time I stood at the fence and watched the cattle. They hadn't sensed the evil creature that was so close. Domestication had dulled their sense of survival. Five white egrets soared above the cattle's heads, finally landing only inches away. As the cattle pulled at the grass, disturbing the roots, the egrets feasted on the wriggling insects.

A small bird fluttered above the cattle. Dark and swift, it zipped across the scene before settling onto the back of one of the cows. I recognized the glossy black body and brown head of the male cowbird. A female, brownish and dull, joined her mate on the cow's back.

They were interesting birds. They laid their eggs in the nest of another bird, usually a warbler. The mother warbler hatched out the egg, along with her brood, and then fed and nurtured the strangeling chick. But the cowbird was bigger, stronger, and ultimately it pushed the warbler chicks out of the nest to their death.

A bush on the other side of the field began to quake violently. Though the storm hovered over us, there was no wind. The clouds waited for the moment when they would split and spill millions of gallons. There was no natural reason for the shrub to move so violently.

The creature stepped out into the open. Again the swirl of features as Margo transmogrified into Donald. Nausea washed over me. I knew now what the creature was. I could name it, if I chose. A nester. A child who wanted to climb into the nest of the Henderson family. The evil child before me was the spawn of Annie's doppelganger. This was Annie's master plan. Her vile creation. Once the children were gone, the way would be open for her. And she meant to get there, no matter the means.

A blinding headache smacked my forehead and arced to either temple.

The creature giggled, that soft, sweet sound of innocence. It did not speak, but I heard it. *Now you know me*, it said. *Now you've named my nature.*

I had to stop it. Battling the headache, I ran toward it. It moved fast now, sprinting down the path and finally disappearing at the edge of a bayou. I was sick from the pain in my head and disoriented, but I realized I'd tracked in a huge circle. I was behind the old hotel on the edge of Bayou Abondant that ran beside the Paradise and eventually emptied into the Sound.

The bay of a hound came so close, my heart jumped. As I spun around, my head swam with dizziness. Nausea overwhelmed me and I dropped to my knees, retching up breakfast.

Two dogs burst from a huckleberry bush. The last thing I remembered was their hot breath on my face and neck before I lost consciousness.

35

Dr. Adams filled a syringe. "You know better than this, Mimi." He prepared the antibiotic injection and came to my bedside. "Cora is downstairs worried sick. The Hendersons are blaming themselves, but this falls on you. Your feet are infected. If you don't take care of them, you may lose them."

I swallowed and nodded. Dr. Adams had never been stern with me. I couldn't see my feet because of the huge bandages, but I could assume they were not good.

"I'm going to give you several shots, including tetanus. Then oral antibiotics. Also something for pain. Take your medicine and soak those feet. Stay off them. Are we clear?"

My head moved up and down.

He motioned for me to roll over and pull up my nightgown. I felt the jab of the needle in my hip.

"Thank you for coming to the house." Dr. Adams was one of the few doctors who still made house calls, but it was normally limited to the elderly and shut-ins—people who had trouble getting into town to the doctor's office or the hospital. The only reason he came to Belle Fleur was Berta. She and Bob had developed a friendship with the doctor and his wife.

He sat on the edge of my bed. "What were you doing off in the woods like that?"

My throat ached with a bottleneck of words. I wanted to tell him. I wanted to tell someone. I had no proof, but in my heart I knew the nester meant harm to the Henderson family. Someone had to stop it, and I wasn't strong enough. I'd known Dr. Adams most of my life, but still I couldn't trust him. He was a man of science, of order and fact. What I'd seen was impossible. "I was looking for Margo."

"You're lucky those dogs found you, Mimi. You could have lain out there for a long time." He got up and prepared another injection. This one he put into the vein of my arm. Warmth spread over me and my limbs grew heavy. The effect was so instant that I was caught unprepared. "Tell Bob . . . Bayou Abondant . . . Margo. Look there." I had to make him see how important this was. The nester had drawn me there for a purpose. I didn't know what, but there was motive behind everything the creature did.

Moving to sit on the side of the bed again, the doctor brushed my hair off my forehead. "Berta has told me you've been upset, Mimi. The night of Erin's party you seriously damaged your feet, for no apparent reason. Bob and Berta are worried about you. They think you've taken Margo's disappearance to heart, and I think finding Margo's shoe has caused . . . unbalanced thoughts." As I'd feared, my stability was in question.

I fought to shake my head. My lips were huge, thick, and wouldn't form the word "no." A tear leaked out of the corner of my eye, but I didn't have the strength to even lift my head.

"The shot will relax you. Now I urge you to take care of yourself. Heal those feet. Sometimes an infection can cause . . . problems. It's the fever, and you are burning up. In a day or so, that will be gone and things will be clear again."

My fingers found his suit jacket and curled around the edge. I had to make him believe me.

"Bob has gone back to the search with the dogs. Everyone is hurrying before the storm hits. So you concentrate on healing and feeling better."

He stood, snapped his bag shut, and walked to the door.

The drug held me in a grip close to paralysis. My eyelids eased shut and no willpower could open them. The last thing I heard was a crack of lightning followed by a rumble of thunder and the lashing fury of a hard rain.

36

By the time I woke up the next day, it was nearly noon. The rain had halted the search for Margo and Andrew, but the men were back at dawn. They'd been in the woods for six hours, Annie said, when she brought me coffee and a Danish.

"How are your feet?" she asked, and I thought I caught the hint of a smile.

"I'm fine." I pushed up in the bed and was rewarded with a white-hot jolt of pain. Even the weight of the cool sheets angered my wounds.

"Berta said she'd be up here in a little while." Annie went to the door.

"Did they find any trace of Margo?"

"Not yesterday. The dogs found something near the old hotel, they think, but the rain came down hard and confused things."

"Why aren't you out with the searchers today?"

She turned back to look at me. "Berta asked me to stay here and watch the children since you were injured."

Annie in charge of the children was the most dangerous situation of all. "The private investigator is looking into your past, Annie. With any luck, Jimmy Finch will find your real family and you can go home."

Her smile was amused. "I wouldn't count on that."

"You haven't lost your memory at all, have you?"

"You say the darndest things, Mimi. Why would you even think such?" Smug didn't begin to describe her attitude.

"Call it intuition. Tell me about the other girl, the one that waits outside. What is she to you?"

She came closer, and now she wasn't smiling at all. "I don't have a clue what you're talking about. Keep it up, though, and you'll end up in Searcy mental institution. I heard the doctor talking to Bob and Berta. He said you were self-destructive. If you persist in talking crazy and making ridiculous accusations, you're going to find yourself in more hot water than Cora can get you out of."

She left the room, closing the door firmly behind her.

Although I was worried about my feet, I managed to get out of bed and make it over to the chair beside the window. From that vantage point, I could see the path to the Paradise Inn. When the searchers returned, that was likely the route they'd use. I itched to be downstairs with Berta and the children during this awful time.

The day was filled with golden light and a cool breeze. I loved the fall. Crisp days, cold nights when a fire flickered orange and welcoming. A store of oak was in a shed in the backyard, dry and seasoned, ready for a good fire in one of the numerous fireplaces. My room even had one.

The painkillers Dr. Adams left made me woozy. My thoughts drifted like leaves on a slow river. No matter how hard I tried to avoid it, I returned to the cowbird and what I knew to be true about the dark-haired girl and her progeny, the little blond children who could morph into replicas of the Hendersons.

From downstairs I heard Jim Croce singing about Leroy Brown. Annie played the radio while she worked in the kitchen. It made me want to strum the guitar I'd neglected for the past several weeks. Since I was laid up, I had nothing better to do. I reached for the case and brought out the beautiful instrument.

My left hand formed the chord patterns as I picked with my right. "Tecumseh Valley" was a Townes Van Zandt song I loved. I heard footsteps outside my door. Donald loved for me to play for him. I picked up "Pancho and Lefty," another Van Zandt song that was his favorite.

A light scratching at my door made me smile as I continued with the saga. Donald was messing with me. Any moment he would pop into the room.

When I glanced out the window, my fingers faltered on the strings. Berta and Annie stood in the side yard with the children. Both children. They stared down the path, and in the distance I saw Mark coming toward them.

The scratching sounded at my door again.

I put the guitar aside. The house was so quiet I heard the creak of a shutter outside my window.

"Mimi," the singsong voice called to me from outside my door.

Gripping the sill, I wanted to call to Berta, but I couldn't. The way Mark was moving, I knew it was bad. He marched toward Berta, his back rigid, hands hanging at his side.

"Mi-mi, we want to play with you. They know about Margo. She's no fun now." The giggle filtered under the door, followed by more scratching.

I lurched across the room and tore the door open. The hallway was empty. The only sign that anyone had been at my door were the strange claw marks just below the doorknob.

From outside the window, a bloodcurdling cry came from Berta. Margo had indeed been found, and the news was not good.

37

Using the crutches Dr. Adams had insisted on, I made it to the front porch as Bob scooped Berta into his arms and carried her into the house. She clung to him, sobbing. Mark stood alone in the yard, his mud-smeared face a testament to his exhaustion and sorrow.

Bob brushed past me, eyes glazed. I automatically opened the door for him.

"I'm sorry," Mark said, still standing in the yard.

I motioned him to the porch. "What did you find?"

"We believe it's Andrew Cargill's car."

"You believe?" I couldn't put it together.

"It's submerged. In the bayou beside the old Paradise. The tides have been working on it and it's buried in silt. The sheriff's got a call out to some local divers."

"Bayou Abondant?" I could barely utter the words.

"That's right. After we found you yesterday, we decided to try on the other side of the bayou. When we were crossing the water, the dogs caught a scent."

"But it might not be his car, and it might be empty. . . ." I stopped because his face told another story.

"There are two bodies in the car. One of the search-and-rescue guys dove down to check. He couldn't hold his breath long enough to identify either person, but the girl has long blond hair. It's a black Mustang."

Maybe I'd known all along, but the news didn't shock me. "When I found the shoe I think I knew. But how did the shoe get into the woods?"

"We don't have all the answers yet. Hell, we don't have any. But my guess, and this is just between us, Mimi, is that Margo met Andrew in the woods. Someone else was there, too. Maybe the drug dealers, maybe a buyer. I don't know. But something went very wrong. They probably cut off Andrew's hand to make him talk about something, and after that, they had to kill them both. Then they drove them to the Paradise and ran the car into the bayou."

I motioned for him to take a seat on the steps. My feet were throbbing, and I had to take the weight off them.

"If you hadn't passed out in the woods, we would never have thought to cross the bayou."

I didn't say it, but I wondered if it would have been better if the bodies had remained submerged. At least Berta would have her hope. In a sense, I'd taken that from her. Or the nester had. The bastard creature had lured me into the woods, led me to the shoe, knowing I would tell, knowing somehow that the bodies would be found. But why? What did it matter to the creature?

"Mimi?" Mark's hand grasped my arm. "Are you going to faint?"

I pulled myself together. "Take me to the hotel."

"That's not a good idea. They're going to use divers to bring the bodies out and then a wrecker to pull up the car."

"I have to go."

"No. You don't." Mark was firm. "If it's Margo, she's been in the water for two months. You don't know what that looks like, but I do. You shouldn't put that in your mind. The fish and the crabs. . . ." He shook his head. "No. As you tell me all the time, your place is here with the children. This is one time I concur. Those kids are going to need you, and so are Mr. and Mrs. Henderson. In fact, the sheriff sent a cruiser to get Mrs. Eubanks and bring her here."

"What about the Cargills? Andrew's parents. . . ."

"A deputy is on the way to tell them too."

"Is there any chance it isn't Margo and Andrew?"

He looked toward the Sound rather than at me. "I'd be lying if I said yes. I think it's them, Mimi. Best prepare yourself." He stood. "Now I have to get back to the bayou. The sheriff will return with the divers any minute."

"Will you catch the person who did this?"

He took a long breath. "I'll do my best, Mimi. I promise. I really thought those kids had run off and that they'd come home after a while or at least call their parents. I never thought it would come to this. Not even with the hand."

"Thank you, Mark." I hobbled across the porch and into the house.

The house ticked with silence, the old heart-of-pine boards seeming to flex and pop with the cold November day. Donald and Erin were in their rooms. Annie had disappeared. I needed some time alone, so I didn't search for her.

I put on a pot of coffee and hobbled up to my room. Dr. Adams had left a few tablets of fentanyl to help with the pain of my feet. I shook two out of the bottle and brought them back to the kitchen. As the coffee brewed, I crushed them up and put them in a cup, which I then laced with a dollop of brandy and lots of sugar. Berta could get mad at me later, but she shouldn't be waiting for the law to drag up the body of her daughter. Bob would thank me for doing this.

I prepared Bob's coffee and put aside my crutches to carry the tray to their bedroom. Standing outside the door, I heard Berta's sobs and Bob's voice, calm and reasonable, comforting her. Berta had lost a child, but she had the best husband on the planet. I tapped, and when the door opened, I gave Bob the tray. "That's Berta's." I met his gaze. "Make her drink it if you can."

The door closed and I hobbled back to the kitchen just as Cora came in the front door. Her hair was wild and her face pale. "My Lord, Mimi, this is just awful."

I waved her into a chair at the kitchen table, poured us both some coffee, and sat.

"Where are the children?" she asked.

"Upstairs." From the quiet of the house, it was obvious they weren't. I sprang to my feet and ran upstairs to check. Their bedrooms were empty. They were gone. When I looked out the window, I realized what had happened. Behind my back, Annie had taken them.

I was calmer when I returned to the kitchen. Cora would find my concerns unfounded, and I couldn't level accusations at Annie without proof. "Erin and Donald must be with Annie. The station wagon is gone. I guess she took them to town."

Cora sighed. "That's good." She drank the coffee as if it would sustain her.

"Bob is with Berta in the bedroom. She's determined to go to the hotel, to be there when they bring up. . . ."

"That's not a good idea." Cora ran a hand through her wild hair. I'd never seen her so frazzled. "Do they know what happened?"

"Mark thinks they were murdered. Some run-in involving drugs." I shrugged, unable to breach the wall that separated me from my emotions. It was self-preservation, but I felt as if my head were stuffed with wet cotton.

"Drugs? That's. . . ." Cora was at a loss. "This is going to break Berta."

"You have to get Annie out of here." I blurted the words against all of my good intentions. It wasn't the way I wanted to talk to Cora about Annie, but I had to make her understand. Annie was at the bottom of Margo's death, and she was free to take Donald or Erin wherever she chose.

"What are you talking about?" She got up and poured herself another cup of coffee. The cup clattered against the saucer as she held it.

"She has to go, Cora. She's up to no good. *She's* going to break this family apart."

Cora sank into a chair. "Annie's just a child, Mimi. Your jealousy—"

"She isn't a child. She a very experienced young woman. The night of the scavenger hunt, didn't you notice that she was coming on to Bob? At the grill, at the bonfire. Back here at the house. She seduced—"

"Stop it!" Cora grasped my wrist in a punishing grip. She was old, but she was strong. "Stop that talk right now." She shook my arm. "Where do you come up with the things you say?"

I snatched my arm free. "I saw them. Everyone else was too busy to pay attention, but I saw them."

"What I saw that night was you, out of control. You frightened Donald half to death, and you injured yourself so severely you required medical attention." Her pale blue gaze held mine and dared me to say more. "Now you get hold of yourself, Mimi. You have everything a young woman could want—a wonderful job, living with a great family in a beautiful house. Do you really want to risk this because you're jealous of another child?"

"She isn't a child."

My tone must have frightened her, because the anger in her face gave way to something else. "What do you mean?"

"There's more to Annie than she lets on. You know that. The story of finding her on the streets of Mobile, that's not true, is it?" I thought I saw fear flicker in her eyes.

"Are you sick, Mimi?" She reached a hand toward my forehead. "Your feet! The infection has made you delirious."

I ducked to avoid her touch. "I'm not sick and I'm not stupid. Where did Annie really come from?"

Cora pushed her chair back and stood. "Mimi, you're irrational."

"Let me tell you what's irrational." I was beyond control. "She fucked Bob. That's what's going on under this roof with precious Annie."

Cora fell back as if I'd slapped her. She started to speak but stopped herself.

"I saw them. The night of the scavenger hunt. In Annie's bedroom when they thought I was in bed. They brought me back here, remember?"

"That's an awful accusation." She spoke as if her mouth was deadened by Novocain. The words came out, but they didn't match the shape of her lips.

"What's awful is that it isn't just an accusation. It's a fact. Annie wants Bob, and she will use any opportunity to seduce him, even Margo's death. You get her out of this house."

"Get a grip on yourself before it's too late." Cora looked beyond me and then stood and walked out of the kitchen to check to see if anyone else had heard me. "You can't be saying this kind of thing out loud."

"Why not?"

She grasped my shoulders. "Trust me, Mimi. You cannot do this."

"But—"

She shook me lightly. "No buts. Never say such a thing again." Her hand touched my lips, stopping my protest. "I will take care of this. But you cannot do this to Berta right now. Do you hear me? She's lost her firstborn. She cannot hear even a whisper of talk that Bob has betrayed her."

"Even if he has?"

"I will handle this."

"How?"

She pushed me toward the sink. "Wash the dishes. Try to be as helpful and kind as you can. I'll do what has to be done."

Her answer didn't satisfy me. "What do you mean?"

"It means that you stay out of it now. Keep your mouth shut. If you start this with Berta, it could send her into an institution. She isn't strong enough for accusations of Bob's betrayal. If she collapses mentally, the family will leave Belle Fleur, Mimi. Think about that. If Berta requires hospitalization, the family would no doubt return to California."

The hall clocked ticked and chimed. I didn't count the number. I forced myself to be calm. "Okay," I said. "I understand."

"Do you?" she asked. "You have as much to lose as Annie."

I nodded.

"Not a word." She picked up her purse and left.

38

I slipped the keys to Berta's Thunderbird off the hook and headed for town, searching for Annie and the children. Though I drove to all the places we frequented, I found no trace. When I returned to Belle Fleur, the station wagon was parked out front, but a quick search of the house revealed they weren't inside. I could only assume Annie had returned with the children and taken them somewhere on foot. Perhaps to the stables—anywhere away from the pall of doom that hung over Belle Fleur.

She was alone with them—in total control of their safety. And I could do nothing but wait for her to bring them back. My feet prevented me from searching for them on foot.

Berta's soft sobs told me she was in her room. If I pressed my ear against the door, I could hear Bob's consoling murmur. Though he was as grief-stricken as Berta, he had to be strong. Without Bob, the Henderson family would disintegrate, which made Annie's seductions all the more dangerous. Berta was a wonderful mother, but she wasn't strong enough to hold the family together without him.

Neither Bob nor Berta needed to be at the Paradise when Margo was retrieved. I would be there. Somehow, I kept hoping the discovery of a car with two bodies was a mistake, that the Search and Rescue divers had been mistaken, that no Mustang was submerged in tidal silt and the feathery tendrils of aquatic life. I wanted to discover that the cadaver dogs had picked up the decaying scent of a cow or some other livestock or that there were other blond teenagers, other black Mustangs . . . other boys with an arm that ended at the wrist.

But even as I tried to convince myself, I knew the truth. And while I wouldn't admit it even to myself, I knew what had happened. The nester had edged one fledgling from the nest.

I put on my old boots, the most comfortable shoes I owned, put the crutches in the back of the station wagon, and drove to the Paradise.

The scene came straight from hell. Red lights on the ambulance flashed like the spinning headache that smacked my forehead every few seconds. At least a dozen sheriff's cruisers, doors open and blue lights spiking, mingled with the yellow flashers of the massive wrecker backed up to the bayou.

Using the crutches, I made my way to the water's edge. Several deputies made to push me back, but Mark stopped them. He came over to me.

"You shouldn't be here."

"So I've been told." The morning was chill, but not cold. Even so, my teeth chattered, and I was reminded of the first day Annie came to Belle Fleur. She'd certainly changed from a trembling, skinny, unwanted child into a lush and voluptuous little vixen. Now I was the one shaking as if afflicted by an ague. "I've come to identify Margo's body. I don't want Bob to have to do that."

"You could do that at the morgue, after they've had a chance to clean her up some. Why not spare yourself this horror?"

"I want this behind us."

He stepped slightly away from me. "How did you end up at Bayou Abondant yesterday? I mean, your feet—" he pointed at them. "You shouldn't have been walking. What were you doing in the woods?"

He'd caught me unprepared. "I wanted to help."

"But why take the trail you took? How did you know?"

Now was a chance. "I saw Annie going that way yesterday. I wondered where she was going, so I decided to try and figure it out, while everyone else was with the search groups."

"Annie was with Bob and the others."

I steeled myself for the lie. "Part of the time, yes. But I saw her. Why else would I hobble around on my damaged feet? I wanted to see what she was up to."

"Up to?"

"I don't trust her. All of this started since she came into the house. I don't have any proof, only suspicions. I tried to tell Cora, but she won't listen." I shrugged. "Maybe I'm overreacting. I didn't find anything in the woods. I just fainted."

His gaze slid from me and I turned back to the water. A rubber-suited diver surfaced and lifted a hand. The winch on the wrecker began to turn, the thick twisted wire cable inching out of the water. Something large stirred beneath the surface.

The sheriff called to Mark, who gave me one last look of pity and walked away. I was glad he was gone. It would be hard enough to see this without having a witness to my reaction. But I would do this so Bob or Berta wouldn't have to.

The front of the car broke the water's dark surface. I was facing the driver's side, and as the passenger compartment came up, water gushed from the open window. Andrew Cargill's head, savaged by crabs and other aquatic creatures, flopped out the window. A moan escaped me.

No one heard me over the shriek of the cable as the wrecker slowly crawled forward and dragged the streaming car onto the bank. Ignoring the deputies, EMTs, firemen, and other curiosity-seekers, I walked to the passenger side.

Margo had floated out of her seat and resettled on the floorboard of the car. I looked inside and saw her, curled like a gray, decaying fetus. She wore her favorite blue jean shorts and a red blouse that she'd loved.

"Margo!" I reached out, but before I could try to touch her, Mark swept me away. He turned my face into his shirt, smelling of sweat and starch.

"It's Margo," I said. "And Andrew."

"I know, I know." He eased me back to the station wagon.

"I should. . . ." But I didn't know what I should do. What did one do with a body so badly decayed?

"Go back to Belle Fleur, Mimi. I'll come with you and tell the Hendersons."

I nodded mutely and let him put me in the passenger seat of the station wagon.

"Were they dead when they were put in the water?"

He didn't answer immediately. "It's hard to tell. The coroner will be able to help us with that."

"Berta will want to know everything."

"And so will the Cargills," he said. "As soon as we have information, I'm sure the sheriff will be in touch."

"Do you think you'll catch the person who killed them?"

We were fifty yards from the Mustang and he turned back to look at the car. Water seeped from it and the deputies and emergency workers stood around it, defeated by the bodies inside. In the cold gray morning light, it was an image of sadness.

"Water washes away a lot of evidence," Mark said. "The medical examiner is good at his job. Maybe he'll find something that will give us some leads."

"And if he doesn't?"

Mark put his arm around me and started walking back to the station wagon. "We'll do our best, Mimi. The sheriff's been in office a long time. He has a lot of experience, and the homicide detectives are good."

"But you are viewing it as a murder?"

He hesitated.

"Andrew didn't cut off his own hand, you know."

"That's a fact." He sighed. "I'll stop by Belle Fleur later today, maybe around eight or so. I have some questions for Annie. And I want to see how you're doing. I am so sorry, Mimi. I was wrong to criticize you for caring about this family. In the end, you were right to worry."

I touched his chest with the flat of my hand. "I'd better get home. You don't have to come. It would be better if I told Bob and Berta."

"Are you sure?"

"I'm positive. Let me handle this." I pulled the car keys from my pocket and limped back to the car. My feet throbbed with each beat of my heart. While I dreaded facing Bob and Berta, I was eager to get home. When I was gone from Belle Fleur too long, I grew anxious. The house sheltered me in a way I found impossible to explain to Mark or anyone else.

As I drove slowly along Shore Road, I let the sound of the water console me. Belle Fleur rose above the trees and I stopped to admire the gingerbread trim of the upper balconies, the ornamental shingles that decorated the eaves. Bob had painted them a darker yellow than the main body of the house. In the pale morning light of November, the house seemed to glow with an inner light. It was a beacon leading me toward home.

⚜

When I entered the house, I was struck by the silence. The narcotics I'd slipped into Berta's coffee had taken effect; she was soundly sleeping. Her bedroom door was shut, and I could hear nothing when I eavesdropped with an ear against the solid door. I wouldn't wake her.

A note on the kitchen counter told me Bob had gone to Mobile to meet with the medical examiner. It was obvious the sheriff had telephoned Bob, or maybe stopped by and told him. He, too, had decided not to wake Berta.

It was almost noon and Annie and the children still had not come home. Worry and frustration ate at me.

I put together sandwiches I knew no one would eat, as the routine actions made me feel useful, productive, in control. I thought about driving to Cora's, but I hesitated to do so. For some reason I felt I should stay close. If Berta was deeply asleep, she was vulnerable. To what, I didn't want to say. But I stayed in the kitchen, cleaning the refrigerator, then the oven, organizing the flatware drawer, taking inventory of the canned goods and glass jars of preserves we'd put up over the summer. There was enough food at Belle Fleur to see a family through several months. The thought was strangely comforting.

When the hall clock chimed one P.M., I climbed the stairs to the second floor. The slim possibility that somehow the children had slipped back in the house without my awareness sent me for another check.

Donald's room was empty. His toys were scattered about the floor, mixed with dirty clothes. In the past, Berta would have skinned him if she came up and found such disarray. But she wasn't coming up here any time soon. And I seriously doubted she'd fuss at her youngest. Loss took the starch out of discipline.

I moved down the hall to the end bedroom where Erin had been sleeping. The room was still a bit austere. She'd moved some of her books, but she'd left the blue-checked bedspreads on the twin beds in the room she'd shared with Margo. I detected Annie's influence in the bedspread striped in the colors of the sunset. Annie loved vibrant colors, and Erin was emulating her. But Erin had brought her stuffed animals and lined the room with teddy bears, carnival prizes Bob had won for her, princess dolls, and Breyer horses. Caught on the cusp of young adulthood, Erin still fell on the side of child at times.

While her room showed recent occupancy, there was no sign of Erin.

On the off chance she'd returned to her old room, I checked the bedroom she'd shared with her older sister. The beds were neatly made, and all of Margo's things were in place. Books, posters on the wall, stuffed animals, a radio and eight-track tape player, the things of vital importance to a teenager. All of this would have to be removed, and preferably before Berta came up here. It choked me up to think of her looking at this, these last reminders of the daughter she'd lost.

I closed the door and started to the third floor. Maybe they'd gone up the exterior stairs and slipped into Annie's room.

In the quiet of the house, I heard a sound like something being dragged. The hair on my arms stood at attention, and my foot faltered on the next rise. I listened intently, but there was only silence. My imagination was in overdrive. I'd taken only two steps when I heard it again—the distinctive sound of something being dragged along the upper hallway.

"Annie." I spoke softly because fear clamped my throat. The noise stopped. Whoever it was heard me.

"Annie." I whispered her name again.

There was only silence.

"Donald?" Surely he would answer. Donald was not a cruel child. The panic in my voice was clear. If this was a prank, he'd give in and respond. He would—if he could.

"Annie!" She could hear me. She was deliberately making it hard for me. "Annie!"

"An-nie!" My voice echoed back to me in perfect imitation followed by a giggle. It came from the third floor. The sound of nails clicking on the hardwood was distinct. "Mi-mi, let's play Hide and Go Seek."

Fear made my body clench. "Where are the children?" I asked.

"You're *it*!" The creature scuttled above me. The giggle came again, so sweet and innocent in the beginning but turning dark and smoky at the end. A child maturing into evil in the space of ten seconds.

"I want Donald and Erin right now."

"Find them, Mimi. Find them if you can."

The nester was on the third floor—had been in the house all morning. A thousand terrible images climbed through my brain. Had Bob really gone to Mobile? Was Berta merely sleeping? The creature had gained access to the house earlier. It had scratched on my door hours before, but I'd thought it had left. Now I had to find it, and quickly.

The third floor was smaller in size than the second or first. Part of it was under the eaves, so the walls angled in. A narrow hallway led down to the door of Annie's room, which was in the center of what must have once been an attic, until it was fitted out for Chloe's room. Chloe's prison. The story Chad Petri had told resurfaced in my mind. Horrible things had happened in Belle Fleur. I pretended they hadn't, but now I couldn't escape the past.

The hallway was empty, but that didn't mean anything. There were nooks and alcoves with windows that threw the pale November light on the carpet runner that went straight to Annie's door.

Steeling myself, I walked down the hallway, my feet pulsing with blood and pain.

The door was unlocked, and I pushed it open, half expecting the children to jump out and scare me. But this wasn't a game of hide and seek. This was deadly.

The wind gusted through the open windows, sending the material billowing all around the room like a mini-cyclone. If Annie and the children were in the room, they were completely quiet.

I heard something else. A whisper. A tickle of toenails on wood. A wallowing gurgle.

Moving deeper into the room, I followed the sound. It came from Annie's bathroom.

The door was closed. I pushed it open slowly. Water coursed into the tub in a strong jet, but no one was in the room. I entered, startling myself with my own reflection in the bathroom mirror. At first I didn't recognize the pale face with huge eyes.

The water in the bathtub was running full blast. Stumbling across the tile floor, I reached for the faucet and froze. Donald's pale face floated beneath the surface. He rested at the bottom of the tub as if he were asleep.

"Donald!" I didn't know what to do. "Oh, Donald!" I sank to my knees beside the tub. As I reached to pull his lifeless body from the water, his eyes blinked open. His lips drew back to reveal sharpened teeth.

He exploded out of the water, snapping his jaws together only an inch from my face. My reflex sent me hurtling backward into the

223

vanity, and my head struck with such force it stunned me and sent a cascade of cosmetics onto the floor.

The nester perched on the edge of the tub. "You found me, Mimi," it said before it leaped over me and disappeared into the swirling fabric in Annie's bedroom.

It took me a moment to find my breath. On my hands and knees, I gathered up the lipstick tubes, mascara wand, pressed powder, and blusher. I stood on shaky legs and tried to remember where the items had been on her vanity top. At last, I opened one of the drawers and tossed everything inside. She'd know I'd been in her room, but so what? What was she going to do, report me to the police?

I was about to close the drawer when I noticed a bill of sale from a jewelry store. Margo had talked incessantly about Ambri's Jewelry in the Bel Air Mall. She'd wanted a pair of opal earrings for her birthday, and she'd let everyone know.

Pulling the paper out, I read over the item that had been purchased. A silver spoon ring engraved with an M. Size six.

39

Standing on Annie's balcony, I watched for the children to emerge from the woods. Gut-wrenching worry and my encounter with the nester had left me numb. I'd drained the tub, dried the floor, and replaced the bill of sale in the drawer. No one would believe me, so the less said the better. The nester's intentions were clear, but efforts to make the adults understand would be futile.

I knew, and I was forewarned. I'd seen the creature stalking Donald along the edge of the Sound. Now I knew what it meant to do. There had been no forewarning for Margo. Her rash actions, in sneaking out of the house to meet Andrew, had given the nester an opportunity it had acted upon. Now she was dead, and if my presumptions were correct—and I knew they were—Donald was the next victim.

When I saw Donald's golden head bobbing along the path to the woods, I went downstairs to meet them. Berta slept, and she would not be awakened to the reality of Margo's death by Annie's careless laughter or the slamming of a door.

Erin was the first to spot me, and she stopped on the path. My face revealed everything—the death of her sister and the horror of Margo's final hours. I didn't have to tell them. Children are intuitive in that way. Erin burst into tears. Behind her, Donald, too, began to cry.

"*Someone* killed Margo and Andrew," I said. I had to frighten them enough to make them cautious. "I've been worried sick about both of you."

Annie put an arm around each of them and hugged them to her as she faced off with me. The faintest hint of a smile touched her lips. "You're cruel, Mimi," she said.

"Am I?" I only wished I could be half as cruel as she was. I would kill her in her sleep. *If* she slept. I wasn't certain she required the necessities of other humans, for I had come to believe Annie was more than human. She was something else entirely. It wouldn't surprise me to learn she could levitate or live without sleep or food. She was evil.

"What's wrong with you? You're standing there like you aren't going to let us in the house." Annie pointed at the door.

"I'm not going to let you rush into the house." My fists clenched and unclenched at my side. "Berta is asleep. She's about to have a breakdown over Margo's death. Bob has gone to Mobile. Don't slam into the house and wake Berta up."

"You're probably lying. It probably isn't Margo." Annie was defiant, and she hugged the children against her so they couldn't see the delight in her eyes.

"I saw her. It's Margo. She was in the passenger side of Andrew's car in the bayou by the hotel."

Erin's crying increased to a howl. Donald looked at me with confusion.

Huddling the children against her, Annie pressed forward, determined to get past me and into the house. "Come on," she said to the children, "Berta will tell us the truth."

"Don't wake Berta."

"Step aside." Annie's face flushed with anger. "There was no need to tell the children this way. Why do you want to hurt them like that?"

I grasped her arm and held it tightly. She'd gained weight, but her upper arm was still slim. "I know what you're up to, Annie. I intend to stop you."

Above the children's heads, she glared at me. "I don't know what's wrong with you, Mimi, but you're frightening the children. You're the one who'll be stopped." She shook free and herded the children into the house.

Once Donald and Erin were inside, she came back to the edge of the porch. "You're losing your grip on reality, and everyone sees it. Cora knows. Bob and Berta know. Even Mark can see it. You won't be here much longer if you don't stop acting like a freak." With that she closed the door, and I heard the lock click into place. She'd locked me out of Belle Fleur. But at least the children were safely home.

The keys to the station wagon were in my pocket. Berta would sleep another four hours or so. I didn't want to raise a ruckus by pounding to be let in, and I had time to drive to Pascagoula and talk with the private investigator. While Berta would no longer pay him— Margo was found—I'd saved my entire salary for months. Annie's secrets would be dug up. No matter the cost. She was practiced at this insidious infiltration of a family. It was probable she'd done this before, nesting in with people and then slowly destroying them from the inside. No wonder she had no memory. Very convenient.

I backed the station wagon onto the drive and headed to Jimmy Finch's office. His contacts in the sheriff's department would have let him know that Margo was found, but I didn't want him to lose a minute on the search for Annie's past.

Twenty minutes later I was sitting in a chair in his reception area. The woman who worked for him, a bottle blonde in her fifties, kept glancing at me as if she feared I would bite her. I went in the restroom to discover my hair was wild and my eyes ringed by dark circles. I looked like an addict coming off some kind of drug high.

I dashed cold water on my face and used wet fingers to comb my hair into a semblance of order. I seldom wore make-up, but I wished for some foundation to even my skin tone, which looked splotchy. When I'd done the best I could, I went back to the reception area to wait.

Finch's office was utilitarian, but it was clean. And Sarah Waters, his receptionist with a nameplate on her desk, typed with great efficiency. When Finch's door finally opened, a middle-aged man, his face strained with tension, raced out of the office without a glance to either side. Unhappy husband was my guess.

"Mimi," he said, coming to me. "I'm so sorry to hear about Margo."

"I know."

"There was no point coming here. You could have called. Mrs. Henderson can settle her bill whenever she feels better."

I cleared my throat. "We want you—I want you to continue with the other aspect of this."

He motioned me into his inner office and closed the door behind me. "Let's talk about this."

When I was seated in front of his desk, he sat on the edge. His green eyes studied me. "I've really turned over every rock I can," he said. "To continue with this would be unfair. I'd be taking your money for nothing. I've checked everywhere, and there simply is no one looking for Annie. There's no record of her birth that I can find."

I leaned forward. "Don't you find that strange?"

"I do. But that doesn't mean I can solve it. I know private investigators don't have the best reputation, but I can't continue to take your money when I don't have a reasonable expectation of finding a result for you."

His attempts to be kind only annoyed me. He didn't understand what was happening at the Hendersons. Unlocking Annie's secrets was the key to safeguarding Donald and Erin, and even Berta and Bob.

"I found a bill of sale in Annie bathroom for a ring, a spoon ring with an M engraved, like the one found on the severed hand."

That gave him pause. "Why wouldn't she say so?"

I didn't answer. It was best for him to draw his own conclusions. "There's one other avenue to check, and I realize it's going to sound very strange." I gave him my best smile to show I understood I was about to make an irrational statement. I began to recount the tale I'd concocted as I drove to his office. "Annie was telling a story to the children, and it involved the death of a family, one by one. It started with the children." I paused and let him put it together.

His eyebrows slowly rose on his forehead. "You think it wasn't made up. You think this teenage girl who couldn't weigh a hundred and twenty pounds killed members of her family?"

"I don't know. I don't. But if it happened once, it could be happening again. Margo was determined to push Annie out of Belle Fleur." My voice started to shake and I clamped down on my emotions. One hint of instability and Finch would back away. "I understand this sounds nutty, but, Mr. Finch, I had to come and talk to you. What if I'm right and I ignored it? What if something happens to another one of the Hendersons because I didn't do everything I could to check Annie out?" I put my hand on his wrist. "I couldn't live with myself if I didn't try everything. You should know, I'm paying for this. Not Berta. It means that much to me."

He eyed me as he considered my words. "You honestly believe that kid could kill?"

I slowly shook my head to show my own puzzlement. "I don't know. But what if she can? What if she did? I'd go mad if she hurt someone else and I hadn't at least tried to stop her."

He stood. "Okay. I'll check for families with unusual deaths." He went behind his desk and sat down. Pulling a pad from a drawer, he started to make some notes. "Do you have any idea where to start? Has she ever mentioned a place or person?"

"Not one single one. She's perfected the amnesia act."

He tapped the pencil on his pad. "Can you help me with this?"

"I can try."

"Find that suitcase she arrived with. Check it thoroughly. If she keeps a dairy, read through it. Can you do that without getting caught?"

I kept my face solemn. "I can."

"As soon as possible. This will give us a starting place."

"Thank you, Mr. Finch." I stood up and pulled the cash I'd withdrawn from my checking account out of my purse. I handed it to him. "When I owe more, let me know."

The heft of the envelope told him it was not an insignificant amount, half my savings. I was at the door when he stopped me.

"Mimi, I did check into Belle Fleur. Like you asked. The house was sold by a corporation, Trident Inc."

I thought a moment. "I've never heard of that. There's Azalea Realty and Skinners here in Coden. They're the only two."

"A strange fact. I checked with the local real estate agencies, and they'd never heard of Trident. Neither real estate agency knew Belle Fleur was up for sale. The house had been empty for decades, so it never occurred to them it might be a property they could list. It wasn't until Bob and his renovation crew arrived that they considered the opportunity they'd lost."

"So how did Bob learn about the property?"

"I'm working on that." Finch pulled his cigarettes from his jacket pocket and extended them to me. I knew I shouldn't, but I took one. My nerves were shot. "Trident is supposedly based in Montgomery."

"Did you check?" I leaned forward to accept his light and inhaled deeply.

"I did. I can't find a phone listing for them anywhere in the state. They're a blind corporation, a front for someone."

My mouth went dry. "What does that mean?"

"I'm not sure, but it is curious. I'll give you that."

"Keep looking."

For the first time he smiled. "Oh, I intend to. This has piqued my interest. I don't believe you have a murdering sixteen-year-old at Belle Fleur, but I have to admit, something strange is going on. Cargill's severed hand, the hidden company owning Belle Fleur, how the Hendersons, living in Cambria, California, and with no connection whatsoever to Coden, became aware of the property for sale. I'm still trying to track it down. And I will. Trust me."

For the first time in weeks I felt a ray of hope. Jimmy Finch was on my side. I had someone to help me get to the bottom of what was happening before anyone else was harmed. I stubbed out my cigarette and walked out the door.

40

The visit to Finch had taken only two hours, so I turned down the tree-shaded drive to Cora's. The horror of Margo's death would have reached her ears by now. Cora had many sources in Coden, and she was seldom without the latest news. Her roots ran deep, like her love of the community. She would be crushed by what happened to Margo, but my trip there was twofold. I wanted to check on Cora and also to try, once again, to probe her for any secrets about Annie. Or at least to try to understand why Cora was so emotionally invested in a sixteen-year-old girl who appeared on a downtown Mobile street. What was it about Annie that had rendered Cora so totally under her spell?

I considered telling her about the ring with the engraved M, but I realized the sales receipt proved nothing except that Annie had not told the truth about the ring. And based on past reactions, Cora would only say Annie was trying to spare Berta and Bob. I would stay quiet until I had more proof.

I'd never thought the day would come when I'd view my own grandmother as an obstacle in my path. It was only that her heart was too soft for girls like Annie, and perhaps this was the answer I sought. Cora helped girls who hadn't had the chances I'd had, waifs desperately seeking love. Those female children were her weakness, and Annie was the most needy of all.

She simply didn't see the danger.

Cora's car wasn't in the driveway when I pulled up. She never locked her door, so I went in and walked automatically to the refrigerator. I hadn't eaten all day, and my stomach churned with emptiness and emotion. I found a chocolate pie, my favorite, and sat down at the table to eat a piece. Unless she was working, Cora was never gone for long. I'd wait an hour, and if she wasn't back by then, I'd leave her a note.

I'd taken only two bites of pie when I heard a car pulling in. Glancing out the kitchen window, I saw my grandmother. She got out of her car and stared at the station wagon as if it were a spaceship. When she glanced toward her house, her face held tension and stress. I lowered the fork and went to the front door to greet her.

"Mimi," she said, coming slowly up the steps. It seemed she'd aged a decade since the last time I saw her. "I heard about Margo. What a tragedy. What a nightmare. Poor Berta."

"And Bob," I said, wiping the stickiness of the meringue from the side of my mouth. "I don't know what they're going to do."

She came to me and wrapped her arms around me. "Honey, they'll cry and grieve, and then they'll begin to live again. Same as we all do when tragedy takes our loved ones. Same as you'll do. I know Margo pushed your limits at times, but I also know you'd grown to love her."

The tears caught me by surprise. I'd been so focused on saving Donald, on stopping Annie, that I'd failed to fully grasp that Margo would never return to Belle Fleur. She was dead and gone. I would never again hear her laughter, or suffer her gentle teasing, or witness her beauty parlor sessions where she practiced putting on different styles of make-up. There would be no more gossip about what television shows were good, no door-slamming complaints about curfews or studies. Leaning against Cora's ample shoulder, I cried with abandon for all I'd lost.

When I was a child, Cora soothed away my tears, and she did so now. Holding me close, she helped me into the kitchen. When I was at the table, sobbing into my arms, she put on a pot of coffee and rubbed my shoulders while it brewed.

"Oh, Mimi," she said. "You've been so strong for the Hendersons." She kissed the back of my head and combed through my hair with her fingers until she had the tangles out. I felt her begin to braid it, a ritual that always served to calm me. "Come home for a week and let me take care of you."

The offer was too tempting. What a relief it would be to walk out the door of Belle Fleur and not think about Annie or the nester or what might happen next. "I can't." I spoke with more force than I intended. "It would be awful to leave Berta now," I said in a softer tone. "There's no one to help her and Bob."

"It isn't your responsibility," she told me as her fingers worked my long hair. "You've taken on too much at Belle Fleur. You're practically a child yourself."

"I feel I have a duty to the family." Here was the opportunity, the moment perfectly formed. "Someone murdered Margo. What if they come after the other children?"

Cora dropped the long dark braid over my shoulder. The ends were untied and it slowly began to unravel. "I think drugs were at the bottom of what happened to Margo and Andrew. There's no reason for anyone to harm the smaller children."

"What if it wasn't drugs?" I turned sideways in my chair so I could face her. Her gaze slid from me to the floor.

"What else would it be, Mimi? Margo was high-handed sometimes, but that's not really a reason for anyone to kill her. It had to be Andrew they were after. They cut off his hand. Margo just got in the way."

She wanted to believe what she said. I wished I could. "What if it's someone from Annie's past?"

Tears filled Cora's eyes. "What are you saying?" She put a hand on my cheek and turned my face up so that our gazes met. "What are you implying?"

"Annie isn't who she says she is. She's something . . . more."

The first tear oozed out of Cora's right eye. It tracked down her cheek, through the powder she applied so carefully, to the corner of her lip. "Oh, Mimi." She pressed my face into her stomach. The scent of Evening in Paris filled my nostrils, and for a split second I was small and safe against her.

I let her comfort me, her body trembling with her own tears. When I pushed back, she hesitated before she stepped away. "Honey, it isn't Annie. She isn't a threat to that family."

"She wants Bob. I told you—"

"I asked her. She denies it, Mimi. I confronted Bob, too."

I felt betrayed. "You told him I said he'd screwed Annie?"

She shook her head. "I asked him if Annie had behaved inappropriately, if there was any reason I should find another home for her. He assured me she was not a problem." She touched my cheek. "He's worried about you. He says you're always up and guarding the house, going off into the woods, hurting yourself."

Somehow it had all been turned around. Fighting it was pointless. Annie lied and everyone lined up to believe her. "One day you'll discover that I'm right. Annie is a threat to everyone."

Cora started to embrace me, but I ducked her arms. "I'd really hoped you and Annie would hit it off. I wanted you to help her. She has no one else."

"Annie isn't my concern. I care about the Hendersons, and so should you. Everything bad started to happen after she came."

Cora didn't deny that. "I know Margo felt Annie was an intruder. I tried to persuade Bob not to give Annie the third floor. It felt wrong. Margo wanted that room. She'd pinned her dreams on having it." Cora sipped her coffee. "Margo was jealous of Annie, that's true. Berta was aware of it, but she felt her children had all the benefits. Annie had none."

"She scares Donald and Erin. There's a darkness in her, Cora."

My grandmother didn't disagree. "There is. I see it, Mimi. The loneliness, the way she tends to stay by herself in her room. Children who grow up hard are often afflicted with depression and an attraction to the dark elements of life. But living with the Hendersons could impact that positively. That's why I worked so hard to get her there."

But what about me? I wanted to ask her. Did you consider how this would affect me? But I didn't say it. "What if she impacts them negatively?"

Cora pushed the piece of pie I'd ignored toward me. "Eat something, Mimi. You're too pale and too thin."

Obediently I forked a bite into my mouth.

"How could Annie, a sixteen-year-old girl, negatively impact this family? Think about what you're saying, Mimi."

I had to keep it solid, factual. "Someone followed her to Belle Fleur. I've seen her."

"This is the stranger you saw and Mark went to check on. He said he didn't find anything."

My heart pounded in my chest. "Not anything human."

Sadness touched her face. "What's that supposed to mean?" She came around the table to me. Her hands, the skin so smooth because of her age, pressed both of my cheeks. "Mimi, I'm worried about you. Not human? That sounds . . . crazy."

I'd taken it one step too far, time to retrench. "Annie's friend was in the yard the night Margo disappeared, I don't care what Mark or anyone else says. Donald saw her, too. I'm not saying Annie is responsible. Maybe it's just a person who followed her. Maybe Annie's in danger, too. Maybe we all are."

"Donald is susceptible to ghost stories and spooky talk. He's a child. But you're twenty-one, Mimi. You have to think before you make accusations. What you're accusing Annie of is serious. That she has intentions to harm people."

"Next time you're having a chat with her, ask her about the spoon ring with the engraved M. Just ask her. She bought it for Margo and she lied about it." I flung that fact at her like a gauntlet.

"I will ask her."

I stood up. "I have to get back to the Hendersons." Anger throbbed in my temples. Annie had wormed her way into Cora's confidence, and nothing I said now would make any difference. Cora might act like she was listening, but she didn't believe anything I said.

"Stay the night here, Mimi. Like the old days."

"I feel I should be at Belle Fleur."

"I need you, too."

"No, I don't think you do. Not the way Berta and the children do." I had no proof, nothing I could show her. I left the pie unfinished and the coffee barely sipped. I walked out of the house to the front lawn.

Cora followed to the screened door, where she stopped. "Mimi, please stay with me."

"Call Annie." I couldn't help the bitterness.

"Oh, child," she said, "it isn't like you think at all. I haven't chosen Annie over you."

"But you have," I told her. "And maybe Bob and Berta have too. Maybe it's time for me to leave Belle Fleur and Coden and get a teaching job somewhere else." For a moment freedom opened to me like a shot of silver light from a cloud.

Cora came out on the porch, the screen banging behind her. "Come in and let's talk about it."

"Another time. But when Annie does something terrible, don't say I didn't warn you and everyone else." I got in the car and slammed the door. Berta would be waking at Belle Fleur. Bob might be back, but if he wasn't, Berta and the children were alone. I wasn't sure how far Annie would push to have exactly what she wanted.

41

Bob's car was in the garage when I pulled up to the house. The day was overcast, and the yellow paint of Belle Fleur had taken on a sickly cast in the storm light. The front door was unlocked when I turned the knob. I went inside, closed the door softly, and listened. There was only the ticking of the hall clock. The house yielded no secrets about its occupants.

Belle Fleur. Home of the Desmarais family.

I walked into the parlor and couldn't help but notice the blood hues trapped in the plush puddling of the velvet draperies. The hand-carved sofa, also highlighted in carmine, was original with the house. Berta had planned the décor of the room around the brocade upholstery—she'd been so pleased to find some of the original pieces. Cora had known exactly where to look.

I thought about calling my grandmother and asking her about Trident, but something held me back. Guilt was part of it. I'd worried Cora, and I'd been happy when I did. But there was also distrust. Cora knew more about Annie than she'd let on. A lot more. It stood to reason she knew more about Belle Fleur. She'd withheld the facts from me, and while I presumed her reasons were innocent, doubt niggled at me.

All of my life I'd been painted a picture of this house as the cultural center of the town, of a place where locals had found employment in the most beautiful of places—flower gardens filled with exotic blooms and heavenly scents. Belle Fleur had represented an ideal. The Desmarais family had been held up for admiration, and then pity at the young death of their only child. It had all been a fabrication, a complete lie.

If Chad Petri were to be believed, horrible things happened in this house. A young girl had been held prisoner, her infant thrown into a well and left to die. The idea of it made my throat catch. Cora had to know the true history, yet she and everyone else in town had buried it.

From the parlor I went to the den. Bob had modernized this room with a television and leather sofas and two recliners. A fire had been laid but remained unlit. The past didn't reside as heavily here; there was more comfort and less coldness. From the den a hallway led to Bob and Berta's room. I went to the door, careful not to betray my presence by stepping on a squeaky board. Pressing my ear to the wood, I listened.

Silence.

Berta remained asleep, and I hoped Bob was curled beside her, holding her against the grief and loss. He'd betrayed her with Annie, but I knew how manipulative Annie could be. I wasn't excusing him, but I also knew he was the backbone of the family. He was Berta's strength, the core of stability that gave Erin her confidence and Donald his humor. My job was to see that Annie never again had a chance to get her hooks into him, because I no longer doubted it was her goal to have him for herself.

Easing away from the door, I went to the back staircase—poorly lit with steeper stairs and narrower treads. Normally I avoided it because it was steep and dangerous. Sigourney's theory, I supposed, was that if a servant broke her neck, she would be easy enough to replace. Today, I wanted to move to the upper levels without being seen. I wanted to know what Annie was up to so I could search her room and plunder through the suitcase she'd brought into Belle Fleur.

For a moment I paused on the landing of the second floor. The main staircase split the floor in the middle, but I was at the far south end of the hall. My room was across from the stairs. Erin's was nearest the servants' stairs. Donald's at the far end of the hall. Not a sound came from any of the rooms.

I was ready to move up to the third floor when the door to Margo's old room slowly creaked open. "Come in, if you dare," it seemed to say.

My ribs ached from the pressure of the fear that swept over me. My impulse was to run downstairs and out of the house. To keep running until I was back at Cora's. Light from a beautiful stained-glass window colored the hall in fragments of green, red, yellow, and blue.

From the third floor, Donald's sweet voice came to me as he sang "Stop and Smell the Roses." He was obsessed with Mac Davis. Relief touched me. It was only a draft that had blown open the door to Margo's room.

I put a foot on the tread to go upstairs to Donald when the door to Margo's room shut. Softly. As if someone had closed it. Maybe Erin had gone there to mourn her sister. To remember their time shared in a fine room in a new home with the future before them. She would be heartbroken.

Since Donald was okay, I walked down the hall toward Margo's room. The thick carpet absorbed the sound of my footsteps. When I got to the door, I tapped lightly.

"Come in," Erin said.

I stepped through the door into gloom. Erin had closed the curtains, and the day outside was gray to begin with. Margo's bed was tumbled but empty. Erin's bed was neatly made. Erin was in the room, but in the dim light I couldn't spot her.

"Erin, where's Annie?"

"I don't know." Her voice came from a dark corner of the room. She sounded empty, hollow.

"I know how upset you must be. I'm so sorry." I could take a moment from my quest to comfort her. When she didn't answer, I stepped fully into the room and closed the door. I caught a whiff of a peculiar odor. Sweet, but sickly. Rancid. I inhaled. "Erin?"

The room was completely silent.

Anger began to burn. "Erin! Stop doing this. Where are you?"

The branch of a tree outside the window raked across the screen. The sound was like ice down my spine. "Erin!"

I went to the curtains and pushed them back. When I looked down into the front yard, my heart almost stopped. Annie, Donald, and Erin were sitting down by the water. Erin wore her favorite navy coat, and Donald was bundled in a gray windbreaker, a cap on his head against the cold stormy wind. Annie's hair billowed around her, a cloud of dark curls that the wind caught and tossed.

Around me the odor became stifling, nauseating. I started back to the door, but it grew stronger. I moved slowly to Margo's bed. My hand shook as I found the covers and pulled them back. Weeds and muck from the bottom of the bayou smeared the sheets, as if something dragged from the bottom of deep water had lain on the bed. My hand trembled as I reached toward the debris.

"What the hell are you doing, Mimi? Where have you been? Bob's looking for you." Annie stood in the doorway.

Her unexpected appearance almost made me scream. I stopped myself. "I had some errands to run." I struggled to regain my composure. She'd frightened me, and I didn't want her to see the dirty sheets. I started toward the door.

"You'd better have a good explanation. Bob's upset. You're just making more trouble for yourself." She leaned closer to me. "You can't best me. You shouldn't try."

I pushed past her and went into the hall. "Have the children eaten?"

"I gave them the sandwiches you'd made. I'm making soup for Berta. She has to eat."

Good luck with that, I thought, but I didn't say anything. Once Annie was busy in the kitchen, I would snoop. And I would have her out of that house before Thanksgiving. But I had to be very careful how I handled myself. Annie was smart. More than smart, she was cunning. And if I became an impediment, she would do whatever it took to remove me.

"I'll help you chop vegetables for the soup," I said. "Berta does need to eat. And the children, too." I smiled at her and thought how I, too, could play the wolf. The game had changed, but I couldn't let her know it.

⁂

Night had fallen when Bob gathered us around the kitchen table. I hadn't had a chance to explore Annie's room, but I hadn't given up. Now, we sat at the table, all except Berta, who refused to leave her room. "We've agreed on the funeral arrangements," Bob said. "We'll have a service Thursday at St. Mary's by the Sea." His voice wavered, and he put a hand over his eyes for a moment as he composed himself. "The burial will be here, in the cemetery. Tomorrow I've arranged for someone to come out and repair the broken angel."

"I thought we'd go back to California." Erin looked shocked. "Mother wants to bury Margo here? What if we move away? What if we go home? She'll be here alone."

I got up and went to the sink. I couldn't bear this.

Bob pressed her against him. "This is our home now," he said. "What happened to Margo is a tragedy, but it could have happened in California or Maine as well as here. We aren't leaving Coden, Erin."

"I don't want to stay here. I don't! Someone *murdered* my sister!" Her howl echoed off the red walls of the kitchen. A place I'd always viewed as so homey and safe now held only pain.

"We can't just pack up and leave, Erin. I've put everything we own into this house, into building my reputation here. Alabama is our home now."

Erin pushed away from him with a violent surge. "I hate this place. And I hate *you*." She ran out of the room, and I heard her footsteps pounding on the stairs.

Donald remained at the table, large tears rolling down his face. I went to him and put my arm around him. "Erin's just upset. This is an awful thing." I ruffled his hair.

"I'm sorry," Bob said. "Berta is upset, too. She doesn't understand that we can't just leave."

"It wouldn't matter if you were here or in California," Annie said. "She would be upset. We all are. What can I do?"

Bob shook his head. "I wish I knew."

I'd never seen him so defeated. I had to keep a sharp eye on Annie. He was prime pickings now—an angry, grieving wife, children who were mad at him, his own grief swamping him like a tidal wave. Oh, Annie could smell the opportunity.

42

Storm clouds massed behind Father Lorett, the Episcopal priest from St. Mary's. In contrast to the mores of Coden, Bob and Berta had opted for a graveside service. Their decision had caused gossip to fly around the community, but Cora had quelled most of it—a child dead for months, submerged in water, it was best to conclude the service as quickly and quietly as possible. There was only so much loving parents could bear. Still, the lack of a wake and funeral service in a church drew a stark contrast between the Hendersons and the rest of Coden.

"Let us pray," Father Lorett said.

I gazed through my eyelashes at the handful of mourners. The family, Cora, Annie, me, and Andrew Cargill's family, who stood in a corner of the cemetery, paying respect but not intruding.

Margo's coffin, a sleek bronze, rested on the frame over the open grave. The mound of dirt was covered by a green carpet.

Wind whipped off the water and blew the priest's black robes around his legs. The pages of his Book of Common Prayer fluttered, and he glanced up from the service for a moment. The storm was bearing down on us. Dead leaves blasted across the small cemetery, and a sob tore from Berta's throat.

"Ashes to ashes, dust to dust, we return our daughter, Margo, to the ground from which she came." Father Lorett concluded the funeral service. The mechanical lift slowly lowered the coffin into the ground.

Unable to watch, I assessed the clouds. The storm had been building for a week, and with each passing hour, the day grew darker and heavier. Though it was 11 A.M., it was as dark as twilight.

Berta sobbed against Bob's shoulder, and Donald clung to his mother's other side. Erin stood alone, still angry at the indignity of burying her sister in foreign soil. I hung back, finding a spot beside the wrought-iron railing of the small cemetery. Cora stood with me.

Mrs. Cargill cried silently into a handkerchief, her remaining children beside her, stoic and dry-eyed. Andrew's funeral, a less formal Baptist service, had been conducted the day before. It had been an orgy of grief and emotion, so different from this bitter calm ritual. Bob, Cora, and I had attended, but Berta couldn't bring herself to go, which was a good thing. And I'd made sure Annie remained with Erin and Donald, though constant worry for their safety nagged at me.

When the coffin was in the ground, each family member walked forward to throw a pale yellow rose. Bob tossed in the first dirt. And then it was done.

"Please join us at the house," Bob said.

Supporting Berta, he led the way out of the cemetery. I lagged behind, and when everyone else was gone, I knelt by the open grave. "I'll find out who did this, Margo. I will."

Movement near the gate almost made me cry out, but it was just old Junior Motes and Abraham Leggin, the gravediggers. They'd been hiding out of sight until the service was finished. I had no doubt they'd been told to cover the coffin as fast as possible. The open grave would be like a wound to Bob and Berta. Best to get it covered and the sod put back in place.

I'd found out from the funeral director that Bob had commissioned an arch decorated with butterflies and ivy for Margo. It would rival

Sigourney's angel, which had been repaired. I was tempted to push the angel over, to destroy the last monument to Sigourney's power, but it wasn't my place to do so.

Dead leaves crunched beneath my feet as I walked back to the house. I dreaded the social convention of the funeral feast. To me, it was macabre to shovel food down my gullet in response to death, but in Coden it was how the community showed support. Casseroles, pies, fried chicken, and cakes—handmade goods showed caring hearts— had been arriving for two days.

While people had respected Berta's wishes for a private ceremony, they'd gathered at the house. I understood the kind impulse behind the act, but I also knew it was the last thing Berta should have to endure.

When I walked up on the front porch, I was surprised to see the sheriff and Mark standing awkwardly in their uniforms. Mark's face brightened when he saw me.

"Mimi." Mark came down the steps two at a time and pulled me into an easy embrace. "You okay? We didn't want to intrude on the service."

I stiffened and he released me. "Why are you here? Do you have a lead?" They'd both been at Andrew's funeral the day before—along with most of the town. Andrew had been a bad boy, but apparently a damn good mechanic. He'd worked on the cars and trucks of half the people of Coden.

"We came to pay our respects. I'm sorrier than I can say that it turned out this way."

"Mark, how did Margo die?" No one had told me and I couldn't ask Bob. I couldn't. "Did she drown?"

He glanced at the sheriff, who nodded. "Her neck was broken, Mimi. At least it was quick. Andrew wasn't so lucky. He bled to death."

"Are there any new leads?"

Mark grimly shook his head.

I hid my disappointment behind a smile. "Come inside and get something to eat. There's enough food to feed the town."

"Thank you. We'll be inside in a minute."

I walked past him and into the house. Cora had taken over as hostess, and Berta, who had been given a sedative by Dr. Adams, sat in a straight-backed chair, her eyes glassy, her breathing shallow. This whole funeral feast was a cruelty. I started to go to her, to help her to her room, but Bob lightly grasped my arm.

"She's okay," he said. "If she goes back in that room, she'll want to stay forever."

He was right. "I'll sit with her."

"If you could help Cora. She's doing everything."

"Sure." I glanced around for Annie, but I didn't see her. She had perfected the art of disappearing when she was needed. In front of Bob and Berta, Annie was so earnest and helpful. The minute their backs were turned, poof, she was gone. But her days in the bosom of the Henderson family were numbered. I intended to see to that.

For two hours, I brewed and served coffee, collected dirty plates and saucers, washed and dried dishes for the next round. Cora shaped the facts about Margo's death as she spoke with everyone.

"She'd fallen in love with Andrew," Cora told Mrs. Baker, one of the town's gossips. "Bob and Berta felt she was too young, but Andrew was a hard-working young man. No one is certain exactly what happened. They went on a date, to the movies in Mobile. Apparently they never got there."

"Who would kill two teenagers?" Mrs. Baker asked, a rhetorical question since she knew the cops had uncovered no leads.

"We don't know. It could have been someone passing through, someone drawn to the Moonies but not involved with them—the sheriff has checked that angle thoroughly and found no reason to suspect any involvement by the Unification Church."

I poured coffee and listened to Cora's spin. Obviously she and Bob had decided to put to rest the rumors that Andrew had abducted Margo or unduly influenced her. Or harmed her. Which didn't seem likely, since he was the one missing a hand, not her.

All suspicions where thrown on a "stranger wandering into the community."

Well, they were partially right. But Annie hadn't wandered in, she'd been brought in by my grandmother. Cora simply refused to visit the idea that Annie was behind anything bad.

"Where are Donald and Erin?" I asked Cora when I hadn't seen them for several hours.

"Annie took them over to my house. We felt it would be easier for them."

"That's not a good idea." Coffee slopped over the top of a cup as I poured. My hands shook. "I should go get the children."

"No need for them to stand around here. Funeral feasts are hard on youngsters. They're better off at my house."

But not with Annie. I simply couldn't make Cora understand the danger. "I think they should come home and get some rest. Berta needs their support."

"Berta is going to have a hard time of it. "

"She hates it here. I heard her telling Bob."

Cora sighed and patted my arm. "I know, honey. She wants to leave here. She thinks California is a place where nothing bad will happen. She's scared. It's important that you help her feel safe in Coden. Don't make it worse by pointing blame at Annie. Let things settle. I told Annie to bring the children home by six. If they aren't here, then we'll worry."

I didn't trust Annie with the children, but I couldn't do a thing about it. Until the adults believed me, Annie was sacrosanct.

"Do you think the Hendersons will leave Belle Fleur?" I almost couldn't bear the idea, though I understood Berta and Erin wanting to leave.

"Bob has put his heart into this house. Leaving now would mean financial ruin for him, especially since he got that renovation job on the Bienville Hotel in Mobile. And he's got backers to begin work on the Paradise. That's a lot of money, and he can't do the work here and live in California."

"My head is splitting wide open. I'm going upstairs for a few minutes." The majority of guests had departed. Only a few diehards remained, and Cora could easily manage them. Annie was out of the house for at least another half hour. Now was my opportunity to search her room.

"I can finish this, Mimi. You were a tremendous help. Bob and Berta are lucky to have you here with them. They know that. But I worry for you. Maybe this weekend you can come home for a night or two. I want to pamper you and give you some time to grieve. You've had to be the strong one, the one everyone else looks to. Even rocks get worn down and need a respite."

Cora knew exactly how to comfort me. "I'd like that. If Berta is better, I will."

I was halfway up the stairs when Chad Petri came in the front door. He looked stronger, better nourished than the last time I'd seen him. He stopped at the parlor and looked around, and not with happiness. The house had awakened unpleasant memories for him.

Even though I wanted to search Annie's room, I sat on the stairs. Chad was not a friend of the Hendersons, nor of Belle Fleur. Cora went to him immediately, and I could tell by her expression that she was upset.

"I intend to tell them," Chad said. "They deserve to know."

Cora grasped his arm firmly and moved him away from Berta and Bob, who hadn't noticed Chad enter. "Calm down, Chad," Cora said. "This isn't the time or place."

"That girl is dead. The boy too. It's this house, Cora. It never should have been opened up again. You know that as well as I. You've always believed Belle Fleur would bring Coden back to life, but I know it won't. The only thing that happens in this house is death and suffering."

Cora almost dragged Chad back into the kitchen. The door shut, and though I could hear their voices, I couldn't understand what was being said. I'd caught the gist of it. I didn't need to hear any more, and my opportunity was slipping away.

I hurried up the stairs past the second floor and on to the third. If there was anything like a diary or journal to tell who Annie really was and how she was connected to Belle Fleur, I intended to have it in my hands before Annie returned.

43

The old suitcase was stowed in the very top of her closet, covered with a comforter and blankets. It looked to me as if she'd attempted to hide it. Taking care to remove everything so I could put it back exactly as it was, I finally dragged the suitcase down, surprised at the heaviness. She hadn't arrived with much, but it felt as if she'd weighted the thing with bricks.

Before I opened it, I checked the road from both the front and back balconies of Annie's room. There was no sign of her. I had to search quickly and thoroughly and put everything back.

The suitcase had a lock, but it was flimsy, and I used a bobby pin to wiggle it open. When I lifted the lid, an old smell escaped, as if the past had been trapped there by some magic and I'd finally released it.

I removed some of Annie's clothes—things she hadn't worn since she got to Belle Fleur. In the months she'd been in residence, Berta had taken her shopping in Mobile on several occasions for new jeans and tops. Beneath the clothes was a jewelry case. I opened it and found some trinkets of costume jewelry and what appeared to be a pearl necklace. Jewelry wasn't my forte, but the necklace looked real. The pearls were a creamy white and when I tried them on, they glowed against my skin. Where had Annie gotten pearls?

I was tempted to take them to Jimmy Finch, but I couldn't risk Annie looking for them and finding them gone. I'd describe them as best I could, and perhaps he could find out something. Maybe she'd stolen them from her previous family. I put the jewelry case away and dug deeper. At the bottom of the suitcase was a photo album so old the pages were crumbling.

So, little orphan Annie who claimed to have no knowledge of her past was stupid enough to drag a photo album with her. I should have thought to look in the suitcase long before now. Margo might still be alive if I'd routed Annie when I first began to suspect what she was up to.

I carried the album to the window and sat down in an old rocker to examine it. The overcast day was almost too dim, but I didn't want to turn on a light. If Annie walked home through the woods, she'd be able to see it and know someone was in her room. I made do with the natural light and opened the crumbling cover. There was no name, no markings, no indication of where the photos came from.

On the first page, I recognized Belle Fleur. The photo was taken in the mid-1800s when Belle Fleur was brand new, a sparkling white gem of a house with new camellias and azaleas—only two feet high. The oaks, a grove of young trees, shaded the front lawn where a family sat in straight-backed chairs. A man, a woman, and a young girl. The Desmarais family. I couldn't determine the details of their features, but I knew them. The photo was so old, it was a tintype.

I flipped the page, and stopped at a picture of boats docked in the small Coden harbor. Same era. I moved through the photo album, amazed that Annie had found a history of Coden that no one else could produce. Where had she gotten the album?

Why had she arrived with it?

How did she know she would come to live in Belle Fleur? Cora said she found her wandering the streets of Mobile and within days, Annie was with the Hendersons. How had she found these pictures, this album in that length of time? Or had she had it all along, had she come to Mobile, sought out Cora, and manipulated her to get to the Hendersons and Belle Fleur?

I continued through the album that captured Belle Fleur at the beginning, a jewel in the heart of lower Alabama. The house built on the hope of Henri Desmarais. The house that had become a prison, and finally the home to a new family.

The last photograph in the book was a portrait of Sigourney. Though there wasn't a name, I knew her. She'd once been beautiful, but there was darkness and cruelty in her eyes and the set of her lips. Haughty defined her, and ruthless also came to mind.

Closing the book, I glanced out the window and jumped to my feet. Annie and the children were coming across the front lawn. They were only moments away. I jammed the album in her suitcase, put in the jewelry case and her clothes and shut it. Heaving it into the top of the closet, I put the comforter and covers on top and closed the closet door. I darted into the hallway, closed her door and made it to the servants' staircase as she and the children came up the main staircase. By a matter of seconds, I escaped detection.

And I'd escaped with a better than average lead. Wherever Annie came from, she'd studied Belle Fleur and its history. Not library research, but she'd found original source material. Things like that could only have come from a family descendant or from someone who'd known and been a confidante of the Desmarais family. Another possibility was like a punch. Maybe Chloe hadn't died, as Annie had noted that day in the cemetery at Chloe's grave. Maybe her baby had lived. Maybe Sigourney and Henri had another child.

I slumped to the wooden treads of the back staircase. The constant coming and going of servants had worn the wood so it was slightly cupped. Hidden in the shadows there, I calmed myself.

As I thought through Annie's arrival and all that had happened, I faced the fact that my own grandmother had been manipulated by a very smart teenager. Cora's tender heart had been played, and in a way that was much, much darker than I'd anticipated. Annie had come to Belle Fleur not because Cora had brought her. She'd come because she'd manipulated Cora. I had no doubt that Margo was dead because of her. Now I just had to prove it.

44

The days bled into mid-November, and I minimized my role in the Henderson family until I became part of the background. As Annie's influence grew, I allowed mine to wane. I tutored, did the chores, and kept my opinions to myself.

Singed by the ugly gossip and rumors regarding Margo, Erin dropped out of public school. She walked the four miles home from school one morning, her face streaked with tears, and refused to consider going back. Bob allowed her to quit. I don't know if Berta was consulted or not, but I was glad that Erin had returned to me. I worried that her sister's death had severely marked her. She withdrew from contact with the outside world and rode Cogar obsessively, meeting four times a week with her riding coach.

She was up at dawn and rode before breakfast and her studies. Each afternoon, she returned to the stables and the big gray horse. I was glad she had her riding, because there was little else for her in Coden.

Donald found solace in the woods and his fishing. He never brought fish home—he'd lost the desire to hunt and kill—but I watched him casting into the bay, the yellow sally winking in the sunlight as it flew through the air to land in the water. Moving deliberately, he'd reel the false bait in. Some days, I tracked him down to Crystal Mirror Lake. More than once I found him sitting on the bank, staring at his reflection in the still water, and I wondered what he saw. I could not forget the small creature that mimicked him so perfectly, except for the sharpened teeth and claws of a dog. Margo's death had robbed him of his joy in the natural paradise of Coden, but I was afraid the nester would take more than that.

If the nester's desires had been satisfied, time would heal both children, and the parents, too. Cora said it often, and I believed it. Time was their greatest ally. I had not seen the creature for two weeks, nor the dark-haired girl. To that end, I allowed Annie to have her way in the house. As she ascended to power, perhaps her needs would be met and the nester wouldn't remove another child.

But I never assumed they were gone. Only waiting.

Bob threw himself into his work. When he wasn't in Mobile on a project, he was in the small room next to the library that he'd turned into his office. He was obsessed with beginning renovations on the Paradise Inn. He worked late into the night, but Berta didn't notice. He'd begun to drink heavily each evening, but Berta didn't take note of that either. She found her own escape in the prescription drugs that rocked her into a slumber so deep her grief couldn't touch her. She'd made a dangerous decision, but I hoped in time she would come to her senses and return to her family.

If she didn't, Annie would totally usurp her. I saw it play out, hour by hour, as Annie moved from teenage ward to Bob's companion. If he didn't come out to eat, she prepared a tray and took it to him. Late at night, she took brandy or wine into his private sanctum. A bottle and *two* glasses. If he walked over to the Paradise, she threw on her coat and gloves and went after him. When she caught me watching them, she would only smile, confident she would succeed, that I was powerless to stop her.

Oh, but I had other plans. Even as I lurked in the shadows, the obedient tutor, the governess who did the daily chores of existence to run the household, I was plotting and taking small, secret steps.

I made an appointment with Jimmy Finch and told him about the pearl necklace and the photo album. *Intrigued* was a mild description of his reaction. Little by little, I began to convince him of Annie's plot. Once he found some solid evidence—and I knew he would find something—I would try again to convince Cora. If I could only make her see Annie in a true light, I could win. If I could win one adult to my side, just one, maybe I could stop what I knew would happen.

To that end, I made it a point to call Mark and talk with him about insignificant things. Respecting my grief, he didn't press me for intimacies. He stopped by the house at least twice a week, at my request, for dinner or to watch a TV show or play a game or listen to some records. He made Erin and Donald laugh as he imitated the dances of our high school years like the Monkey or the Swim. I had quite a collection of '60s and early '70s albums, and we'd gather in the family room and put them on the stereo. Mark was a good dancer and a total exhibitionist. He loved making Erin laugh, and sometimes even Bob came out of his lair to watch. It lifted my spirits considerably to see him smile and interact with his children.

Annie was always on her best behavior. Those were the nights she volunteered to clean up the kitchen and then went up to her room "to read" instead of disappearing into Bob's study. Watching her, no one could fault her conduct on those evenings. Only I knew her dark intentions.

Cora had given up trying to get me to stay with her, but she came to the Hendersons almost every day. She brought home-baked goodies and sometimes sat with Berta in her room. While I cleaned the house or cooked, I sometimes heard her talking, her calm and lulling voice sharing inconsequential moments of the day with Berta, keeping her in touch with national news, local events, and a sense of community. I wondered if it did any good, but I was glad she tried. My attempts to reach Berta failed utterly.

She acknowledged the breakfast tray of coffee, toast, juice, maybe a scrambled egg, that I brought her each morning. She'd drink the coffee—everything else remained untouched. In the matter of the two weeks since Margo's funeral, Berta had become skeletal in appearance.

"Berta should see a doctor," Cora told me one sunny afternoon as I dried the dishes she'd washed. Cora liked to help out, and over the past few days, the breach in our relationship had begun to heal. I'd learned the hard way not to go after Annie without proof, and if her name wasn't mentioned, Cora and I settled into our old relationship.

"I've talked to her and so has Bob. She refuses."

"She told me the last time she got so depressed that you helped her." Cora rinsed out the sink and faced me. "Whatever you did, do it again?"

Annie was in her room and Donald and Erin were on the front porch doing lessons. The day was incredible—temperatures in the upper sixties, the sun bright and the waters of the Sound a clear blue. I itched to be outside, but I had my chores to finish.

I'd given Berta hope with Jimmy Finch, and it had proven to be false. "I can't. Margo's dead. There's no hope to spare."

"I see." Cora sat down at the kitchen table. "Hope. It's what we all live on, isn't it? No matter how silly or how improbable, we hope. We hope that this time things will be different, that this time it won't be as bad as we've been taught to expect, that people can change and happiness is real and can be found by those determined enough to search for it."

I sank into a chair beside her. "Wow. You sound depressed, too."

"It's hard not to be. The brutal death of two young people—that's a harsh thing to swallow without gagging." Cora put a hand over her eyes for a moment. "This must be hell for Berta. I know she's reliving Margo's death again and again."

"I don't believe they were killed over drugs. Andrew sold a little pot. He wasn't any kind of dealer, no matter what people say."

"What do you think the motive was?"

I had prepared for this. It was my opportunity to get Cora to at least think about the deaths from a different perspective. "I think Margo was the target and Andrew was collateral damage."

Cora's eyebrows, still dark even though her hair was gray, inched up her forehead. "Who would want to kill Margo?" She was shocked.

"Someone who was jealous of her."

Cora stiffened, and I wondered if I'd taken it too far. My fists clenched and I moved my hands to my lap so she couldn't see.

"Who might that be?"

"Maybe another girl who liked Andrew? He was a handsome boy. Popular. He had his own car." I shrugged. "Or maybe a boy in town Margo flirted with and then brushed off. Margo was no saint. She liked attention from the boys, and she flaunted herself and her family's money." Pointing the finger at Annie was out of the question, but if I could shift Cora's thinking just a little, I could push for another inch later.

"After she disappeared, I heard talk." Cora leaned back in her chair. "She would go up to the Esso station in halter tops and short shorts and flirt with Andrew and anyone else who came up. I never heard or I would have told Berta."

My fists unclenched. "She was sixteen and beautiful. She was just becoming aware of her power over boys. She had to try it out. She didn't do anything really wrong, but she could be callous about other people's feelings. You know, flirting without thinking. She was filled with her ability to make boys want her."

Cora chuckled. "I remember those days. I know you don't believe it, but I was young once."

I'd heard a little about those days. "Did you dance at the Paradise? Were you a flapper?"

She laughed out loud, pleased to remember those times. "Yes, I was as close to a flapper as a Coden girl could get. Zelda Fitzgerald had an influence on me and my girlfriends. Short dresses, stockings with seams, cloche hats, and binding our breasts. Those were fun times. I've got a picture somewhere of me in my favorite flapper dress. It was a scandal here in Coden."

"Sigourney was still alive then, wasn't she?"

"In the '20s, yes. She was very old. Belle Fleur was falling into ruin." Cora looked around her. "Bob has brought this place back to her heyday. When the Hendersons moved here, I anticipated Belle Fleur returned to her grandeur. Bob far exceeded even my dreams."

"How did Bob find out about Belle Fleur being up for sale?" I played it innocent.

"Real estate agents list houses like this one on a national level. I suppose he saw it in some catalogue. Maybe one of those travel magazines." Her fingers tapped on the tablecloth.

"I don't remember ever seeing a FOR SALE sign." I stood. "I think I'll make us a bit of coffee. It'll give me an excuse to check on Berta."

"Good idea." Cora gazed out the kitchen window, lost in thought. "I guess the real estate agency got tired of putting up the signs. Someone always stole them. Anyway, no one ever asked about Belle Fleur. The estate is so large, and we had several bad hurricanes. Waterfront property looked pretty risky, but I guess if you live in a place where an earthquake could send you shuttling off the edge of a cliff into the ocean, a hurricane doesn't seem so bad."

"Excellent point." I turned on the stove to heat water for the dripolater, then spooned coffee into the basket of the pot.

"If Bob hadn't fallen in love with Belle Fleur, no telling what would have happened to the house."

"There are plenty of people in Mobile with the money to buy her. Why didn't someone local?"

Cora hesitated. "What's with the sudden interest in real estate?"

"I've always been curious, but Mark and the sheriff were asking some questions about how the Hendersons came to be here." It was only a tiny white lie. "They said some company out of Montgomery sold Belle Fleur, a realtor or something, but they couldn't find out a lot of information. I told them you might know."

"Me?" Cora was startled.

"Belle Fleur was always special to you." I shrugged. "I figured you'd know. You or Chad Petri."

Cora's face showed concern. "There's nothing to know."

"After Sigourney died, who owned Belle Fleur? There were no descendants. So who inherited the property?"

"Why, I'm not certain. It seems there was someone who worked at the perfume factory who bought the property, but that was such a long time ago. I was busy working in Mobile, and I don't recall. Why would the sheriff care about that?"

"I don't know." I went to the fridge and got an apple pie I'd baked the day before. I cut three slices and put them on saucers. When I glanced over my shoulder, I saw worry on Cora's brow. "Are you upset?" I put a slice in front of her.

"No."

She was lying. Cora gave herself away when she couldn't hold my gaze. She knew more about the sale of Belle Fleur than she was letting on. "Do you think Mr. Petri would know more? In case Mark asks."

"He might."

The kettle began to sing, and I poured the hot water into the top of the coffee pot and got cups and saucers down. While the water dripped through, I fixed a tray with pie and a coffee cup for Berta. "I'd like to know more about this house. I've heard some things about Sigourney. Unpleasant things. A very different picture than what you told me about Belle Fleur." I poured the freshly brewed coffee into the cup in front of Cora.

"Every old house has stories attached," Cora said. She'd regained her balance. Her voice was strong. "There's always been foolishness about Belle Fleur. Sigourney was a mean woman in her last years. She hurt local children. She broke Si's leg when she struck him with her cane, and he's held a grudge all these years. Those are facts. The rest is just foolishness." She stabbed her fork into the pie and took a bite. "This is wonderful, Mimi. You've become an excellent baker."

"Berta probably wouldn't approve of all the sweets, but the children enjoy them." I poured another cup. "I'll be right back. Let me take this tray to Berta."

Cora stood up abruptly. "Let me do that. I want to have a word with her and then I've got to be on my way."

"But you didn't eat your pie."

"Wrap it up for me, Mimi. I'll take it home. I think I should try to reach Berta."

There was no point arguing. She was more hardheaded than I. "Okay."

She took the tray and I heard her tap lightly on Berta's door before she entered. Then the door closed and I was alone in the kitchen.

After I filled a cup with coffee for me, I sat at the table and ate my pie. The kitchen window was open, and the starched white curtains lifted and fell on a breeze that came from the woods. Normally the wind came from the south, crossing the water and picking up the tang of salt. This smelled of pine. I sniffed it, savoring the difference.

I'd just taken the last bite of pie when I heard something scratching beneath the kitchen window.

I ignored it. Two weeks had passed. Annie was ruling the roost. She had everything she wanted, so perhaps the creature wouldn't return.

The scratching came again, more insistent. The claws scoured the wood. It wanted in, and it would not be denied.

45

Easing away from the table, I went to the kitchen window and looked out. The yard rolled toward the woods in the perfect November light. A breeze rustled through the trees, and some dead leaves blew off the scuppernong harbor and scattered toward the front of the house. The empty swing shifted slightly. Nothing was amiss in the yard, but I went to the closet and selected a heavy wooden croquet mallet. I'd moved the set from Annie's room, knowing the time would come when a weapon would be necessary.

I'd thought to get a gun—had almost asked Mark to help me find one—but I knew such a request would be met with concern and skepticism. A sudden interest in a firearm would be a red alert. I'd have to settle for various baseball bats Donald left around the house and yard, and the croquet mallets and whatever club or weapon I could find. I didn't relish the thought of beating the nester to death, but I would if I got the opportunity.

Grasping the mallet, I went to the back door. Again, I scanned the yard and saw nothing. The scratching sound could have been the wind moving a branch against the side of the house. Or it could have been something far more sinister.

I wasn't going to wait in the house to see what came inside to harm us. I opened the door and slipped into the yard. Checking beneath the kitchen window I found the telltale claw marks.

The fragile calm that I'd worked so hard to maintain was over. The creature wanted only one thing—to destroy the children. To push each one out of the house, to make room for its mistress.

The thick carpet grass hid the creature's tracks, but I walked to the edge of the woods, looking for any sign, any evidence of where it had disappeared. It wouldn't be far. If I could only sneak up on it, I would do what was necessary.

"Mi-mi." It called my name from within the shelter of the thick woods. "Play hide and go seek, Mimi. We love that game."

My fingers gripped the mallet so tightly my fingernails dug into my palm. "I'm coming," I answered.

Branches from a young Tibouchina plant were snapped, the beautiful purple flowers trampled into the dirt in what looked like a place where a dog had dug. The nester had come this way. I stepped into the woods and felt the temperature drop a good ten degrees. Overhead, the trees canopied. Some of the natural hardwoods were bare, but there were enough live oaks to give a dense shade.

"Mimi." The voice was soft, enticing. "You're *it!*"

I glanced back at the house. Annie sat on her balcony, watching me. Her amusement made my temper rise, but I stepped deeper into the woods, where she couldn't see me, and kept going. If I found her cohort, I would put an end to this in a brutal way. Then I'd see what she had to smile about.

The deeper I walked into the woods, the more the gloom settled around me. The November light was weaker than the full blast of summer sun, but I'd never had the sensation that the forest drank the sunshine. I pulled my coat together and zipped it against the sudden chill and kept walking, my stride long and quick, my chin tucked and my focus on the path.

"Mi-mi, where are we? Find us. We want to play."

I didn't answer. If I got close enough, I'd whack the little beast with the mallet. To practice my swing, I struck a tree on the side of the path. The solid thwack was gratifying. I could imagine the mallet striking the flesh of the nester.

"Find the present, Mimi." The childish giggle came from the woods not too far away. The creature was toying with me. "We made you a gift."

I stopped and listened, my breath harsh in my ears.

"You're getting warmer." This was a vile thing. The voice seemed to come from different places, and I waited, hoping it would speak again and give me an indication of where to look. When I didn't hear anything, I walked forward slowly. I was half a mile from Belle Fleur deep in the woods. I'd walked out without a word to anyone, and I'd left the children alone on the front porch.

"Warmer! Warmer, Mimi!" The creature sang the words.

I rounded a bend in the trail and saw something buried in leaves in the middle of the path. Dread twisted my gut, and the copper taste of fear filled my mouth. I couldn't tell what it was by staring at it. Finally, I kicked it.

Long blond hair attached to a head rolled across the carpet of leaves. When it struck the base of a sweet gum, the blue eyes popped open. It took an eternity to realize it was not Erin's head, but that of her favorite doll, Savannah.

I went to the doll's head and picked it up carefully by the hair. At last I had proof. Something to show Mark, maybe something to get fingerprints off. I had no doubt I'd find Annie's prints on the doll—she had to have taken it from Erin's room. But I hoped for some other prints, those of a creature that was not human, not Erin.

Holding the doll head by the hair, I started back to Belle Fleur.

46

When I came out of the woods, Erin and Donald had moved to the back yard. Erin swung, her blond hair almost touching the ground when she used her legs and body to push higher. Donald nudged a plastic road-grader truck to make pathways for his other toys. He saw me first and jumped up, smiling, to greet me. The smile faded when he saw what I held.

"Savannah." He said the doll's name in a whisper. "What did you do to her?"

I realized then how the nester had played me. "I found this in the woods."

Erin stopped swinging. When she realized what I held, she jumped from the swing and ran toward me. "What did you do to Savannah?" Her face was drained of all color.

"I found this in the woods." She grabbed for the doll head, but I snatched it away. "I have to call Mark."

"Mark? Why are you calling Mark?" She made another grab for the doll, but I eluded her.

"He can check for fingerprints." She was furious at me, and I could tell she wasn't listening.

"What good will that do?" Erin's fists clenched and unclenched at her side. Donald tried to touch her arm, but she flung her hand and struck him in the face. He was so stunned, he didn't even cry.

"Erin, someone did this to your doll. I have to find out who."

"Look in the mirror, you sick freak! You did it. You did it!" She swung blindly and hit my shoulder with such force, I stumbled backward.

"Erin! Stop it." I put up my hands to defend myself, but she kept swinging.

"I hate you. Why would you do that to Savannah?"

She was out of control, and I had no choice. I slapped her. The shock and sting of the blow numbed my hand and stopped her in her tracks. The fury left her face as if washed away. She stared at me and then burst into tears.

"Oh, Erin." I pulled her into my arms and held her as she sobbed. Donald started crying, too. Together, we huddled in the yard and cried. I couldn't stop myself. While I knew it was the pent-up emotions of weeks of horror and grief, and I also knew it was my job to remain in control, to guide the children through these hard times, I couldn't stop the tears.

When I looked up, Cora stood on the top step, her brow furrowed with worry. Behind her, Annie waited. Her smile slowly widened, and she gave me a big wink before she turned back inside.

⚜

"Mimi, you really want me to fingerprint a doll head?" Mark sat beside me on the front steps. Even with the potential evidence in a paper bag at my feet, no one believed me. Nor did Mark touch me. I wasn't surprised, but it still hurt.

The early darkness of winter had fallen, and with the loss of sun, the temperatures were chilly. I pulled the car coat tighter around me and resisted the urge to jam my hands in my pockets. I needed Mark to do this. Physical evidence was the only thing that would convince people of Annie's role in what was happening. She'd masterfully played it, time and time again, so that I looked like the bad person, but if her prints were on the doll head—I would get her prints on a glass or something else for comparison—I would have something to fight back with. And if there were unknown prints, nester prints, I could prove that someone was lurking in the house.

"I know it sounds ridiculous, but someone took that doll's head into the woods and did this. It's a warning, Mark."

"A warning to whom?"

To Erin. But I couldn't say that, either. The nester had returned to Belle Fleur to rid the house of another child, to make more room in the nest. I knew it with the core of my being; but should I be foolish enough to express such an idea, I would be the one removed and put in a place for the insane. "You heard how upset Erin was. Savannah was her childhood friend, a link to her past in California. For god's sake, the doll looks like Erin. I have to know who did this. Someone is terrorizing the children, and if I find proof, I can stop it."

"Frankly, it sounds more like something Donald would do to get back at his sister. I mean, it's been rough on both kids. Maybe he's acting out."

"Donald isn't like that." Why wouldn't anyone believe me? Cora had blown me off, too, saying some animal had found the doll in the yard and dragged it into the woods and the head had conveniently become buried under leaves in the middle of a trail. "Would you just check it for prints? Just do that. Please."

"Sure." That one word was like pulling teeth.

"Thank you, Mark." I gathered his strong hand in mine, surprised at how much I wanted him to touch me in the old, possessive way. "Really, thank you."

He shifted so that we faced each other. "I'm doing this for you, Mimi. Not because I expect to find anything. For you. I'm worried about you. If this will set your mind at rest, it will be worth it, but if the sheriff finds out, he isn't going to be happy with me."

The relief was so intense, I closed my eyes and leaned against him. In that moment, I wanted him to kiss me. I needed him to take an action that showed he cared for me, that someone could love me, even if only for an evening.

I lifted my chin, offering my mouth to him. His lips found mine and he kissed me. I relaxed and kissed him back, a long, slow kiss that promised many of the things I'd withheld. It was a pleasure to let his strong arms surround me and offer shelter from the horrible things that had happened. A truth revealed itself to me at that moment. I *needed* Mark in my life. I'd trained myself to be strong and independent, to handle whatever crossed my path. Now I couldn't handle this alone. In the past few weeks, I'd come to rely on him, and he'd been there for me when no one else had shown up. My passion intensified, and he pulled me against him and kissed me harder.

"Mark and Mimi sittin' in a tree, K-I-S-S-I-N-G." The sarcastic, superior voice came from behind us.

I pushed back from Mark and turned to find Annie standing on the porch less than four feet away. She'd moved so stealthily, neither of us had heard her.

"You two should take it somewhere private," she said, her smile sly and suggestive. "Another few minutes and I would have had to get the hose to separate you. Do you really think Donald and Erin will benefit from watching a make-out session?"

Mark rose slowly to his feet, then offered his hand to me and tugged me to my feet. "You're pretty good at sneaking up on people, Annie." There was a flintiness to his eyes I'd never seen before.

"Most people don't make out on the front porch of their employer's home," Annie said. "Just be glad it was me instead of Bob who came out. I don't think he'd be happy with that kind of . . . public display. You two were hot and heavy."

Mark drew me to his side. "Mimi's twenty-one and old enough to kiss a man. We weren't acting inappropriately."

Annie arched her eyebrows. "I see." She noticed the paper sack at our feet. "Oh, the doll's head. A new case for Deputy Mark. Are you going to nab the doll killer?"

"What's wrong with you today, Annie?" Mark spoke softly, but his body was tense.

"I'm incensed that a teenage girl and a young man are dead, and the sheriff and his deputies can't find any answers about who killed them. But you're making out on the front porch of a house and playing with a doll's head. That's a little upsetting to me."

She turned abruptly and went back in the house.

"She's arrogant and sneaky," Mark said.

"You don't know the half of it. She's worse than sneaky." I spoke softly. At last, at last, Annie had shown her true self to someone other than me. "Thank you."

He picked up the paper sack with the doll's head. "I'll get the prints for you. I'll have to wait until Friday, when Howard is working in the lab. He'll do it as a favor for me."

I kissed his cheek. "Thank you, Mark." I almost cried with the simply pleasure that his support gave me. "Thank you."

"Hey, it isn't that big of a deal." He kissed me again. "It'll take a while for me to get this done, but I'll be by tomorrow night, okay? Maybe Erin and Donald would want to go to Mobile, maybe go bowling or play some putt-putt."

"I'll look forward to it." The coldness was gone from his beautiful gray eyes, and I smiled as I watched him walk to the patrol car and drive away.

Those fingerprints would bolster my theories. Annie was on the way to being caught.

47

The next evening, Donald and I waited for Mark on the front porch, ready for an evening of bowling. The weather had turned cold, too unpleasant for putt-putt. Indoor recreation was called for.

Erin, predictably enough, refused to go with me. I felt a gaze on my back, and when I turned, I saw her half-hidden behind the sheers of the front-door sidelights. The cut glass fractured her features, making her grotesque. I walked across the porch and opened the front door. "Please come with us, Erin. We won't be long and it would be good to do something fun."

"I told Dad not to let you take Donald, but he wouldn't listen to me. I'm not stupid enough to go off with you and that halfwit deputy you've got wrapped around your finger."

Those were some of the same words Annie had hurled at me the evening before, after Mark left with the doll's head. She'd poisoned Erin against me. "I'm sorry you feel that way. I'd do anything to help you and Donald and Bob and Berta. Anything."

"And Annie?" she asked.

"I don't trust Annie." I could be honest with Erin. Not too honest, but I didn't have to pretend to like Annie the way I did for the grown-ups. "When I get the evidence of what she's been up to, you'll feel differently."

"Don't hold your breath." She turned away from me and went to the beautiful staircase. I watched until her feet disappeared, blocked by the second floor.

"She's mad all the time," Donald said.

"People handle grief differently. Sometimes getting angry is the only way to survive. She can be angry at me, because I'm an outsider. I don't mind."

Donald took my hand as Mark's headlights came down the driveway. "Forget about Erin and everything that's happened here. We're going to have a couple of hours of fun, Donald. It will be good for both of us."

"I wish Dad and Mom would come." I'd asked Bob and Berta, but my invitation had been quickly quashed. They didn't realize how much Donald missed having time with them.

"Maybe next time." I goosed his ribs and then dragged him behind me as I ran to Mark's car and slipped across the seat to snuggle beside him. Donald took the passenger seat.

I welcomed Mark with a warm kiss, and then we were off. Camellia Bowling Lanes was a good thirty-minute drive, and I didn't want to be out too late.

Mark kept up easy banter with Donald on the drive, and when we arrived at the bowling alley, we found a lightweight ball for him and then let him beat the socks off us. For the first time in weeks, Donald's laughter rang clear and unhampered by worry or sadness. He ate most of the pizza we ordered, and on the way home he slumped against my shoulder in a blissful rest.

"Thank you, Mark." I stroked his face with the knuckles of my left hand. It was all I could manage supporting Donald.

"It was a good thing, Mimi. And I'm taking the doll head to Mobile tomorrow. My buddy has agreed to run the prints for me as a favor."

"Thank you." I captured one of his hands and brought it to my lips for a kiss and a slight tickle with my tongue.

"You're treading on dangerous ground." He brushed my cheek with his fingers. "I care about you, Mimi. A lot. I don't want to ruin this by pushing too hard."

It had happened without any effort from me. My gratitude and appreciation for Mark's help, for the way he treated me, had blossomed into stronger feelings. "Maybe tomorrow evening we can go to your place."

"It's a poor showing compared to Belle Fleur."

I laughed. "It has one superior ingredient. Privacy."

His arm pulled me hard against him and we drove the rest of the way home pressed tightly together, the promise of intimacy bonding us even closer.

Belle Fleur was quiet, the house settled for the night, though it was only nine o'clock when Donald and I latched the front door behind us. The hall clock ticked in the emptiness.

"Good night, Mimi." Donald reached up for a hug, and I held him tightly for a moment before releasing him to go to bed.

"Want me to tuck you in?"

He shook his head. "I'm not scared tonight. I'm just tired. A good tired."

His smile almost broke my heart. How long it had been since I'd seen him free of stress and worry. Tonight, he was truly physically depleted from three hours of bowling.

He trudged up the stairs without even a thought of saying goodnight to his parents. Berta, with medications, and Bob, with work, had effectively shut him out of their lives. He was a little boy alone except for me.

I stopped in the kitchen for a glass of milk and another small slice of apple pie. I loaded up a tray and went up to the second floor. On an impulse, I checked on Donald. He slept with one arm trailing on the floor, his tousled blond hair looking as if someone had rumpled it deliberately. At the far end of the hall, I opened the door to Erin's room. She, too, slept soundly. To my extreme discomfort, I saw that she'd put Savannah's headless body on the shelf with her other dolls. Morbid and creepy.

I entered my room and opened the windows. I liked to sleep under several quilts without the central heat. I forked a piece of pie into my mouth and reached for the milk when the sirens kicked in.

Walking out to the balcony, I leaned over the railing and tried to catch a glimpse of Shore Road through the wind-tossed limbs of the beautiful oaks. For a moment I thought I caught a wink of a flashing blue light, but I couldn't be certain. I was about to go back in when I heard something on the balcony above me. Annie was awake and moving around.

I started to go up the stairs and confront her. Without an audience, the honeyed-veneer would be gone. Pretending wasn't necessary with me, for I knew her and she understood that. I was halfway up the exterior staircase to Annie's balcony when another set of sirens was blocked out by the sound of an explosion.

A plume of flames leaped thirty feet into the night sky, and it came from a location on Shore Road between Belle Fleur and Coden.

"Holy shit." I raced up the stairs. "Annie!" As I neared the top, I looked through the white spindles of the balcony railing and my heart almost stopped. Erin sat on one of the wicker chairs, her legs crossed and one paw twitching mid-air.

"Annie's not here anymore, Mimi." She laughed and before I could move, she jumped over the railing. I reached out for her, but I was too late. She looked so much like Erin, so much like the thirteen-year-old girl I'd left asleep in her bed. But it wasn't Erin.

I stumbled to the rail and looked down, expecting to see her broken body in the dirt. Instead, the creature rose slowly from the crouch it had landed in. It looked up at me and took off across the yard in a gallop, a gait like a young girl would use to imitate a horse. She disappeared around the corner of the house.

48

When I ducked back into my room, the telephone rang. It was nearly eleven o'clock, and no one called that late. Or no one with good news or good manners. It could only mean trouble.

Bob had modernized the house with numerous phone jacks. There were phones downstairs in the hallway, the kitchen, and Bob and Berta's bedroom. Bob had also installed a phone in my room. Margo and Erin's room had a blue princess phone, and on the third floor in Annie's room was a pale yellow one. I picked up the receiver and said hello.

"Oh, Mimi." Cora's voice broke and she began to cry.

"Cora, what's wrong?" Had she fallen and injured herself? I'd never heard her so defeated.

"I'm so sorry," she said.

"What's wrong?" My voice was sharper than it should have been, but she was frightening me.

"It's Mark."

"What about him?" Now she was really scaring me.

"Honey, he had a wreck. His car exploded. He's dead. It happened half a mile from my house. I heard the crash and called the sheriff's office." She struggled to keep control of her emotions, but her pain washed around me. My body no longer belonged to me. My hand holding the phone refused to put it down. I couldn't breathe. I couldn't think or feel. The image of Mark walking to his car kept playing again and again in my brain. He'd opened the door and turned to me. His grin was cocky, and he'd given me a nod that confirmed our romantic plans for the next evening.

"Are you sure he's dead?" The words came from me, but I didn't understand how. My throat was paralyzed.

"The sheriff came by here himself. He's positive. Mark must have been coming back from seeing you."

"Yes, he took Donald and me bowling." My tone was robotic.

"The sheriff thinks something ran across the road in front of his car and caused him to swerve. He struck an old culvert hidden in the saw-grass. The gas tank ruptured, and a spark caused the explosion." She cleared her throat and choked back a sob. "He didn't suffer, Mimi. He didn't suffer."

"I'm coming to get you. Get dressed." I hung up the phone and stood in the middle of my room. It didn't make any sense. Not any. Mark was dead and the doll's head in the trunk of his car had been burned up. This wasn't an accident. The spark that led to the explosion wasn't of unknown origin. I knew very well where it had come from. This was Annie's work.

I stormed up the interior steps to her room. She'd had plenty of time to get back to Belle Fleur if she cut through the woods. It wasn't even a mile. When I pushed the door open, the blowing material gave me a terrible fright. Shadows darted and swirled in the fabric that danced on the wind. The door to her balcony and all of the windows were open, even though the night hovered in the low forties.

"Annie!" I thought I might strangle her. "Annie!"

But she wasn't there. The room was empty.

49

I drove white-knuckled from Cora's house while she sat in the passenger seat bundled in her coat and wiping at her tears with a tissue.
When I turned right from her drive and went around the only curve
on that stretch of Shore Drive, I saw the accident. The blue lights of
the police cars flashed, along with the red lights of the ambulance and
fire truck. It was a scene from hell.

As we got closer, I could see at least a half dozen deputies and six
or eight firemen all standing in the road, wandering back and forth,
talking in the way that men who can't show emotion do. These were
men of action but there was nothing they could do to help Mark. It
was over. A heap of twisted metal that was once Mark's car steamed
in the ditch, smoke and vapor rising, metal hissing and groaning like
the charred skeleton of some prehistoric monster. No one could have
survived the accident and then the explosion and fire.

I slowed and pulled off the road. The volunteer firemen began
rolling up their hoses. Smoke still spiraled into the night sky. I opened
the car door and Cora's fingers dug into my wrist. When I tried to
shake her off, she clung more tightly.

"Let's go home," she said gently. She didn't want me to witness the removal of Mark's burned body from the car. Some kind of wild animal sounds came from me, but I couldn't control them or even register what I was doing.

I pulled free of Cora, jumped out, and ran toward the wreck. Two deputies waylaid me and held me. I struggled, kicking and trying to bite them. "Easy there, Mimi." They knew me, though I didn't recognize them. "Easy there. Nothing you can do to help now. You don't want to see that." They delivered me back to Cora.

"Oh, Mimi." Cora pressed me into her bosom and held me until I stopped making a sound that ranged between a bark and a groan. "My poor, poor girl." She stroked my hair.

When I'd regained my composure, I eased out of her embrace. "This isn't fair," I said. "It isn't fair. Mark was a good person."

"He was indeed." She got me turned and walking back to the station wagon I'd borrowed. Bob would be wondering where I'd gone in such a hurry. It wasn't like me to dash out of the house at midnight and take a car. My life was unraveling in all directions.

Cora tucked me into the passenger seat and drove back to her house. We went into the kitchen and she reached behind the canisters and brought out a bottle of bourbon. She poured two stiff drinks and handed me one. I drank it without question, welcoming the heat that raced down my throat. A moment later, I rushed outside to vomit.

The retching turned into sobs, and Cora came to stand beside me until I'd cried myself out. Her phone rang and she started to ignore it, but I motioned her to answer. I could hear her conversation from my position on the porch, and I knew it was Bob calling. She told him what had happened, her voice ragged with emotion.

"Mimi should stay here with me," she said. "I'll look after her."

When she came back to the porch, she drew me into the house and led me to my old bedroom. She helped me undress and tucked me under the handmade quilts that had been in our family for generations. I remembered their names, the Wedding Ring, the Rose of Sharon, the Friendship Bow.

As I fingered the bright cloth, I asked her, "Do you think Belle Fleur is cursed?"

My question was like a slap. She drew up sharply. "Why would you say that?"

"The Desmarais family was ultimately destroyed. Now the Hendersons are suffering and even me, because I live there. Chloe supposedly fell to her death. Her baby was tossed in a well and left to die. Margo was murdered. Mark, who was visiting me there, was killed in a freak accident. Is there something about Belle Fleur I don't know?"

Cora stood where the light of the bedside lamp didn't fully reach her face. "It's only a house, Mimi."

If it wasn't the house, then Annie was involved in these tragedies. In my heart, I believed that Annie had engineered his death. I couldn't prove my theory, but it went back to the doll head and what it might have told us. She couldn't afford for Mark to check it for prints. What would he have found? Something to incriminate her—I was willing to stake my life on it.

⚜

The rest of the night slipped away from me as I maneuvered through tormented dreams of Mark's headlights picking up the image of a dark-haired girl darting out of the saw-grass into his path. He swung the wheel to miss her and went into the ditch, expecting a soft landing in swamp and mud. Instead the cement culvert caught the front of the car with brutal force. And then there were flames.

Though I knew I was dreaming, I couldn't stop it. I also accepted that my dreams replicated the events that had taken Mark's life. Annie's doppelganger had caused the wreck. Deliberately. My dreams were a window on that dark world that Annie brought into Belle Fleur when she arrived.

When I woke, I was completely disoriented. It took several moments for me to realize I was at Cora's. I heard her in the kitchen, and I caught the scent of something good cooking. My stomach growled with hunger, and I got up.

"Mimi, how about some chicken and dumplings?" Cora asked. A bib apron covered her dress and she held a large spoon in her hand as she stood at the stove. "They're piping hot."

I nodded and slipped into a chair at the table. I wanted to believe Mark's death was a dream, but I knew better. I checked the time— three P.M. Darkness would fall in another two hours. I ate the chicken and dumplings Cora put in front of me because I knew she'd never let me leave the house if I didn't.

"I'm feeling better," I lied. "I want to go back to Belle Fleur and shower and change clothes."

Cora lifted my face with a gentle hand under my chin. "I love you, Mimi. More than you know."

But not enough to get Annie out of my life. Cora didn't see in Annie the things I knew were there, the things she kept hidden. "I know."

"Run along then. Tell Bob I'll be down in a bit. I'm going to bring the rest of the chicken and dumplings for supper tonight."

"They would be wonderful." I kissed her cheek and hurried to the car.

Instead of turning left to Belle Fleur at the end of her drive, I went right. When I came upon the skid marks on the highway and the patch of charred grass, I got out and looked around. The story of Mark's last moments scored the asphalt. Something had darted out of the high grass, and he'd slammed on brakes hard enough to leave rubber in two long, black streaks. He'd cut the wheel, thinking he'd land in the soft shoulder, but he hadn't counted on the culvert.

It took some careful examination, but I found the strange, sharp claw marks I'd known would be there, about twenty yards before the skid marks began. She'd timed it perfectly. I knelt down and traced the marks with a small stick. A skeptic might say they'd been made by the wrecker dragging the car out of the weeds, or any number of other causes. But I knew the truth. I'd seen the dark-haired girl on this very road.

For a long time I sat in the station wagon beside the ditch where Mark had died. Trying to help me had cost him his life. When the light disappeared from the sky and the wind grew colder, I turned the car toward Belle Fleur.

50

When I got back to the Hendersons, Cora was there, and she was plenty worried. As was Bob. Even Berta had come out of her room and was making cornbread in the kitchen. She gave me a hug and kissed the top of my head. "I'm so sorry, Mimi," she said. "We're here for you."

"Where did you go, Mimi?" Bob asked.

"I took a drive. To think." I lifted my hands in a gesture of helplessness. "I just wanted to be alone."

"Next time, just call us. I don't mind you using the car, but you have to let me know. I was worried."

"Of course," I said.

Annie was pleased. She stood behind Bob and smiled at me. I'd earned Bob's displeasure, and that made her gloat. I wanted to demand the details of where she'd been at the time of the accident, but to do so would label me as irrational. Now, of all times, I couldn't afford to look unstable.

I took the children up to my room on the second floor to work on a history assignment while Berta and Cora finished preparing the meal. Had I been in a different frame of mind, I would have taken pleasure in seeing Berta back in command of her kitchen. As it was, I didn't want the scrutiny of the adults on me—not any of them. I could deceive the children about my emotional state, and there was safety in pretending that our studies held importance, that I was clinging to the normalcy of routine instead of nose-diving into emotional turmoil. They already suspected I was irrational. I could not give them another single incident to question.

"Our town was founded by the French on Bayou Coq I'nde. The name Coden, as we call it today, is an English translation. There are many interesting facts about this place you call home." Oh, there were things I could tell them.

"It isn't really our home," Erin said. "Mother wants to go back to Cambria, and so do I." Donald, who was normally the bastion of defense for Coden, said nothing.

"Times haven't been happy here lately, but we have to make the best of it. All of us." My voice trembled and I turned away from them and looked out the window. Although it wasn't late, darkness covered the yard. "Open your history books to page 103."

When they settled at the table, I started the lesson. History had always been one of my favorite subjects, especially state history. Facts were indisputable, safe.

"As you've learned, Coden, like most of the coastal region, was settled by American Indians, tribes that fell under the Creek or Choctaw nation." From there I moved the focus to Dauphin Island, one of several barrier islands that separated the Mississippi Sound from the Gulf of Mexico. I had fond memories of picnics on the sandy beach as the water raced forward and retreated in frothy, white-capped waves, and I felt my rational thought returning. There were times when I honestly believed I might be insane. Maybe this was all me—the dark-haired girl, the nester, the house, Sigourney, maybe every bit of it was fabricated in my head and I was somehow sharing my delusions with the children.

As I put the children to reading about the history of Dauphin Island, I walked to the window and looked out at the bare winter lawn. There were plenty of places for the duo to be hiding, waiting. I wasn't crazy. Donald had seen the Margo creature on the path home. Mark had seen something when he wrecked his car. Even if I wanted it to be a fabrication of my sick brain, it wasn't.

"Mimi, are you okay?" Donald asked.

To my surprise, I was crying.

He put his hand in mine. "I'm sorry about Deputy Mark, Mimi. I liked him. A lot."

I fought back the desire to give in to my grief, to really wail. "I liked him, too."

"Was he your boyfriend?" Erin asked. Her voice was gentler, kinder, as if she'd finally acknowledged that I, too, had lost something I loved.

"I knew Mark when I was in high school. I've known him for a long time."

"But was he your boyfriend?" she persisted.

"Yes, I suppose he was." I combed my hair with my fingers. In the winter, when the humidity was low, my curls were softer and less violent. "Now let's focus on our lesson. I don't want to talk about this."

"How long did you live with Cora before you moved here?" Erin asked.

I hesitated. "It feels like always."

"But she's your grandmother, not your mother."

"That's true." There was something in Erin's tone that made me wary. "After my parents died, I went to live with Cora."

"How old were you?" Erin closed her history book. "This is much more interesting than French settlements more than two hundred years ago on a barrier island made of sand."

"But my personal history is of no consequence. We study history to learn from our past mistakes." My hand fell lightly on Donald's thin shoulder. "Dauphin Island was originally called Massacre Island because the skeletons of sixty people were found when the first explorers went there."

"Who killed them?" Donald asked.

"I don't know. It was never discovered."

There was a tap on the door and Bob entered. "Cora has supper ready downstairs."

Grief didn't tamp down Donald's appetite. He was a healthy boy. He closed his book and stood to leave. "Are you coming?" he asked me.

"I am."

"I want a word with Mimi," Bob said. He waited until the children left the room and then closed the door. "I'm very sorry, Mimi. I know you and Mark were developing a relationship. He seemed like a fine young man."

Grief held me in suspension. I concentrated on breathing in and out. At last I could speak. "Mark was a good person. I just don't understand how this could happen to someone who only wanted to help people."

"Why don't you spend some time with Cora? I'm concerned about you. Berta is worried. You're not acting like yourself."

"Is Berta even aware how I'm acting?" Anger made my tone sharp. "If I don't mind the children, who will? Annie? I wouldn't count on that."

Bob came toward me. His hands settled on my upper arms and he squeezed gently. "Your emotions are raw, Mimi. I'm trying to help you. Berta is stronger. She can manage the children for a few days. You owe yourself space to heal."

I shook him off. The words I bit back were mean and ugly. I wanted to tell him to keep his pants zipped around Annie, but I didn't dare. "Let me do my job. I have an obligation to the children."

He eased me to the bed, where he sat beside me. "You're not much more than a kid yourself, Mimi. You aren't resting. I hear you moving around the house at night, checking the doors and windows. You're always on the alert. I see you looking outside, frightened. What happened to Margo. . . ." He took a moment to compose himself. "I don't think anyone singled her out. She was in the wrong place at the wrong time. I don't think anyone is out to hurt me or my family. Mark's death was a tragic accident."

"That's where you're wrong!" I tried to stand up, but he caught me and held me beside him on the bed.

"Mimi, calm down." He pulled me into his chest and held me tightly. I couldn't stop the sobs then. I pressed my face into his chest and let him hold me. "It's okay, it's okay," he said again and again. But it wasn't, and it never would be.

Someone at the doorway cleared her throat. Bob stiffened slightly and let me go, but I still clung to him. I hadn't realized how much I needed him to hold me. I'd never had a father, never had that masculine sense of safety and protection.

"Mimi." Berta's voice cut me like a blade.

I shifted back from Bob and glanced at the doorway. She steadied herself on the doorjamb with one hand. "Dinner is ready," she said. She turned away, and I couldn't help but notice how painfully thin she'd become. She'd lost her curves and the soft lushness that had always been the major aspect of her beauty. Her face, gaunt now with puffy circles, made her blue eyes faded and tired. But those eyes had registered shock and hurt at what she'd witnessed. I knew how it must look to her. Bob in my bedroom and me clinging to him. She'd never understand that her husband was merely comforting me. I wasn't the threat to her. It was Annie. But it was me she'd witnessed in his arms, not Annie. I'd screwed myself this time.

"Come down and eat, Mimi." Bob walked to the doorway. He didn't look at me.

"In a minute."

He didn't argue. He just went away, his footsteps fading as he descended the stairs.

51

The dynamics of the household were changed—and charged. To Cora's disappointment, and Berta's puzzlement, I refused to attend Mark's funeral. I couldn't. I was trapped in that place where I was neither friend nor lover, the in-between. I'd spent most of my life in that spot.

If I attended Mark's service, it would appear that I was claiming more of Mark than I owned, so I left his final rites to the people who truly knew him, to those whose connection was true and pure. Had he lived one more night, I would have been rooted in his life, committed in a way that gave me license to sit among his family and friends. But that hadn't happened.

Though I did my best to win back Berta's high regard of me, she treated me with a reserve that broke my heart. She was kind and considerate of my loss, but she was also cool. The spark we'd shared when I'd first gone to work at Belle Fleur had been tamped down. Possibly exterminated. My only option was to bide my time and hope we could get past the wrong impression she'd gotten of me the day after Mark died.

Berta returned to her duties as wife and mother, but she didn't sing in the kitchen or play the radio and dance as she dug in her garden. She worked in silence. When Bob came home from work exhausted, she found a smile for him, and she tried harder with Donald and Erin. Inch by inch she reestablished the bond that had taken such a severe beating when she retreated into her grief.

And Annie was always there, her right-hand man, her assistant, her confidante.

Sometimes, early in the morning when they were cleaning the kitchen after breakfast, I would hear Annie whispering with Berta. They'd grown closer, while I was excluded. I didn't blame Berta. Annie was behind this. She'd wormed her way into Berta's good graces and painted me as a desperate person who would grasp another woman's husband. And I'd played right into her hands.

The worst part was that I couldn't even defend myself from her charges because none were spoken aloud. I made it a point to steer clear of Bob. If I was alone in a room and he entered, I left. My weakness in seeking his comfort had brought this on, and I could never be that vulnerable again. Bob wasn't my father and he wasn't my husband. I could lay no claim to his consoling.

Over time, we would work through this—if I could only get rid of Annie. That was easier said than done. For the moment, I was stuck with her, until I could prove what she was up to. My hopes were pinned on Jimmy Finch.

Because I could do nothing else, I concentrated on teaching. I found real joy in having Erin back in my schoolroom. As Thanksgiving approached, the family began to move along more smoothly. There were still plenty of bumps and upsets, especially if Margo's name came up unexpectedly, or a reference to a past holiday was made. But each day it got a little better.

Donald and I made pinecone turkeys for decorations, and we planned two recipes that might have been served by Native Americans at the first Thanksgiving—corn pudding and one of my favorites, pumpkin pie. While Berta and Cora cooked the main dishes, I helped the children with our "Indian offering." To my surprise, Annie joined us in the kitchen and went into a lengthy—and gory—retelling of the Salem witch trials, which really had nothing to do with Thanksgiving. Still, Donald and Erin were enthralled.

As I rolled out pie crust, the children begged Annie for each gruesome detail of those awful trials and the foolish children who'd caused the execution of nearly two dozen people.

The day before, I'd made a call to Jimmy Finch, only to discover he was in Natchez, Mississippi. His secretary, who clearly disliked me, refused to tell me what case he was working on. He would be back on Friday after Thanksgiving.

Thursday morning, I threw myself into the final preparation for the meal. Erin and I set the table. Cora arrived on a blast of crisp fall air with an apple pie and green bean casserole. Donald filled the tea glasses, and Annie helped Berta bring out the golden turkey. When we sat down, Bob said grace. His voice broke, and Berta stifled a sob, but they regained their composure and the meal went flawlessly.

Berta had served a light white wine, and she filled our glasses. Even Annie got half a glass. The food was delicious as always, and I had a sense that perhaps we were over the worst of the grief. For Margo *and* for Mark. The grief, but not the guilt. Had Mark not been involved in helping me, he would still be alive.

In a lull in the conversation, Erin spoke. "Mother, the Grand Prix Horse Show is in Gulfport next week. I want to go."

I wiped my mouth with the linen napkin and waited, my gaze on my nearly empty plate. This confrontation had been in the wings for a long time, but Erin's decision to broach it at a holiday dinner wasn't wise. Bob's face registered his dismay.

"I don't think so, Erin. It's too dangerous. It's bad enough you take those jumps here, but in the confusion of a show, Cogar could spook, or another horse could misbehave . . . you could be hurt." Berta put her napkin beside her plate. "Maybe next year."

"Cogar is ready this year. And so am I." Erin's voice held firmness.

"No." Berta put her hands on the table. "I can't. I can't do it. I won't let you put me through that kind of worry."

"Berta," Bob said softly, "she deserves a chance. She's been working at this all fall. She's been riding with Mason Jones, and he thinks she's ready."

"Mason Jones? When did she start taking—" She pushed back from the table. "It would seem there are lots of things happening in this family I don't know about."

"Berta!" Bob stood up, too. "Erin is a talented equestrian. She deserves a shot at her dream."

"And I deserve a family. A safe family." She left the dining room. In a moment, Annie stood and went after her. Erin excused herself and left the house, no doubt to go to the barn. Donald, Bob, Cora, and I remained, each of us unwilling or unable to say a thing. Finally Bob left the table without a word.

"That went well," Donald said, then sighed. "Mom is scared. She doesn't want Erin to get hurt."

"I know. This is difficult for her. She's afraid of the horse, and of the jumping. Each time Cogar goes over one of those huge jumps, she thinks of Erin falling under his feet."

"I'll clear the dishes," Cora said. "You two find something fun to do."

Donald pushed back from the table. "No one ate our pumpkin pie."

"I'm sure they will later this evening. Let's take a walk." I grabbed his arm in the old way, before tragedy visited us, more like we were friends than teacher and student.

He brightened instantly. Anything outdoors was always preferable to inside.

Cora turned around in the doorway. "Mimi, don't leave the yard, okay?"

I stopped in my tracks. "Why not?"

"We're all on edge. Stay where Berta can find you."

"Sure thing." As I walked down the hall to the front door, I wondered if she was worried about Donald, or if she was concerned that

I couldn't be trusted to take care of Donald. It was a bitter question to contemplate.

"Mimi, come on!" Donald rushed down the front steps and into the yard. "Let's go to the old hotel. Daddy said the work crew was starting there next Monday. Let's go before they tear everything out. I brought Mom's camera so we could make pictures of things before they get torn down."

Bob hadn't mentioned that the crews would begin so quickly. I knew his plans were moving along well, but this was a big step. He'd become less talkative about his work on the Paradise, probably because Berta no longer supported it. She wanted to leave Alabama, and she'd begun to view the Paradise as competition for her husband's affections. Margo's death was fertile ground for two disparate ambitions to sprout.

"Quit dragging your feet!" Donald yelled. He didn't wait for me to respond. He was gone, running across the lawn to the trail that went through the woods to the Paradise. I followed at a stroll, deliberately disregarding Cora's request to stay on the Belle Fleur grounds. I was angry and hurting and determined not to yield to anyone else's wishes, especially if it seemed that I was being viewed as unreliable or damaged. Not when Annie traipsed around as if she were a queen, everyone bowing and scraping to her. That Cora did it too hurt the most.

Up ahead I caught a brief glimpse of Donald running by a wall of scuppernong vines that shaded from forest green to apple with yellow mixed in, a pointillist vision come to life. He wore a burgundy jacket and a yellow cap that advertised treated wood products. Bob had given it to him, and he loved it on his closely cropped head.

Soon enough he'd notice the long hair on the boys around town. Fashion trends moved into Coden at a snail's pace, but the longhair boys had been driving school authorities crazy since the late '60s. Even Bob's hair was a little longer, a la Robert Redford. Donald kept his short, but that would change when he realized that girls preferred the longer style.

I mused about some of my high school friends as I walked. Scottie Logan didn't earn a diploma, but he had hair down to his waist. Nice hair, a honey brown as thick and shiny as any girl's. I'd seen him in the five and dime store in Tillmans Corner only the week before. We said hello, but there was no common ground for conversation. Brady McCant's carrot top was a thicket of curls. He'd driven his truck past the Esso station while I was filling the station wagon with gas. If Brady could straighten his curls, his hair might reach to his knees.

Because of his work, Mark's hair had been short. But in high school, it had been a glossy black, cut like David Cassidy's, that same, luxuriant weight. If I thought hard enough, I could almost feel my flingers gliding through it.

Passing the cemetery, I glanced at Margo's grave. The stone marker had already been erected. Bob hadn't mentioned it, which probably meant that Berta disapproved. If they moved back to California, I wondered if they'd disinter Margo and move her, too.

The old wrought-iron gate creaked as I walked in to get a better look at the beautiful monument. A stone bench centered the arch that was elaborately carved with ivy vines and what looked like wisteria flowers. The words "Margo, Beloved Daughter of Robert and Berta Henderson" were centered at the top of the arch. Below that was "She graced our lives for sixteen years, a span too short." And then the dates of her birth and death. The coroner had listed the date of her disappearance as her death date. Fact or simply a kindness, I couldn't say.

Even though Donald would be expecting me, I took a seat on the bench. The bright afternoon sun warmed my shoulders. Ten minutes alone wouldn't hurt anything. This was a fitting place to think about Mark. My claim on him was a romantic fumbling that felt diminished by my hesitation, my unwillingness to commit to a real relationship. I was such a coward, hiding from his family, because I knew they wondered why he'd put me safely out of his car and then died. Maybe it was all my imagination. Maybe I was the only person who asked that question, but I did.

The creaking of the gate pulled me out of my thoughts. The view of the entrance was blocked by statuary. I looked around the angel that marked Sigourney's grave, expecting an impatient Donald. Fear laced my gut into a tight knot.

The nester stood at the cemetery entrance, blocking my way. When I stepped toward it, it didn't retreat. Blood dripped from an open gash on the creature's wrist. The amorphous features seemed to swirl, a fetus going through the stages of embryonic development. It grew taller, thinner. Paralyzed by fear, I didn't move. I watched the transmogrification. Fish, sheep, beast, until at last the bones length-ened and the visage of Berta emerged.

"No!"

"She won't last long now," the creature said before it darted away, running on back paws and hands, taking the same path Donald had run down earlier.

"Donald!" I cried his name as I started to run. It was only when I glanced at the tombstone over Chloe's grave that I saw the fresh blood and the writing.

"Mimi." My name was scrawled across the gray marble in red.

But there was no time to investigate. I had to get to Donald before the nester did—if I was not too late already. I knew the game now. It would kill Donald and push Berta over the edge of sanity.

52

I arrived at the Paradise breathless and panicked. Though I fought to compose myself, I couldn't calm the images that sliced through my mind. Donald alone with the nester. Donald running for his life. Donald captured in the grip of a malevolent creature that could snap his neck or drown him. I wanted to call out to Donald, but I had only the element of surprise to assist me. I'd seen the nester run and jump. It had far superior strength to mine.

Afternoon sunlight slanted across the front of the hotel, basting the columns and steps in a deceptive golden glow. I climbed the marble steps where I'd sat the night of the scavenger hunt and scanned the shoreline as far as I could see. A clear blue sky met calm water. Saw-grass rippled in a teasing wind. The shore was empty. Where had Donald gone? I abandoned the stairs and went into the skeleton of the building. Scuppernong and honeysuckle had twined around the columns, and I thought of Margo's gravestone, so elegant in design.

There wasn't much left of the hotel. The foundation was still good, and I wandered into what would have once been an elegant lobby.

Piles of rubble and debris had been pushed to the front of the slab. Bob was clearing out the old to make way for his dream. But where was Donald?

I moved cautiously, easing from one column to the next, trying to make my way as stealthily as possible while looking for a small boy who had no idea his life was in danger. I should never have let him get away from me. Cora had warned me to stay on the grounds of Belle Fleur, but in my hurt and anger at her, I'd disobeyed. If anything happened to Donald, it would be my fault. It was always my fault.

I found no trace of the child in the lobby area, so I moved along the ruins, hoping for a glimpse of his burgundy jacket or bright yellow cap. With each passing minute, my fear grew. I was about to give up when I heard the soft murmur of conversation. Donald was talking to someone. Surely not the nester. Donald wouldn't be fooled into thinking the vile creature was his mother. He wouldn't talk to the thing that meant to kill him! I eased toward the voices.

"How many rooms will there be?" Donald asked.

"Initially, about a hundred." Bob's calm voice stopped me in my tracks.

"When will you be finished?"

"Hard to tell. I've got a couple of projects in Mobile that are must-do. But the crews will work here when we can and on weekends. The investors are committed. The Paradise is going to be a showcase for me." Bob laughed. "I've dreamed about this a long time, Donald. It's good to finally start."

"Mom doesn't want to stay here." Donald sounded so sad. "She said if you wouldn't go with her, she'd leave you here."

"She's upset."

"She doesn't want me to do anything." Donald hesitated. "She doesn't want Erin to ride Cogar."

"She's only worried, Donald. Give her a chance to get her feet under her."

I finally saw them behind the hotel at the swimming pool. Stagnant water had filled the bottom of the pool. Dark green and slimy looking, the water rippled as Donald tossed a rock into it. Bob knelt beside him and put a hand on his shoulder. "Your mother needs time to get over what happened to Margo. It's hard for a mother to lose a child. It's not the normal order of life."

"She can't keep us in the house all the time," Donald said. He tossed another rock.

"She'll ease up as time passes."

"She's going to leave here."

Bob tried to comfort Donald, but the child pulled away. "She is, Dad. She said she'd give you until Christmas, and if you wouldn't go back to California then, she would take us and go without you."

"She doesn't mean that, Donald."

Donald hunched his shoulders. "Oh, yes, she does. She means it. She's going back to California, and she's going to make me go with her. She has some man looking for a house to buy back where we used to live."

The force of his anguish made me catch my breath.

"That won't happen, Donald." Bob was calm. He put his arms around his son. "Everything will be fine."

There was nothing I could add to the scene, so I eased back. Donald was safe with his father. The nester wouldn't take on Bob. My place was back at Belle Fleur. I had to make Berta understand how torn up Donald was, how worried. Maybe I could talk to her and show her what was at stake.

On the way back to Belle Fleur, I detoured to go by the stables. Just as I suspected, Erin was riding Cogar. The big gray sailed over jumps that were nearly as tall as I was. Erin ignored me at the rail. She concentrated on the pattern of the jumps.

"Nice job," I said, when she finished a round.

"Tell it to my mother."

She wasn't in the mood to listen to explanations or reasons. "Be careful, Erin. Your mother—"

"Is *my* mother! Stay out of family business." She rode out of the arena and set Cogar into a canter as she headed into the woods toward Crystal Mirror Lake.

Four months earlier, her conduct would have cut me to the bone. I didn't expect better now. I was a hired tutor, a governess who "lived in." Erin had made that perfectly clear. And perhaps she was right. If the Hendersons left Coden, I would apply to teach at the local high school. They would have hired me for this year, had Cora not urged me to take the job at Belle Fleur.

Walking to the house, I thought about my life away from the family. At Belle Fleur, I was isolated from everyone my age. I'd lost touch with friends in Coden. I had no professional stimulation from others in my field. It would be sad to see the promise the Henderson family brought to Coden leave with them, but it wouldn't be completely bad for me. It wasn't as if they were really my family, abandoning me.

I chose the back door and entered the house. Silence owned the first floor, and I wondered where Cora had gone. When I checked in the front yard, I discovered her car was missing. She'd gone home.

But where was Annie?

I went upstairs. It felt peculiar to be on the third floor, because I'd come to view it as Annie's domain, the enemy camp. Not that I was above spying. I did it on a regular basis when I knew Annie was away. The problem was that I had no idea where she was. She could be in her room or she could have gone somewhere with Cora. I didn't care where she was as long as I didn't get caught snooping.

At her door, I hesitated, then knocked lightly. There was no response, so I eased the door open. Annie had closed her windows, and the gauzy fabrics hung limp. I checked the bed to be sure she wasn't playing possum. The night of the scavenger hunt came back to me. Bob had betrayed Berta that night. Things had begun to change at Belle Fleur.

I'd searched Annie's room numerous times and found only the photo album she kept in her suitcase. I pulled it from the closet and again went through it. The pearl necklace was missing from the jeweler's box where it had rested. I didn't care enough to search for it. The photos were what I wanted.

I went to the window and opened the album. Belle Fleur, newly painted and beautiful, was front and center. The small family standing in front had to be Henri, Sigourney, and the elfin Chloe. She was probably Donald's age, but small. Even at the beginning of her time at Belle Fleur, she looked tentative.

I turned the page and studied Henri. He wore his weakness in his face. Not so with Sigourney. Proud, defiant, determined to have her way. The edge of cruelty touched her lips. Even from the photo she spoke to me.

Flipping back and forth, I hunted for evidence of Chloe's pregnancy. The photos covered a span of maybe eight years. The shrubs and trees around Belle Fleur grew and thrived. Not so with Chloe. She diminished, almost fading into the background of the photos. I knew what that felt like—to be only background for someone else's dreams and ambitions. Everything she'd ever loved had been taken from her.

When I looked out the window, I noticed Cora turning back down the driveway as Bob and Donald came out of the woods. Bob had his hand on Donald's shoulder, and it made my heart swell to see that Bob, at last, was tending to his son's needs. A movement to Bob's left, just at the edge of a stand of live oaks and less than thirty yards from the trail they walked, caught my eye.

The woods were full of squirrels and deer, sometimes wild turkey. The crisp fall weather had brought them out to forage. I'd always love the wildlife, but now, any unexpected movement made me wary. Bob and Donald continued to walk and Cora's car eased down the driveway. Everything was normal. We'd had a good day, with the exception of Erin's outbreak. Things were better. Steady.

The nester stepped out of the treeline. The royal blue silk shirt it wore belonged to Berta. Blond hair cut at the shoulders glowed in the late afternoon sunlight. The creature stood perfectly still, staring up at me in Annie's window, as Bob and Donald made it safely to the front porch and Cora got out of the car to walk in with them.

I wanted to scream at the creature, to make Bob see it, but I knew the moment I opened my mouth, it would disappear. And I would be revealed as invading Annie's room. I held up one hand. The nester mocked me by holding up a hand smeared with red. From the distance of the window, I couldn't be certain, but it looked like blood. The creature smiled, snapped the air with vicious teeth, and leaped back into the woods.

I put away the photos and the suitcase and slipped out of Annie's room. I met her on the stairs, her face pinked with wind.

"Were you in my room?" she asked.

"Of course not. I went up to look for you. I knocked and you didn't answer so I was leaving." I wanted to go outside to hunt for the creature, but she grabbed my arm.

"What do you want?"

There was no one to hear my answer. "I want you to leave Belle Fleur."

"I'm not the problem, Mimi."

"To hell you aren't." I matched her stare. With everyone else I had to play a role, but I wanted Annie to know I was on to her. "Ever since you came here there's been nothing but tragedy."

"You're upset over Mark."

I couldn't be certain, but I thought a smile of victory passed across her lips. I wanted to smack her so hard she tumbled backwards down the stairs.

"I'm going to bust you, Annie. If it's the last thing I do. So let's go downstairs and pretend that we never had this conversation."

Annie brushed past me. "I'll be down in a moment, after I wash up."

My heart thudded as I descended to the first floor. A pot of coffee was in order. And some pumpkin or apple pie. Maybe both.

The front door opened and Donald came rushing into the kitchen.

"Dad wants some of our pumpkin pie," he said.

"I'll make some coffee. Let's play Monopoly."

"Yes!" Donald danced and jiggled as he shook off his jacket. "We haven't played a game in a long time."

I turned the gas on under the pot of water and spooned the coffee into the pot. "Where's Cora?" I asked.

"Talking to Dad."

"Oh, really." I crossed the room and glanced down the hall to the front door. Cora and Bob were deep in conversation. Cora glanced in at me and put a hand on Bob's shoulder. They both came inside, smiling.

"Donald says you have homemade pumpkin pie," Bob said. "I'll have a big slice."

"Me, too." Cora gave me a hug. "Mimi makes the best pie crust."

"Let me get Berta." Bob excused himself and went down the short hallway to the master suite. I cut slices of pie for all of us and put them on saucers. Maybe Berta would come play with us.

As I lifted the pot to poor the hot water into the dripolater, a cry of outrage and alarm stopped me. My gaze swept the room. Cora and Donald were fine.

"Call an ambulance!" Bob came out of his bedroom. "Call an ambulance. Hurry!"

He carried Berta in his arms. They were both soaked, and water poured from him. For one mad second, I thought he was melting. It took me a moment to register the red stain that swirled down Bob's khakis and dripped from Berta's fingertips. Her blood mingled with the water and fell to the floor.

"Sweet Jesus." Cora rushed toward them and assisted Bob in putting Berta on the floor. "Mimi, call for an ambulance! Now!" She grasped Berta's wrist and wrapped it in a dishcloth she held.

The crack of her voice galvanized me into action. I grabbed Donald and tore him away from the awful scene. I held him pressed to my belly as I dialed the operator and got emergency help. It would take an ambulance at least half an hour to get here.

"We have to take her in the car," I said.

But Cora's face told another story. She knelt beside Berta and carefully closed her wide blue eyes. "Get Donald out of here. Stop Erin before she comes in," she said.

I didn't have to be told twice.

53

Holy shit. Holy shit. Holy shit. The mantra was a drum-line in my brain. Donald and Erin huddled in my room, crying softly. Hysteria had given way to shock. Dr. Adams was on the way, the sedatives in his black bag the only comfort available for the children. Cora was with Bob, keeping him away from Berta's body, which was stretched out on the dining room floor, the gashes in her wrists a red jagged symbol of her desperation. Bob had tried CPR and mouth-to-mouth, even though Cora told him Berta was dead.

Cora and Bob believed Berta had been unable to handle Margo's death and the possibility that Erin would be injured riding. They were wrong, though. Very wrong. Berta hadn't killed herself. Someone had sedated her and then used the double-edged blade from Bob's razor to slice up her wrists, opening the veins.

I paced the second floor hallway, listening for Annie's footfalls. No one knew where she was—but I knew where she'd been. She'd come downstairs when she heard the commotion, and she'd run from the house as if the hounds of hell were on her heels. No one had seen her since.

I used the servants' stairs to bypass Bob and Cora and went into Berta's bathroom to drain the bloody tub and clean up. The room smelled of death and its thievery of dignity. The scene was classic suicide, and my intention was to clean up before Bob had to go in there again. Something stopped me, though. As painful as the pink-tinged water was to look at, perhaps there was evidence that would point the finger at Annie. I closed the door softly, leaning against it for a moment to rope in my grief. I had to be strong now. Stronger than I'd ever been. I returned to the second floor to stand guard over the children.

Dusk settled outside the house. Each time I paced the hallway, I stopped at the stained-glass window, original to the house, that depicted The Lady of Shalott. Shards of brightly hued glass told the story of her patient weaving while waiting for Lancelot to claim her love. According to legend, she died en route to Camelot. Berta had told me once, when I first moved in, that it was the window that sold her on Belle Fleur. She loved Arthurian legend, and the beauty of the stained glass had sealed the deal for her. In a blinding moment of impotent rage, I wanted to destroy the window, but I didn't.

When Annie returned, Cora caught her downstairs and brought her up the servants' staircase to avoid Berta's body. I heard their footsteps, their whispers, and I longed to confront Annie, to beat a confession from her while Cora was with her. Instead, they passed by the second floor, my grandmother supporting Annie to the third floor. They never even noticed me. Cora's solicitations of Annie made the top of my head tingle like fire ants were biting. Little did Cora know she was consoling Berta's murderer.

The sheriff arrived with the coroner. Surely this medical doctor, a man schooled in illness and the secrets of the dead, would see what others couldn't—that Berta had not taken her own life. There had to be evidence of a struggle. Bruises, medication in her system, something to show an outside force or person had played a role in her death.

I checked on the children and found them huddled on my bed, both asleep, exhausted by emotion and tears. I closed the door and went to Margo's old room to look out over the front lawn. The nester would not be far away. The creature was drawing closer and closer, confident now of its ability to win. The dark-haired girl who did Annie's bidding—she could be in the house already.

The flashing lights of a patrol car caught my attention. A deputy led the hearse into the yard. I watched from Margo's empty room as the attendants took Berta's body away. There would be no answers today, but soon. Soon. I let that word wrap me in the warmth of ultimate revenge against Annie for what she'd done to a loving family.

Dr. Adams arrived, and Erin and Donald gave no complaint when he filled two syringes with a mild sedative. They were beyond grief. Their brains refused to accept Berta's death, and so they sought the release of sleep. With Cora insisting, Bob allowed the doctor to administer a sedative to him. Annie stayed in her room, and I refused the doctor's offer of the gray emptiness of sleep. Someone had to remain vigilant.

The nester had struck while I was out mourning the loss of Mark. I should have known. It had appeared to me at the cemetery, mocking me, showing me Donald; and when I rushed to save the child, it went after Berta. Because Berta wanted to move back to California, Berta became the enemy. Annie had marshaled her forces to quash Berta's resistance to staying in Alabama. The one thing Annie and the nester would never allow was for Bob Henderson to leave Coden alive.

Like the cowbird, the nester was pushing everyone out of the way. Only Annie wasn't a baby bird wanting mother-love. No, she was older with more mature drives. Bob was what she desired, and she would remove anyone who got in her path.

The itch to take action was like salt in a wound. My body ached, and I went downstairs.

"I'm going into town," I told Cora. She sat on the front porch. Her face was gray, drained of color and expression. "Can you stay with the children?" I asked her.

"Bob should pack up the children and go back to California. I was wrong to ever. . . ." She waved a hand, indicating Belle Fleur.

"Cora, it's not this place. It's Annie." I glanced behind me because I had the sense that she stood at the door eavesdropping. She moved so quietly, so stealthily, and often came up on me when I least expected her.

A wind whipped off the Sound and sent leaves skittering across the floorboards of the porch. The sound was eerie, the wind biting. Cora shivered and wept without restraint.

I got a comforter from the house and wrapped it around her. In the November light, I saw the wrinkles in her face and neck. Age spots marked her hands. Cora was growing old before my eyes. She was in her seventies, but I'd never thought her old until now. "If we can get rid of Annie—"

"Stop it, Mimi." She caught my shoulders in a harsh grip. "It isn't Annie. You can't live in that delusion. It's never been Annie."

I spun out of her grasp. The proof was right in front of her, but she wouldn't see it. "You're keeping yourself blind, and as long as you do, tragedy is going to visit this house." I ran down the steps to the station wagon. It was Thanksgiving Day, but I had to find a private phone. I had to find Jimmy Finch.

As I drove toward town, I tried not to look at the place where Mark had died. I drove blindly past and sped along Shore Road to Coden, but I didn't tarry there. I kept moving along Highway 90 into Pascagoula. The parking lot at Jimmy Finch's detective agency was empty, the white shells of the drive crunching softly as I eased around the building to the back, which was overgrown with ligustrum and oleander. The shrubs made a thick, convenient cover as I pried off the screen to a window and worked the glass up. It was a simple matter to break in.

Hefting myself over the window ledge, I was in Finch's private office in a matter of moments. I went straight to the bitchy secretary's desk and found Finch's appointment book. He was at the Eola in Natchez. The number to the hotel was right beside his information.

I placed the call, counting the seconds, wondering what a long-distance call on a holiday would cost. Whatever it was, I would pay him back. I had to talk to him.

The desk clerk connected me to his room, and when the phone rang six times without an answer, despair almost overwhelmed me. I could leave a message, but when would he call me back? I couldn't talk in the Henderson house and there was no other phone number I could leave for a return call.

"Hello. Finch here," he finally said.

"It's me. Mimi. I had to talk to you."

"How'd you find me?"

"I'm in your office." I expected him to say something but he didn't.

"How'd you get into my office?"

"Through a window. Annie killed Berta because she wanted to move back to California." The words rushed out of my mouth in a blur.

"Hold on. What?" Finch was calm, and his control helped me regain mine.

I repeated what I'd told him.

Silence met my statement.

"Mr. Finch, did you find anything about Annie? We have to—" My voice collapsed, but I fought down my emotions. "She murdered Berta. I know she did, but there's nothing I can do to stop her. You're the only person who will even listen to me."

"I'm coming home. I was going to stay until tomorrow, but I have enough information. I'll head out now."

"What kind of information."

"You should see this in person."

"Can we meet somewhere?" I asked.

"Meet me at my office at seven A.M. tomorrow," Finch said. "Be careful, Mimi."

"You found something, didn't you?" I hardly dared to believe it.

"I did. Tomorrow at seven." He hung up.

⚘

Cora stayed the night at Belle Fleur, but it was as if the spring in her body had broken. She sagged. She moved from chair to chair, trying to order the chaos of Belle Fleur. Her voice, weakened by grief, held no authority. At last, I put her in the recliner in the family room and crushed up one of the pain meds I'd hoarded from my injured-feet incident. I put it in a glass of bourbon and coke, which she drank without complaint.

Annie wandered the house like a ghost. She knew better than to mess with me, and I left her alone. For the moment. No doubt she was planning something special for me, but soon enough I would have the goods on her and she would be in jail, or at least a mental ward. My concern was Erin and Donald. And Bob. He'd gone into Mobile with the sheriff. Three deaths, four if you counted Andrew Cargill, all associated with Belle Fleur, was too much for the sheriff to ignore. Questions had to be asked and answered.

The grandfather clock in the hall marked the minutes and the hours as I waited for dawn and my date with Annie's destiny. Bob returned around midnight, and I made a bed for him on the sofa in the den. He couldn't return to the bedroom he'd shared with Berta. As I covered him with a blanket, he grasped my hand.

"They'll have to do an autopsy," he said. Tears leaked from his eyes, tracing down his temples. "They'll have to cut her up and—"

"Shhhhhh," I said, wiping the tears with my fingertips. "It doesn't matter to Berta now, Bob. It doesn't. They have to check." Please god, let them find evidence of Annie's wrong-doing. If Berta had to die, please let it count toward ridding the family of Annie and her evil obsession.

"I don't want them to cut her up." Bob tried to master his grief, but exhaustion made him weak.

"Don't think about it now. Don't." I snapped out the light beside the sofa. "It's after one in the morning. Cora's asleep in the recliner. Try to rest. Tomorrow we'll do everything that's necessary. The children are asleep in my room and I'll take care of them."

"This is too much," Bob said. "Too much." But his voice was already fading.

When his grip on my hand eased, I covered him and also pulled the comforter around Cora in the recliner. Standing in the den, I listened to the house. Belle Fleur held its breath, or so it seemed to me.

I went to the second floor to check the children. They remained as I'd left them, both asleep on my bed. I watched them for a moment, the gentle exhalation of their breath, the movement of their eyeballs beneath the thin lids that signaled the dream state. I could only hope that in their surrender to sleep they'd found a place of joy and comfort, even if it was only for a few hours. I snapped off the light beside the bed.

Using the servants' stairs, I went up to the third floor. If I could, I would have locked Annie in her room. I considered throwing her off her balcony and calling it an accident, but I knew I was outmatched. She had helpers. Clever little nesters with superhuman speed and strength. No, I would not take Annie on, head to head. Deception was the ticket. I would be as cunning as she was.

Sometime between the hours of two and three A.M. I fell asleep in Erin's bedroom. I'd gone there to lie down, not wanting to disturb the children in my room. At first, I didn't understand what had awakened me—a sound, a dream, a fragment of memory, or the wrenching twist of grief that came when I realized Berta was dead and that each day I would awaken to that reality.

I rolled over in Erin's single bed and tried to go back to sleep, but it was pointless. Belle Fleur's hundred-year-old frame ticked and settled, each sound an alarm to my hyper-vigilant mind. The house was wide awake now, and I sensed there was a reason for it.

With Berta gone, I was the children's protector. It was the only thing I could do for Berta now.

I got up, straightened my jeans and top, and eased out of Erin's room to go down to mine. My thoughts had unnerved me, and I would sleep on the floor beside Erin and Donald, a physical guard against whatever mischief was afoot in the house. Halfway down the hall, I realized the door to my room was open.

I'd left it shut.

Panic made me want to throw the door open, but I restrained the impulse. Claw marks under the doorknob made me cautious. Barely pushing the door, I slipped into the room. In the darkness, I could make out two lumps in my bed. Tiptoeing, I eased to the bed. Donald, his features still malleable, not yet formed into the visage he'd carry as an adult, rested on my pillow. Erin had pulled the covers over her head.

Terror immobilized me. What if it wasn't Erin? What if it was the creature who'd slithered into bed with a sleeping Donald? I prepared myself to grab the nester by the throat.

Catching the sheet by the top edge, I pulled the covers back. Erin slept on her side, blond hair covering her face. My fingers caught the fine, heavy sheaf of her hair and pulled it back to reveal the thirteen-year-old, lips slightly parted showing normal teeth as she breathed in a deep slumber. I wanted to sink to the floor and thank god. Before I could move, I heard the scratch of claws in the hallway.

"Mi-mi." The voice called softly to me from just outside the door. The creature was in the house. Bob and the children were drugged. Cora was old. There was no help other than me.

"Come and find me, Mimi, or I'll come in there. It's time to play."

The creature was threatening me. I could go out and meet it, or it would come into the room and possibly harm the children in front of me. I replaced the covers over Erin and stepped back from the bed. I knew when I turned around the nester would be in the doorway.

Dread made me want to run, to escape, to flee, but duty held me in place, and I slowly faced the door. The nester blocked my escape. Its features were hidden in shadows, but it wore what looked like a black riding jacket.

"Poor Mimi," it said in Erin's voice. "You lost another mama. No one loves Mimi anymore." It giggled.

"Get away from the children." I spoke calmly, almost a whisper. If Donald or Erin woke now and saw this abomination, it could snap their minds. I advanced toward the creature. "I'm going to kill you."

It darted out of the door and down the hall to Erin's room. "Catch me if you can," it trilled.

"Oh, I'm going to catch you." I had one thought in mind. Murder. I would kill it, and then I would kill Annie. She'd come into this house with her obsessive need for love and brought this monster with her. It fed on her desperation, and it destroyed anything that got between

Annie and what she wanted—Bob. I saw it. Margo, Mark, Berta. Now Erin and Donald were in the way. She would kill them to get Bob all to herself. She wouldn't share him with his children or his wife. She'd kill me, too, but I wasn't nearly the threat that Donald and Erin were.

The creature giggled and ran into Erin's room. The door closed behind it.

I followed, but first I slipped into Donald's room and got a baseball bat. I would have preferred a gun, but I couldn't risk going downstairs. I had to stay between the creature and the children.

Once the nester was dead, I would go up the stairs to the third floor and beat Annie to death. This had to end. It had to. Annie was the source, and so she had to be removed, one way or the other.

"Mi-mi. Hide-and-seek. Play with me, or I'll play with the children."

Oh, I wanted to play. Gripping the bat, I pushed open the door to Erin's room and stepped inside.

Moonlight filtered in the window through the branches of a live oak. The tree grew close enough to the house that the branches grazed the glass when the wind was up. The creature had opened the window, and a brisk November breeze chilled the room.

I closed the door behind me and flipped on the overhead light.

The nester was nowhere in sight. The bed where I'd slept was rumpled, and Erin's dolls and stuffed animals had been knocked from the shelf where she kept them. Her closet door was open, and things were tumbled onto the floor. The nester had scrambled there to hide.

Excellent. It would be easier to bludgeon it in a confined space. I knew it could run far more quickly than I could, but if I cornered it, I could kill it.

"Come out, come out, wherever you are," I sang to the creature. "I have something for you, Nester."

"Mimi is very mad," it said in Erin's voice, but there was a darker, smokier note beneath. "Mimi wants to play ugly."

"I do." I stepped toward the closet where the voice came from. "I want to beat the living shit out of you." I grabbed Erin's clothes and threw them onto the floor with one hand while I hefted the bat with another. Movement in the far back corner of the closet prompted me to swing with everything I had in me. The thwack of the bat into something solid was one of the most satisfying things I'd ever felt.

"Gottcha!" I said and beat the thing in the corner covered by an old comforter. I struck without mercy. After repeated blows, I stopped, winded. Whatever had been in the closet had to be dead.

I pushed aside the comforter and found Erin's china doll, an antique Bob had found in the attic. The face was irreparably smashed. But that wasn't the worst of it. If the nester wasn't in the closet, where was it?

I surveyed the room, the bat still hefted. There was no other place to hide, except under the bed. I walked slowly to the spot where I'd been sleeping only half an hour before. There was a ruffled duster around the bed and I knelt down and lifted it slowly. When I lowered my face to the floor, I was eye to eye with the nester. Saliva dripped from the pointed teeth that were blasphemy in Erin's beautiful face.

"Soon they'll all be gone." It blew rancid breath across my face.

Despite my terror, I reached for the creature. It lunged at my hand, teeth snapping like a rabid dog. Spittle sprayed my hand and face and gagged me with the horrible odor.

The creature giggled and slammed into me, knocking me onto my side. And then it was out from under the bed and at Erin's window. With one final giggle, it leaped into the branches of the oak tree.

I raced after it, still wielding the bat. It stopped on the branch, just out of reach, looking so much like Erin that my heart dropped at the sight of her perched so precariously on the tree limb, the ground at least twenty feet below her.

The nester stared at me, smiling, nasty teeth glinting white in the moonlight. It lifted its arm up and with a viciousness I'd never seen, it bit. Blood spurted from its arm, from Erin's arm. "Erin's mine," it said before it scampered along the limb to the tree trunk and ran down it like an animal.

I stood in the window and watched it race across the yard, running on two legs and sometimes four. It disappeared into the woods and I knew if I went to look I would find only claw marks in the dirt.

The bat slipped through my nerveless fingers and I sank onto Erin's bed, wondering what I could possibly do to prevent further tragedy.

I had to get Annie out of the house. Perhaps I would go to jail for killing Annie, but at least the children and Bob would be saved.

For the rest of the night I sat outside my bedroom door, the bat across my lap, waiting. Guarding the door didn't mean the creature couldn't get in another way. With the nester, there were no guarantees. But while I sat, I planned the future. One way or the other, Annie would be gone from Belle Fleur before darkness fell again.

54

Jimmy Finch actually wore a trench coat and carried a manila envelope when he got out of his car and walked across the parking lot to where I sat on his steps. A cigarette dangled from his mouth and his eyes were tired.

"Why didn't you just break in again?" he asked.

"Not necessary. You were coming, and the heat isn't on in your office." I followed him inside but kept my coat on. The place was freezing. I wondered if he was aggravated that I'd broken in, but there was only worry on his face.

He handed me the papers he'd brought in. "Take a look at that."

I shook out the handwritten pages and scanned them.

"Annie lived with a family in Natchez?" I couldn't be certain what I was reading. Finch's handwriting was atrocious.

"Yeah. She was fostered by a rural family just outside of Natchez. They got her when she was six from a shelter home in Jackson. According to the state records, she was dropped in front of the shelter, obviously a victim of some kind of trauma. She didn't speak for the first six years, and she was shifted from home to home for a while, until the Fultons near Natchez took her in. By all accounts from the family, she was happy there, though always distant. She ran away from the Fultons back in July. She was seen talking to an older woman in a shop where she'd gone to buy a new blouse. She never returned to the Fultons and no one has seen her since. Natchez police have her listed as a runaway, presumed dead."

"Are you positive?"

He nodded. "Mr. and Mrs. Fulton identified her by a photo. It's Annie all right. Annie Fulton. They gave her their last name because she couldn't remember—or wouldn't say—her own. They've been searching for her. They never gave up hope. They never dreamed she'd come to this area. She has no connection to Mobile that they knew of."

"Did they say what the older woman she was talking to in the shop looked like?"

"You're pretty astute," Finch said. He sat on the edge of his desk.

"It was my grandmother, wasn't it?"

"Can't say for sure, but she fits the description. In her sixties or seventies, dressed in business clothes, drove a newer model Cadillac, blue."

"Cora's car is blue." I didn't feel anything. I didn't understand. Why would Cora go to Natchez, Mississippi—a five-hour drive one way—and encourage a teenage girl into running away from a family to show up in Coden? If Cora actually drove Annie across a state line, she had risked a kidnapping charge. "Were the Fultons abusing Annie?"

"Not from what I could tell. They seemed like decent, compassionate people. Religious, but not crazy. They lived out from town, but Annie attended the local school. I checked with the middle-school authorities, and Annie was a good student, smart, if not well-adjusted. She caused no trouble. She had no friends and she didn't talk except when asked a direct question. But there was no sign of abuse or unhappiness with her family situation."

"Did they say how they came to have Annie?"

"The story they got from the caseworker at the state shelter was that she'd lost her family in a fire, and that the trauma had sent her into a depression that affected the way she interacted with others. She never spoke of her family or cried. They thought that was strange, but they were willing to accept what the caseworker told them—children react differently to such horrible loss. They didn't press for details. I've got a call in to the Jackson shelter to see if more information is available, but what I understand is that she was found sitting on the front steps of the shelter. Abandoned. Now that I have a time period, I can do more checking on house fires, but I daresay your grandmother can fill in a lot of the blanks."

I didn't know what to say. "Have you talked to Cora?"

"Not yet."

"She's a wreck because of Berta."

"I thought I'd wait until Monday. Give everyone a chance to recover a bit. I have to report this to the sheriff, though. He'll probably want to talk to Cora immediately."

"Give me a chance to talk to her first. Please."

Finch tapped a forefinger on his thigh as he considered my request. "Okay. I'll wait until noon. But it's my duty to report this, Mimi. If your grandmother did something unethical, we have to tell the truth. If she was actively involved in Annie running away, it could be serious charges."

"Whatever Cora did, she did because she meant to help. I don't understand this at all. She wouldn't take a child from a loving home. But I have to ask her and give her a chance to explain."

"Do you know when services for Mrs. Henderson will be held?" he asked.

"They had to do an autopsy." I blinked back the tears. In twenty-four hours, I'd emotionally lost the woman I considered to be my mother and physically lost the woman I'd grown to love like a mother. "Bob and the children were given sedatives last night. I don't know what's going to happen at Belle Fleur."

"If I were Bob Henderson, I'd put that house on the market and get out of town as fast as possible."

I looked at Finch. "Why? It isn't the fault of the house."

"They've had nothing but bad luck since they came. I never believed the stories about the house, but I swear, now, I'm reconsidering."

"What stories?"

Finch shook his head slowly. "Once I started asking around about Belle Fleur, there are stories, actually different variations of the same story. Belle Fleur is supposedly haunted."

"By the ghost of Sigourney Desmarais?"

"That would make sense, but that's not what I've heard. It's a young girl. Supposedly beautiful. Folks have seen her in the third floor windows staring out."

"Chloe?" Or worse, Annie. Had Annie become possessed by Chloe's spirit? The idea was terrifying.

He stood up. "It's local legend, Mimi. You've been living in the house. There's no ghost."

Something was roaming the rooms and woods of Belle Fleur. But even as much as Jimmy Finch believed the things I told him, he would never believe me about the nester. I restacked his papers and put them in the manila envelope. When I started to leave, he stopped me.

"I'll get Martha to type up my report for you. She's the only person who can really read my handwriting."

"Sure thing." I gave his notes back.

"You want to call me when you finish with Cora?"

"I can do that. In fact, let me call the Hendersons and tell them where I am."

He waved me to the phone at his secretary's desk. Instead of dialing the Hendersons, I thought better of it. I didn't want to wake them, so I called Cora's house on the off chance she'd gone home when she woke up. She was normally up with the sun, and it was nearly eight o'clock on a sunny day, the last Friday in November.

When Cora answered her phone, I wasn't surprised. "I have to talk with you," I told her. "I know about Annie. I know she lived in Natchez."

"It's a relief that you know," she said. I'd never heard her voice so worn and without hope. "When I first brought Annie here, I thought it best for her to leave everything about her past behind. That was a mistake."

"Why did you do this, Cora?" I knew Cora didn't see it the same way I did, but she'd betrayed me. Out of the corner of my eye, I watched Finch in his private office going through some files.

"Annie belongs here, in Coden," Cora said. "Like you. I was only trying to bring it all back together, to fix it so that the past could be made whole."

"What are you saying?"

"What do you know of Annie's birth parents?" Cora's voice was almost a whisper.

"They died in a fire." I hesitated. I saw it—the parallel. "Like mine."

"Annie is your sister, Mimi. The fire was an awful tragedy, and I took you, and Annie went into foster care. She was so young. She had a better chance to be adopted. You were so badly scarred by the fire, by what you'd seen. You forgot everything, even the fact that you had a sister."

Finch's office was freezing, but a flush of heat ran from the telephone through my head and along my body. Sweat popped out on my forehead and cheeks. "She's my what?"

"Your younger sister. Look in the mirror. Really look. You'll see it."

Finch's secretary had a glass cover on her desk, and I could see a ghostly reflection in it. When I looked, for one split second, I saw Annie. My hair was lighter, more wave than curl. My eyes were hazel where hers were golden brown. But there was a hint of her in me.

"Everything okay?" Finch called out.

"Fine," I answered automatically.

"Where are you?" Cora asked.

"In town. I have to talk to you."

"Yes, you do. There's more for you to know, Mimi. A lot more."

"I'm headed to your house." Silence filled the line, and unreasonable dread consumed me. "Cora! Cora!"

"There's someone in the edge of the woods," Cora said. "I can barely make them out. My eyes aren't what they used to be. But there's someone standing out by the big magnolia tree on the edge of the woods."

"Who is it?" Holding the phone in Jimmy Finch's office, I was totally helpless.

"I can't be certain."

"Is it Annie?" What would Annie do to Cora now that her secrets were being divulged?

"No, it looks more like . . . why, it's Erin. But she's standing in the edge of the woods just watching my house. She's acting peculiar. Let me get her inside and see what's wrong with her."

"No!"

"Mimi, I think she's hurt."

"Do *not* let her inside. Lock the doors, Cora. Lock the doors and get in the bathroom. Lock that door, too!"

"What's wrong with you, Mimi?" She was frightened.

"That isn't Erin. It is something vile and evil. Get in the bathroom and barricade the door!"

"I have to go, Mimi." The line went dead.

Finch heard my frantic orders and came into the front room. "What's wrong?"

"Someone is at Cora's house and I think they mean to hurt her." I pulled the car keys from my pocket. "I have to go."

"I'll call the sheriff in Mobile. I'll come with you."

"Call the sheriff and catch up with me," I said and ran out the front door to the station wagon. It was only fifteen minutes to Cora's house, but in that amount of time, the nester could do anything.

55

The sun climbed the morning sky, but I felt as if darkness surrounded me. I raced along Shore Road, oblivious to the gulls crying over the water or the fishing vessels out in the Sound. My world had narrowed to the gray strip of asphalt that led to Cora's and the grass and trees that bordered the road. When I got to the turn to Cora's house, I was traveling so fast I almost lost control, but I righted the car. I slid to a stop at the front of the house.

Cora sat on the front porch in her favorite rocker. For a split second, I felt relief. Then I realized something was wrong. She wore a blue dress, one that she often chose for a workday, but her feet were spaced wide apart in a pose no lady of her generation would ever assume.

"Cora!" I rushed up the steps. "Cora!"

She didn't move. Her neck was covered in vivid red that had seeped onto the book she held in her lap.

"Cora!" I dropped to my knees beside her. The front of her dress was soaked in blood, and a gash sliced her throat. The blood bubbled at the wound, and I saw her eyes fixed on me. She was alive!

I tried to stop the flow of blood by pressing my hands against it. A butcher knife was in her lap, and I picked it up and threw it into the yard.

"Help!" I called out for anyone, but there was no one near enough to hear me. "Help me!" I tried to press the blood back into her. I could feel her breath bubbling beneath my fingers. I felt something else, too. Uniform, round pebbles. I looked more closely. Cora wore the pearl necklace, the one I'd last seen in Annie's suitcase at Belle Fleur.

I could feel Cora slipping away from me. Her body was growing limp, and as I watched, the flicker of life left her eyes. "No, Cora, no." I rocked back and forth. "Don't leave me. You're all the family I have."

She'd claimed that Annie was my sister, but that had to be wrong. It had to be. How could she be?

I heard the sirens blowing to the west as a sheriff's deputy blasted toward Cora's. Too late. Just like me. Too late to do anything to save my grandmother. A gust of wind grabbed at the pages of the book in Cora's lap and I pushed it aside.

The patrol car slewed into the yard and a deputy I didn't know jumped out, his weapon drawn. "Step away from her," he said.

I heard him, but I didn't understand. I picked up her lifeless hand and held it. "She's my grandmother."

He saw the knife in the grass of the front yard and came toward me, gun drawn. "Move away from her," he said again, his face white.

I realized he thought I'd killed her. "I just got here. She was still breathing." I help up my hands, her blood dripping from my fingertips. "I tried to stop the bleeding. She was still alive."

"Move away. Now." He stepped closer, and I could see the fear in his eyes. If I did anything sudden, he might shoot me. "Okay." I gently put her hand in her lap. Her eyes were flat and empty. I tried to ease to my feet, but the deputy yelled at me to stay on my knees. I carefully moved away from her toward the steps.

Another car pulled into the yard, and I was relieved to see Jimmy Finch. He got out of his car and went toward the deputy. "That's Mimi, the granddaughter," he said. "She was in my office when her grandmother saw someone in her yard. Mimi came as quickly as she could. Obviously not fast enough, though."

The deputy wasn't certain if he should believe Finch or not. "Let me call this in," he said.

"Put your gun away. Mimi isn't going anywhere and neither am I."

The deputy slowly lowered his weapon and eased to the car where he got his radio and called in Cora's murder. This death could not be viewed as suicide or anything other than a vicious, brutal killing. The necklace would prove Annie had been here.

Finch came up to the porch. "You okay?" he asked.

I stared at him. I couldn't answer. My grandmother had just been murdered. Her blood was all over me.

"Any idea who might have done this?" Finch asked.

"It was Annie." In truth, it was likely the nester who'd sliced Cora's throat, but the creature worked at the behest of Annie. If her hand hadn't wielded the knife, it was her will that had caused it.

"How can you be certain?" Finch asked.

"The necklace. The pearl necklace. It's Annie's. I saw it in her suitcase in her room."

Finch walked over to Cora's body. The deputy joined him. Finch kept his thoughts to himself, thank goodness.

"The sheriff and the coroner are on the way," the deputy said. "I have to secure the crime scene. Can you move the girl off the porch?"

"How about I take her inside and let her wash up a little."

The deputy hesitated.

"She was with me. I was ten minutes behind her. She couldn't have done this."

"Okay." He went to his car to open the trunk and get the tape used to mark off a crime scene.

Finch assisted me to my feet and opened the door to Cora's house. I let him lead me to the bathroom. He turned on the hot water and stood over me. I wondered if he was afraid I'd do something to myself.

"I'm okay. Really. I want to wash up and use the bathroom."

He didn't move.

"I can't do that if you're standing here with me."

"Okay." He backed out of the bathroom, his footsteps going into the living room.

I washed my hands and then glanced at my face in the mirror. Blood from her throat had bubbled onto my face. I washed it all away, trying hard not to think about what had happened.

56

The lawmen and crime-scene people worked around me, an object of their curiosity. If I returned their looks, they got very busy. They knew my grandmother had been murdered and that I'd found her in the last moments of her life. They didn't know what to say to me, other than the "sorry for your loss" line that they were trained to repeat with varying degrees of sincerity.

To my surprise, Jimmy Finch stayed at my side like a pit bull. He growled if anyone tried to ask me a question, though he had plenty of his own. He kept jotting things into his pocket notebook. And he kept insisting that I leave Cora's house. Her blood was drying into the boards of the porch, and he refused to leave me by myself, though he was restless, pacing the floral-printed rug in the front room.

The crime-scene techs packed up their gear. They'd found the knife I threw in the yard, and I'd explained that I found it in her lap and had slung it away without thinking.

They'd also told me to come to the sheriff's office to have my fingerprints taken and answer some questions. The sheriff, in a moment of compassion, told me to wait until the afternoon.

"Mimi, let me take you to the Hendersons," Finch said for the twentieth time. "Staying here won't bring Cora back."

"No," I told him. "I won't go back to Belle Fleur. I can't go there. I have things to do here."

"When you were talking with your grandmother, she saw someone in the yard. You have to tell the sheriff what Cora saw." Finch stood over me as I sat in Cora's wing chair in her front room.

I knew what I had to do. Involving the sheriff wasn't in my game plan. "I'll talk to the sheriff later today."

"Mimi, you don't have a choice in this. Tell him you were talking to Cora and she saw someone in her yard, someone she recognized."

"She didn't tell me who it was." I wasn't about to say it was Erin, only not really Erin but a creature that had taken Erin's features. I changed the subject. "Bob has to make funeral arrangements for Berta. I need to do the same for Cora. I wonder if Bob will let me bury her in the cemetery at Belle Fleur. She loved that place as much as any Desmarais or Henderson."

Finch sat down opposite me. "You're in shock, Mimi. This is a terrible thing. Someone should watch out for you."

"There's no one who fits that job description." I didn't mean to sound pitiful. "Look, I'm not going to do anything silly. I just want some time alone." I pressed my knees together until my thighs ached. I wanted to jump and scream, to run and curse, to slug someone. Instead, I sat primly, giving the illusion of total control.

"Oh, I think you're a long way from being okay. I just don't know what to do about it."

"Let me have some time." I looked out the window. They had taken Cora away in an ambulance, but the light was not flashing and there was no siren, because there was no hurry. The nester had come out of the woods and killed her in the time it took me to drive from Pascagoula to her home.

"You can't sit here. Alone." Finch paced again. Stillness made him anxious. I eyed him with some annoyance. If he would only leave, I could take action. Until he drove away, I had to present a calm exterior, a young woman operating in a reasonable way, grieving but not emotionally frenzied.

"I'll go back to Belle Fleur later tonight. That's where most of my things are, and Bob will need help with the children. Right now, I want some time to think. I want to think about Cora here, in this house, happy and laughing with me. I want to remember the times we shared together."

He squatted down so we were on eye level. "What are you up to, Mimi?"

"I'm going to kill Annie." I said it without emotion.

"I was afraid you'd say that." He didn't smile. "We have no proof she did this. No one was here when you got here. It could have been a burglar."

I stared into his eyes. "I know I can't kill Annie. I want to, but I can't. I'm going to do what's necessary to bury my grandmother and find evidence to use against Annie."

He sighed. "It unnerves me that you aren't crying."

"Because I'm a woman?" I almost laughed.

"Because you're not much more than a kid, even though you think you're grown." He patted his pocket for a cigarette. When he had the pack, he shook one out for me. "Women cry, but you're hard as flint."

"I've lost everyone who ever loved me. If I start crying, I won't stop. So I can't. There are things that must be done, and I have to be alone to do them. Please, just go." I accepted the light he offered. "I'm not going to have a breakdown. I'm not going to do anything rash."

"I know you aren't telling me the truth about who Cora saw. It was Annie, wasn't it? I can't let this go, Mimi. I'm going to make certain the guilty party pays for this."

I wanted to tell him that wouldn't be necessary, but if I did that, he would become suspicious. "Annie will pay. Why don't you go up to Belle Fleur and talk to Bob? See if you can find out where Annie was this morning without upsetting Bob and the children." I drew on the cigarette. "What Cora said she saw—it was Annie. In the edge of the woods. She did this, Mr. Finch. This time I'm going to prove it."

He stood up. "I'll drop by Belle Fleur to pay my respects and see if I can talk to Annie alone. I'll get more out of her than Bob. They're going to want to know about Cora. What should I tell them?"

I thought about it. "Tell them the police think it was someone trying to rob her."

"And you're certain it wasn't?"

Finch's doubt infuriated me, but I didn't show it. "I told you what Cora said. That's all I have to go on. But tell them we think it was a robber. Until the sheriff finds real evidence of Annie's work, we should leave it at that."

Finch finally went to the door. He turned back and watched me for a long moment, but I kept my gaze fixed on the front window, which gave a view of the woods. I smoked the cigarette, ignoring the ash that fell to the floor.

In my mind, I could see exactly what Cora had seen. The nester had stood right at the edge of the woods beside a magnolia that had weathered innumerable storms. The creature was close enough that it could probably hear Cora's conversation with me. Superior in strength and speed to an old woman, it had felt no need to rush or hurry. It had slipped into the house while she wasn't looking, selected a butcher knife from the kitchen, and then tricked her onto the front porch. Without a qualm, it had sliced her throat and pushed her into a rocker and left her to bleed out.

I took another puff of the cigarette, aware that Finch was watching me. At last he left. He went slowly down the driveway, and I could see he was searching the woods from some sign that Annie had been there as I insisted. The only sign he would find would be the claw marks. Like everyone else, he would think they belonged to a dog or wild creature. They were half right. But it was the half-wrong part that had cost Andrew, Margo, Berta, and finally Cora their lives.

Cora had wanted to tell me something. Something other than the fact that Annie was my sister, which I didn't believe. It was impossible. It couldn't be true. Why she would make up such a thing didn't make sense to me.

I got up and went to the bathroom where Cora's blood still stained the washcloth and hand towel I'd used. The mirror gave me back my reflection. We were not related. Cora had made one last effort to bond us with a lie. But why did she care so much? My reflection gave me no answers, so I decided to investigate the house. The sheriff hadn't bothered to look through Cora's personal things. He'd assumed it was a burglary gone wrong, and I'd told him nothing of value appeared to be missing. Perhaps there was something I hadn't discovered yet. Something Annie wanted.

I'd lived in Cora's house most of my life, but I'd never been one to paw through the belongings of others. Now, though, I had to search before the sheriff realized Cora's murder was not some random burglar and came back to look for reasons.

Cora's room held a vague scent of Evening in Paris, her favorite bath powder. I found it on her dresser and held it close to my face, drawing in her scent. Her dresser top contained a jewelry box, which I had investigated in the past. Nothing new was inside. The pearl necklace—that had come from Annie. The nester had put it around Cora's throat as she was dying. I was positive of it. I was about to put the jewelry case back when I realized there was another drawer, a flat enclosure for documents or letters. A flimsy lock held it shut. I got a dinner knife from the kitchen and pried it open.

A half dozen old photographs dropped onto my lap.

The first one showed Belle Fleur, sparkling new in the sunlight. Men and women dressed in gardening clothes stood lined along the front porch. On the steps were Henri, Sigourney, and Chloe. It was a photo of Belle Fleur and the garden staff Henri hired for the fledgling perfume business.

I studied the men and women, who seemed happy and proud. This must have been in the beginning, because Chloe was very young and the plants around the house were small. But why would Cora have this photograph of the gardening staff? Why had she never shown it to me?

The next photograph was of Chloe, blooming with joy and caught sitting on the front steps. Her pose almost concealed her pregnancy.

Almost. I flipped to the next photo and stopped. Sigourney, her hair perfectly coiled, stared back at me. A pearl necklace adorned her throat.

The next photo was of a young woman I didn't know, but it was of a similar time period. She wore the pearl necklace and she held an infant in her arms. Her smile was serene, and the baby was fat and happy, but I had no idea who these people were. I flipped it over and found the name Anna Nyman written in pencil. Anna was Cora's grandmother, my great-great-grandmother. The baby's name was Delphine.

It was the final photo that stopped me. Sigourney wore the necklace, but this time I recognized her. It was the same photo I'd found in Annie's room. Either Annie had left the photo here in Cora's jewelry box, or she and Cora had a copy of the same photograph, circa 1860.

It was impossible, but there it was.

57

I found nothing else of interest in Cora's room. I remembered the book and went outside to retrieve it. The deputies had examined it but found nothing of interest. There had to be something, though. Cora had said there was more to tell me. More lies? More distortions of the truth? Perhaps the book she'd died with in her hand could tell me something new. If Annie was my sister—and I didn't believe that for a moment—was there anything about my life that was real and true?

At the edge of the porch, I picked up the book and went back inside. I knew the volume I held. It was a collection of fairy tales and poems. Cora had sometimes read to me at night when she put me to bed. It wasn't that I couldn't read on my own, but I loved the sound of her voice as I drifted off to sleep. I loved the fairy tales from around the world, "Wasilla, the Beautiful," or "Little One Eye," or "The Two Sisters." There were poems, too. I flipped through the book and stopped at "Little Orphant Annie" by James Whitcomb Riley. It was the poem Annie had recited to the Henderson children when she first arrived.

I read the words and felt the chill of fear march along my skin. Goblins. Nesters. Most people would think that such creatures populated only the imagination of poets and writers, but I knew better.

At the bottom of the poem, Cora had written something. It wasn't her normal, clear script. "Secretary." Just one word.

In the front room was a small desk, an antique that Cora was exceptionally proud of. Cora had called it a lady's secretary, a place where the woman of the house could sit to write out notes and pay bills, a small, feminine piece in contrast to a man's desk. I went to it and opened the main drawer. An envelope with my name on it was on the top of a stack of papers.

From the kitchen, I selected a knife. I went out to the front porch and sat on the steps where the light was strong, a reminder that the sun did shine, even in Coden. The note was dated only a few weeks earlier, November 17. A premonition must have prompted Cora to put her story in writing. Or more likely, the string of tragedies that had befallen the Hendersons reminded Cora of her own mortality.

Mimi,

"I've kept many secrets from you, waiting for the time I thought you could handle the truth about your past.

I could almost hear her voice as I read.

When your home burned and your parents were killed, you and your baby sister, Annie, survived. The trauma was so severe, I took you into my home because I didn't trust anyone else to care for you. I've known your family for years. You are not my grandchild, but we share a bond much closer than blood.

Something moved just out of sight in the woods. The wind fluttered the pages in my hand and I pulled my coat tighter around me. I couldn't see anything, but I hoped it was the creature. I wanted it to come to me, to try to savage me. My free hand found the knife handle. It gave me a good bit of comfort as I returned to my reading.

> *I wanted to tell you about your family in person. I know how difficult this will be for you to accept, how betrayed you're going to feel. I thought each day that I had to tell you the truth, Mimi. But the time was never right. You seemed to forget about the fire, about the horror of how your parents died. When you first came to me, you woke up every night with terrible nightmares. After a few weeks, the nightmares stopped and you forgot. I couldn't bring myself to remind you, to take you back to the horrible event. Not even for your own good. I was weak, and now you'll learn the truth in the most brutal way.*
>
> *I knew your parents well. In fact, I helped raise your mother, Amanda Bosarge. She was a good person, kind and gentle. Your father, James, was a talented man, a painter. Amanda got pregnant with you, and she married James and left Coden. Back then, girls who got pregnant out of wedlock were scorned. I helped them find a house in Fort Bayou Bluff, just across the state line in Jackson County, Mississippi. They rented a little cottage, and they were very happy. You were born and you were the most beautiful baby I'd ever seen. I couldn't look at you without thinking of Chloe Desmarais.*

The name stopped me cold. Cora's obsession with Belle Fleur went back to my birth. But why?

> *Your family was secure and happy. James began to sell his work, and he built a studio in the garage beside the house. The years passed. Amanda got pregnant again, and Annie was born. You were almost ready to start school, and your parents thought you were a genius. You painted and drew the*

most fantastic pictures. Some of them were very dark, scary even. But you were a child who loved a ghost story more than anything else. I should know, I told you plenty.

For the first five years of your life, Mimi, you enjoyed a perfect life. After Annie was born, things changed. Most children resent a new sibling, but with Annie, it went much deeper than that. Your mother was afraid you would hurt the new baby. You were extremely jealous. You drew pictures that showed Annie dead. No one could understand why, but from the moment Amanda brought her home from the hospital, you hated her. You said she was evil. Your words. "Annie is evil. She wants to hurt Mama."

We found a psychologist, but before you could make the first appointment with him, the house caught fire and Amanda and James died. The last thing they did was put Annie out a window to the ground. She made it to safety in the woods behind the house. You were found standing in the front yard in your nightgown, staring at the flames. You were in a deep, walking coma, and for months no one knew if you'd recover. You were seven. Annie, who was two, seemed less traumatized. Amanda had no family in the area, and James was from Buffalo, New York. None of his people even came for the funerals. So I took you and Annie. My intention was to raise you both as my granddaughters. But every time you saw Annie, you became hysterical, and Annie refused to speak. Child welfare wanted to put you into a mental institution. But you were docile as long as Annie was not near you. It broke my heart, but I made a choice. I kept you with me, and Annie was put into a shelter home in Jackson and adopted by a family in Natchez from there.

I never told you the truth, because I couldn't hurt you. You'd lost so much, even your sister. But you never seemed to remember anything about the past. You accepted me as your grandmother and never asked a single question. I told you

*your parents had died in a fire, and that was true. But I never
told you the truth.*

*This part is very hard, Mimi. The fire chief believed you
were in the garage, perhaps playing with matches. You were
a child who investigated and explored. James smoked. Back
then a lot of people did. His cigarettes and Zippo lighter were
in the garage. The fire chief theorized that you knocked over
paint thinner and accidentally set it on fire. The fact that you
were outside the garage on the front lawn seemed to support
that theory. No formal report was made—at my request. We
both believed it would do no good to put that in the record of
a child with emotional problems.*

My hand shook so hard, I had to stop reading. Cora believed I had
set the fire that killed my parents. Though I didn't remember James
and Amanda—had no memory of anything Cora wrote about—I
knew I hadn't killed anyone. It was Annie. If I had hated her, even
then, it was for cause. She was only a toddler at the time of the fire,
but she was cunning. She learned things by osmosis, and I could see
her in the converted garage, eyeing the Zippo, wanting the blue flame
that leaped when the wheel was struck. If the fire was set deliberately,
then it was by her hand, not mine. Yet once again, I received the
blame for her actions.

I could not remember the events Cora wrote about, yet I sensed
the truth of her words. And it made sense that for me, the hatred of
Annie went back much longer than our time at Belle Fleur.

I had to finish the things Cora had written. I was almost to the
end. I had to know.

*From that point, I kept up with Annie. I checked with her
foster parents, and I waited for the opportunity to bring her
home to Coden, to reunite her with you, her sister. I waited
and planned for that day. When the Hendersons bought Belle
Fleur, that was the perfect opportunity. I could bring you both*

home. Home to me, and home to the place that is your birth-right. Belle Fleur.

The telephone in Cora's house rang, and I stopped reading. There were only a few paragraphs to go. I considered not answering, but if it was Bob or the sheriff or Jimmy Finch, if I didn't answer, they would come looking for me. And I didn't want to be disturbed. I answered the phone in a monotone.

"Are you okay?" Jimmy Finch asked.

"Yes."

"The sheriff wants to see you in Mobile, Mimi. I told him I would drive you."

"Okay."

"I'll come and pick you up."

"Okay."

He hesitated. "Are you sure you're okay?"

"I think I understand a lot now. Things I didn't know." I tried to keep the thoughts in my head from swirling too fast. "Did you ever find out who sold Belle Fleur?"

"Trident Company, the realty group, wasn't very helpful. They only said descendants of the Desmarais family. They wouldn't be more specific, but I haven't given up. That there are descendants of the Desmarais family is a big lead. I can track that."

"Don't worry about it, Mr. Finch."

"It's a point of curiosity, Mimi. I'll keep on it, no charge."

There was no sense arguing. Finch was a stubborn man once he got his teeth into something.

"Thank you."

"I'll be by Cora's house in fifteen minutes. Twenty at the latest. I just think it would be best for you to have someone with you."

"Thank you. If I'm not here, I'll be at the Hendersons." Twenty minutes wasn't enough time, but it was all I had. I returned to the pages. Cora had called Belle Fleur my birthright. I had to find out what she meant.

I think you've guessed the rest by now, Mimi.

I think from the moment you first saw Belle Fleur, you knew. You feel it. The house, the property, the history. Even as a child, when I would bring you there, to sit on the lawn, you were drawn to the house. And now, you live there as you were always meant to. You are a Desmarais.

I didn't need Cora's words to tell me anything else. I had to find Annie.

58

Pulling into the driveway of Belle Fleur, I had a sense that the house was already empty, Bob and the children gone. Belle Fleur had always been a fantasy for me, a place where the glamour of the past lived on, a place where I had a family. Now, the sight of the empty windows, like soulless eyes, frightened me. I hoped Bob and the children had escaped. I wanted that to be true more than anything. I couldn't protect them—I accepted that fact. Their only hope was to leave Coden as quickly as possible. And to leave without Annie, though she would do anything to keep Bob there.

The sensation of being watched followed me as I opened the door and checked the garage. Berta's car, the convertible that she'd loved to drive with the summer wind blowing her blond hair, was to the right. I touched the trunk, seeking a trace of what? The past? Berta's joyful essence? A time that had been too brief? I could almost see her in the driver's seat, sunglasses shielding her eyes and a wide smile because her world was good.

Bob's car was gone. He was probably in Mobile making arrangements for Berta's funeral. I prayed the children were with him. Surely he wouldn't have left them alone in the house. But where was Annie?

I walked to the backyard. The windows of her room were open, and the curtains blew out onto the balcony and back inside again, as if her room breathed. In and out. In and out. Strange, because there was no breeze to stir the material, or none that I could detect.

Whatever Annie was, she wasn't my sister. She might have been born into my birth family, but she was something other than ordinary flesh and blood. Cora had brought her to Coden in an effort to help her, but it had destroyed the Hendersons and my happiness. The family that had accepted me with open, loving arms was gone. Bob would never recover. Erin and Donald would bear the scars of Belle Fleur for the rest of their lives. It was all for nothing.

I went back to the front door and entered the house, the emptiness echoing all around me. Blood marred the hardwood floor where Berta's body had lain, a pool of rusty red and black stains. For a long time I stared at the blood. There seemed no option open to me. None that I wanted to take. I knew what I had to do, and while a part of me wanted it, another part rebelled. Cora had taught me that all life was precious, but the instinct to survive, to save what I loved, was stronger.

The one truth I knew was that Bob would never be rid of Annie unless I killed her. That creature she'd spawned, the nester, would never leave Belle Fleur. Like Annie—like me—it had come home to this house. With Cora's help, the last of Sigourney's line had returned to Coden. But Cora had never anticipated what Annie would bring with her. The blood of the Desmarais family pumped through the nester's evil veins just as it did mine and Annie's. Sigourney, who had imprisoned and mistreated her daughter Chloe, who had thrown her own grandchild into a well, was the root-stock of the nester. The cruelties Sigourney had inflected on Chloe and her baby had changed the infant in unfathomable, physical ways. Emotion was made manifest.

And I was descended from that unwanted bastard.

I could see it clearly now. Cora's ancestors had worked at Belle Fleur. In the old photograph of the garden workers, Cora's people could be found. She'd mentioned all of this in passing, how the gardens had been a paradise for the workers. From others, I'd learned of Chloe's love affair gone wrong, and the child that resulted, tossed into a well to drown.

Only the workers had intervened. Cora's grandmother had taken action to save the baby. Anna Nyman and Delphine. She'd been unwilling to let the child die alone and frightened at the bottom of a well.

Cora's connection to Belle Fleur went back generations. And when Belle Fleur was sold to the Hendersons by descendants of the Desmarais family, that was me and Annie. That's how Cora had settled my college debt. I'd never stopped to ask her where the money came from or why she'd volunteered to treat me as her own. Now I knew. It was what her family did for Chloe and those who came from her.

The problem was that Annie was far more Sigourney than Chloe. She was Sigourney to the tenth power. She was able to take her anger and rage and desperation and create from it a creature that did her bidding. The nester. Wanting all the love and willing to push everyone else out of the nest.

I'd watched it transform into Margo, Berta, Donald, and Erin, and if I didn't stop it, it would kill the last Henderson children. And sooner rather than later. And me? Would it come after me? I had no way of knowing.

I went into Bob and Berta's bedroom and found the gun in the closet. I would kill Annie and the creature she'd spawned.

The nester was a physical manifestation of her need, her endless, unfillable desire for love. How she had accomplished this, I had no idea. How did one create such an entity out of emotion? It was impossible, except I'd seen it for myself. Cora saw it, too. It was the last thing she saw.

While I would kill the nester, I wanted to kill Annie first. Chop off the head of the snake. It was a smart lesson for one who'd grown up in south Alabama where moccasins and rattlers coiled along paths, waiting for victims.

No one could give Annie what she so desperately craved, and when they failed, she killed them. When they got in her way, she eliminated them. Mark and Margo were obstacles she removed. Cora and Berta, both mother figures, had failed her. Ultimately, we were all hurdles in the path to Bob. I had no doubt that Erin, Donald, and I would also find a brutal death if Annie was not stopped.

The gun was heavier than I'd expected, but my hand gripped it with assurance. My finger fitted to the trigger. I tested the pull. An automatic was so much easier than a revolver. I checked the clip to make sure I had a full load. I pushed the clip back into place and started up the servants' staircase to the third floor.

59

Annie's room was alive with whirling fabric. A small cyclone of energy emanated from the bed. While Jimmy Finch believed much of what I told him, he'd never understand this. Even I didn't, but I believed it because I witnessed it.

Creeping to the bed, I steadied the gun. No warning. Whatever Annie was doing in the midst of the shifting bed hangings, I would end it. I pulled the trigger and the gun fired three times into the bed. Even before the echo of the bullets died, all motion in the room stopped. Dead calm.

Chop off the head.

Grasping a fistful of the gossamer material, I pulled it back. The bed was empty.

Where was the bitch?

A gut instinct told me to look beneath the bed. Gun extended, I braced myself as I leaned down. The space was empty. I'd been tricked. Again.

I went to the balcony and stepped out. At the edge of the woods the nester waited. It wore a replica of Erin's riding jacket and breeches. It didn't require boots. The dog-like claw feet required nothing.

"Mi-mi." It sang my name. "Come down and play. A last game, Mimi."

I aimed the gun and fired without thinking. If not the head of the snake, the tail would do.

Bullets bit into the ground and the oak it stood beside, but my aim was off. I didn't stop until the gun was empty, but I missed the creature.

"Come and play, Mi-mi. Soon Erin will join us. We'll play and play until she dies of exhaustion." The creature giggled. "You know the game."

I wanted to throw the gun at the vile thing, but I didn't. Instead, I went back inside and ran down the stairs to Bob and Berta's bedroom. From the top of the closet I found two more loaded clips.

Above me, I heard footsteps on the second floor. Annie! She'd abandoned her room and hidden on my floor.

Slamming a clip into place, I hefted the gun. A sound outside the bedroom stopped me. The front door creaked open. Footsteps in the foyer. Someone paused, waiting.

The creature was inside the house. It had come to torment me face-to-face. Swollen with bloodlust and power, it had no fear of me. Perhaps I could not kill it, but I would damn sure try. But Annie first.

Instead of going to the front, I headed to the servants' staircase. If I was quiet, I might take Annie by surprise. If I could kill her, I hoped the nester would die. Step by step I moved up the worn stairs. There was definitely someone on the second floor moving around. A door creaked open, then closed. What was Annie looking for? The children were gone. What did she hope to find?

When I got to the second floor, I scanned the empty hallway. At the far end, light filtered through the beautiful stained glass. It was as if the window had come alive. I'd never seen it so vibrant.

"Looking for me?" Annie stepped out of the doorway of my room.

"Yes." I brought the gun up from my side.

"I'm your sister." Annie didn't flinch. "Cora told you, didn't she?"

"Cora is dead. But then you know that."

"You're such a liar, Mimi. You've lied about everything your entire life. You can't face the truth." Whatever else Annie was, she was not afraid. She walked toward me, her hands hanging empty at her side. I could kill her with one bullet.

Or perhaps not. It hadn't occurred to me that Annie might not die if I shot her.

"You're nothing to me, Annie. Once you're dead, the Hendersons will be okay. They'll heal and grow strong again. I'll help them." My hand shook slightly from holding out the weight of the gun.

"You'll destroy them, Mimi. Like you do everything you touch. The irony is that I'm the only one you can't kill, but not from lack of trying."

I wanted to shut her up. I wouldn't listen to anything else she had to say. As I steadied the gun and began to squeeze the trigger, the front door slammed. The momentary distraction was all she needed. Quicker than I ever imagined, she ran toward me. She slammed into me, knocking me off my feet and against the staircase railing.

"You'll never get another chance at me. I know you for what you are," Annie said. She rushed down the stairs and disappeared before I could scrabble to my feet.

I scrambled up and chased after her. As I rounded the alcove where the staircase fed onto the first floor, I heard her in the hallway headed to the foyer and front door. Darting out, I fired. The clock in the hallway splintered. Plaster blasted from the walls. Nine bullets, until the hammer fell on an empty chamber. I ejected the empty clip and pulled another from my pocket. "I will kill you," I said as I walked forward. "I will pursue you relentlessly."

When I rounded the corner, I stopped. Jimmy Finch lay on the floor of the foyers in a pool of creeping blood. He looked up at me, realization dawning in his eyes. His hand went to his jacket and I saw the edge of a manila folder there.

"Mimi. . . ." He coughed blood.

"Mr. Finch!" I knelt beside him. "I'll call an ambulance. I thought you were—" I ran for the hall phone and called for help. By the time I replaced the phone, Finch was dead.

Annie and the nester had tricked me, had forced me to become what they were—murderers. I'd shot a man who was trying to help me. I'd been driven to act irrationally, out of fear. I'd killed the only true adult who'd thought to help me. Annie had defeated me.

I took the envelope from his jacket and sat down on the stairs to wait for the law officers or Bob, whichever one came first. Annie was gone now. She'd accomplished more today than she'd ever dreamed possible. Cora was dead, Finch was dead, and I would be charged with murder. She had an open playing field. Erin and Donald wouldn't last a week.

60

Deputy Frank Grange sat with me on the porch as the crime-scene men and the sheriff went through the house. They hadn't handcuffed me. Not yet. They'd allowed me to tell how I'd gone to get Bob's gun to defend myself and the children, how Finch had slipped into the house, and how I'd fired, thinking he meant to harm me. Self-defense was the way Frank viewed it. I made no mention of Annie's presence in the house.

"Where is the other girl, Annie?" he asked.

"I don't know." She wasn't far, I would be willing to bet on that.

"Do you have any idea why someone would want to kill your grandmother?"

"Berta was murdered, too. She didn't kill herself. Someone did that while I was looking for Donald."

The deputy wrote in his notebook. "This house has seen a lot of tragedy."

"More than you'll ever know." I didn't elaborate. I could tell he thought I was in shock. Perhaps I was; but more than that, my spirit was broken. Annie had won.

"Mrs. Eubanks brought Annie into the Henderson home. The girl has no known history. Deputy Walton had looked into her past before he died, but without much success. Did you ever learn more about her?"

I shook my head. What could I tell him? That Annie was my sister, an evil creature with tainted blood in her veins that could create monsters out of her will and emotions. Right. Searcy Mental Hospital would become my new home if I talked like that. Cora wanted me to know Annie was my blood, but that secret would die with me.

Bob's car turned off Shore Road and stopped. The sheriff's car, the emergency vehicles, it was enough to warn him. I thought for a moment he would turn around and flee, but he came on, slowly. To my relief, Donald and Erin were in the car with him. He got out slowly but waved the children to remain in the vehicle. Deputy Grange stood to speak with him, and they stepped away from me, where I couldn't hear. I didn't have to listen to know what was being said. I watched Bob's face, gray and unemotional, crack for one moment before he resumed a blank expression.

"Bob?" I stood.

"What the hell, Mimi? Where's Annie?"

"I don't know."

The sheriff arrived and walked onto the porch. He went to speak with Bob and I heard the mention of bullet holes in the third floor bedroom. I'd have to fabricate a lie, and quickly. I settled on denial. They couldn't prove I'd fired those shots.

Donald and Erin got out of the car. They came slowly toward me, crying silently.

"It's okay," I told them. "It was an accident." I was crying, too.

Bob took them to the back door and up to the second floor bedroom. He was gone a while, but when he came back, he spoke to the sheriff. "I called my sister in California. I'm sending the children there right away."

"That's a good idea, Mr. Henderson."

"We should have left after Margo. . . ." He didn't finish. "Berta wanted to leave. She wanted to take our daughter home to Cambria, but I wanted to stay here, to renovate the Paradise, to—" He covered his face with his hand. "I should have listened to my wife."

"Annie is missing." The sheriff glanced at me. "There are bullet holes in her bed, but no blood."

"She shouldn't be far. She's on foot."

"We'll search for her. Is it possible she was in any way involved in the things that have happened here at Belle Fleur?"

Bob glanced at me and our gaze connected. I willed him to say yes, to say he finally saw her for what she was. "She's just a kid. Why would she do such things?"

The sheriff pursed his lips, and his gaze, too, found me. "You didn't know much about her. You've got a good heart, but that doesn't safeguard you. Look at Mrs. Eubanks. We believe she knew her killer. We believe she talked with the person who killed her. Whoever it was got a butcher knife from the kitchen and walked right up behind her and slit her throat."

Bob staggered. "I have to pack the children. What about Mimi?"

"We're taking her to town. We want a doctor to speak with her."

"Is she hurt?" Bob's glance held concern, and I wanted to rush into his arms, to let him hold me and tell me it would all be okay.

"Physically she's not injured."

"Are you going to charge her with the private detective's death?"

Bob did care what happened to me. He did. I closed my eyes for just a second and savored the relief.

"I can't say. The story she tells, it was accidental. She found her granny dying and came here. Finch came in on her unannounced. She reacted by emptying nine rounds at him. Three hit."

"Once the children are on a plane, I'll come and talk with Mimi. But we have to find Annie. She's out there . . . somewhere."

Good luck with that, I thought. She would be found when and if she desired.

Deputy Grange took my arm and lifted me to my feet. I'd never noticed he was beside me. I still held the manila envelope Finch had carried with the discovery of Annie's past. I didn't want anyone to ever know she was my sister.

Grange opened the back of a patrol car and assisted me inside, closing the door that had no handle. A screen separated the front from the back, which was nothing more than a prison. Ironic that I'd ended up as Chloe had, a prisoner on the grounds of Belle Fleur.

"Bob!" I slapped my palm against the window that wouldn't roll down. "Bob." I couldn't leave without telling him goodbye. I had to warn him.

The sheriff gave a nod and Bob opened the back door so we could speak.

"Take care of the children," I told him. "Don't leave them alone in the house. Whatever you do, don't find Annie."

His hand touched my forehead. "You're burning up with fever, Mimi. You're sick."

"Promise me! Promise me you'll leave Belle Fleur tonight. Promise me! And don't hunt for Annie. Let her go."

"Everything will be okay." He bent and kissed my forehead, a gentle fatherly kiss, and I knew I would never see him again.

The sheriff got behind the wheel, and the deputy in the passenger seat. They turned the car around and started down the drive.

I looked out the back window, watching Belle Fleur recede. The yellow paint looked sickly, the shutters bracketing dark, empty windows. Belle Fleur had returned to the empty mausoleum she had been before the Hendersons bought her.

I glanced up at the second floor. Donald and Erin stood in the window of her old room, the one she'd shared with Margo. She had her arm around her brother, and I thought for a moment what a luxury it would be to have a sibling who loved me, who cared what happened to me. Perhaps they would recover from this on some sunny stretch of California shore.

My gaze wandered to the third floor, and I uttered a cry of terror.

"What?" the sheriff demanded.

I didn't answer. My entire focus on was the third floor window. Annie's window. The nester was there. It wore Donald's favorite red jacket. It stood in the window, a Zippo lighter in hand. It flicked open the top and spun the striker wheel that ignited a spark. Blue flames leapt. When the creature smiled, its sharpened teeth dripped with saliva.

"Mimi! What's wrong?" The sheriff stopped the car and got out. He opened the back door and grabbed me because I was clawing at the back window. I had to get out, to get back to the house, to save the children.

"Mimi!" He grabbed me and got into the back seat with me, his big strong arms restraining me as I fought to escape. "Drive!" he ordered the deputy. "Get us the fuck out of here."

61

AUGUST, 2013

That was forty years ago. My last glimpse of Belle Fleur was Bob in the yard beside emergency vehicles and Donald in the second-floor window, while above him the nester waited to catch him unaware.

Donald and Erin left that night for California. Bob closed down the house, disinterred Margo, and took the bodies of his wife and daughter away.

For nearly forty years, Belle Fleur has remained empty. The harsh coastal winds have blistered the paint until it curled and fell flaking from the boards. Shutters have blown away. Children, drawn by the lure of something dark and frightening, have broken windows, and rain has splashed onto the floors, once so beautifully waxed.

The stained-glass window of the Lady of Shalott remains amazingly intact. A jungle of trees has grown up around the house, and perhaps the branches have shielded the beautiful glass image. Or perhaps the house has protected itself. Throughout the years, several teenagers have been hurt on the property. One boy fell into an abandoned well

344

and broke his neck. I heard the stories, because I made it my business to keep up with Coden and what transpired here.

Annie was never found. The sheriff searched, but to no avail. Eventually, I was released and no charges were brought against me. Cora's murderer was never discovered, but Jimmy Finch, before he died, had alibied me. I could not have been in two places at once. I tried one time to tell the sheriff about Annie and her creatures. For my pains I was given a psychiatric examination and a week-long stay, at the county's expense, in the mental ward of a Mobile hospital.

When I was released, I left the area. I made a new life, but I always kept an eye on Belle Fleur.

Cora had established a trust for Belle Fleur. Or I should say that the trust established several generations back still held. Bob gave up payments on Belle Fleur, and the house returned to the trust. To me. Many, many times I considered burning it down, but I couldn't bring myself to do it. And now there's a lovely family eager to move in. Belle Fleur is to be resurrected once more. Annie has come home.

Like it or not, I am linked to the house. To the past. To the horrors committed in the name of love.

And now I am back in Coden. My name today is Elaine Alcut. I've had more than a dozen names. As each one grows too painful, I change. It allows me the illusion that I have some control over who I am and my fate. Elaine is so much more refined than Mimi. Some would say I've grown into the name.

I've returned to Cora's house, because it gives me easy access, through the woods, to the new family moving into Belle Fleur. Another architect, if you can believe it. I placed the ad for the sale of Belle Fleur in *Architectural Digest*. Scott McRay answered.

He looks like a young Lawrence Olivier, very polished and properly British. His wife won't last two months. She reminds me of a delicate bloom. But the children are incredible. Twin girls, and a younger boy. I believe she calls them Madeline and Miranda. The boy is Scott, like his father.

I watch them because I know Annie has returned. I've seen her. A glimpse here, a movement at the corner of my eye. She hasn't aged a lick, but then she was never quite human. She is still a teenager. Perhaps a tad older than the sixteen she was back in 1974. She looks to be more college-age now. Why am I not surprised? If I knew the name she was using, I'll bet I could find her enrolled in the local university. Education major. Oh, she has a plan this time. One far better than the last one.

But I am watching. It is August, and I have come to the end of this story. I've written it down as Cora asked me to do in the final paragraphs of her letter to me. "Annie is your sister and you must love her." Those were Cora's words. I'd sooner nestle a snake at my bosom.

The papers Jimmy Finch found, the ones that linked me to Belle Fleur and the Damarais family, I destroyed. There is no record of my connection to Belle Fleur. I couldn't afford it. This time I shall stop her. This time there will be an end to the horrors Sigourney set in motion so many decades ago.

As I wander through the woods, peeping through the dense foliage, I hear the sound of saws. This new family, Scott and Belinda McRay, are clearing the trees grown too close to the house. Talk in town is that he plans a grand renovation of Belle Fleur and the Paradise Inn.

I wonder if the McRay family knows the history of Belle Fleur. As I once told Donald Henderson, history is the road map of past mistakes. Learn it and avoid repetition.

Now I must walk to the road and make my way to the front door of Belle Fleur. A proper introduction is in order. Perhaps the McRay family will require a music instructor. I'm quite proficient at the piano.

THE END

Acknowledgments

Ghost stories and creepy tales were my first love as a reader, and it's been a circuitous journey back to this dark terrain as a writer. My grandmother, a remarkable woman, often recounted Poe's gothic tales to us grandchildren, all huddled beside her under a handmade quilt. The flames from the fireplace cast shadows in the high-ceilinged room, as her voice with a faint Swedish accent pulled us slowly into the realm of imagination.

She was a lover of literature and poetry, and she could bring us children to heel in a matter of moments with her rendition of "Little Orphant Annie," James Whitcomb Riley's chilling poem that is at the center of this tale.

My parents, both journalists, were also great storytellers, and with their tales came the added authority of supposed fact. "Did I ever tell you about the McDonald house where Highway 26 curves on the way to Central?" Real places populated by what was presented as real people. Or at least real dead people.

Sometimes late on a dusky summer evening my mother would load us and the neighborhood children into the car and drive us through the twilight to a haunted bridge where a love triangle had ended tragically, or a cemetery where a grief-crazed man dug up his dead child, only to find the grave empty.

I've always loved stories of ghosts and hauntings, and I've had an encounter or two with an entity from "the other side." Luckily, none have left a physical mark on me, though I did prematurely gray.

There are many people who believed in this story, and they know who they are. Thank you, cheerleaders of the macabre. I also want to thank Ed Stackler and Suzann Ledbetter for helpful advice on shaping the story. And also a nod to Sarah Waters, whose wonderful book, *The Little Stranger*, reminded me that the tradition of scary tales is alive and well.

I want to thank my agent, Marian Young, for her many years of support. With *The Darkling* we have come full circle.

And I am thrilled to be publishing with Pegasus Books. My editor Maia Larson is a joy to work with. Incisive yet gentle. And the book cover so rocks. Many thanks to the artist Michael Fusco, who captured the spirit of my book.

To everyone who reads this story, I wish you the nerve-twitching chill that was such a pleasure of my childhood. The possibilities of what might be there, in the dark, feeds our imaginations.